ISBN 978-1-331-12479-5
PIBN 10148096

FB &c Ltd, Dalton House, 60 Windsor Avenue, London, SW19 2RR.
Company number 08720141. Registered in England and Wales.

For support please visit www.forgottenbooks.com

HUMOURS OF THE COUNTRY.

❧ ❧

W Robinson

CHOSEN ~~by R. U. S.~~

London :
John Murray, Albemarle Street.
— 1909. —

CONTENTS.

HUMOURS OF THE COUNTRY.

CHAPTER I.

FARMING AND FARMERS.

"Is Marriage a Success? I should say so," remarked a farmer. "Why, there's my Hesba gits up in the mornin,' milks six cows, gits breakfast, starts four children to school, feeds the hens, likewise the hogs, likewise some motherless sheep, skims twenty pans of milk, washes the clothes, gits dinner, et cetery. Think I could hire anybody to do it for what she gits?"

The Crows.—The farmer was very short-handed, and had been compelled to engage a town boy, whose knowledge of agriculture and kindred subjects was extremely limited. One day he sent the youth to a wheat field to see if there were any crows among his wheat. When the boy returned from the field his master asked him if there were any crows there. The boy said he counted twenty-two.

"Did you drive them away?" asked the farmer.

"No," replied the lad; "I thought they belonged to you."

Singular.—"How is it, Mr Brown," said the mill-owner to the farmer, "that when I came to measure those five barrels of apples I bought from you I found them nearly a barrel short?" "Singular, very singular, for I put them up in some of your own flour barrels. "Ahem! Did, eh? Well, perhaps I made a mistake. Fine weather, is'nt it."

The Amateur Farmer.—"But your amateur farming doesn't pay expenses, does it?"

"I hope so. I am going to write a book about it."

All Grow.

Alas! when we our wild oats
sow
With blood and sweat and toil,
How few of them we ever throw
On rocks or sterile soil!

Why he Left.—An Irishman in this country, was one day remarking in a village inn on the cheapness of provisions in Ireland.

"Shure," said he, "there

ye can buy salmon for sixpence, and a dozen mackerel for twopence."

"What made you leave such a fine country then, Pat?" asked one of the company.

"Arrah, me boy!" answered the son of Erin, "but where was the sixpences and twopences to come from to buy 'em with?"

The Limerick Farmer: "This land is not like your miserable Kerry land, where a mountain sheep can hardly get enough to eat. The grass grows here so fast and so high, that if you left a heifer out in the field there at night, you would scarcely find her in the morning."

Kerry Farmer: "Bedad, yer honour there's many a part of my own country where if you left a heifer out at night the divil a bit of her you'd ever see agin."

The Agricultural Department.—First Farmer: "Blest if I think the Agricultural Department is any good!"

Second Farmer: "What's the trouble?"

First Farmer: "Well, I wrote to 'em to find out how high the price of wheat was goin' to go an' I couldn't get no satisfaction at all."

The Greater Calf.—A gentle-

easy to work, but it's a good deal easier to gather the crops."

Theory and Practice.—"You should lay something aside for a rainy day," said the man who gives advice.

"Mister," said the Kansas farmer, "you talk like a theorist. What we people need to do is to lay something aside against a drought."

Jes' for the fun of it. "I understand that your boy, Josiar, is a good deal of an athlete," said a neighbour. "Yes," answered Farmer Corntossel, "I'm kind o' worried about Josiar. Sence I saw him jumping over parallel bars an' turnin' somersaults jes' for the fun of it, I'm downright afeared he will work hisself to death when he gits here on the farm where there's business to 'tend to."

As hard as bullets.—Lord Carlisle used to relate an experience he had with a waiter at an agricultural dinner in Galway while he was Lord Lieutenant of Ireland. This waiter was specially appointed to attend to the wants of the Viceroy, and he passed remarks on every dish which he handed him. With a dish of peas he said, "Pays, yer Excellency," adding in a whisper, "an' if I was you, the divil a wan iv thim I'd touch, for they're as hard as bullets!"

Times be Changed. A golf enthusiast got leave from a farmer to use a meadow for his hobby, and among the players were some ladies. A servant on the farm, scandalised by the sight of girls in scarlet coats, armed with clubs, striding over the fields, one day said to his master—

"Them girls in the meadow scare our cows!"

Farmer: "Ah, Thomas, times be changed since we were young. Used to be the cows which scared the gals!"

A French Peasant, by means of economy and judgment, had become the owner of several farms. One of his farmers, who had been about the renewal of his lease, and was agreeably surprised to find him more accommodating than he had hoped invited him to drink.

"I drink no wine or spirits."

"Very well, what you please," the farmer insisted politely; "but you have something!"

"Well then, if it's all the same to you, I'll take a postage stamp."

Providence and Another.—Minister (to old parishioner): "I have not seen you in church for two Sundays!"

Old Parishioner: "I canna' get away; I have to watch the crops."

"Can you not leave them to the Divine protection for one day?"

"Man, they boys are sic deevils, it taks us baith to do it!"

An inducement.—This advertisement from the "Times" reads well:—

A GENTLEMAN FARMER, on a large mixed farm, would take a pupil. Good hunting and all kinds of port.

Not fit to hold a plough.—The late Bishop of Ely was once talking to a labourer, and he let fall a remark which plainly showed that he had no idea how turnips should be sown. Hodge looked at him round-eyed in amazement.

"'E a bishop indeed! Whoy, 'e aint fit to 'old a plough!

Getting and Earning.—"What are men earning at harvesting in these parts?" said a bristly looking member of the travelling army of the unemployed to a Devonshire farmer.

"Half a crown a day."

"What's that? I was told that they were getting six shillings a day."

"So they are. You asked me what they were earning."

The Long and the Short of it.—Somewhere in Kent there is a farmer who was born with one of his legs longer than the other. A gentleman from town went over there to see about a summer boarding place for his family. The ruralite is very touchy concerning his legs, but the other didn't know it. He met the farmer at the hotel one night.

"Will you tell me, sir, how it happens that one of your legs is longer than the other?" he asked. "Met with an accident when you were young, I suppose."

"No sir, 'twasn't no accident. They was made so at my request."

"Ha! ha. That's funny. Tell me about it."

"Well, sir, I wanted to be a farmer from the very day I was born. That right leg, the longest one, when I'm ploughin' can go into the furrow, and the short one on top ground, without bobbing up and down, as one of you ordinary city folks would do it. See?"

Sandy and the Laird.—Laird: "Well, Sandy, you are getting very bent. Why don't you you stand straight up like me, man?"

Sandy: "Eh, man, do ye see that field o' corn ower there?"

Laird: I do."

Sandy: "A' weel, ye'll notice that the full heids hang down an' the empty ones stand up."

Secretary of Agriculture Wilson. in an address to a delegation of farmers, won hearty applause with the following anecdote:—

"I overheard a dialogue between two well-dressed men at lunch the other day. The first man, as he helped himself to asparagus, said:—'By the way, you said Johnson was a farmer, didn't you?"

"'Good gracious, no!' returned the other man. 'I said he made his fortune out of wheat. Did you ever hear of a farmer doing that?'"

A wee bit late.—On the afternoon of the judging day at a Highland and Agricultural Society of Scotland's Show, after the awards had been announced, the following encounter between two Clydesdale exhibitors occurred. Mr. Montgomery of Netherhall entered a refreshment tent in which Mr. David Riddell was seated along with three of the judges:—

Mr. Riddell: "Come here, Andrew! I'm treating the judges."

Mr. Montgomery: "It s all right, you're a wee bit late. I treated them yestreen!"

The "Boon" Ploughing.—The late Rev. Dr. Robertson of the Cathedral, Glasgow, was having part of his glebe ploughed by his neighbours when he became minister of Mains and Straithmattine. One of the farmers, an elder, who had arranged the "boon" ploughing suggested to the young minister that he should go out to the field and see the ploughmen.

But the elder gave him a caution. "Dinna talk to them aboot ploughing, sir! Ye see they ken aboot ploughing and ye dinna, and if they find oot frae your talk that ye dinna ken they'll begin to suppose that ye ken aboot naething else."

A Wonderfu' able Man.—Scots people like a minister who is well informed in farming and kindred matters. The late Rev. Robert Whyte, minister of Dryfesdale, had a thorough knowledge of farming. A shepherd who had been in charge of a flock of sheep near his manse after having had many talks with him, said of him to his master: "He's a wonderfu' able man! he's bye-ordinar' clever a'together! In fact, he is clever enough to be a farmer."

In their naitral state.—A Duke of Gordon continued the practice of attending the "rent dinners," and after his Grace took his departure the conviviality was prolonged for some time. After the principal toasts had been proposed and responded to, the Duke rose to leave. On noticing this one of his old tenants, who was a bit of a character said: "Yer Grace, you're no gaun awa to leave us, are ye?"

"Oh! yes, James, you see the night is dark, the roads are not good, I am getting an old man, and I must get home in good time."

"Oh! yer Grace, ye micht stay an hour or twa and see yer tenants in their naitral state!"

Muck and Science.—An enthusiastic advocate of applied science was very earnestly impressing on an old-fashioned Scottish farmer the advantage of science as applied to agriculture when the latter said: "For my pairt, a' believe in the auld saying, that 'Muck is the mither o' the meal chest.' Gie me a cheap fairm and plenty o' muck, and a'll be contented."

No time to die.—City Man: "Well, Uncle Reuben, you people have something to be thankful for—the death-rate is much smaller in the country than in town."

Uncle Reuben: "Yaas; folks who have to keep a farm a-goin' don't git time t' die."

Farming in Vermont.—"How did you like farming in Vermont?" was asked of a Michigan man who went there because he was told that the bulk of the wealth was in the Eastern States.

"Oh, I guess it would have been all right, only fur one thing."

"What was that?"

"I'll be durned ef I'll work ground so hard and rocky that you have to plant wheat with a shot-gun!"

Had him there.—A man who was very miserly hoarded up his stacks of hay year after year in the hope of making double the price he was offered for them. A well-known hay and straw buyer in the district one day asked the price of a stack. A high price was asked, which the buyer accepted.

"How about the terms of settlement?" asked the owner.

"Well you see my terms are to settle when I fetch the last load away."

"That's a bargain!" The old chap watched every load go away except the last and that the buyer never did fetch away.

The Overworked Farmer.—A farmer, it is said, once came home from a rent-dinner, and said to his wife: "I am aboot tired out! Is cows in t' barn?"

"Yes," answered his hard-working wife, "long since."

"Is t' hosses unharnessed and fed?"

"Yes."

"Fowls locked up?"

"Yes."

"Wood chopped for mornin'?"

"Yes."

"Them ducks plucked and dressed for market?"

"Yes."

"Waggon wheel mended, and ready to start in t' mornin'?"

"Yes."

"Oh, then," he said, with a sigh, "let me have my supper and turn in! Farmin' is beginnin' to tell on me!"

More than he wanted.—An Irish tenant farmer, returning from a somewhat distant market late one afternoon, missed his way and got into a boghole, where he stuck fast. His landlord, chancing to pass shortly afterwards on horseback, shouted out, 'Hallo, Pat—you've got fixity of tenure now!" "Shure," ejaculated Pat, "and I'd be moightily obliged if yer honour wud evict me!"

The Farmer's Responsibility.—At a so-called "literary" meeting in Georgia an old farmer spoke for one hour on corn-raising, fodder-saving, and cotton-picking. The local preacher was present, and rose to a point of order.

"I do not see," said he, "what a literary meeting has to do with corn-raising and fodder-saving."

"Well," replied the old farmer, "it's got jest this to do with it: Ef it warn't for corn, cotton, an' bacon an' greens, there wouldn't be a literary man in the whole blessed country!"

At a dinner given to tenants on an estate in Berkshire a few days ago, the steward in the chair, a discussion came on with reference to farming.

"Mr. Green," said the steward, "you have got that ten-acre field in capital order. What do you think of planting it with?"

"Well, sir," replied Mr. Green, "I have hardly made up

my mind yet: but I don't think I could do better than plant it with gentleman stewards, as they appear to thrive as well as anything on the land now."

"This farm for sale."—Smith was riding, and saw a board nailed up on a post in the yard of a farmhouse, with a sign painted on it—"This farm for sail." Always ready for a little pleasantry, and seeing a woman picking up chips at the wood pile in front of the house, he stopped and asked her very politely when the farm was to sail. She went on with her work, but replied to his question instanter—"Just as soon as the man comes along who can raise the wind!"

Got it in the neck. A countryman sowing seed was accosted by two would-be smart fellows on horseback, and one remarked with an insolent air, "Well, honest fellow, it is your business to sow, but we reap the fruits of your labours." To which the countryman replied, "It is very likely you may, for I be sowing hemp."

Making the Most of it.—A Scottish clergyman in a moorland parish received a visit from an English friend in the month of December. From an unkindly season operating on an ungenial soil, it so happened that the little crop of the glebe was only then under the scythe of honest John Fairweather, the minister's man. In spite of sundry small artifices to turn the Englishman's attention another way, and prevent him from spying the nakedness of the land, he stumbled upon John busy in his work, to whom he expressed his surprise at what he saw. John, whose zeal for the honour of his country was quite equal to that of his master, assured the Englishman that this was the second crop within the year; and the Englishman shortly after went away, grudging Scotland her more fortunate climate. When John was reproved by the minister for practising a deception, he said, "Sir, it's as true as the Gospel; ye ken yoursel' the last crop wasna off the ground till Januar' this blessed year."

Not Made in Germany.—An American firm recently issued a number of show cards representing the Goddess of Liberty arrayed in scanty garments, driving a harvesting machine drawn by a pair of black and orange tigers, and forwarded a number to their German agents, who returned them, however, with the following letter:

"The picture of your admirable machines, of which I the receipt acknowledge, is not useful in this country, and it is of much regret to me that I request to return them permission. The women of our country, when by circumstances to do agricultural work compelled, do not dress as your picture shows is the custom in your wonderful country, and would not deem such garments with modesty to consist. Also we do not tigers for draught purposes cultivate, they not being to the country native, nor in our experience for such work well suited. I have to my customers explained with earnestness that your picture is an allegory, and does not mean that your admirable machine should be operated by women too little clothed, but I cannot use the cards as you instruct, and your further advices respectfully await."

Forkibus, cartibus, et manuribus.—A farmer, whose son had been for a long time ostensibly studying Latin in a popular academy, not being satisfied with the course and the conduct of the young fellow, recalled him from school, and, placing him by the side of a cart one day, thus addressed him:

"Now, Joseph, here is a pitchfork, and here is a heap of manure and a cart. What do you call them in Latin?"

"Forkibus, cartibus, et manuribus," said Joseph.

"Well, now, said the old man, "if you don't take that farkibus pretty quickibus, and pitch that manuribus into the cartibus, I'll break your lazy backibus.

Joseph went to work forthwithibus.

Thinkin' to mak' a minister o' him.—A certain popular teacher of the present day, son of a worthy Perthshire farmer, was of a retired, studious disposition when a young man, and preferred "burning the midnight oil" to catching the proverbial worm in the early morning and assisting in the daily work on the farm. His father, though not averse to learning, would rather his son had studied agriculture instead of polemics, and one day a friend, knowing this, asked if he intended the lad to be a farmer like himself. "Na, na," replied the father seriously, "it tak's a man wi' a head to be a farmer, but I was thinkin' to mak' a minister o'. him."

Zomerzet Speech.—At a rent audit in Somersetshire, the oldest tenant on the estate had to propose the health of the landlord. He did so in these terms. After rising, looking helplessly around, and scratching his head, he said: "Wull, zur, all I can say is, 'Yer's to yer good health; and if all the landlards 'ud do as you do, tenant varmers 'ud do better than they do do.'

A Second Crop.—Gregson: "Why are you following that young man at the plough with a whip?" Farmer Heyson: "Stranger, that's my son. He kem from college with his hair parted in th' middle an' a-smoking a cigernet. They sent me a whoppin' big bill an' sed he'd bin a sowing of his wild oats. I'm makin' him sow sum tame ones now.

Once bitten, twice shy.—Owner: "So you think you have a customer for my farm?"

Agent: "I've been negotiating with a man who says he used to own one."

Owner: "Don't have anything to do with him. He's a fraud. No one who ever owned a farm would want to buy another."

The language Difficulty. — A Scottish farmer recently paid a visit to a South of England cattle show, and while walking round got talking with a native farmer. Neither could well understand what the other said. The Scotsman got a little nettled at this, and put it down to the Englishman's stupidity. "Man," he at last said, "yer kye moos a' right, and yer cocks craw quite plain, but I'm hanged if I can mak' you oot."

Observing Tourist.—"Aw—this is a delightful spot! I wondah now if I could succeed in—aw—agwicultural pursuits."

Farmer Weedle: "Don't ye try it. It's all we folks kin do to make a livin' outen farmin,' and them which tries 'agricultural pursoots' is durned sure to git left."

Good Pay, Little work.—A Kansas farmer who simply could not get harvest hands, put this sign upon his fence: "Harvest hands wanted. Servant girl pretty and genial. Music in the evening. Pudding three times a day. Three spoons of sugar with every cup of coffee. Rising hour nine o'clock in the morning. Three hours' rest at noon."

Full heads and empty.—"Why don't you hold up your head as I do?" inquired a lawyer of a small farmer.

"Squire," replied the farmer, "look at that field of wheat. All the valuable heads hang

once for all. A live young farmer can sink more hard cash in grain, wire-netting, horse-shoeing, ploughs, harrows, repairs, harness, and fences to keep his herds from his neighbour's cornfields than a man who hadn't tried it could ever guess. Of course, he doesn't want any clothes. It's a pleasure to show up at town meetin' lookin' like a pauper. His wife doesn't want any clothes either. She just naturally hates them—especially the ones she's wearin'. She sees sunrise every day it doesn't rain. Maybe she loves the sunrise, but it's a wonder she doesn't hate the sound of the silence, and the sight of milk-pans sittin' in a row. Now, you folk in the city have regular workin' hours and regular playin' hours, and money to spend for something besides hoes and harrows and fertilisers. You are the most independent folk on earth! Why——"

Mr. Swift cut Mr. Bean off short: "Independent? Man, you're crazy! I tell you, we're bound hand and foot, soul, body, mind and spirit. We can't move or stand still without paying tribute to a corporation or a landlord. We go deep down in our pockets feeling for money we havn't earned yet to meet last month's meat bill! Look at you farmers! You can stroll from one end of your farm to the other, and you own everything in sight. Think of the satisfaction of taking a half-mile stroll and being able to order off the premises any man whose face you didn't like, while your honest, kindly neighbours stood by and cheered. Think ——"

"See here," said Mr. Abner Bean, "while a man is struttin' around over his property orderin' folks off he doesn't appreciate, about how many neighbours do you s'pose are gathered around, cheerin'?"

"Well, of course, metaphorically,——"

"Precisely — farmin' and struttin' are great sport metaphorically, but sometimes I get so lonesome for the sight of a face that I don't like, that when it comes along I'm inclined to invite the owner to stay over-night."

A reasonable retort.—In a debate on the Agricultural Appropriation Bill, Congressman Rixey, of Virginia, was denouncing the agricultural committee vigorously because it had been promising for years to do something for Virginia, and had not done it yet. Chairman Wadsworth tried to pour oil on the troubled waters. "The gentleman from Virginia must remember," said he, "that Rome wasn't built in a day." "I know it wasn't," retorted Rixey, "and if Romulus and Remus had been on the agricultural committee it wouldn't be built yet."

His last words.—A miller noted for his keenness in money matters, was in a boat trying his best to get across the stream which drove his mill. The stream was in flood, and he was taken past the spot at which he wanted to land, and the boat was upset. His wife ran along the side of the stream crying for help, when she was brought up by her husband yelling out: "If I'm drowned, Maggie, dunnot forget flour's gone up two shillings a sack!"

Explosive. — Mr. Binks: "The paper says a big flour mill out west blew up yesterday."

Mrs. Binks: "La sakes! I s'pose it's where they make the self-raising flour."

A fuss-rate farmer.—"Sambo is your master a good farmer?"

"Oh! yes, massa, fuss-rate farmer—he make two crops in one year."

"How is dat, Sambo?"

"Why, he sell all his hay in de fall, and make money once; den in de spring he sell de hides of de cattle dat die for want of de hay, and make money twice."

Only Fair.—Some years ago when the price of wheat and other agricultural produce had fallen to the lowest point ever reached, a farmer entered a barber's shop for the purpose of being shaved. On taking his seat for the operation he noticed on the wall a card with these words: "Shaving, one penny; farmers, twopence." The farmer inquired the meaning of this strange distinction. Said the barber to the farmer: "Well, you see, since farming has become so unprofitable farmers have such very long faces, so we are obliged to charge them double." And that farmer paid his twopence in grim silence.

Proof Positive.—Fat Rider to yokel: "Can I get through yon gate, my man?"

"Yes, sir. I zaw a wagon load o' hay go threw 'ee only this vere marnin'."

Disappointing. — A farm labourer was lately told by a friend that on account of the slackness of work during the winter, he ought to put by a sum when in full work in case he should be thrown out of employment.

The man thought for a moment or two, and then replied:

"Well, aw know a chap as once saved about twelve pounds agen the frost cooming, and it never did coom that year at all; an' he had all that there money thrown on his hands!"

He was a plough boy.—"All our best men are public-school men," once remarked a gentleman to Charles Lamb. "Look at our poets. There's Byron, he was a Harrow boy."

"Yes," grimly observed Lamb, "and there's Burns, he was a plough-boy."

Not Lonesome.—A man who was travelling through Arkansas on horseback stopped before a mountain region farmhouse to inquire the way. "What's the news?" asked the mountaineer as he leaned his lank frame against the fence.

"As far as that? You must find it rather lonesome here."

"No, I can't say as I do."

"Perhaps you are not one of the lonesome kind?"

"No, I'm not. But, you see, I mortgaged this farm for four hundred dollars. I couldn't pay, and they foreclosed or me."

"I see."

"That was two years ago, and the sheriff has been trying to get possession ever since. He comes now and then, and we have a shot at each other, and betimes some fool comes along and wants to know if I ain't lonesome; and when you add the claim jumpers, the rattle snakes and the skunks, my life is anything but lonely."

Sympathy.—A lady invited a party of "mothers" from Whitechapel to spend the day at her house in the country. All went well, and the young lady of the house accompanied them to the station in the evening. "Well, miss," said one of them to her as the train appeared in sight, "we've 'ad a very nice day; but lor! 'ow I do pity yer poor dear ma 'aving to live always in such a place as this!"

Feudal Customs. — The splendid manor of Farnham Royal is held by the service of putting the glove on the King's right hand and by supporting the arm that holds the sceptre on Coronation Day. There is no other payment. The rental of the manor of Aylesbury is three eels in winter and three green geese in summer, besides a litter of straw for the King's bedchamber thrice a year if he come that way so often. The manor of Addington's rental is a pair of gilt spurs, a pair of tongs, a snowball on Midsummer Day, and a rose at Christmas. The rental of the manor of Coperland is the holding of the King's head, if needful, as often as he crosses the sea between Dover and Whitsand.

No more "fatted Calves."—"I've a sight o' sons—thirteen altogether," remarked a prosperous old farmer, "and all of 'em's done me credit save the three eldest, who sowed wild oats at a pretty rapid rate, and then come home and saddled my shoulders with the harvest. Well, I own I was glad to see 'em back and I feasted 'em, and petted 'em, and set 'em on their legs again, only to see 'em skedaddle off afresh, when things had slowed down, with all the cash they could lay hands on. That thereabouts sickened me, so I called the rest of 'em together, and said: 'There's ten of you left, and if any of you 'ud like to follow t'other three I won't try to stop you. But, understand this, though there may be a few more prodigal sons, there'll be no more fatted calves. I've killed the last of 'em.' And," continned the old man, triumphantly, "I've had trouble wi' none of 'em since."

The busy bee.—Jones (who has foresworn town life for a more healthful existence, to hired compendium of agricultural knowledge at 14s. 6d. a week, with cottage and 'tater patch): "Do you know anything about bees, Isaac?"

Isaac: "Yes, they stings!"

Ignorance rebuked.—The Earl of Aberdeen, who owns about 63,000 acres of land in Scotland, was once out walking in a country district where he had rarely been before, and paused beside a cottage garden fence to watch an aged labourer at work. "Is this a good soil," he questioned.

"Ay," responded the other.

"What is your next crop to be?" was the next interrogation.

The worker looked up, gazed disapprovingly at the stranger, and finally remarked: "You don't know anything about crops, young man. Just you hire a nice little allotment somewheres, an' take to cultivatin' it, and you'll have something better to do than to come chattern here."

No social hops.—Kate: "Well, it's a mercy you left Wurzelspire and have come to spend a few days with us, Cousin Joe! I suppose down where you live the people know nothing of concerts or even social hops?"

Cousin Joe! "Aw! My father ha' ten acres o' nowt else but hops, but I dunno about social hops. We call um Kent hops.'

As deep as its broad.—In districts where the only wells are artesian, the necessary depth of these sources of water supply is often something appalling. A traveller relates that he once met a farmer driving a load of water.

"Where do you get the water?" asked the traveller.

"Up the road about seven miles," answered the farmer.

"And you actually drag water seven miles for your family and stock?"

"Yes,"

"Why in the name of common-sense don't you dig a well?"

"Why, because it happens that the water is jest as far one way as it is the other—that's why."

The idea.—Agent: "Talk about unreasonable people, that man wants me to be sure to let his farm to somebody who has had experience."

Friend: "What is there unreasonable about that?"

Agent: "The idea of anybody who has had experience wanting a farm nowadays!"

A good cup.—A piece of good advice was given by a late chairman of the Royal Agricultural Society on presenting a silver cup to a young man who had won the first prize at a ploughing match. "Take this cup, my young friend, and remember always to plough deep and drink shallow."

An Ignorant Captain.—Farmer on board a steamer (suffering a good deal from the rolling of the vessel) to friend: "This capt'n don't understand his business. Why don't he keep in the furrows?"

A good time coming.—Landlord: "Well Awlford, glad to see the farm looking up so well; (jokingly) I shall have to raise your rent."

Awlford (tenant): "Glad to hear 'ee say so, sir, for 'tis more than I've been able to do these three years."

The Seat of honour.—In Norfolk, at a feast given at the end of harvest, the hostess, thinking to honour one of her principal men, asked him to come and sit at her right hand. " Thank you, my lady ; but if it's all the same ter yew, I'd rather sit opposite this 'ere pudden."

Why is a rook like a farmer ? " Because he gets his grub by following the plough.

Not easily frightened.—One must admire the firmness of an absentee Irish landlord. " Stop where you are," he wrote to his agent, " and if my tenants think they will alarm me by shooting you they little know the man they have to deal with."

A Poser.—" He," screamed the park orator, " who puts his hand to the plough must not turn back."

" What's he to do when he he gets to the end of the furrer," asked the man in the crowd.

Got mixed —An agricultural editor was asked by two subscribers, respectively : 1. Which was the best way to get a couple of twins safely through the trouble of teething ? and 2. How to protect an orchard from a plague of grasshoppers ? He answered the questions rightly, but mixed the initials. The happy father of the twins was told to cover them carefully with straw and set fire to them." and the man plagued with grasshoppers to " give a little castor oil and rub their gums with bone rings."

The last straw.—In olden days some of the Shetland farmers were notably bad payers of rent, looking upon the payment as something to be avoided if possible. One such man had given so much trouble that his landlord, after repeated reductions, at length left him alone, and he was asked for no rent for about five years. He then appeared on rent day, and his landlord laughingly asked him : " Well, Robbie, what is it now ? Do you want a further reduction ?" " Na, na, it's jokin' ye are ; but I cam to say 'at if ye dinna build me a barn, I maun flit."

Not encouraging.—" I suppose," said the farm hand, who was looking for a job, " that you believe in the eight-hour day ?' " That I do," said the farmer. " I do eight hours in the forenoon and eight in the afternoon, but along about hay and harvest time I put in two or three hours extra.'"

Cool.—A collier, being late going to his work one morning, thought he'd take a short cut across a farmer's field, but had not gone far when he heard the farmer shout:

"Hey, ma lad, there's no road across this field."

"Noa," said the collier, "it's not a very gooid rooad, but it'll do for me, an' Aw've noa time to mak a new un this mornin'," and he went on his way.

Merely that.—"Thought you said you had ploughed that ten-acre field?" said the first farmer. "No; I only said I was thinking about ploughing it," said the second farmer. "Oh! I see; you've merely turned it over in your mind."

Not the same thing.—"Wal," said Farmer Wilkins to his city lodger, who was up early and looking round, "ben out to hear the haycock crow, I s'pose?"

"No," replied the city lodger; "I've been out tying a knot in a cord of wood."

Sarcastic.—There is a firm of commission agents in the neighbourhood of Smithfield who make it a rule to get as many discounts and reductions from their accounts as possible and they have a special clerk who attends to this branch of the business. A farmer in the country had been in the habit of sending them up live turkeys for sale, but this Christmas he had sent up the dressed birds instead. The clerk, however, was not advised of the change, and he wrote to the farmer, as usual, to advise that four of the turkeys were found dead on arrival, and that they must be deducted from the consignment note.

The farmer wrote the following in reply: "It is with regret that I have to inform you that I cannot make the deduction. If you had wished me to send live dressed turkeys you should have notified me in advance, so that I could forward them in a heated motor-car. Owing to the snowy weather, turkeys, without feathers or insides, are liable to take cold if sent by ordinary goods train. The mortality among dressed turkeys was very large this year. Please, therefore, remit full amount due by return of post, and oblige."

The Crime of Paying Rent.—An Irish farmer who had paid his rent and been visited by the penalties of the Land League wrote the following letter of apology:—

"Ballinrobe, Mayo,
Jany 8, 1881.

"To the Honourable Land

Lague.—Gintlemin, in a moment of wakeness i pade me rint, i did not no ther was a law aginst it or i wud not do it. the people pass by me dure as if the smal pox was in the hous, i heer ye do be givin pardons to min that do rong, and if ye will sind me a pardon to put in the windy for every one to rede it, as God is me judge i will never Komit the crime agin. Misther Scrab Nally will give me a Karacter if ye write to him at Bal.

Yours thruly,

The Farmer Feeds them all.

The King may rule o'er land and sea ;
The Lord may rule right royally ;
The soldier ride in pomp and pride ;
The sailor roam o'er the ocean wide.
But this, or that, whate'er befal,
The farmer he must feed them all.
The writer thinks, the poet sings ;
The craftsman fashions wondrous things ;
The doctor heals, the lawyer pleads,
The miner follows the precious leads :
But this, or that, whate'er befal,
The farmer he must feed them all.
The merchant he may buy and sell ;
The teacher do his duty well ;
But men may toil through busy days,
Or men may stroll through pleasant ways.
From King to beggar, whate'er befal,
The farmer he must feed them all.
The farmer's tread is one of worth ;
He's partner with the sky and earth ;
He's partner with the sun and rain,
And no man loses for his gain.
And men may rise and men may fall,
The farmer he must feed them all.
God bless the man who sows the wheat,
Who finds us milk and fruit and meat ;
May his purse be heavy, his heart be light,
His cattle and corn, and all go right,
God bless the seeds his hands let fall,
For the farmer he must feed us all.

Overheard in Essex.—Gossipy cyclist meets a rustic and gives him good-day.

"Marnin'. fair roky this

marnin'." ("roky" meaning hazy.)

"How's farmin'? No great shakes, I tell 'ee. It don't pay to grow nawthin' now, an' it gits wusser'n wusser. All the fields goin' under grass for ship'n cattle. An' the land's fair poisoned with weeds. Yow see them 'ere beece in that there close down along o' the chutch? There's a mort o' docks'n that 'ere close. More docks'n grass, an' I thinks warsley o' the chantst of cattle gettin' a fair bite off'n it. Don't know what docks is? Wish I didden! I've bin a-pullin' of 'em till my back's well-nigh broke, an' I'm fair dunted with 'em. Where do they come from? Lord knows! They don't want no cultiwation, bless 'ee. There ain't no land so choice but what it'll grow docks.'

Defined.—Farmer Greene: "Oh, yes; there are several 'gentlemen farmers round here.

The Stranger: "And what is a 'gentleman farmer?'"

Farmer Greene: "Oh, one that knows enough to run a farm as it should be run, and is rich enough to stand the loss!"

Farming in Kansas.—Through the hot, dusty roads of Kansas a would-be homesteader was pursuing his way to the Cherokee strip in search of one of Uncle Sam's free homes. He had his family and goods in a shaky waggon, which was drawn by two feeble old horses.

"Whar you bound?" asked a farmer at whose house he stopped for water.

"Fer a hundred an' sixty acres o' Government land in th' strip."

A few months later the same man stopped again at the Kansas farmer's for water, this time travelling north.

"Watcher done with yer hundred an' sixty acres?" said the farmer.

"See them mules thar?" pointing to a fine pair of animals which were harnessed to the "prairie schooner." "I traded eighty acres o' my claim fer 'em.

"Watcher do with th' other eighty?"

"Don't give it away till I git further off. Th' fellar wer an innercent, an' I managed to run th' other eighty acres in on 'im without his knowing it!"

Hale and Gay at Seventy.—A farmer, who is over seventy years old, is proud of being still hale and gay. One morning he and his two sons began to wrangle over their respective strength, and the farmer declared that he could load hay as fast as they could pitch it.

So they went to the field, and the old farmer climbed into a hay waggon with his fork, and the two sons began to pitch the hay up to him as fast as they could. The old man worked bravely and well; he loaded with lightning speed, and all the while he kept calling down:

"More hay! More hay!"

The boys were kept mighty busy, and their youth told in their favour. The farmer began to load more untidily. Still, scrambling on top of the uneven mounds, he kept on shouting, "More hay!" Suddenly he tripped as he dug in his fork, and fell from the waggon to the the ground.

"Aha," said the eldest son, "what are you doing down here?"

The old farmer answered, as he rose from the ground:—

"You're too darned slow; I came down for more hay."

That Cockney again.—A Cockney whose education pertaining to rural life had been sadly neglected, recently paid his first visit to the country. Whilst viewing the rustic scene, he observed a large hayrick near a farmhouse, and asked his companion what it was.

"Why, that's hay!" said his pal.

"Wot, all 'ay!" exclaimed the benighted Cockney. "Blow me, Bill, don't the 'ay grow in big lumps down 'ere?"

"I should be awfully fond of country life," said the newly-married Cockney pet to her devoted lord, "if we could only go to the theatre or a music-hall at night."

"Quite so, baby. What you want is a farm-house in the middle of Victoria Park."

Overheard in a third-class carriage near Northampton:—

Commercial Traveller (to neighbour, a farmer): "Hay looks nice here. Nearly all cut, I see."

Farmer: "Yes, very fair; and 'ave they cut all t' hay in Lunnon?"

Not Satisfied.—The man who
has a little farm
Of trouble has no dearth;
And yet he reaches out for
wealth,
And tries to own the earth.

The Ploughing Match.—A Dumfriesshire parish minister had sent his man to compete at the parish ploughing match.

When the man returned the minister said: "Well, Andrew, how did you get on? Did you get a prize?"

"Yes sir, I got the sixth prize."

"How many ploughs were there?"

"There were twenty-four, sir."

"So few as twenty-four competitors, Andrew, and you have only got the sixth prize! I'm ashamed of you, Andrew, and you ought to be ashamed of yourself.' The minister kept nagging at Andrew still further, until the latter at length rejoined:—

"Weel, sir, if ye had been at a preachin' match wi' as mony at it, ye mightna hae been sae far forrit yoursel'."

Don't mention it —"I regret James, that owing to report made by my steward, I have to dispense with your services, as there is not, I believe, sufficient work for all."

"Faith, your Grace, there is no necessity to dismiss me on account of scarcity of work, as very little does for me."

His ready reply amused the duke, who let him bide.

The new tool.—John Rogers revolving, expanding, unceremonious, self-adjusting, self-contrakting, self-sharpening, self-greasing, and self-righteous Hoss Rake, iz now, and forever, offered tew a generous publik. Theze rakes are az eazy tew keep in repair az a hitching post, and will rake up a paper ov pins, sowed broad kast, in a ten aker lot ov wheat stubble. Theze rakes kan be used in the winter for a hen roost, or be sawed up into stove wood for the kitchen fire. No farmer, ov good moral karakter, should be without this rake, not even if he haz to steal one.

"Both togidder."—"Where is the hoe, Sambo?" "Wid de rake, massa." "Well, where is the rake?" "Why, wid de hoe!" "Well, well, where are they both?" "Why both togidder, massa; you 'pears to bery 'ticular dis morning!"

A picture.—Miss Townley: "I think the country is just sweet. I love to see the peasant returning to his humble cot, his sturdy figure outlined against the setting sun, his faithful collie, by his side, and his plough upon his shoulder."

Is he steady.—Farmer Haye: "That Jones boy that used to work for you wants me to give him a job. Is he steady?"

Farmer Seede: "Well, if

he was any steadier he'd be motionless."

Those Cheering words.—Farmer: "I'm afraid that times are so bad that you will not be able to get a job anywhere about here."

Tramp: "Oh, thank you! Thank you kindly for those cheering words."

The hop grower's lament.—
Prosperity's fled from our gardens and grounds;
How spindly our bines and how scanty our crops!
Wealth may be "advancing by leaps and bounds."
It certainly isn't by hops!

Never at a loss.—When a Scotsman has no argument at his tongue's end to defend his own line of conduct which another may have criticised, it may safely be inferred that his ancestry has a strain from some other nation.

A man who has an estate in Scotland took his new ploughman to task for the wavering furrows which were the result of his work.

"Your drills are not nearly so straight as those of Angus's work," he said, severely.

"Angus didna ken his work," said Tamas, calmly, contemplating his employer with an indulgent gaze. "Ye see, when the drills is crookit the sun gits in on all sides, an' 'tis then ye get early 'taters."

So bad as that.—A rich Bostonian bought an estate in Scotland called Glen Accra. He bought it without having seen it. He believed that he could trust the man he bought it from. And last summer he went over to have a look at the place. The drive from the nearest railway station to Glen Accra was a matter of twelve miles. The Bostonian hired a Highlander to drive him. As the cart jogged along, the Bostonian said: "I suppose you know the country hereabouts, well, friend?" "Aye ilka foot o' 't." "And do you know Glen Accra?" "Aye, weel," was the reply. "What sort of a place is it?' "Aweel," he said, "if ye saw the de'il tethered on it, ye'd juist say, Poor brute!"

Slap in between.—Farmer Button walked into the Market Place with one arm in a sling, his head bandaged, and the general appearance of having been in a very bad accident.

"How did it all happen?" a crowd of sympathetic inquirers hastened to ask.

Farmer Button shifted his bandages uneasily and explained: "Driving home from market t'other night it were terrible dark up Black Hill, and presently I says to the driver: 'Look out, Jim; there be a light comin' down left side, and one comin' down right side; mind where you be a-going to.' 'Right,' says Jim: 'I'll drive slap in between 'em.' And he just up and did so, and hanged if they warn't both on 'em on to one cart—one on each side!"

Choice of a profession.—"I suppose your son will adopt a profession?" said one farmer to another.

"Well," was the answer, "that's the way Josh talks about it now. But I shouldn't be surprised if he'd see the wisdom of lookin' for a profession that'll adopt him!"

The Glorious West.—Eastern man (writing home from the Far West): "The rush of business in the glorious West is simply marvellous—things move like lightning. I stepped into an estate office on my arrival, to buy a lot, and they made me out the receipt and filled out the deed in exactly three minutes." Same man (writing home five years later): "I'll come back as soon as I can sell my lot. I have been trying to sell it for four years now, and I think in a few years more will find a customer."

A Bargain.—John was returning home from a spree one morning when he came across Farmer Jones digging his potatoes.

"Look here," said John, "if you give me a couple of shillings I'll lift some of your tatties."

"Man," said the farmer, "I'll gie ye twa shullin's if ye promise tae lift nae mair o' them."

In Praise of Oats.—Oats are the food of the most sagacious of animals, viz., horses and Scotsmen. No kind of intoxicant is made from oats, excepting the oaten posset, which is, after all, not so very heady. Oats are reckoned an all-round crop, although you do now and then hear of a corner in oats. Oats are wild or tame. Wild oats have come somewhat into disrepute through being cultivated mostly by men who are not farmers.

Down in Essex.—"And you say that you ran your Essex Farm without actual loss?"

"I did," answered the man who has just bought a country place.

"How did you manage it?"

" Sent to London and bought my meat, fruit, and vegetables in the City market."

Honesty Rewarded.—The death of Earl Fitzwilliam recalls an incident in the career of his father, who died in 1857. One of his tenants informed him that his wheat had been seriously injured by the hounds, appraising the damage at £50, which the peer paid. After harvest the farmer came again, and said that the wheat, far from being injured where most trampled on, seemed strongest when cut, and he had brought back the £50. " Ah ! " said his lordship, " this is as things should be twixt man and man." Then he wrote out a cheque for £100, saying, " Take care of this, and when your eldest son is of age present it to him, and tell him how it came about."

Not so easy.—Sydney Smith used to say there were three things which every man fancied he could do—farm, drive a gig, and edit a newspaper, but if he lived now he would find farming not so easy for every man.

Agricultural statistics.—Policeman (in Ireland): " I have called for the agricultural statistics."

Mrs. Shearer : " Ye've what ! Sticks ! Och begorra, the sorra a twig we kape here. Phil carries his blackthorn wid him when he's from home."

Man, that's the Crop.—A distinguished Judge owns a farm and finds pleasure in walking about the place commenting on the condition of the crops. The grass had been cut during the day—a very thin crop—and was lying on the ground. The Judge saw it, and, calling his man, he said :—

" It seems to me you are very careless. Why haven't you been more particular in raking up this hay ? Don't you see that you have left little dribblings all about ? "

For a minute the man stared, wondering if the Judge were quizzing him. Then he replied : " Little dribblings ! Why, man that's the crop ! "

Jiu Jitsu.—" Jeems ! " bawled Farmer Gehaw on the day after his son returned from college.

" Yes, governor."

" What's this new-fangled business called, that I hear you braggin' so much about ? "

" Jiu Jitsu."

" Jiu Jitsu, eh ? Pretty husky thing, is it ? "

" That's what it is."

" Well, Jeems."

" What is it, governor ? "

"S'pose ye jest hustle out and see what Jiu Jitsu'll do fer that air wood-pile yander."

Squaring Accounts.—A famous war correspondent, while a reporter on an American paper, one day approached a farmer in a Kentucky town and asked him if there was any news in his neighbourhood.

"Not a bit," said the farmer. "We are all too busy with our crops to think of anything else."

"Pretty good crops this year?"

"Splendid; I ought to be in my field this minute, an' I would be if I hadn't come to town to see the coroner."

"The coroner?"

"Yes. Want him to hold an inquest on a couple of fellers down in our neighbourhood."

"Inquest? Was it an accident?"

"No. Zeke Burke did it a poppus. Plugged George Rambo and his boy Bill with a pistol."

"What caused the fight?"

"There wasn't no fight. Zeke never give the other fellers a show. Guess he was right, too, 'cause the Rambos didn't give Zeke's father an' brother any chance. Just hid behind a tree and fired at 'em as they came along the road. That was yistiday mornin', an' in an hour Zeke had squared accounts.

"Has Zeke been arrested?"

"No. What's the use? Some of old Rambo's relatives came along last night, burned down Zeke's house, shot him and his wife, an' set fire to his barn. No, Zeke hasn't been arrested."

Sarcastic.—Boarder: "I suppose you take summer lodgers so as to help you out?"

Farmer Winrow: "I s'pose so. I wouldn't know how to farm it nohow if it wasn't fer th' good ideas I git from summer lodgers."

Makes no difference.—"I've been thinkin' of workin' for old Beaton," said one farm hand to another, "an' I'd like to know what kind of a place it is to work at. Is the livin' fair?"

"First rate. Plenty to eat, an' all of it good."

"Is the pay sure?"

"Certain as the month rolls round."

"What kind of lodgin' do ye git there?"

"Well, I don't know; but the fact is, ye ain't in 'em enough when ye work with old Beaton for that to make any difference."

That Girl.—" There's mighty few people," said Farmer Corntossel, " that knows what to do with a farm after they get one."

" I have noticed that," answered the girl with frizzes. " They always insist on filling the whole place up with corn and oats and things when they might have such lovely tennis courts and golf links."

Do as Adam did.—" To succeed," said Lord Selborne to the Middleburg farmers the other day, " you must do as Adam did—sweat."

Agricultural Colleges.—Uncle Josh: " You've heerd of them agricultural colleges, haven't you ? "

Uncle Silas: " Yes, but what do they amount to ? I read there one of them graduated a lot of fellers the other day, and not one of them is willin' to take up farmin'."

Uncle Josh: " Well, that kind of looks as if they'd learned a good deal about it."

" Are you going to send your boy to the agricultural college ? '

" I don't see the use," answered Farmer Corntossel. " The first thing a college professor does when he gets a bright idea is to publish it. I'd rather subscribe to the newspaper."

He told a droll thing about Lord F—— at a farmer's dinner at Exeter the other day. Speaking to some toast his lordship had occasion to name one of the most important farmers present, and alluded with sympathy to a recent family affliction which had befallen him, the man's wife having died a short time before. The farmer having to speak by and by thanked his lordship very kindly for the way he had spoken of him. " But as for my old woman, she were a teasy twoad, and the Lord's welcome to her." —W. Allingham's Diary.

Laying for b'loons.—The farmer sat on the top rail of his fence with his sawed-off gun across his bony knees.

" Layin' for crows ? " queried the Weary Willie, who came limping up the dusty highway.

" No," the farmer gruffly answered. " I'm layin' fer b'loons. See that sign ? "

The wayfarer saw the sign. It was rudely lettered with white chalk on a blackboard. He read it aloud:

" All b'loonists is warned that these is private groun's. Any b'loonists trespassin' on these premises will be give the ful pennalty of the law."

" Understandable, ain't it ? " the farmer asked.

"Couldn't be plainer," said the way-farer "Been annoyin' you, have they?"

"Annoyin' is mild," returned the farmer. "The fust one of 'em dropped in the middle o' my onean bed. I'll admit I wuz rather tickled to see him, an' didn't say nothin' 'bout damages. Second feller tipped over seven of my beehives an' ripped the roof off the corn-crib. I wuz too dern busy dogin' bees to put in any bill, an' afore I could look 'round—both eyes bein' pretty nigh stung-shut—the feller was a-sailin' away over Plum Creek. The last chap didn't come clear down, but he dropped his anchor, an' somehow it caught in my cucumber vines, an' away he flew with 27 o' the finest an' ripest you ever see a-danglin' at the end of his drag-rope. Then I writ that warnin' over there an' loaded the gun, an' the fust arrynot that flies low enough I'll blow his old gas-bag full o' holes ez sure ez my name's Lige Hawkins!"

Came over with the Conqueror.—He was a new and aristocratic curate, and he was paying his first visit to a good old Yorkshire yeoman farmer whose forbears had held the farm in direct descent since Saxon times. The curate thought fit in conversation to tell the old man that his ancestors came over with the Conqueror.

"Coom over wi' Coonqueror, did they?" drawled the old farmer. "Lot of moock come over with Willum. We was here then."

Be Aisy now.—"Didn't you tell me you could hold the plough?" said a farmer to an Irishman he had taken on trial. "Be aisy, now," says Pat. "How could I hould it, an' two horses pullin' it away? Just stop the craytures, and I'll hould it for ye."

What else?—A man engaged by the Australian Lands Department to spread rabbit poison was out in the country, and came upon a disconsolate chap sitting on a fence.

"Hot?" said our man.

"Damnable," said the settler

"And dry?" said the rabbiter.

"Aye, as 'ell!" said the other.

"How are things otherwise?'

"Rotten," replied the bushie. "The drought's killed me cows, me old woman's run away with a cane-grower,, and the Jew money-lender in Mel'ne's foreclosed the mortgage."

"S'truth!" said our man. "Then in that case what are you waiting here for?"

"I'm waiting for the drought to break."

"But if the mortgage is foreclosed, and nothing is left to you, what do you want water for?"

And the man on the fence replied, with some disdain, "To drown meself, of course, you fool!"

More Light.—Captain of County Fire Brigade (called out to subdue an outbreak in local hay-ricks) to over-zealous comrade: "Not so fast, Jarge. Let 'un burn up a bit fust so as 'ow we can see what we're a doin' of."—Punch.

CHAPTER II.

CATTLE.

Get rid of that Cow.—The following note was received by a schoolmaster from the mother of a pupil:—

"Mister sir, my Jason had to be late to-day. It is his bizness to milk our cow. She kicked Jase in the back to-day when he wasn't looking or thinking of her, an he thot his back was broke, but it ain't. But it is black and blue, and the pane kept him late. We would get rid of that cow if we could. This is the fourth time she kicked Jase but never kicked him, late before."

Scottish Caution.—The subjoined proclamation was actually publicly read, some years ago, by the common crier, in a burgh north of the river Tay. "O yez! O yez! O yez! There is a cow to be killed at Flesher Gillies on Friday next, gin there sall be encouragement for the same. The Provost is to tak a hale leg; the Minister to tak anither leg for sartin; the Dominie and Gauger a leg between them. Sin there is only anither leg on hand, gin there sall be ony certainty of taking this odd leg, the cow shall be killed withouten fail, for the Flesher himsel is to tak his chance of seling the head and harragles."—Elgin Courier, 1828.

It maun be good.—Smith (and bride, on a tour, lunching at a clachan inn): "We can't eat this steak; it's not good."

Servant: "Ye're surely jokin', sir. It maun be guid. It's a bit o' the minister's auld coo."

Non-Committal.— Overheard at the door of a public hall near Benachie.

Farmer: "Good evening, John. Do you know if there is a meeting of the Agricultural Improvement Association here to-night?"

John (scratching his head): "Dod, I dinna ken; bit there's a meetin'o'the cattle show folk up the stair."

A Whistler story.—Once, in the country, and walking through a field, Whistler suddenly found that a huge bull was making straight towards him. He ran as he had never run before, and succeeded in getting to the other side of the fence before the bull got to him. When he reached the other side he saw a farmer, the owner of the field, coolly watching the proceedings. Mr. Whistler was furious, and shaking his fist at the farmer, said: "What do you mean, sir, by letting a savage bull like that roam at large? Do you know who I am, sir? I'm Whistler." "Are you?" replied the farmer "What's the good of telling me. Why didn't you tell the bull?"

A fair test.—Fair Visitor: "But how can I know if a bull is mad?"

Farmer: "Oh! just twist his tail or punch him in the ribs with the sharp end of a pitch-fork."

Cause and effect.—An American farmer lost a cow in a singular manner. The animal, in rummaging through a camp kitchen, found and swallowed an old umbrella and a cake of yeast. The yeast, fermenting in the poor beast's stomach, raised the umbrella, and she died in great agony.

Give him a lead.—Farmer (to lady): "Have you seen my bull?"

Lady: "Mercy, no! Where is he?"

Farmer: "He got loose. And if you should see him, will you please keep on that there red cloak and run this way?"

A pardonable error.—"I was once attending a show," says Lord Onslow in the "County Gentleman," "at which a bull named after me took first prize, and I accepted the invitation of a celebrated stock-breeder to visit his farm. He wired to his bailiff to meet a certain train, adding, 'I am bringing the Earl of Onslow.' The bailiff thought he had brought the champion bull, and brought a stick and ring instead of a carriage to meet us.''

An investment.—In the Post Office Savings Bank, where the sum standing to the credit of depositors must not exceed a certain limit, it is customary, when the limit is reached, to notify the depositors of the fact, asking them if they would like to invest the money in ''Government stock,'' and so make their ordinary account available for more deposits.

On one occasion this form of letter was sent to an old country-woman who had been a regular saver for many years. A few days later the official dealing with the case was astonished to receive the following answer:—

'' Dear Sir,—Thank you kindly for looking after my interests. I have never had any stock, but as you are willing to see to it for me I should like a nice cow.''

Fisk got the cream.—Commodore Vanderbilt had a strong rival in James Fisk, and he once set a trap for him. As they ran competition lines to Chicago, Vanderbilt proposed they should contract with each other to fleece the public by charging sixteen shillings per head for bringing cattle to New York. Fisk readily agreed.

Suddenly, without a warning, Vanderbilt's road announced a reduction in rates to six shillings a head. He thought he could thus break up the freight business of the other road.

Fisk, prince of schemers, sent an agent to Chicago, bought up 40,000 cattle, and had them shipped by Vanderbilt's road at the reduced fare. One hundred thousand dollars on the cattle alone he made as a private specnlation, besides loading up Vanderbilt's line so that he could not take paying freight of other kinds; while Fisk's road made money.

'' The Commodore got the cows, but Jim Fisk got the cream,'' Fisk said.

Appearances are deceptive.—Mr. John Barrett, now United States Minister to Panama, had a unique experience during the Presidential campaign. While speaking in a New England town, he made the assertion that he knew well what it was to work on a farm. A young farmer in the crowd, made sceptical by the speaker's faultless coat, immaculate shirt-front, pale grey trousers, and shining tile, shouted out:—

'' You work on a farm? Bet

yer never milked a cow in your life.''

''I take your bet,'' said Barrett. ''I will put up £20 against the same amount that I can milk a cow faster than you can.''

The bet was accepted; the Democrats raised a purse of £20, two cows were brought round. At the cry of ''Ready! Go!'' the milk rattled into the bottom of the pails, and Barrett's pail was full first, the meeting winding up in a blaze of enthusiasm.

Lacked good breeding.—An old Scottish farmer recently went to a cattle show to exhibit a favourite cow for which he had high hopes of winning first place. On learning the result, and that his cow had been placed fifth, his anger knew no bounds, and, rushing into the ring, he attacked the judges. ''Why is my cow not first? What are her faults, I'd like to know?''

At this point one of the judges approached him and answered: ''Her faults, my good man, are somewhat akin to your own. She lacks good breeding.''

Train up a cow.—''T. P's Weekly'' relates how Major Malony, of Ballyduff, saw from his bedroom window a lad driving a cow back and forward again and again over a ditch and through a fence on his land, and he rushed out to question the trespasser. ''What are ye after with that cow? Is it to kill the beast ye want?''

''Kill her! Shure, it's to keep her alive I want.''

''Keep her alive?''

''Shure, it's taiching her to get her own living I am. There isn't a ditch or fince in the barony that'll hold her in afther I've done wid her.'' Then the Major understood.

A strange animal.—Circus man (hunting for a stray elephant): ''Have you seen a strange animal round here?''

Irishman: ''Begorra, Oi hov that. There was a bull around here pulling up carrots wid his tail!''

The udder side.—A lady and gentleman were walking across a field in which some cows were grazing, the man asked the girl if she had to milk cows which side would she start.

''Right side,'' said she, after a little hesitation.

''No; the udder side,'' said he.

A failure.—''Yes,'' said the old inhabitant; ''he was a failure, poor fellow. A mule kicked him 'crost a 10-acre field, an' when he landed a bull tossed him into a pine saplin', an' when he got thar a cyclone blowed the saplin' down, an then he give up farmin' forever! ''

Irresistible.—Captain X —, who commands a company which is recruited from amongst the agricultural labourers of the district, is an enthusiastic volunteer. Recently he called a parade for Saturday afternoon in order to exercise his men in the tactics of active service. Dividing his company into two sections, he dispatched one, under Lieutenant Z—, to hold a certain position, and later set forth at the head of the remaining section to attack it.

Unfortunately the captain stumbled and cut his leg, but as the afternoon was waning he sent his men on under command of the colour-sergeant, whilst he sat by the hedge to bandage his leg with his handkerchief. Presently rose the sound of firing, shouts of alarm, and back down the stony lane came his men in ignominious flight.

"Cowards!" roared the captain, pausing in his bandaging. "Have you let Lieutenant Z—'s men repulse you?"

"It ain't Lieutenant Z—'s men, sir," gasped the portly and terrified colour-sergeant, as he led the flight past his indignant officer; "it's the farmer's bull!

And as it came into view the captain, in spite of his injury, fled too.

The social test.—The social standing of people in parts of Victoria is fixed by the number of cows they possess. If you have fifty or more you waltz above the chalk line in the local "Assembly." Below that the grading goes by tens. Mrs. Jimson, who "milks forty," says of Mrs. Jackson, who only "milks thirty," "A very nice person, but hardly in our class."

The relationship ceased.—"And so I understand that Patrick O'Flaherty was your uncle?" said a counsel to a witness.

"He was—till a bull killed him."

The dinner bell.—Jimmy: "What's dat bell around dat cow's neck fer?"

Jammy: "Oh! that's what she rings when she wants to tell the calf that dinner's ready."

What Nature never did.—A well-known artist overheard a countryman and his wife ridiculing his picture, which represented a farm scene, and, indignant, said:—

"That painting is valued at a hundred pounds. Allow me

to ask if you are familiar with works of art ?"

Farmer: "Not very familiar with art, but I know something about Nature, young man. When you make a cow get up from the ground by putting her fore feet first you do something nature never did."

How it struck him.—Farmer Greene: "Glad t' see ye home, Silas! How's things up in town?"

Farmer Browne: "Bustling, Joshua, bustlin'! Why, the way folks rush roun' there y'd think the cows wuz loose in th' cabbages th' hull tarnation time!"

Can do her no harm.—A V.S. not a hundred miles from Inverness, having been consulted about the health of a cow, recommended a quart of stout for the trouble, and undertook to administer the dose himself. One of the farm servants, who was rather sceptical in the matter, looked through the door and saw the vet. drink the medicine himself. On coming out, the vet. remarked, with a pawky smile:

"Weel, if that dose does not do her any good it can do her no harm."

The Governor's Cows.—There used to be a small green opposite the Government House at Plymouth, over which no one was permitted to pass. Not a creature was allowed to approach, except the Governor's cow. The sentries had particular orders to keep trespassers off the forbidden turf. One day, old Lady B—— called on the Governor, and, in order to make a short cut home, was going across the lawn, when she was challenged by the sentry. She remonstrated; the soldier said he could not disobey orders. "But," said the Lady B——, with a stately air, "do you know who I am?" "I don't know who you be, ma'am," replied the man, "but I know who you bain't—you bain't the Governor's cow." So Lady B— wisely gave up the argument and went the other way.

Not the same.—The Earl of Glasgow tells of an amusing experience he had when Governor of New Zealand. There was an Ayrshire bull in the colony which had an unvanquished career in the show-ring, and out of compliment to the Governor its owner called it "Lord Glasgow." His Lordship was walking along a narrow lane near the entrance to a showyard, behind two or three colonists who were carrying on a brisk conversation, and whose tongues gave unmistakeable evidence that they were natives of the old country. One of them said: "A' havena seen Lord Glasgow the day." His lordship good-naturedly sought to oblige his countryman by saying: "If you look round you will see him." The Scotchman looked round, and added, "it's no you a' mean—it's the bull."

Wore his Cow's medals.—The commanding officer of a Yorkshire yeomanry regiment was congratulating the "A" troop on its appearance, and referred proudly to the medals worn by some army veterans in the ranks. Private Harvey went home that night in a thoughtful mood, and next morning he came on parade with several medals on his chest.

Sergeant: "I didn't know you had been in the regulars?"

Harvey: No, I ain't."

Sergeant: "What about the medals, then; they can't be yours?"

Harvey: "Can't they, indeed? But they be. My old coo won 'em all at Otley Show!"

I told you so.—An old lady who was in the habit of saying after any event that she had foretold it, was one day "sold" by her husband, who had got tired of her eternal "I told you so!"

Rushing into the house, he dropped into a chair, raised his hands and exclaimed: "Oh, my dear! what do you think? The old cow has gone and eaten the grindstone."

"I told you so! I told you so!" was the reply; "you always let it stand out of doors."

A correction.—There is a story told of the present Earl of Antrim, who is well-known in the North of Ireland as a lover of agriculture and any kind of farming. An aristocratic gentleman sent a letter to his lordship complaining that his conduct was not that of a titled earl, but rather that of a country farmer. "I saw you myself," he wrote, "driving three cows to market, and consider it disgraceful," etc. In reply to this extremely personal epistle, the Earl thanked the writer, and merely added that a mistake had been made, "for it was not three cows you saw me drive to market, but two cows and a bullock!"

Had enough o' that systhem.—At a certain cattle market the other day a well-known Irish dealer accosted the owner of a fat bullock. "Oi'll give ye nine pounds," he said, after a critical inspection from a safe distance.

"Nonsense," responded the owner. "I want twelve for him. It isn't like you, Mr. M—, to be making a blundher like that. Come and feel his points."

"Be jabers, I won't," he remarked. "I've had about enough o' that systhem. The lasht toime I thried it on, the ongrateful baste lifted me over a ten-fut wall."

He knew.—Smart Tourist (in New Hampshire, where cobble stones and granite are the principal crops): "I say there, friend, what are you building a wire fence around that field for? There isn't anything in there that any animal could possibly eat."

Farmer: "I'm putting up this fence for fear some of my cows might stray in there and starve to death."

But she did.—Maiden (in summer lodgings): "How that cow looks at me."

Native: "It's your red parasol, mum."

Maiden: "Dear me! I knew it was a bit out of fashion, but I didn't suppose a country cow would notice it."

It worked admirably.—It is said that, if you have presence of mind enough to face a raging bull and look straight into his eyes, he is powerless to do you harm. We tried this experiment once, says an agricultural contemporary, and found it worked admirably. The fierce animal tore the ground with his feet and bellowed with all his might; but something seemed to hold him back like magic, and he did us no injury. Perhaps we ought to add, in order to be correct historically, that the bull was on the other side of a fence.

The Cow with an iron tail.—Two small boys of my acquaintance one evening at the tea-table heard their mother remark to a visitor that she thought Mrs. Jones (who supplied her with milk) kept a cow with an iron tail. The boys listened to this remark with open ears, but passed no comment on it at the time. Afterwards they discussed together the wonderful phenomenon, and as a result they next day presented themselves to Mrs. Jones. She was the presiding genius of the village shop, as well as the owner of "strange" cattle. "Please, Mrs. Jones," the elder boy began with wide open eyes of expectation, and yet very clearly and deliberately, for he was rather slow of speech, " mother says that you keep a cow with an iron tail; would you let us see it ? "

The local band.—For a recent fat stock show in a northern town a local brass band had been hired, and towards the close of the show some of the men had been having a good deal of drink, and this did not improve the music.

At the close of a " selection " —all brass bray and burst and bang—one of the bandsmen turned to his wife who had just entered, and asked :

" Weel, lass, how's ta loike it ? "—meaning the show.

" Oh, weel," was the reply, "it don't hurt me. Aw's gettin' used to it. But Aw pities them puir beasties ! "

" Why ? "

" I wonder you ask. Ain't they had to stand that racket all day, puir things ? "

The Amateur Farmer.—" How you must enjoy getting out to your little farm and casting dull care to the winds after your hard day's toil in the City ! "

" Casting dull care to the winds ! You wouldn't call it amusing to chase a runaway cow three miles after dark, would you ? "

Why they were not milked.—Londoner (to boatman on Norfolk Broads), " There seems to be a large number of cattle hereabouts, boatman."

Boatman : " Yes, sir."

Londoner : " But I don't see any houses anywhere near. How are the cattle milked ? "

Boatman : " They ain't milked at all."

Londoner : " Not milked ? How's that ? "

Boatman : " They're all bullocks."

The Quaker's retort.—A Quaker went into a book-store, and an impertinent salesman, wishing to have a little fun, said to him : " You are from the country, aren't you ? "

" Yes."

" Then here's just the thing for you," said the clerk, holding up a book.

" What is it ? " asked the Quaker.

" It's an essay on the rearing of calves."

" Friend," said the Quaker, " thou hadst better present that to thy mother."

The Cure's Gratitude.—A curé, taking the air one morning, and reading his breviary, received on his bald head the droppings from a passing bird. Instead of being put out, he showed his grateful nature by exclaiming: "Merci au bon dieu de sa bonté que les vaches ne volent pas!" ("Thank God that cows don't fly!")

"Watered Stock."—Daniel Drew added to the language his contribution, "watered stock," and it grew out of the fact that when he sold a drove of oxen he weighed them to the buyer immediately after they had drunk quantities of water. After the old rover got to be a magnate of Wall Street, this practice of his gave addition to our financial nomenclature.

"Do animals have fun?" asks a correspondent. Of course they do. When a cow switches her tail across the face of a man who is milking her, steps along just two yards, and turns to see him pick up his stool and follow, she has the most amused expression on her face possible; and if she can kick over the milk pail she grows hilarious.

Sir Wilfrid Lawson's Epitaph.—The late Sir Wilfrid Lawson, who kept a herd of shorthorns, at Brayton, once bought a bull for £1,200 from the Duke of Devonshire. When the animal died shortly afterwards, Sir Wilfrid wrote the following epitaph:—

"Here lies Baron Oxford, quiet and cool,
Bred by a duke, and bought by a fool."

Irish Bulls.—An Irish peasant was once asked whether he knew what an Irish "bull" was. "To be sure I do," he replied. "If you was dhrivin' along a high road and you seen three cows lyin' down in a field and wan ov thim's standin' up—that wan is an Irish bull." The Yorkshire and Lancashire Agricultural Society fell into a laughable error on the appearance of Miss Edgeworth's essay on Irish "Bulls," several copies of the work were ordered for the use of members of the Society, who were mortified to find that the bulls were mere creatures of the brain, and not, as they had expected, robust animals pastured on the rich grazing lands of Meath and Limerick.

The power of the eye.—A Yorkshireman who had been listening to a lecture on the power of the eye and its hypnotic influence, asked the lecturer if he really believed "all he'd been a-telling of 'em."

"Yes," he answered.

"Whya then, ah'll tell ya what, just cum doon ta mah place to-morrow mornin' and you can hev a few minutes in t' paddock wi' my bull; we-ve tried everything but eeying him to quieten him, an' ez you're used to that business, ah'll leave it to you."

Barefitted about the forehead.—A young lady in a perfumer's tells of a rustic who hung about the shop for a while, and then shyly ventured in, and asked if she had "ony hair restorer."

He was shown some bottles, and having fixed on one he remarked:

"Ye ken, it's for the bull. We're sending it to the show, an' it's gey barefitted about the forehead."

Embrocation extraordinary.—"I guess you won't have heard about that embrocation we have in America," said the imaginative Yankee. "You just simply cut off a cow's tail, rub the embrocation on the stump, and you have another tail on the cow in a week's time.'

"Ay, that's nowt," the Briton said, "Yo' want to see the embrocation we have at the place I come fro'. Yo' just simply cut a cow's tail off, stick part of the cow's tail that yo' cut off in the embrocation bottle, and there's another cow grown on in about four days' time!"

Hyperbolic.—A speculative Scottish gentlemen wanted to dispose of some bees, so, to attract purchasers, he printed the following placard:—"Extensive sale of live stock, comprising not less than one hundred and forty thousand head with an unlimited right of pasturage."

A Testimonial.—"Sirs: We fed our baby on 'modified' cows' milk the first six months, but the milkman did not understand how to modify his cows properly, and in consequence the child lost flesh till he weighed but one pound. I now procured some of your celebrated Infants' Food. This the baby managed to trade off to the dog for some dog-biscuit, which he ate, and is now well and hearty. The dog died on the infants' food, but dogs are cheap. We are grateful to you indeed, and you may use my name if you like."

Advice to a young man.—Never take a bull by the horns. Take him by the tail instead, then you can let go.

If!—An English tourist in the west of Ireland met a farmer driving some young cattle to a local fair, and encountering him again in the evening, asked him how much he had got for his stock. " Four pounds a head," replied Pat. " Only four pounds a head!" said the tourist. " Why, if you brought them to my country you would have got at least £6 each for them." " Och, maybe so, yer honour," rejoined the farmer, " an' if I cud bring the lakes of Killarney to Purgatory I'd get a pound a drop."

I'd like him changed.—" A man was charged at the Nenagh Assizes, a few years ago, with cattle lifting. After the jury had been sworn, the judge, observing the prisoner was unrepresented, said to him: "Have you no counsel?"

" I have not, me lord judge."

" I must tell you what, perhaps, you do not know, that you are charged with a very serious offence, and if convicted you may be sent to prison for a considerable time. Surely you have at least a solicitor to say something for you?"

" Sorra a wan, me lord; I've several good friends among the jury, but the judge has convicted me several times already, and I'd like him changed!"

When last seen.—" I know of nothing," said a gentleman, " that will kick up an excitement sooner than a mad ox. I saw one the other day rush up the street, followed by all the boys within a circuit of two miles, the whole led on by a brindle bulldog, two parsons, six butchers, two policemen, and an alderman. They were chasing the ox."

" Well, did they secure him?"

" I am not in a position to say; but when last seen the animal was chasing them."

The cow refused to use it.—One of the speakers at a missionary meeting told the audience that, in response to an appeal for various articles for use on an African farm, a milking stool was sent to him from England. He gave it to the servant whose duty it was to milk the cows, with strict injunctions to use it. On the first day the man returned home bruised and battered, and with an empty pail.

When asked for an explanation he replied, " Milk stool very nice, baas, but she won't sit on it!"

The golden milk.—" Gentlemen," said the orator, " a cow may be drained dry, and if Chancellors of the Exchequer persist in meeting every deficiency that occurs by increasing the income tax they will inevitably kill the cow that lays the golden milk."

When the trouble begins.—Tenderfoot (on the Texas ranch) "I should think it would be a lot of trouble for a man to pick out his own cattle from among so many."

Cowboy: "Oh, that's an easy matter. The trouble begins when he picks out some other man's cattle. See!"

Our local agricultural show.—Scene—A Country Drawing Room. Visitor (to old lady and daughters, one of whose hobbies is the keeping of a small herd of Jerseys): "By the way, I didn't see you at our local agricultural show."

Daughter: "Oh, no! We never go unless we exhibit ourselves."—Punch.

Bad for the cow.—In the Fishing Gazette an angler tells a story of Scotch coolness:—He was one day fishing the Ness, when he noticed a cow examining some things left by the waterside. On landing, he found she had eaten up the whole of one side, the button half, of a new mackintosh. Meeting the miller, whose property she was, he showed him the mangled evidence of her misdeeds, expecting at least, to meet with something like sympathy for the loss. The miller's sympathies were, however, all on the other side. He surveyed it for some time in silence and with an air of dejection, and simply exclaimed, "Eh, but she'll no be the better o' the buttons!"

Improving stock in Kentucky.—President Scott, of the Cincinnati Southern Railroad, was greatly annoyed when he first took hold of the road by the claims for horses and cattle killed by trains on their way through Kentucky. It seemed as though it were not possible for a train to run north or south Kentucky without killing either a horse or a cow. And every animal killed, however scrawny, scrubby, or miserable it may have been before the accident, always figured in the claims subsequently presented as of the best blood in Kentucky.

"Well," said Scott one day, after examining a claim, "I don't know anything that improves stock in Kentucky like crossing it with an engine."

County Society.—Mrs. Waldo (of Boston): "I have a letter from your Uncle James, Penelope, who wants us to spend the summer on his farm."

Penelope (dubiously): "Is there any society in the neighbourhood?"

Mrs. Waldo: I've heard him speak of the Holsteins and Jerseys and Herefords. I presume they are pleasant people."

Exchange no robbery.—For several mornings a cow at Neuchatel gave little or no milk. Suspecting theft, the owner quietly placed a bull in the cow's place, and the next night had the satisfaction of seeing two Italian railway labourers put to ignominious flight.

A Kite-flying Cow.—A cow flying a kite was the unusual spectacle witnessed recently near New York.

A boy had been flying the kite in a pasture and had laid it on the turf where the cow was grazing. The animal, in browsing about, swallowed the ball of twine, which was lying about thirty feet from the kite.

As the cow moved off the kite moved too, and cow, eyeing it curiously, started again. The kite followed. The cow quickened her gait. The kite gracefully rose in the air and remained suspended until the frightened animal was caught.

No offers.—A countryman had lost his wife and a favourite cow on the same day. His friends came to console him for the loss of his wife; and as the farmer was highly respectable, no time was lost by some busybodies in giving hints and offers towards getting another for him. "Ou, ay," he at length replied, "you're a' keen enough to gie me anither wife, but no yin o' ye offers to gie me anither coo."

Make yourself useful.—'Arry and Araminta strolled lovingly adown the green and perfumed meadow, prating playfully of love.

In the course of their perambulations they chanced upon a bull—a skittish bull; for his head lowered coquettishly, charmingly he pawed the ground, and then——

"Oh!" cried Araminta to her valiant swain, "he's making straight towards us! What shall we do?"

"Here," roared the resourceful 'arry "don't stand there doing nothing! Come and help me climb this tree!"

Tautological.—"He was gored by an angry bull," wrote a reporter, in describing the death of a farmer.

"Don't be tautological," said the editor. "Strike out the word 'angry'; of course, a good-natured bull wouldn't do such a thing."

CHAPTER III.

HORSES, MULES AND DONKEYS.

A thin horse.—At a provincial county-court recently, a case was brought before the judge concerning some horses.

One of the witnesses for the plaintiff was asked if the horses were thin.

"No," said the witness.

"What is your description of a thin horse?" he was asked.

"Well, sir," he said, "I think a horse is thin when you can hang your hat on its hip-bones."

Sold.—"Appearances are deceptive" is a proverb the truth of which has just been brought home to a young auctioneer who was wont to look upon himself as being exceptionally smart.

It was his first sale, and was of the live and dead farming stock variety. The bidding for a certain horse had, by reason of the young man's eloquence, risen in a very few minutes to eleven and a half guineas.

"Eleven guineas and a half, gentlemen," said the auctioneer scornfully, "only eleven and a half for this splendid chestnut cob, rising seven, and warranted sound in wind and limb. Going for eleven guineas and a half. Gentlemen! Gentlemen! Aren't you to be tempted?"

"Oh, well, I don't mind giving you twelve pound, mister," said a little man who was chewing a straw.

"Thank you, sir. Going at twelve pounds! Going at twelve! Gone!"

As his hammer fell triumphantly a laugh went up, but it took some time to convince that smart auctioneer that the man who bought the horse had taken him down one-and-sixpence and several pegs in addition.

About George III.—It is told of George III that having purchased a horse, the dealer put into his hands a large sheet of paper, covering with writing.

"What's this?" said his majesty.

"The pedigree of the horse, sire, which you have just bought.

"Take it back, take it back," said the king, laughing; "it will do very well for the next horse you sell."

Cabby's humour.—A lady bargained with a cabman at a station to take her into the town with her parrots and cats, a dog, the boxes, and the baskets.

Cabman : " Beggin' your pardon, ma'am, but you ain't expecting a flood, I 'ope ? "

" Dear me, no ; whatever made you ask that ? "

" I thought I'd ask," said Jehu, " 'cos I ain't certain as 'ow my horse can swim, and I fancied that you were a-takin' my keb for a Noah's Ark l "

Knowed he was a muff.—There is a story of the Duke of Clarence (William IV.), whose bluff sailor-like bearing embarrassed his Ministers and scandalised his courtiers when he came to the throne. He used to tell it himself :—

" I was riding near Hampton unattended when I was overtaken by a butcher's boy with a tray of meat. 'That's a nice cob of yours, old gent,' said the boy.

" Pretty fair,' I answered.

" 'Mine's a good 'un, too, and I'll tell you what, I'll trot you to Hampton Wick for a pot o' beer.'

His Royal Highness declined the offer, and the boy galloped off, calling back over his shoulder " I knowed you was only a muff."

Inquire within :—A Gentleman who had left his bony steed in the street a few minutes while on business, upon returning a short time afterwards discovered to his amazement, that some jovial friend had placed on the fleshless ribs a card, bearing the inscription — " Oats wanted. Inquire within."

The cab horse as trooper.—The sun blazed down on a field of hot, tired horses and excited troopers, all waiting for a rawboned animal to obey the urgings of the starter and get into line.

" Bring up that horse ! " shouted one of the officers. " You'll get into trouble if you don't ! "

" I'm as tired of it as you are, sir, but I can't help it. He's a cab horse, sir, and he won't start till he hears the door shut, sir, and I haven't got any door to shut ! "

The poet puzzled.—When Coleridge was staying among the Quantock Hills he was fond of riding over to Taunton. One day his horse cast a shoe, and he stopped at a village to have it replaced.

" What time is it ? " he asked the smith, chiefly with the desire of making conversation.

" I'll tell 'ee presently, sir,"

said the man. Then he lifted a hind foot of the horse, and, looking across it attentively, said "Half-past eleven."

"How do you know?" asked Coleridge.

"Do'ee think I have shod horses all my life and don't know by sign what time it is?"

The poet went away puzzled, but returned in the evening and offered the blacksmith a shilling to show him how he could tell time by a horse's hoof.

"Just you get off your horse, sir. Now, do 'ee stoop down and look through the hole in yon pollard ash, and you'll see the church clock."

A K. C.'s story. — At the annual dinner of the Union Society of London, Mr. Rufus Isaacs, K.C., told a story of the late Lord Chief Justice. A witness in a running-down case, when asked: "Were you driving this cart on the day in question? persisted in replying in emphatic tones "No, I was not."

At last the Lord Chief Justice himself put the query but could only elicit the same reply. "Then what were you doing?" demanded his lordship.

"I was driving the horse."

Plaguey bad luck.—A farmer became bankrupt. In the course of his examination before the Official Receiver he admitted that he had been speculating on the Turf and he had experienced what he described as "plaguey bad luck."

"Did you know anything about horse-racing?"

"No; that's why I engaged a fellow who did to buy some 'osses for me."

"And these horses turned out badly I suppose?"

"Very, though I don't blame the 'osses for that. They tried hard but summat were bound to turn up to upset 'em. They nearly allus ran second."

"How do you account for that?"

"Weel sometimes they ran second 'cos they'd over much weight to carry, sometimes they ran second 'cos the jockey had backed another and wanted 'em there. But more often than not they ran second cos the judge would have them there. Sometimes, again, they ran second 'cos there wor nobbut two 'osses in the race!"

Father (to the seven-year-old son besides him in the dog-cart, cutting the whip sharply through the air): "See, Tommy how I make the horse go faster without striking him at all."

Tommy (in an eager tone of happy discovery): "Papa,

why don't you beat us that way?"

A Knowing Horse.—"I engaged," says a traveller, "a chaise at Galway to conduct me some few miles into the country, and had not proceeded far when it pulled up at the foot of a hill, and the driver, coming to the door, opened it. "What are you at, man? This isn't where I ordered you to stop," said I.

"Whist! your honour; I'm only desaving the baste. If I bang the door, he'll think you're out, and he'll cut up the hill like blazes."

How goes the ass?—A young man was once proceeding along the road on a beautiful horse, when he overtook an old monk riding on a donkey.

"How goes the ass, father?" he asked.

"On horseback. my son, on horseback."

Chief Justice Doherty used to relate an experience which befel him during a visit to a country house in Ireland. His friend, the host, sent a car to the railway station to bring him to the place. He had not gone far when the horse became very restive, and finally upset the car into a ditch. The judge asked the driver how long the animal had been in harness.

"Half an hour, sur."

"I mean, how long since he was first put in harness."

"Sure, I've tould you, half an hour, sur," answered the driver, "an' the masther said if he carried ye safe he'd buy him."

Sweet simplicity.—She was young and beautiful, and had never been on a racecourse before and he was trying to explain everything, and to make her day pleasant for her.

"Now you must have a bet on this race,' he said. "I'll put you a sovereign each way on the favourite."

She thanked him with a smile.

The race was run, and the favourite came in with the crowd.

"How much do I win?" she said.

"Well-er-in-fact nothing."

"Oh, but I thought each way meant whether the horse won or lost."

A sure way.—She: "Is there any sure way of telling the age of a horse?"

He: "Yes, ask the dealer, and multiply by two."

A good ladies' horse.—"You told me he was a good ladies' horse," angrily said the man who had made the purchase.

"He was," replied the deacon

"My wife owned him, and she's one of the best women I ever knew."

The Artificial Horse.—One of the mechanical contrivances of our boasted times is the machine that gives its owners a substitute for horse exercise. As told in the Sporting Times :—

It is well known that one of the very best boys in "the House" only contrives to live high, and at the same time look fit, by taking horseless horse-exercise in his bedroom every morning on a machine that looks like a blacksmith's bellows with a hunting-saddle on top of it. But the thing got out of hand last week, and our hero had several cuts and contusions.

One reason.—"Why," asked the racehorse, sneeringly, "do you have that great bunch of useless hair on your fetlocks ?"

"One reason," said the Clydesdale, "is that I want to look as much unlike a useless sporting animal as I possibly can."

Goin' home.—Purchaser (angrily) : "You told me this horse could go with the speed of the wind. It was all I could do to get into town before noon."

Dealer : "He ain't had no fair show yit. Wait till ye turn him home'ard. Goin' home he's greased lightnin' !"

Philosophy.—Having a bad day makes a philosopher of a man. "Here am I," said a well-known backer of horses, "I have worked for my money like a horse, and now I am losing it like an ass !"

No last legs.—"Why, that is a very spirited horse. I thought you told me it was on its last legs." "No, I didn't or if I did, I meant that it was always on its hind legs."

A Poetical Traveller, stopping at a Georgia inn, dismounted from his horse and called to the landlord, who was lounging on the verandah :—

"Wrinkled 'ostler, grim and thin,
Here is custom come your way ;
Take my brute and lead him in—
Stuff his ribs with mouldy hay."

"Ef you say that ag'in," said the landlord "I'll lamm you side the head with this hickory. Thar's a nigger here to look after the horses !"

"My good man," explained the traveller, "I meant no offence. I was only quoting Tennyson to you."

—"Hang Tennyson !" exclaimed the landlord, "an' tell him

I said so. Neither him nor you kin make a stable boy o'me."

A saddle no doubt.—

He ordered a saddle of mutton,
The waiter brought it of course:
Said he after trying to carve it;
"'Tis a saddle, no doubt, of a horse."

Had him there.—"Well, you're a veterinary surgeon—what do you know about a horse?" asked a brow-beating attorney.

"I don't pretend to be a horse doctor," replied the witness, "but I know a good deal of the nature of a horse."

"That means to say you know a horse from a jackass when you see them."

"Oh, yes, just so! For instance, I should never take you for a horse."

The Schoolmaster abroad.—Inspector of Village School (questioning class): "Now, my boy, what is an ?"

Pupil (dejectedly): "I dunno sir."

Inspector: Well, for instance, could I ride from here to France?"

Pupil (brightening up): "Noa sir, that yer couldn't; for feyther saw you on hossback t'other day, an' sed as how he'd lay a shilling yer couldn't roide a moile without a-wobbling off."

He knew.—Referring to a man who owns and trains a few horses, a race-course habitue said to another trainer:

"He's a mystery. He lives well, and is always well dressed, and yet he never wins a race. I can't make him out."

"Well, you see," said the other, "wot little bit he does make he makes reg'lar, without no risk. It doesn't cost yer nothin' for backin' 'em, don't you know, when yer bit's always the other way. Take it from me, never tryin' and always losin' is a bit better for the bank balance than always tryin' an' 'hardly ever winnin'. I know, cos I've played the game both ways!"

Mixed.—A Cavalry sergeant was out of patience with an awkward recruit, and thus spoke to him: "Never approach the horses from behind without speaking. If you do, they'll kick that thick head of yours, and the end of it will be that we shall have nothing but lame horses in the squadron."

Misplaced sympathy.—"It must make those poor horses dreadfully tired to go running round the race-course," said the sympathetic woman.

"No," replied the guileless

man who bets, "the horses are all right. It's the man who went over there with a sure tip who is tired."

What the cob missed.—A clergyman in a town in Hertfordshire recently took a great fancy to a cob ridden by a butcher's boy who brought the meat supply for the house from the nearest town, and the horse changed owners. The clergyman was the head master of the grammar school, and he rode his new mount to his daily duty; but neither whip nor spur would get it out of a shuffle, while jibbing and buck-jumping brought one or two spills. He called in great indignation on the butcher, who, in his turn, asked the boy what it meant.

"He'll be all right again," said the boy, "if you'll only carry the basket!"

Artful.—A man entered the bar-parlour of a country inn on a very cold day. A group of loungers were huddled about the fire, and the stranger could not get near it.

"Got any oysters?" he asked the landlord, and receiving an affirmative reply said, "Take a dozen out to my horse."

All hands crowded to the door to see the horse eat oysters, and the stranger secured the most comfortable seat. The landlord returned soon, and said the horse refused to eat the shell-fish.

"Well, give 'em to me, then," said the artful visitor, in his warm corner.

No impediment.—"Never was glad for this im-im-pediment in my speech but once," said the man from the North.

"When was that?"

"Fe-fe-fellow asked me h-h-how much I would take for a-a horse, and while I-I-I was t-trying to tell him t-twenty p-pounds, he offered me f-fifty."

As the poet says.—Dealer: "Well, sir, you must take the 'oss or leave 'im. There he is, 'with all 'is himperfections on 'is 'ead,' as the poet says!"

Customer: "Ah, your friend the poet can't have looked at his legs!"

That settled it.—"I have several reasons for not buying the horse," said the man. "The first is that I haven't enough money, and—"

"You needn't mention the others," interrupted the owner.

No harm meant.—"Is she gentle?" asked the city man, who thought he wanted to buy a steed.

"Gentle? Why, she's as gentle as a suckin' dove. Hain't

got a fault or failin' in the world —nussir. She don't kick, or strike, or bite——''

At that instant the mare swung her head viciously around and snapped off a piece of the seller's ear.

"That is, not with the deliberate intention of doin' any harm. The mare is sorter absent-minded at times, an' I kinder guess she must 'a' mistook my ear fer a cabbage leaf."

He knew better. — The coachman had bought a load of hay for the horses, and it was nearly unloaded in the yard when his master made his appearance.

"This hay is not good," he said, "it is mixed."

"Beg your pardon, sir, the horses eat it very well, I have given them some."

"No doubt, but I tell you that hay is not good."

"All right; if the gentleman knows hay better than the horses do."

Each one his turn.—While Henri IV. of France was once being harangued by deputies in a provincial town, an ass started to bray. Said the King:—

"Pray, gentlemen, allow him to go on; each one in his turn."

Made a difference.—In an Irish paper was an advertisement for horses to stand at livery, on the following terms:—

"Long-tailed horses at 3s. 6d. per week. Short-tailed horses at 3s. per week."

On inquiry into the cause of the difference, it was answered that the horses with long tails could brush the flies off their backs while eating, whereas the short-tailed horses were obliged to take their heads from the manger.

An Excuse.—In past coaching days there was an old Jehu who was not over choice in his language when driving. Seated on a box beside him was a Quaker, who was much shocked, and begged him to remember the patience of Job. Turning round, with an indignant expression on his face, he said: "Job never druv two blind hosses and a bolter."

The life to come.—Lucy Larcom the author, was one day driving with Mr. Whittier. The hill was steep, and Whittier was driving. The horse was gay, and the load was not light. Lucy was talking, and she talked on. The subject was the life to come. The horse grew unruly. The buggy lurched and rolled. Whittier grashed the reins valiantly, anticipating a possible accident. But Lucy talked on serenely. The horse threatened to break. The danger redoubled. The buggy sagged heavily on Lucy's side. Still she murmured on. "Lucy," said the poet at last, "if thee does not stop talking till I get this horse in hand, thee will be in heaven before thee wants to!"

No use telling.—A story is told of a County Court judge, who, for some little time, had a house in a Yorkshire village, and whilst there did a bit of "hoss swapping" with one of the farmers. Unfortunately, his horse did not turn out well, and on meeting the farmer one day he said:—

"Robert, you took me in with that horse. It has turned out very badly."

"Hez't noo?" replied Robert. "Whye, that's a bad job; but you maun't gan blethering aboot as Ah-ve-ta'en ya in, or else fau'k 'll get it i' ther heeads 'at yu're nobbut a verra poor judge."

Knew that very well.—An ostler was sent to the stable to bring forth a traveller's horse. Not knowing which of the two strange horses in the stalls belonged to the traveller, and wishing to avoid the appearance of ignorance in his business, he saddled both animals and brought them to the door. The traveller pointed out his own horse, saying: "That's my nag." "Certainly, your honour, I knew that very well, but I didn't know which was the other gentleman's."

No inducement.—"I've got the very thing that you want," said the horse dealer to the farmer in search of a horse, "a thorough-going road horse, five years old, sound as a quail; £20, cash down, and he goes ten miles without stopping."

The purchaser threw his hands skyward. "Not for me," he said, "not for me. I wouldn't give you five shillings for him. I live eight miles out in the country, and I'd have to walk back about two miles."

A runaway team.—Two old darkies, lounging on a street corner in Richmond, Virginia, one day were suddenly aroused by a runaway team that came dashing towards them at breakneck speed. The driver, scared nearly to death, had abandoned his reins and was awkwardly climbing out of the waggon at the rear end. One of the old negroes said: "'Bier' Johnson, sure as you born man, de runaway horse am powerful monstrous fine sight to see." Johnson shook his head doubtfully, and then replied: "Dat 'pends berry much, nigger, on whedder you be standin' on de corner obsarvin' of him or be gettin' ober de tailboard ob de waggin'."

A Courageous Animal.—City man: "A safe family horse?"

Farmer: "Yes-siree! Why, that 'ere hoss ain't even afraid of a woman in curl-papers?"

What's wrong. — Dealer: "'E jumps well, 'e trots beautiful, 'e's as quiet as a lamb, and I'll let you 'ave 'im cheap."

Purchaser: "Why—what's wrong with him?"

Simply impossible.—An Irishman was boasting about his horsemanship, and to let his mates see how good he was at it he got on to the back of a nag. The horse began to kick and fling, and the rider was nearly thrown off, when one of his mates shouted out, "Paddy, can't you come off?"

"How can Oi get off when Oi can't stay on?"

Knowing.—"Ef yer real interested," said Deacon Skinner, "I'll tell ye what I want fur thet horse."

"Oh! I wouldn't care to know thet," replied Farmer Shrude.

"No?"

"No; but I wouldn't mind knowin' what ye'd take."

The making of him.—"Be careful there," called a policeman to a man who was whipping up his horse the other day in Oxford Street.

"What for?" asked the man, as he pulled up.

"Hi'll have you up for furious driving."

"What is furious driving?"

"Why, over eight miles an hour."

"I say, old fellow, take me into Court at once, will you? If you will only get it into the papers that this old hoss was going over two miles an hour I can sell him for fifty shillings."

Just so.—A Hereford gentleman met the other morning an eccentric old squire of his acquaintance riding with only one spur.

"What have you done with the other spur, squire?" he asked.

"Why, what would be the use of the other?" said the squire; "if one side of the horse goes the other can't stand still."

Simply unrideable.—The showman on the steps was inviting the public to "step inside and see the wondrous wild horse of Tartary."

"There's no deception, ladies and gentlemen," he was saying; "with this hanimal Mazeppa would have stood no hearthly chance. 'E's simply unrideable. Yer can't stick on im. Before I met this hanimal, ladies an' gentlemen, I used to fancy that I could ride a bit. If there's a gentleman within the sound o' my voice as can stop on his back for thirty seconds, 'e can have the horse for his trouble. I've had years of practice, an' 'e shakes me off in ten seconds."

"Why don't you get inside him?" demanded a witty young fellow.

"I've tried that, my lad, but his mouth ain't quite so big as yours."

The secret.—A cavalry officer tells of an old horse, who had gone blind, and of the manner in which he was sold by his owner. Here is the story: I remember poor old A., of the Queen's Bays, on a memorable election riot in Dublin, when a mob lighted large fires across College Green to arrest the advance of cavalry. A. alone dashed through the blaze in full swing of his gallop, while the whole leading file turned and bolted. "Splendidly done!" cried the major. "What will you take for that horse? I never saw a horse face fire like him."

"A hundred and fifty, major, was the answer. "It took five years before I brought him to that." The bargain was made, and the secret of the five years' training only discovered in the morning—the horse was stone blind!

That native.—At a remount depot in India a large number of stallions are always kept. The superintendent of this depot scratched his head when his orderly handed him a telegram addressed, "The Government Stallion - in - Chief." When he found that it came from a native he realised that no chaff was intended.

Conscientious.—A well-known M.P. relates that during a recent visit to the North he spent a few days at the country seat of one of his sporting friends.

On the morning after his arrival he looked out of his bedroom window, and saw a couple of grooms holding one of the servant maids on a horse, which was being led round the yard.

"I say, my lad," he asked, "what is the meaning of all this performance?"

"Weel, ye see, sir, the hoarse

is gaun to the market the day to be sellt, an' we want to be able to say that he has cairret a leddy."

Got it for nothing.—In the North of England recently an old couple were driving down a steep hill in their cart. Somehow the horse was startled, and it set off at full gallop down the hill. This terrified the old lady, who said to her husband: "Eh, John, I'd give a sovereign to be out o' this."

"Keep th' brass in th' pocket tha'll be out for nought in a minute!"

And she was.

A good lively creetur.—A party who was bargaining for a mule asked the youth who owned the mule:—

"Is he a good, lively creetur?

"I reckon he air. He kicked dad through a circus tent, broke Uncle Bill's leg in two places, and throwed a preacher three times on a Sunday mornin'!"

Not quite an ass.—James Boswell, the biographer of Dr. Johnson, was distinguished in his private life by his humour and power of repartee. He has been described as a man in whose face it was impossible at any time to look without being inclined to laugh. The following is one of his good things. As he was pleading one day at the Scotch Bar before his father, Lord Auchinleck, who was at that time what is called Ordinary on the Bill (judge of cases in the first stage), the testy old senator, offended at something his son said, peevishly exclaimed:—

"Jamie, ye're an ass, man."

"Not exactly, my lord" answered the junior—"only a colt, the foal of an ass."

Preferred something with ears.—"Have you heard that Jones is offering to exchange his car for a horse?" said a member of an auto club to an acquaintance.

"Yes," was the reply. "Its quite true. He says, if he has got to indulge in violent language he prefers to talk to something with ears!"

A sharp lad.—It is told of the son of a horse-dealer, a sharp lad, when once unexpectedly called upon by his father to mount a horse and exhibit its paces, the little fellow whispered the question, in order to regulate how he should ride:—

"Are you buying or selling?"

Presence of mind.—"That woman showed wonderful presence of mind when her horse ran away."

"Is that what you call it?

She threw down the reins and yelled."

"I know, and the horse ran straight down the street. If she had held on to the reins she would have steered him into a shop window."

The kind word.—A benevolent gentleman, while walking about the streets of a large city, saw a driver whipping a jibbing horse. "Stop that, you brute,' he exclaimed, "or I'll have you locked up! Why don't you try kindness on the animal? Don't you suppose a horse can be reached by a kind word, the same as a human being?" "I b'lieve ye're right, sor," replied the driver, a quick-witted Irishman who, with all his faults of temper, was not bad at heart; "an', if a horse has feelin's, sor, don't ye s'pose his dhriver has, too? Thry a koind wor-rd on th' dhriver, if ye plase."

Sold.—A Yorkshireman was bargaining at a fair for a horse, the price to be thirty pounds, and was just about to hand over the money when he said:—

"The bridle goes with the horse, of course. I have none with me."

"Oh, no; if you want the bridle, I want my pay for it."

"How much do you want for your old bridle?"

"Five shillings."

"All right; here's your five shillings. That's just such a bridle as I've been looking for."

And as he passed over the change, he quietly took off the bridle, put the thirty pounds into his pocket, stepped into his trap, and drove away, leaving the overgrasping owner to lament the loss of a good sale, and trying to catch his bridleless horse.

To identify 'em.—'Arry (about to mount hack hunter with kicker's badge on): "'Ere, Gov'nor! Wot's that bit of red ribbon on its tail for?"

Job Master: "Oh, that aint nothing. You see, we let's out a lot of horses 'ere, and we wants a little bit o' something to identify 'em by."

"**Hawkins** is very fond of his horse, isn't he?"

"Why, no; he hates him."

"That's queer. I saw him riding in the park the other day, and he had his arms about the animal's neck."

The village blacksmith.—Beneath the spreading chestnut tree the village blacksmith stood, a-shoeing Higgin's old brown mule the best way that he could.

Beneath the spreading chestnut tree, the mule, with smile divine, still stood the while the blacksmith soared beyond the county line.

What made him late.—" You are an hour late this morning, Sam."

" Yes, sah, I know it, sah. I was kicked by a mule on my way here, sah."

" That ought not to have detained you an hour, Sam."

" Well, you see, boss, it wouldn't have if he'd only have kicked me in this direction, but he kicked me de other way ! "

A cabman's shaft.—A Cabman once called to a " mate " : " What's that thing yer got atween the shafts o' yer cab, matey ? "

" Why, can't you see ? That's my 'oss. What do you think it is ? "

" Oh, I thought it was one of these 'ere X-ray photographs. Yer can only see the skelington."

Not to be bribed.—It was a sorry-looking nag for a Manchester cabman to drive ; nevertheless, the would-be passenger was in a hurry, and, seeing no other vehicle handy, he said :—

" I'll give you an extra half-crown to get me to Victoria Station inside of five minutes."

" Well, sir," was cabby's deliberate reply, " you might corrupt me, but you can't bribe this 'ere hoss,"

Curiosity satisfied. — An inquiring man thrust his finger into a horse's mouth to see how many teeth he had, and the horse closed its mouth to see how many fingers the man had. The curiosity of each was fully satisfied.

From an Indian Station.—He was a major in an Indian station, and he rode an awful screw, an old mare, as a charger. There came a day when the commanding officer could stand this no longer, and he ordered the major to get a new charger.

Time went on, and the major still rode the old mare. The C.O. sent for him and told him that he noted with regret that he had not got a new charger.

" Oh ! yes, I have," answered the major blandly. " My old mare is in foal."

Giles Loflin's compliments.—Somebody has revived this tale of a country editor and a farmer whose speciality was horses.

" One day I read to Loflin—that was the farmer's name—this description of a horse in ' Venus and Adonis ' :—

Round-hoof'd, short - jointed, fetlocks shag and long,

Broad breast, full eye, small head, and nostril wide,
High crest, short ears, straight legs, and passing strong,
Thin mane, thick tail, broad buttock, tender hide:
Look, what a horse should have, he did not lack, save a proud rider on so proud a back.

" 'Giles,' said I, 'what do you think of that ? '

" 'You kin buy a horse from that description if you didn't know one from a mule,' said he. ' Who writ it ? '

" Shakespeare.'

" 'Who's Shakespeare ? '

" ' A great poet.'

" ' Wall, I don't know who Shakespeare was, and don't go much on poetry, but ef yo ever see Shakespeare, tell him from Giles Loflin that he knowed a hoss.' "

Strictly Church of England.—The late Duke of Westminster once received the following letter:—

" My Lord,—I am about to start a horse-breeding establishment in the Midlands. I shall be very grateful if you will finance me. I should like to add that this establishment will be carried on on strictly Church of England principles."

His grace wrote across the letter: " Sorry I cannot finance the man, but should be glad to see the Church of England ' gee-gees ' when they are ready."

It'll dae fine. — A farmer having gone to a fair to sell a horse, was asked by an intending purchaser if it had any faults.

" Weel," said the farmer, " it has jist ane. He's a wee apt to rin awa' wi' ye."

" Oh ! if that's a' it'll dae fine. The last ane I had was gi'en tae rinnen' awa' withoot me."

Setting him down gently.—A groom was giving his master's son some lessons in riding, and teaching him how to handle a hunter when taking a fence. The young man was a very apt pupil, and the obstacles he encountered were so easily surmounted that the groom became quite lavish in his praise of the fine horsemanship displayed. Fired with ambition, the novice essayed a very difficult and dangerous fence, with the result that horse and rider parted company, the rider being shot out of the saddle. The groom, wishing to soothe wounded pride remarked in tones of admiration: " That was a very fine jump, sir, and just the way I do it myself, sir. Only I always manage to take the horse with me ! "

A little ballast aft.—With many a hitch of his trousers and pulls at his forelock in respectful salute to justice, Jack Collins, able seaman, was navigated up to the court-room railing by a policeman on a charge of cruelty to animals.

"He had a paving stone tied to the tail of the horse he was riding, your worship," said the officer who had arrested him.

"What was that for?" sternly asked the magistrate.

"Well, admiral, that wasn't no cruelty to animals, as this officer says, at all," blurted Jack. "I hired that bony craft outside for a short cruise ashore. Soon after getting under way I found the bloomin' old packet wouldn't steer a little bit. She was all down by the head and tacked about the street when the wind was fair astern. Try as I would I couldn't get steady steerage way on her, and she drifted to windward just as often as she did to leeward. Then, thinks I, she's too light by the stern, as her heels were constantly liftin' and racing just for all the world like our propellers on the ship when she tosses on a big sea. 'She wants more weight aft,' says an old shipmate of mine that I met, and then I just got him to help me come to an anchor while I shipped a little ballast aft. That's all, your worship. All shipshape and above board, and no reason in the world why this blue and brass bound corvette here should have overhauled me at all."

"Dismissed," said the justice after Jack had agreed to jettison the ballast and take the "craft" home in "tow," which meant lead the ancient steed back to the stable.

Horses not wanted.—A horse-dealer in Nebraska wrote to a friend in Washington to ask if there was a good chance for him to sell his horses in that city, and received the following reply:

"Dear—,It's of no use. The people here ride on bicycles; the tramcars here are worked by electricity; and at the Government offices they employ donkeys. Therefore, of course, no horses are wanted."

About Dean Swift.—During the time Swift held the living of Laracor, he was out riding one day, when he met one of his parishioners, a farmer, capitally mounted.

"That's a first-class animal you've got there."

"Mr. Dean," replied the farmer, "he is very well, but he is not equal to yours."

"To mine," returned Swift, "why he's a mere pad."

"Ay," replied the other, "but he carries the best head of any horse in Ireland."

The animal's fault.—"What are you doing there, Mike? You are wanted as an ornament for one of his Majesty's horse, and not to be sweeping the ground like a broom!"

Mike: "Oi know that, sorr, but it was the animal's fault intoirely."

Riding Master: "Well, you had better get on that horse again, and if you want to roll about the ground you must get permission. I don't think you received orders from headquarters to lie down there, did you?"

Mike: "No, sorr; it was from the hindquarters, sorr!"

No thanks:—A small boy had charge of a donkey laden with coals in a Midland lane, far away from any human habitation. The wicked ass threw off his load—a load too heavy for the youngster to replace. The boy sat down in despair, looking alternately at the sack and the cuddy, the latter calmly cropping the wayside grass. At last a horseman hove in sight and gradually grew nearer. It was a tall and venerable Church dignitary. "Hallo, thou big fellow!" cried the lad. "I wish thou'd give us a lift wid this ere bag of cwoals! " The venerable rider had delivered many a charge, but never received such a one as this himself, so brief and so brusque. He was taken aback at first, but at last dismounted and played the part of the Samaritan. The big man and the small boy tugged and tumbled the sack and lifted it on to the donkey's back, the Archdeacon retiring with blackened hands and soiled necktie. "Well" shouted the boy, "for sich a big chap as thou'rt the awkwardest at a bag of cwoals ever ah seed!"

Ask the horse.—At the training of a yeomanry regiment in the West of England, one of the trooper's horses became restive, broke out of the ranks, and galloped straight ahead at full-speed. As the man shot by the colonel called, "Hi, sir! Where are you going?"

Yeoman: "Hanged if I know! Ask the horse."

Nothing unnatural. —Stranger (in the Far West): "They tell me that this is a very healthy country; not many deaths here.'

Cowboy: "Well, Broncho Pete died last week."

Stranger: "Ah! but I heard that that wasn't a natural death."

Cowboy: "What! Lemme tell, yer mister, when a feller's ketched stealin' a hoss there couldn't nothin' happen to him more natural than death."

An omission.—The Emperor Francis one day took Lauderer, his eccentric Court chaplain, over his model farm at Laxenburg. On entering the stables, which were floored with marble, and fitted up in finest style, the Emperor said:

"You are much given to fault-finding, I know, Lauderer, but I fancy you will find nothing missing here."

"Nothing your Majesty, except a silk-covered couch for each horse."

An "honest" horse.—A dealer in selling a horse, frequently reiterated that the animal was "an honest horse." After the sale was effected, the purchaser inquired what the dealer meant by "an honest horse."

"Why, sir," was the reply, "whenever I rode him he always threatened to throw me, and he certainly never deceived me."

A pity.—"Yes," said our 'busman, as he passed young Shoddyman's four-in-hand; "it's a pity I can't have his money and he have my hands. 'Cause, if he had my hands he'd be able to drive them horses, and if I had his money I should'nt want to drive these."

Would rather die than run.—A cab owner bought a new horse, and entrusted it to one of his best drivers for its first day's trial. In the evening when the jehu returned he found his master waiting to hear his opinion of the animal.

"Well, John, what do you think of the new horse?" said the boss.

"I think it bears a resemblance to the British soldier."

"What makes you think that, John?"

"Because," said John, "it will die before it will run."

For no other reason.—Buyer: "I don't like this horse you sold me. I can't get him over the bridge."

Seller: "That's the reason I sold him, and I gave my reason for selling him."

Buyer: "Yes, to be sold, you said, for no other reason than that the owner wants to go out of town."

Seller: "Well, if you can go out of town with him I never could."

Something like a jumper.—Purchaser: "Can the horse jump?"

Irish Dealer: "Jump? Bedad, if ye was to put him in a field ye'd have to put a roof on ut to kape him in!"

"**Jist look at their heids!**"—A Scotch gentleman lately paid a visit to a neighbouring farmer who was about flitting, to buy one of the horses, and, after inspecting the stock, the gentleman half settled on one, but while admiring his build and other good points, said he did not like his head. "Weel," said the farmer, "I don't see muckle wrang wi' it forbye bein' jist a wee queer about the heid; but, man, that's naething. Just look at Gladstone an' Salisbury, an' that three-acres-and-a-coo chap; they're a' guid men, and yet jist look at their heids!"

An Episcopalian steed.—A Virginia judge once visited a plantation and the darkey who met him at the gate asked him in which barn he would have his horse put.

"Have you two barns?" inquired the judge.

"Yes, sah," replied the darkey; "dar's de ole barn, and mas'r has jes build a new one."

"Where do you usually put the horses of visitors who come to see your master?"

"Well, sah, if dey's Metodis's or Baptis's, we gen'rally puts 'em in de old barn; but, if dey's 'Piscopal, we puts 'em in de new one."

"Well, Sam, you can put my horse in the new barn; I'm a Baptist, but my horse is an Episcopalian."

The donkeys of England.—A favourite story of Sir Andrew Lusk is that of an old Essex lady who wrote to him after he had passed a heavy sentence on a man for cruelty to a donkey, "thanking him in her own name and in that of all the donkeys in England."

Not in the trap.—The old farmer, intending to go for a drive, ordered the servant to get the trap ready.

When dressed he said to his little niece (who was spending her holidays at the farm):

"Edith, go and see if the horse is in the trap."

Edith, returning, replied coolly: "No, grandpa, the horse is not in the trap, but he is standing between two poles close to it."

Very strange.—A certain major bought a horse from a dealer, and shortly afterwards the following conversation was heard :—

" You have swindled me with that horse you sold me last week."

" How so ? " asked the dealer very much surprised.

" Well, I only had him for three days when he died."

" That's very strange. I owned him twenty three years, and worked him hard every day, and never knew him to do that before."

Unprofessional conduct.—Why, that caps all !—a horse doctor making a call in an automobile.

The only thing.—Two men once hired a horse and trap for a day's outing in the country. When the time came to go home, the two found themselves in a predicament, for neither knew how to reharness the beast. They made many efforts, but with the same result each time. Their chief difficulty was adjusting the bit, the horse making not the least response to their overtures.

" Well," said one of the men, " there's only one thing to do—wait."

" Wait for what ? "

" Wait for the silly animal to yawn ! "

Cabby's sarcasm.—A very stout Irish sportsman, who is a considerable owner of horses, and his friend, who is still stouter between them filled the hansom to overflowing. On arriving at the Raleigh Club, the cabman's disgust was great when a shilling was handed him as his fare.

" The next time you two gents rides in a hansom," he said, " I would advise you to send your fat on in advance by Pickford's."

Voracity in a horse.—In an action brought at Salford over the sale of a horse, the plaintiff said that it not only ate all its food and part of its bedding, but consumed half the manger, and then started on one of the beams of the stable.

The willing horse.—" I'm no sickly sentimentalist, and have nothing to do with the R.S.P.C.A.," said the foremost roof passenger to the somewhat vicious omnibus-driver, " but what the devil do you keep on lashing that willing horse for ; it's the other one—the one on the off side—that won't pull? "

" That's just it ! " readily assented the badged brute, " what's ther use o' floggin' one as won't pull, whip or no whip ? 'Bus-drivin' is like cadgin ; it's no use a-worryin' the coves what won't part, but yer keep on a-bleedin' them as shells out easy!"

A sporting offer.—A gentleman who was anxious to catch a train hailed a hansom, and jumped in. But the horse made slow progress, and the "fare" was afraid that he would miss his train.

"Look here, cabman," he said, "can't you make your horse go faster? He's going very slowly, and I wish to catch the three-forty tιain."

"Yes, sir, he can go faster. But it's like this, sir. He is an old racehorse, and the best way for you to make him go faster is for you to bet me half a crown he won't catch the three-forty train. That'll put him on his mettle directly he hears it, and he'll fly like the wind!"

The cabman won the half-crown.

Thoughtful.—A Jobmaster in the provinces, who was a stickler for neatness and order among his men and horses, recently offered a prize to the man in his employ whose stalls were kept the best.

Visiting the stalls the other day he was greatly pleased with those kept by one man, and was about to hand him the prize when his eye lighted on a spider-web in a rather dark corner.

His man said: "Excuse me, sir, but I left that there one for the sake of the poor horses. We're overrun with flies, sir, and they do torture the horses something awful!"

In Donegal.—A traveller riding a horse that had seen better days, stopped on a country road in Donegal, and asked a peasant:—

"How far is it to Letterkenny?"

Now, every true Irishman, gentle or simple, is a born sportsman, and has a keen appreciation of the "points" of a good horse. So, after surveying the sorry steed with the eye of a connoisseur, the rustic replied slowly:—

"That depends."

"How depends—depends on what?" asked the traveller somewhat impatiently.

"Well," returned Pat in the same measured tones, "ye see, sor, wid a dacent horse it's a matther av five mile or so; widd that quare baste av yours it's fully tin; but," with a sudden burst of energy, "if it was wan av Major Doyle's blood mares, bedad ye'd be there now!"

In Connaught.—A gentleman had occasion to visit Connaught.

Travelling along he overtook a boy who was in charge of a number of donkeys carrying loads of turf in panniers. Noticing that the donkeys were not shod, he asked the reason. "Shure," said the boy, who was barefooted, "it would never do for the bastes to be shod an' their master barefoot."

The parson and the doctor.—A parson in a Hampshire village was the owner of a spirited horse, and while he was driving he overtook the doctor on foot.

"Jump in, doctor," he said pulling up. "I've got a horse here that goes pretty well."

The doctor jumped in and the parson drove off. The horse did go well, in the sense of speed, but ended by tipping over the carriage.

The doctor jumped to his feet and felt himself all over to see if he was injured, and the parson also got to his feet.

"Look here," said the doctor, "what do you mean by asking me to ride behind a horse like that?"

"Well, you see, on such occasions I like to have a doctor with me!"

'Bus-driver's chaff.—A North London 'bus-driver was proceeding in a traffic block behind a scrap iron cart, Being impatient, he called out to the front driver:—

"Now, then, admiral, buck up!"

The cart-driver turned round, and made answer:—

"Oo yer callin' hadmiral, yer whipper-up of cat's meat?"

"Orl right, admiral, don't get 'aughty, even if yer are takin' home the Baltic Fleet!"

As the crow flies.—The following correspondence is pigeon-holed at the War Office:—"The senior commissariat officer requests forage allowance for a second horse, as the distance from A—— to W—— is twenty-two miles. The S.C.O has to ride between the towns three times a week, and the work is too much for one horse."

The War Office replied—

"I am directed by the Under Secretary of State to inform you that your application for forage for a second horse cannot be acceded to, as the distance from A—— to W——, as the crow flies, is but twelve miles."

The correspondence ceased with the following from the S.C.O.:—

"Sir, I beg to inform you that I do not ride a crow—I ride a horse."

The extra forage was granted,

and the S.C.O. got a wigging for "levity in official correspondence."

The carrier's horse.—Old lady: "I wish you would make him go faster. I shall be late for the market."

Carrier: "Well, you see, mum, he always falls on his head if he trots down hill. He can't trot up-hill, for he's broken-winded, and if you hurry him on the level he mostly has a fit of blind staggers. But we'll try if you like, mum. Come up, hoss!"

What it cost.—Jack: "What did that horse cost you?"

Tom: "It cost me all the respect I ever had for the man I bought it from."

That'll Stop her.—Traveller (in Ireland): "Hi, pull her up, man; don't you see the mare is running away?"

Paddy: "Hould toight, yer honner, for yer life; don't touch the reins, shure, they're as rotten as pears. I'll turn her into the river at the bridge below here, shure; that'll stop her."

Cutting.— At Home.— He thought, and always had thought, that he was a born humorist.

"What a large quantity of dry grass you have collected, Miss Mayson," he remarked, glancing round the room decorated with grasses and everlastings. "Nice room for a donkey to get into."

"Make yourself at home then," she said.

For Identification.—Travelling on a stage coach in Ireland, the late Mr. Fraser, the landscape gardener, heard the guard say to the driver that he had better put on a drag, as they were near a steep descent.

"I'll try it without; hold on hard, gentlemen," said the driver, and started his horse at a rapid pace.

"Have you a bit of chalk about you?" said a fellow passenger to Mr. Fraser. "I was just thinking that some of our legs and arms are likely to be flying about before we reach the bottom of the hill, and that it would be best for every man to mark his own."

A Screw Loose.—Owner of Screw (who has taken a toss): "Have you seen a loose horse?"

Sweep: "Yuss, there's a 'oss just gone up the lane."

Owner: "What did he look like?"

Sweep: "Look like? Well, 'e looked like about five bob a leg, I should say."—PUNCH.

An all-round kind a 'norse.—Man (on the look-out for a steed for his master): "Look 'ere, the guvnor wants a norse—a useful, all-round kind a norse. 'E wants a norse as 'e can ride in the Pork of a mornin': a norse as'll gow quiet in a dorg cart for the misis an' the kids ter drive in. Well, then, 'e'd want 'im in the Brorm in the season; and 'e'd 'ave to draw the lawn-rowler now an' agin. An' then——"

Dealer (witheringly): "'E don't want the bloomin' 'orse to wait at table, do 'e?"

Unequal Loads.—A farm servant had been carting hay all day, and at night he and his perspiring steed arrived home. His master, who was a perfect skinflint, and did not pay his employees anything like the average wage, was standing at the stable door, and on his appearance said:—

"John, how comes it that my horse is sweating so much and you so little?"

"Weel, I dinna ken richt," replied the servant, "unless it's because the horse draws the hay an' me the pay."

The Passing of the Horse.—

Every little while they tell us
that the horse has got to go;
First, the tramcar was invented
'cause the horses went so slow,
And they told us that we'd
better not keep raisin' colts no more.
When the street cars got to
moting that the horses pulled before,
I thought it was all over for old
Fan and Doll and Kit,
S'posed the horse was up and
done for,
But he ain't went yit!

When the biking craze first
started people told us right away,
As you probably remember,
that the horse had saw his day;
People put away their buggies
and went kitin' round on wheels;
There were lots and lots of
horses didn't even earn their meals.
I used to stand and watch 'em
with their bloomers as they'd flit,
And I thought the horse was
goin',
But he ain't went yit!

The Donkey's bid.—A story of an auction sale at Farnborough is told. The day being fine, the auction was held on the lawn, and one of the lots brought up was a donkey. On the hammer falling on a previous lot, the donkey brayed loudly.

"Too late, sir, too late," shouted a facetious spectator; "the lot's knocked down!"

In Texas.—"When do you break your horses?" I asked a Texas ranchman.

"Pardner, we have no time to break horses in Texas, we just climb on and ride them."

She had the last word.—Recently a country doctor in the North of Ireland, a bachelor, who was locally noted for his brusqueness, was driving along a narrow lane, when his passage was effectually barred by an old woman who was returning from the bog leading an ass. The woman led the ass to the side of the lane as quickly as she could, but not quickly enough to please the short-tempered doctor.

"Faugh!" he exclaimed, "women and asses are always in the way."

"I'm glad ye have the manners to put yourself last," said the woman calmly.

The doctor drove on without another word.

True to the letter.—Not long ago at a horse market not many miles from the town of G—— a local dealer was disposing of his horse to a contractor, who asked for a guarantee. "Weel," replied the dealer, "I'll guarantee that if ye see nae faults wi' it it'll see nane wi' you." This answer satisfied the contractor, and he bought the horse.

Not long after he called to see the dealer, and told him he (the contractor) had been deceived, as the horse was blind. "Weel, weel," replied the dealer, "did I no' tell ye that if ye saw nae faults wi' it it wid see nane wi' you?"

Unabashed.—The farmer was lecturing one of his farm labourers on his laziness and slowness. "Why, if I was to trust you with a horse and cart, you'd move so slow that the horse 'd step on you."

"He'd have to step into ca-a-art to dew that," answered the unabashed lazy one.

A misunderstanding.—A lady who owns some horses has a groom who has just become entitled to a vote.

"I hear you are going to exercise the franchise?" she said to him.

"I suppose that's the name of one of the new pair that came yesterday, but which of 'em is it?"

During the S.A. War.—A Boer burgher had captured a handsome charger belonging to a squadron of Lancers, and felt so proud of his prize that he mounted the animal and paraded it up and down like a prince in the presence of his comrades. Having finished the performance he jumped off, threw the bridle reins carelessly over the head of the horse, and sat down for the usual talk. Just then a bugle sounded from Ladysmith, whereupon the charger pricked up his ears, looked in the direction from which the sound proceeded, and bolted away so fast that in less than no time he could not be seen for dust.

CHAPTER IV.

DAIRY.

The cow got wet.—A milkman in a country town was brought before the local court to answer a charge of adulteration of milk. "You are charged," said the judge, "with a most serious offence, of selling adulterated milk. Have you anything to say in answer to the charge?"

"Well, your honour," replied the milkman, "the night before it was raining very hard, and the only cause I can give is the cow must have got wet through."

Far better.—A Farmer's son, Thomas Robson, was about to enter on a lease of a dairy farm in Scotland. At a party given at a neighbouring farm in his honour, the conversation turned on the prospects of the principal guest, who, after explaining that he was to manufacture his milk into cheese, wound up by declaring that "he would put his very heart and soul into the cheese!"

Quietly from one of the corners of the room was heard the voice of one of his cronies, who said: "It'll be far better, Tammie, my man, if ye pit the whole o' the cream intil't."

The patent churn.—An agent of a patent churn called on the good woman of the farm and said he had a churn that would get more butter out of cream than any other churn, and do it in less time. He only wanted a chance to demonstrate the churn and he was sure she would buy it.

"Call around to-morrow morning, and you can show me your churn. The next morning the agent was on hand and soon working his churn. He churned and churned, sweated and churned. The woman went calmly about her morning work and let him churn. After he had churned for an hour and a half he said that there must be something wrong with that churning, for he couldn't get any butter.

"Of course not," she replied. "I churned early this morning, and gave you the butter-milk to get the extra butter out with your new fangled machine. You said your churn would get more butter out than any other, so I let you try it."

Ambiguous. — Mr. Vincent Thomas, a well-known South Wales auctioneer, was describing the advantages of Pentresil as an investment for somebody who wanted to keep a milk-walk. He held forth on the fertile meadows, and on their close proximity to the town, and finally remarked, "It has one great recommendation, gentlemen, for anybody wishing to keep a milk-walk. It has an excellent supply of water." When the laugh came, the auctioneer explained that he "did not mean it that way."

Ingenuous.—"What makes the milk so warm?" said Betty to the milkman when he brought the pail to the door one morning.

"Please, mum, the pump-handle's broke, and missus took the water from the biler."

Town Milk.—"I don't like your milk," said the mistress of the house.

"What's wrong with it, mum?"

"It's dreadfully thin, and there's no cream on it."

"After you have lived in the town a while, mum," said the milkman encouragingly, "you'll get over them rooral ideas of your'n."

The Prize Cow.—A lot of poor children were at Rockefeller's farm, near Cleveland. He gave them some milk to drink, the product of a prize cow.

"How do you like it?" he asked, when they had finished.

"Gee, it's fine!" said one little fellow, who added, after a thoughtful pause: "I wisht our milkman kep' a cow!"

The Best Princesses.—At a visit of the King and Queen (then Prince and Princess of Wales) to the dairy department of a certain exhibition, the Princess said to the manager of the department "I have always heard that the best butter in England comes from Denmark. Is that true?" The manager hesitated a moment, and then said: "No your Royal Highness. Denmark sends us the best Princesses, but Devonshire the best butter."

The Wrong Leg.—John Jones lived in Cleveland. While milking he tied the cow's tail to his leg, as the flies kept that appendage flapping. After he was taken three times round the meadow on his back, he remarked, "I recognise my mistake; I should have tied her tail to her own leg instead of mine."

Millions in it.—Bill: "Yes, sir; a vast fortune awaits the capitalist who takes up Norwegian cheese."

Wink: "How's that?"

Bill: "There's millions in it."

"The difference between a cow and a milkman," said the man with a rare memory for old jests, "is that the cow gives pure milk."

"There is another difference," said the milkman, pointedly; "the cow does not give any credit."

A Utilitarian Notion.—An insurance agent stopped at a certain farmhouse in Lincolnshire. Said he to the woman who answered his knock:—

"I observe that there is a good deal of ague in this country. A great drawback. It must unfit a man for work entirely."

"Gener'ly it do," said the woman. "Still when my man, Tom, has a hard fit of the shakes, we fasten the churn-dasher to him, and he brings the butter inside of fifteen minutes."

Came Natural. — Uncle Josiah: "First time you ever milked a cow, is it?" Well, you do it a thunderin' sight better than most city fellers do."

Visiting nephew: "It seems to come natural, somehow. I've had a good deal of practice with a fountain pen."

Not to be beat.—Johnny's grandpa was explaining to Johnny about a conjuror he had seen and the wonderful tricks he did, and finished up by telling him of the hat-trick—how this man could bring oranges, eggs, and fancy boxes all out of an empty hat. Johnny wondered, but then said quickly:—

"Grandpa, that is nothing to what the grocer up our street can do."

"Why Johnny, what can he do?"

"Oh, he can give you the 1s. 10d. and 1s. 6d. butter all out of the same tub."

To save appearances.—In a grocer's shop the other day, a little boy asked for half a pound of margarine. He was being served, and the shopman was about to wrap the margarine up in paper, when the lad exclaimed :—

"Please, sir, my muvver wants to know if yer'll stamp a cow on it, 'cos we're having cump'ny !"

Domestic Economy.—It was a domestic economy lesson, and little Emily was asked to write a short reply as to the best way to keep milk from turning sour. Her answer was certainly brief and decidedly to the point. It ran : "You should leave it in the cow !"

"To the pure all things are pure," as the grocer remarked to the parson when he said the Danish butter smelt of margarine.

Compact.—"I suppose, Subbubs, you get good butter in the country where you live ?"

"Yes ; there is enough butter to the pound to hold the salt together."

Euphemistic.—"Have you got any condensed milk ?" asked the woman at the door.

"No," replied the driver of the milk waggon. "Nothing but the expanded kind."

In union is strength.—Customer : "That last butter was rather strong."

Dealer : "Shouldn't wonder. It was from a union dairy. In union there is strength, you know."

Pudding without Milk.—Mr. E. Conomie : "Did you write to that man who advertises to show people how to make puddings without milk, and have them richer ?"

Mrs. E. Conomie : "Yes, and sent him the shilling."

"What did he reply ?"

"Use Cream."

Limburger Cheese. — "Is Limburger cheese unhealthy ?" asked the man who called in search of information.

"On the contrary," replied the Answers-to-Queries editor, "the organisms of which it is composed are numerous and in the highest state of health and vigour. If you look at a pinch of it through a microscope you will see a picture of active life that you will never forget."

An Expensive Joke.—I had a custhomer played me a grate thrick. A foine upsthandin' sorrt av man he was. He axed fur a pound av butther, an' Oi guv ut him. He wrapped ut up.

"Oi'm the inshpectorr," sez he.

"Are yez," sez Oi.

"This here is marrgerine," sez he.

"Ut is that?" sez Oi.

"Then whoi d'yez sell ut as butther?" sez he.

"Sure, an' ut's April Fool's Day?" sez Oi.

"Oh," sez he, as could as a frosthy night, "ye'll foind ut rather an ixpinsive joke."

• An' ut was at the nixt coort.

Recipe for early rising.—There is a story told of a Hertfordshire farmer. He went home late one night and drank a pint of yeast in mistake for butter-milk. He rose three hours earlier next morning.

The infant son of an American millionaire appears to be about the most sterilised person in existence, if the latest accounts of him are correct. Milk, water, food, bedding and everything about him is sterilised, including his £2,000 Jersey cow. "The milkmaid milks with sterilised hands into a sterilised pail, and a private watchman sees that the cow eats nothing bad."

Might have been worse.—"Milk-ho-o-o!"

The cheery cry woke glad echoes in the sunny street, and Chalkins looked as merry and innocent as it is possible for one of his merry trade to do.

Suddenly his jaw fell, and dismay was plainly depicted on his countenance, for in the distance he saw Tester, the milk inspector, approaching. The memory of a recent forty shillings and costs weighed heavily upon him. What would it be this time?

But Chalkins is clever, and in a moment his foot had slipped, and in falling he tipped his churn clean over; and when Tester arrived on the scene the road was a sea of the milk over which it is useless to cry.

"Bad job, sir!" remarked Chalkins, miserably.

"Yes," remarked Tester grimly; "but it might have been a good deal worse."

Life's Troubles.—"My darling," said a town swain to a country maid—"my darling, let me, aw, share your life's troubles for ever."

"Share 'em?" Of course you may. Come out in the rain with me now to milk the cows. There are six, and you may milk three of them."

The town swain's soul was convulsed, and he soon faded from the scene.

A gentle hint.—A farmer in Canonbie who could not get his milk-cans returned from his customers wrote one to the following effect:—

"Please send on milk-cans, as the railway company refuse to take the milk in bags."

The cans were returned at once.

A profitable transaction.—A farmer was one day selling wool to a carrier, and after weighing it in the yard he went into the house to make out an invoice. Coming back he missed a cheese, which had been standing on a shelf behind the outer door, and, glancing at the bag of wool, he observed that it had suddenly increased in size.

"Man," he said to the carrier, "I hae clean forgotten the weight o' that bag. Let's pit it on the scales again."

The carrier could not refuse. Being duly weighed, the bag was found to be heavier by the weight of the cheese inside. A new invoice was made out, and the crestfallen carrier went away.

The farmer's wife rushed out to her husband, saying that the cheese had been stolen.

Farmer: "Nee, na, Meg, I hae just sold the cheese for twa shillin's the pund!"

Arcadian.—He: "Then, if you are willing, we will be married at once, but we will not live in the close, crowded city. I will purchase a little farm, and we will live in it and be as happy as turtle-doves."

She: "And I shall be a farmer's wife."

"Yes, my darling."

"And what do you think, John?" You won't have to buy a milking-stool for me, for I've got one already."

"You have?"

"Oh, yes; the prettiest you ever saw—decorated with plush and cherry-coloured ribbons."

Cheerfully furnished.—"That milk looks as if it were half water," protested the woman at the kitchen door.

"It is much more than that, ma'am," replied the milkman, a college graduate in reduced circumstances. "I guarantee it to be eighty-six per cent. water four per cent. butter fat, three and one half per cent. casein, and six and one half per cent. sugar and various salts, the combination resulting in the liquid commonly known as milk. Chemical analysis of the same cheerfully furnished whenever desired Good morning, ma'am."

Nobody can touch it.—The humour of the Bermondsey butterman is well up to the average, if one may judge from the following label which appears in a shop window Spa Road way:—

" BEST BUTTER, 10d. per lb. Nobody can touch it."

Just as well.—An old farmer said to his sons: " Boys, don't you wait for somethin' to turn up. You might jest as well go and sit down on a stone in the middle of a meadow with a pail 'twixt your legs and wait for a cow to back up to you to be milked."

Smart.—Wee Miss: " Mamma, mayn't I take the part of a milkmaid at the fancy ball ? "

Mamma: " You are too little."

Wee Miss: " Well, I can be a condensed milkmaid."

Severe.—" You are too hard on Mr. Skinflint. You should treat him with more of the milk of human kindness."

" He'd churn it into butter and sell it if I did."

Not accounted for.—When Thomas drove up to deliver the usual quart of white mixture, the customer inquired:

" Thomas, how many quarts of milk do you deliver daily to your customers ? "

" Ninety-one, sir."

" And how many cows have you ? "

" Nine, sir."

" How much milk per day do your cows average ? "

" Seven quarts, sir."

Thomas looked after the customer as he moved off, pulled out a short pencil and began to figure on the wagon cover.

" Nine cows is nine, and I set down seven quarts under the cows and multiply, that's sixty-three quarts, I told him I sold ninety-one quarts per day. Sixty-three from ninety-one leaves twenty-eight and none to carry. Now, where do I get the rest of the milk ? I'll be hanged if I haven't given myself away to one of my best customers."

The milk maid up to date.—
" Where are you going, my pretty maid ? "
" I'm going a-milking, sir, she said.
" May I go with you, my pretty maid ? "
" Get a doctor's certificate first, she said.
" Can't bring bacteria with you on any terms:
Cows are so apt, sir, at picking up germs.
Take a carbolic plunge and peroxide spray,
Don sterilised rubber clothes — then, sir, you may,
If you can prove that your germs are all dead,
Go with me, milking, sir," she said.
" Might I assist you, my pretty maid ? "

"Get a látologist's licence," she said.
"Then I will let you help clean up my stable;
Polish the floors just as bright as you're able;
Bed them well down with sterilised straw,
Germs have such fondness for milk in the raw!
Then treat the cows to a lively shampoo,
A bath in hot water, and carbolie, too,
Polish their teeth with a sterilised brush,
Spray out their throats, and do all with a rush,
Ten billion more germs'll be born ere you're through.
Get sterilised milk pails and stools for two.
Put a State seal on the sterilised door,
Spray the whole place with carbolic once more,
Then we'll be sure that the germs are all dead.
Yes, you may go with me, sir," she said.

GARRETT SMITH, in "N.Y. Tribune."

Butter v. Margarine.—According to the Board of Agriculture there are over 1,200 fancy names sanctioned for margarine. There will be no excuse now for the absent-minded grocer who calls it butter.

CHAPTER V.

SHEEP AND GOATS.

Cold Mutton made his fortune.—It was simply on account of cold mutton that Mr. Cecil Rhodes became a millionaire. He himself hath said it. "I owe my millions simply and solely to cold mutton," he replied, when a lady suggested "some noble episode," "Oh Mr. Rhodes," said the lady, quite shocked, "what do you mean?" Well, madam," replied Africa's uncrowned king, "when I was young I was so dosed with cold mutton, and I hated it so cordially, that I resolved to grow rich in order to put it on one side for the rest of my life. Yes, madam, cold mutton made my fortune."

More of them.—Whateley once asked a roomful of divines why white sheep eat so much more than black sheep. It was solemnly suggested that black sheep being a warmer colour than white, black sheep could do with less nutriment. Whateley shook his head, and answered "White sheep eat more because there are more of them."

Feed my Lambs.—Village parson (entering country editor's office): "You promised to publish that sermon I sent you on Monday, but I do not find it in the latest issue of your paper."

Editor: "I sent it up. It surely went in. What was the name of it?" Parson: "'Feed my lambs.'"

Editor (after searching through the paper): "Ah—yes—um here it is. You see we've got a new sub, and he put it under the head of 'Agricultural Notes,' as 'Hints on the Care of Sheep.'"

About President Roosevelt.—When President Roosevelt was running a ranch in the West he absorbed many of the ideas of the cattlemen. One is that a man who raises beef is the best man, but a man whe raises sheep is of lesser stuff. A short time ago a Montana friend went to him to plead for a man who was applicant for a position out there.

"No, sir," said the President, "I cannot appoint him. I have promised the place to So-and-So."

"But, Mr. President," insisted the Montana friend, "that man you intend to appoint is a sheepman."

"Now, see here," said the President, "it isn't fair to appeal to my prejudices that way!"

Stan' 'oot o' the road, woman.—One day Queen Victoria was standing on the public road near Balmoral making a sketch of the place, when a flock of sheep were driven along. The boy in charge of the sheep shouted, "Stan' oot o' the road, woman, an' let the sheep go by." The Queen not moving as rapidly as he wished, he shouted again, "Fat are ye stanin' there for? Gang oot o' the gate, an' lat the sheep gae by." One of the attendants, who was at a little distance, hearing his mistress thus rudely addressed, stepped up to the boy and said to him, "Do you know to whom you are speaking in that rude way?" "Na," he replied, "I neither ken nor care, but be she fa she likes, she sudna stan' i' the sheep's road."

The parson's error.—An old vicar at a dinner given by a landed proprietor in Yorkshire to his tenantry, began to wail over schism, and called Dissenters lost sheep, who should be led to the waters of comfort. A practical farmer in the company said, "Lost sheep to be sure, but that aboot bringin' them to the water is a mistak'. When a wether tak's to drinkin' water it's a sure sign that he's got the rot."

Would have had mair sense.—Lord Chief Justice Cockburn, after a long stroll, sat down on a hillside beside a shepherd, and observed that the sheep selected the coldest situation for lying down. "Mac," said he, "I think if I were a sheep, I should certainly have preferred the other side of that hill."

"Ay, my lord; but if you had been a sheep ye would have had mair sense."

Lost Sheep.—A missionary preacher called at a farm-house in America, and, on the farmer's wife asking his business, he said that he was looking for "lost sheep." She called out:

"John, bring that old black ram that strayed into our yard the other day; here's a man looking for lost sheep, and perhaps it is one of his."

Two fat Wethers.—An opulent farmer applied to an attorney about a lawsuit, but was told he could not undertake it, being already engaged on the other side; at the same time he gave him a letter of recommendation to a friend. The farmer, out of curiosity, opened it, and read:

"Here are two fat wethers fallen out together;
If you'll fleece one, I'll fleece the other."

The perusal of this epistle cured both parties.

Peelin' Sheeps.—Mabel, who was visiting in the country, was sent to the barn, where a man was shearing sheep, to look for her grandpa. She soon returned and said: "Him ain't out there; ain't nobody there but a man peclin' sheeps."

Occasionally. — A so-called "happy family" P. T. Barnum used to exhibit consisted of a lion, a tiger, a bear, a wolf, and a lamb, all penned together in one cage. "Remarkable!" a visitor said to Mr. Barnum. "Remarkable, impressive, instructive! And how long have these animals dwelt together in this way?" "Seven months," Barnum answered, "but the lamb has occasionally to be renewed!"

About Sheep.—Why are sheep in general of very bad character?—Because they are brought up on the turf, have many blacklegs among them, are often "Sold," as often fleeced, and their young, without exception, are naturally inclined to gamb(ol)ling.

About Burns.—One day Burns the poet, happening to attend a fair, felt in need of refreshment, and went into a publichouse to rest. The house was full, and Burns could not find a quiet corner. At last he opened the door of a private room, and just put in his head to see if it was occupied. Three jolly farmers were sitting over their liquor, and one of them called out to the stranger: "Come in, Johnny Peep!" Burns went in, sat down, and spent a most enjoyable afternoon with his three new acquaintances. When they rose to go, and called for the reckoning, it came to seven shillings and sixpence for the four. "You can't divide seven and sixpence by four," said one of the farmers. "Let us each write a few lines of poetry, and put them under a plate, then let the verses be read out, and the one who has written the best lines shall pay nothing, while the other three pay two and sixpence each." This was agreed to, and the four pieces of paper were duly deposited under a plate. What the farmers wrote "is hid for ever and eke a day," but Burns' couplet, which fully absolved him from paying his share of the score, was as follows:—

I, Johnny Peep,
Saw three sheep,
And these three sheep saw me.
Half a crown apiece
They pay for their fleece,
And so Johnny Peep goes free!

The Shepherd and the Sheep.—It is related of a certain clergyman that he was once catechising a Sunday-school. When comparing himself—the pastor of the church—to a shepherd, and his congregation to the sheep, he put the following question to the children:

"What does the shepherd do for the sheep?"

To the amusement of all, a small boy in the front row piped out:

"Shears them."

By Coorse.—The sheep of Afghanistan are famed for the great size and fatness of their tails. A lot, purchased by the commissariat in India, having been brought into camp to be slaughtered for the soldiers, two Irishmen stood regarding them.

"I'm a-thinkin', Larry, how do they get their big tails?" exclaimed one of them.

"Aisy enough, my boy. Don't you see they do always be grazing uphill in these mountainous counthries, and by coorse all the fat runs down to their tails!"

How Many Legs has a Sheep?—Mrs. B., a newly-made bride, spent her honeymoon at the house of a friend, who provided for the use of the happy couple a fine sheep of "Welsh mutton." Two of the legs were served up and much relished, and a few days after the young wife sent for the cook, and said they would like another leg of the sheep served for dinner.

Cook: "But, madam, there are only two legs, and those have been eaten."

Mrs. B. (with a knowing air): "Now, cook, it is too bad to make fun of me like that. Though I do come from London I think I know that a sheep has four legs!"

Wool-gatherin'—His Lordship: "Whatever could you have been thinking of to steal the sheep?"

The prisoner: "I dunno, my lord; I must ha' been wool-gatherin'."

That Goat.—"Did ever you keep a goat, Bill?" inquired a grey-whiskered gentleman in a corner seat.

"Did I ever!" answered the little man addressed with such rustic familiarity. "I bought one last Christmas what nearly brought me to the work-us. Eat anything from tins o' blackin' to flat-irons, that goat would. Lucky thing for me the spring killed it."

"I didn't know the seasons affected goats," observed the grey-whiskered gentleman.

"Who's talkin' about seasons?" came the reply. "It was the spring of our alarm clock what 'e made a meal off one day as done it!"

It's Just Charity.—Two Highland farmers met on their way to church.

"Man," said Donald, "I was wonderin' what you will be askin' for yon bit sheep over at your steadin'."

"Man," replied Dougal; "I was thinkin' I wad be wantin' fifty shillings for that sheep."

"I will tak' it at that," said Donald, "but och! man Dougal, I am surprised at you doin' business on the Sawbath."

"Business!" exclaimed Dougal. "Man, sellin' a sheep like that for fifty shullins is not business at all; it's just charity.

Mark Twain on Meanness.—"Coming home on the Minnetonka," said a young girl, "we took up a collection for the widows and orphans of sailors, and Mark Twain prefaced the collection with a talk on meanness. He urged us to be generous in our offerings—not to be like a certain mean old man from Hannibal.

"'The meanest man I ever knew,' he said, 'lived in Hannibal. He sold his son-in-law the half of a very fine cow, and then refused to share the milk with him on the ground that he had only sold him the front half. The son-in-law was also compelled to provide all the cow's fodder and to carry water to her twice a day. Finally the cow butted the old man through a barbed-wire fence, and he sued his son-in-law for damages.'."

"**To** estimate the weight of sheep," says the Field Service Pocket Book, issued by the War Office. "Kill a few and take the average when dressed."—So never ask a soldier to guess your weight.—PUNCH.

CHAPTER VI.

PIGS.

Too slim by half.—Peter Meehan, of Newcastle West, County Limerick, was summoned for allowing his pig to stray on the public road. His defence was that the contrary animal could not be kept in. "Have you a gate to your haggard?" asked the magistrate.

"I have, of coorse, sur; but the pig aisily opens it."

"Have you a latch to the gate?"

"To be shure I have, sur; but he opens that, too."

"I suppose," said the magistrate, "that he also closes the gate after him?"

Peter: Shure, that's the worst of the desaver. He always closes the gate after him, so that we can never tell when he's out." And Peter, who was congratulating himself on having made out so splendid a case, was amazed on hearing the magistrate say, "I fine you five shillings."

All alive this time.—A South Wales paper says:—

Just twelve months ago two

Neath gentlemen visited a village in Pembrokeshire, where at a country inn they partook of two dainty sucking pigs for dinner. Recently, having occasion to go to the same village again, they decided to visit the same inn in the hope of a similar meal.

"We hope that you have a couple of nice sucking pigs in to-day."

Landlady: "No, gentlemen, there's sorry I am; but the old sow did bring 'em all alive this time."

A swine cravat.—The well-known habit of the Americans of avoiding the use of many good English words that they think vulgar, but which to us are of daily use, is well hit off in this from the "Baltimore American":—

"I wish you would build me a swine cravat," said the delicately-nurtured young man who had become a gentleman farmer.

The country carpenter puzzled over the order for a whole day, and at last sought the gentle child of fortune and confessed his ignorance.

"Why, dear me!" said the gentle youth, "I do not like to use the vulgar expression, but if I must I must. What I require built is a pig-sty."

Family pride. — "Get my name right," said the proud owner of the 1175lbs. hog, "it's Judson K. Bimm. My father was Colonel Hiram Hotchkiss Bimm, of Lexington, Ky. He came to Illinois in the year ——"

"Never mind that," interrupted the secretary of the fat show. "Give us the pedigree of the hog."

A friend at Court.—Of a very queer "model" named Bishop, Sir Edwin Landseer tells this story. Bishop was a pig-dealer, and he often found it difficult to get food for his pigs. One day he said to Sir Edwin: "They tell me, sir, you know the Queen."

"Know the Queen? Of course I do. Everybody knows the Queen."

"Ah, but," said Bishop, "to speak to, you know, sir, comfortable!"

"Well, I have had the honour of speaking to her Majesty many times. Why do you ask?"

"Well, sir, you see there must be such a lot of pig-wash from Buckingham Palace and them sort of places most likely thrown away; and my missus and me thinks that if you was just to tip a word or two to the Queen—which is a real kind lady, one and all says—she would give her orders, and I could fetch the wash away every week with my barrer."

The use of tails.—R.S.P.C.A. Inspector: "You'd best be careful how you handle those pigs, young man. If I catch you lifting 'em by the tail again I'll take out a summons against you."

Countryman: "Wull! Whoy wot on 'arth do 'ee think pegs 'as got tails fur, then?"

A pig's time. — Professor: "What are you feeding those pigs on, my friend?"

Farmer: "Corn, professor."

"Don't you know if you feed it wet the hogs can digest it in one half the time?"

Farmer: "Now, see here, professor, how much do you calculate a pig's time is worth?"

The pig the only gentleman.—A noble lord remarked to Dean Swift: "The only real gentleman is one who does nothing."

Swift: "Really! yet in England the man works, the woman works, the horse works, water works, fire works, beer works—there is only the pig that does nothing; so that the only gentleman in England is the pig!"

Satisfactory.— President Tucker, of Dartmouth, has been in the habit of spending his summers on a New Hampshire farm. The family becoming dissatisfied with certain details—the proximity of the pig-pen to the house and the manners of the servant girl—he wrote to the farmer that he could come no more, and mentioned these objections. In a few days he received the following conciliatory reply:—"Dear sir: There ain't been no hogs since you left, and Hannah has went."

Ingenious.—"What are you making that fence of such awfully crooked rails for?" asked the stranger riding by. "So that when them pigs of Thompson's creep through they'll come out on the same side where they started!"

"A Pig in a Poke." — A Soldier Quartering in Cambridge, often observ'd a Young Country Wench that Sold Pigs a Market Days, whereupon he went to her, and desir'd to see some of her Pigs, she having several, he said, he would have one alive, so she shewed him one that she had in a bag. Well, Sweet heart, said he, I live hard by, I will go and shew the Pig to my Captain;

if he like it, you shall have three shillings for it, but in the mean time I will leave the money with you; thus having got the Pig tied up in a bag, he went to his Lodging, and put in a Dog in the Bag instead of it, and returning quickly to the Damsel, said his Captain did not like the Pig, and therefore she took the Bag without looking into it, and gave him his money again. Not long after came a French man in haste to buy a Pig, and he not liking those that were dead, would have a live one; Sir, said she, I have one of the same bigness alive, the Price of it is three Shillings, I will not sell it a Farthing Cheaper; well, said he, if you will not, here is your Money, but how shall I carry it; Why, for a Groat you shall have the Poke and all. Poke, what is dat? said Monsieur. 'Tis a Bag. Is dat de Poke? well, here's a Groat. Thus away he goes with his Bargain home, but when he comes to look in the Poke, he sees the Dog, O de diable, (said he) is dis de Pig? de Diable take me, if I do buy Pig in de Poke agen.—"Humour, Wit, and Satire of the Seventeenth Century."

The awakened conscience.—Don't you know, prisoner, that it's very wrong to steal a pig?"—"I do now, your worship; they make such a row."

Musketry Instructor (after explaining all about the rifle to private): "Now, Macpherson, what is the 'bore'?"

Macpherson (just from the Hills): "The soo's faither." (Class convulsed.)

May honestly differ.—The following is extracted from the report of a committee on hogs, read before an agricultural society "down east": "Some folks accuse pigs of being filthy in their habits, and negligent in their personal appearance. But whether food is best eaten off the ground or from china plates, is, it seems to me, merely a matter of convenience, about which pigs and men may honestly differ. At any rate, pigs are not filthy enough to chew tobacco, nor to poison their breath by drinking whisky. And as to their personal appearance, you don't catch a pig playing the dandy, nor the females among them picking their way up this muddy village, after a rain, in kid slippers.

Speaks "vollums" for the swine.—The swine (almost alway) hav four legs, tho thare iz sum remarkable excepshuns to this rule. Swine are good quiet boarders; they alwus eat what is sot before them, and don't ask enny phoolish questions. The swine kan be larut a great menny amusing things, sich az highsting the front gate oph from the hinges, and finding a hole in the fence to git into the cornfield, but it iz dredful hard work for them tew find the same hole tew git out at, espeshily if yu are in a hurry to hav them. This haz never bin fully explained, but speaks vollums for the swine. Swine can all root well, a swine that kant root well iz a poor job.

Me use de pig.—Many stories are told of Jack using queer things when in a tight place at sea, but the following takes some beating: A few weeks ago we were proceeding through a dense fog off the banks of Newfoundland, when suddenly the loud squealing of a pig was heard right ahead. A few minutes later we ran close alongside of a small washtub of a Norwegian barque, upon whose deck two men were holding a pig up by the ears. By the noise it was making it was quite evident that the pig did not enjoy its position. The barque's captain shouted to us, and in broken English wanted to know why we came so close. Our first mate answered him by wanting to know why in thunder he did not blow his foghorn. At this the former replied, to the amusement of all on board, "Me no got foghorn, me lose him, so me use de pig."

Returned unopened.—"Mr. Thompson presents his compliments to Mr. Simpson, and begs to request that he will keep his piggs from trespassing on his ground."

"Mr. Simpson presents his compliments to Mr. Thompson, and requests that in future he will not spell his piggs with two gees."

"Mr. Thompson's respects to Mr. Simpson, and he will feel obliged if he will add the letter 'e' to the last word in the note just received, so as to represent Mr. Simpson and lady."

"Mr. Simpson returns Mr. Thompson's note unopened, the impertinence it contains being only equalled by its vulgarity."

Disappointing.—"Friend," said a quaker to a man with a drove of hogs, "hast any hogs in the drove with large bones?"

"Yes," replied the drover, "they all have."

"Hast any with long heads and sharp noses?"

"Yes, they all have."

"Hast any with long ears, like those of the elephant, hanging down over their eyes?"

"Yes, all my drove are of that description, and will suit you exactly."

"I rather think they wouldn't suit me, friend, if they are such as thou describest them. Thou mayst drive on."

Outclassed.—At one of the local Christmas fat stock shows in Dumfriesshire a pawky elder was exhibiting a fat bullock, when he discovered that the minister of the parish was also showing an animal in the same class. Before the cattle entered the judging-ring the following conversation was overheard:—Elder: "Judge, it'll never dae for the like o' me to be beaten by a minister. A' tell ye what, man! if a' get the first prize a'll send ye a ham."

Judge: "Hoots, man, gang awa' wi' ye! The minister's a gentleman, for he has promised me a whole swine."

Change of diet.—Tourist: "What do the people round here live on, Pat?"

Jarvey: "Pigs, sor, in the winter, and tourists in the summer."

Living by his pen.—"That man may seem to you somewhat uneducated, and yet he makes a fine living by his pen."

"Why, I would never take him for a writer."

"He isn't; he breeds pigs."

Carlyle's severest critic.—He was an old parish roadman at Ecclefechan.

"Been a long time in this neighbourhood?" asked an English tourist.

"Been here a' ma days, sir."

"Then you'll know the Carlyles?"

"Weel that! A' ken the whole of them. There was, let me see," he said, "Jock; he was a kind o' throughither sort o' chap, a doctor, but no a bad fellow, Jock—he's deid, mon." "And there was Thomas," said the inquirer eagerly. "Oh, ah, of course, there's Tam—a useless munestruck chap that writes in London. There's naething in Tam; but, mon, there's Jamie, owner in the Newlands—there's a chap for ye. Jamie takes mair pigs into Ecclefechan market than any ither farmer i' the parish."

To measure.—Lord Chancellor Hardwicke, who had a very thrifty wife, was fond of telling a story of his bailiff, who had been ordered by her ladyship to procure a sow of a particular description. The bailiff one day burst into the dining room at Wimpole, then full of company, and proclaimed in high glee: "I have been at Royston fair, my lady, and I have got a sow exactly of your ladyship's size."

So he would.—A clergyman met a pitman out one morning exercising his dogs. He expostulated with the collier on the waste of money spent on dogs, and said to him: Why, don't you keep a couple of pigs, and then you would have a chance of them turning out profitably in the end?" "Oh, aye," was the man's reply, "but a chap wad look sae daft gannin' rattin' with a couple o' pigs."

Divil a boar.—A detachment of a crack regiment stationed in Cork was lately marching through that city when they came on a drove of pigs in a narrow street. The officer, finding he could not get past as the pigs more or less blocked the thoroughfare, addressed strong remarks to the pig-drover, who said, "Begorra, you needn't be afeared, yer honour, there's divil a boar among 'em."

A mild reproof.—A countryman, who once went to pay his tithes to the parson happened to call at the time the minister and his family were having dinner. He was, however, brought into the dining-room to wait, while the household went on with their meal.

"Well, any news, Giles?"

"Nuthin' pertic'ler, zur, 'tis only that old Tim's sow has 'ad a litter of thirteen pigs this marnin.."

"Indeed! That is very good."

"Yis; but that ain't the worst of it, zur. It's loike this, zur, t' old sow can only suckle twelve of 'un."

"And what will the other one do, Giles?"

"Oh! he will 'ave ter sit 'imself down and watch t' others, like I'm doing."

Their Master. — Gentleman: "Who do these pigs belong to, boy?"

Chaw: "Why, this 'ere owd zow."

Gentleman: "Yes, yes; but I mean who's their master?"

Chaw: "Why, that there little 'un; he's a varmun to foight!"

Reciprocity. — Parson: "I have missed you from your pew of late, Mr. Stubbins—"

Farmer (apologetically): "Well, sir, I hev' been to

meet'n lately, but—y' see, sir, the Reverend Mr. Scowles o' the chapel, he bought some pigs o' me, and I thought I ought to gi' 'm a tarn!"

As fit to die.—Rector: "Those pigs of yours are in fine condition, Jarvis."

Jarvis: "Yes, sur, they be. Ah, sur, if we wos all on us only as fit to die as them are, sur, we'd do!"

M. Briand, the French Minister for Education, received the following telegram from the prefect of a southern department:—

"Most upset. Have found in seminary from which inmates just expelled calf and two pigs. How feed them?"

The Minister sent back the following reply:—

"Your uneasiness understood. Try find in department enough food for pigs and calf. If unable, eat them."

Whaur's yer bottle.—Two old Scotch women, Mrs. MacWhirter and Mrs. MacBean, met on the road, and Mrs. MacWhirter said: "Losh, woman, yer far frae hame the day."

"Aye," said Mrs. MacBean, "I was just yont at Peebles. Sanders MacNabb o' Peebles keeps rale guid ham. Oor Sandy, ye ken, likes a bit o' guid ham, and is aye yammering about the ham bein' ower fat or ower saut."

"Oor Tam," said Mrs. MacWhirter, "is aye the same. There's nae pleasin' o' him wi' his ham. I'll ha'e to give MacNabb a trial."

So Mrs. MacWhirter journeyed into Peebles and called at the shop of Sanders MacNabb, the grocer. "Gie's two pound o' yer ham."

"What kind," says Sanders, "wad ye like?"

"Oh, just the kind that Mrs. MacBean gets," said she.

"A' richt," said MacNabb; "whaur's yer bottle?"

From the same pig.—She was a pretty little thing, and it was plainly to be seen that she had not been married long. She tripped into a Chelsea shop and said to the proprietor:—

"My husband bought a couple of hams here some time ago."

"Yes, ma'am."

"They were very nice, very nice indeed."

"Yes, ma'am."

"Have you any more like them?"

"Yes, ma'am," said the man of cheese and bacon, pointing to a row of ten or a dozen hanging suspended from the ceiling.

"Are you sure that they are from the same pig?"

"Yes, ma'am," said the shopkeeper, without a quiver.

"Then you may send me two more of them."

Her father.—At a miner's dinner (after sport).—"Who is that ugly swine at the end of the table?"

"The father of the porker who is beside you, sir."

You remind me.—Washington is full of imposters of every variety. An old fellow met an official of the Smithsonian Institution in the surrounding Mall the other day, and grasped the opportunity to unfold a tale of woe, representing himself as a boyhood friend of the famous General Pickett and his wife. Mrs. Pickett resides in Washington, and as she is a personal friend of the official, he took the fellow to her, with a view to helping the unfortunate, if he was genuine. After a moment's conversation, Mrs. Pickett remarked:—

"You remind me of a guinea pig." The man looked blank, till she added: "You know it isn't a pig at all, and it doesn't come from Guinea."

One of the family.—Squire: "Are you going to kill that pig, Hodge?"

Hodge: "Yes, sir; but I be loth to do it. It be like killing one of the family."

Paderewski a Pig Dealer.—"Apart from my music," says Mr. Paderewski, I have no hobbies except whist, billiards, and a fancy for farm stock. This last interest once lead to an amusing experience when I was staying in England. I had just purchased some prize pigs in Essex, and the transaction had been advertised widely in the newspapers. Well, I was looking into the pigsty of a farm when the farmer came up and, scenting a possible customer, entered into conversation with me. After showing me his pigs, and being anxious, apparently, to sell me some, and to impress me with his importance as a breeder he conducted me to a sty I had not seen, and showed me a very fine lot of pigs. 'Do you see those?' he said confidently. 'I've sold them to Mr. Paderewski, the great pig-dealer from abroad!'"

Laconic.—

"Burhans, Supt.:

"Eight hogs dead acc't heat, advise.

"Murphy, No. 78."

At the second telegraph office Dad received his answer:—

"Murphy, Condr. 78:

"What is the present condition of the hogs? Ans. qk.

"Burhans."

Dad grunted and wrote as follows:—

"Burhans, Supt.:

"Hogs still dead."

"Murphy, 78."

"MAGAZINE OF FUN."

The New Proprietor. — Wealthy Pork King (prospective buyer of old Scotch manor, after reading the homely fireplace motto: "East or West, Hame's Best"): ("Wall, I guess the place'll do bang up. But, old man, Hame's advertisement will have to come down."

CHAPTER VII.

DOGS.

A Queer fish.—A faithful old shepherd in the employment of Mr. Bell - Irving, Master of the Dumfriesshire Otter-Hounds, brought down a drove of cattle from one of his upland farms to Knockhill. The beasts becoming leg-wearied and footsore he arrived late, and was reluctantly persuaded to stay the night. The following scene occurred at 10 p.m.:—

Pert Maid: "Now, Thomas, my man, good-night. Would you like a cold bath to-morrow morning?"

Thomas: "Hoots, lassie, gang awa' wi' yer nonsense; dae ye tak me for a trout?"

Curran used to relate a boyish adventure with a miller's dog. Throwing the skirts of his coat over his head, stooping down, and creeping along backwards, he tried to frighten the animal, but found, to his sorrow, that the dog did not care which end of a boy went foremost so that he could get a good bite out of it. "As I had no eyes save those in front, I thought the dog was in retreat, but I was mistaken, for he had attacked my rear, and, having got a good mouthful, was about to take another before I was rescued. I thought for a time the animal had devoured my entire centre of gravity." "Upon my word,' said Sir J. Barrington, to whom Curran related the story, "the dog may have left your centre, but he could not have left much gravity behind among the spectators."

Could not part.—The millionaire had long wished to possess a really well-bred collie, and when he was in the Highlands he saw a splendid specimen which would just suit him, and asked the owner what he would take for the dog.

"Ah! but you'll be taking him back to America?" the canny Scot asked, cautiously.

"Certainly, that is my intention, if you'll sell him to me."

"I no could part wi' Bob," the dog's owner then said, emphatically. "I'm muckle fond like o' him," and even the liberal offer which the millionaire made was no inducement. To his surprise, however, the traveller later saw the dog sold to a drover for half what he had offered, and he asked for an explanation.

"You said you could not sell him."

"I said I could not part wi' him. Rob'll be hame in two or three days from noo, but I couldna ask him to swim across the ocean; na, that would be too muckle to ask."

Breed unknown.—It was near closing time, and the doorkeeper of the dog show was accosted by a hulking individual.

"Called for Bill Smith's dawg."

"Receipt," said the doorkeeper, holding out his hand therefor.

"Lorst it."

"Oh, lorst it, eh? Well, what class was the dawg in?"

"Dunno. It's Bill Smith's dawg, and it is named Jack."

"There's fifty tykes here called Jack," he said. "'Ow am I know which is your'n? Did it win a prize?"

"No; it didn't."

"Well," wearily, "wot breed is it—anything?"

"Breed! 'Ow should I know what breed it is. That's just what puzzled the judge."

Strange.—Farmer A.: "Your dog has been worrying my sheep."

B.: "That cannot be, because he has been all day locked up in my shed, and I let him out only a quarter of an hour ago."

A.: "Quarter of an hour ago! That's strange, for I shot him at four o'clock this morning, when he was killing one of my ewes!"

A sheep farmer in Perthshire, the owner of a fine collie dog, was visited by a gentleman, who took a fancy to the animal. He offered many pounds for the dog, and bought him. Afterwards the gentleman asked the farmer if it would not be more profitable to breed such dogs instead of sheep ?" "No, no," said the farmer, "I can aye get merchants to buy my sheep, but I cannot aye get fools to buy my dogs."

The Show Dog.—First Boy: "Is that a good house dog ?"

Second Boy: "No."

"Good for rabbits ?"

"No."

"Good at birds ?"

"No."

"What is it good for, then ?"

"Nothin', only to take prizes at shows."

Wanted a dogge.—Attention, lyttel chyldrenne, to ye anciente fable of ye Eddytor and ye Merchant:

Once in ye olden time a merchant sayd to an eddytor: "I don't think advertising payes."

"Let me show you," said ye eddytor. "I will pvtte a lyne in my paper and not charge you a pennie." So ye eddytor pvtte ye lyne in his papyr:—

"WANTED.—A Dogge. John Jones, 253, Old Bromptonne Roade."

Now, yt happened that 400 people eache broughte a dogge on ye next daye thereafter, so that ye merchant was overrunne with dogges.

"Since there are so manye dogges," sayd he, "I think I might make some business, and will give you a pennie for each dogge."

"Ye people took ye pennie eache for his dogge, becavse there were so manye dogges, and Mr. Jones skinned ye 400 dogges, and made bootes and gloves from ye 400 hydes, and thys mayd

A Big Fortvne.

and thereafter added to it by advertising in ye eddytor's paper."—Sporting Times.

Not a dog.—A baggage-master was called upon to decide whether a tortoise taken home by a traveller could travel free or was to be paid for. The only rule he had to go by said that dogs must pay, for much was left to the commonsense of the baggage men, and he gave his decision: "Oi niver had t' decoide on wan av thim things before; dogs pays extry, but does it come in th' classification of dogs Oi dunno." He called the station-master, who was also an Irishman. The station-master looked at the tortoise.

"'Tis not a dog," he said promptly. "Dogs is dogs, and cats is dogs and squirrels in cages is dogs, but that there animal is a hinsect, and goes free."

That "Native" again.—A military officer was travelling in Bengal. He had a bull terrier bitch and two pups, and went to the booking office to book them. The native in change glanced at them with the eye of a connoisseur and made out the papers, one of which he gave to the captain. It was as follows: "Captain Dash. One bull terrier and two sons of bitches."

A Dog's Remarkable Intelligence.—A number of drovers and farmers were resting after the heat of the market in the "—— Arms," S——, when dogs became the topic of conversation, and one of the company said:—

"Now, I've a dog here I would not take £20 for. You can believe me or not, but what I am going to tell you is as true as gospel. In the early part of last spring, I lost six ewes, and could find them nowhere, until about three weeks after, when one day, as I was looking across from my house to the edge of the moor opposite about two miles away, I noticed some sheep. I got my telescope, and assured myself that they were mine. I placed the telescope in a suitable position and made Bob look through it. After about a minute the dog wagged his tail and looked at me as if he understood what I wanted, and was off like a shot. In less than two hours he brought the sheep home safe and sound."

The language of flowers.—A Londoner, who was in the habit of giving his dog some small bit on leaving for the city each morning, forgot to do so once; but as he was going out the dog caught his coat-tails in his teeth, and leading him into the garden, stopped at a flower-bed. The flowers growing there were "forget-me-nots."

The pet poodle.—A lady who kept one of those curly poodle dogs lost her pet, and called upon a detective to find it. The next day the officer came with the dog, which was very wet and dirty. The lady was overjoyed, and asked various silly questions, among others:—

"Where did you find the darling?"

"Why, marm," said the officer, "a fellow had him

tied to a pole, and was washing windows with him."

The tramp's request.—" What are you doing here ? " said the woman to the tramp who had got over the wall just in time to escape the bulldog.

" Madam," he said with dignity, " I did intend to request somethin' to eat, but all I ask now is that, in the interests of humanity, you'll feed that dog."

Ower big for its mooth.—" My man,' said an old lady, a notorious busybody, to a collier whose dog was trotting on before him with lolling tongue, " your dog is not safe, and ought not to be at large. His tongue hanging out is a sure sign of rabies.'

" Nae, ma'am, it's tongue's ower big for its mooth, same as some old ladies' tongues."

The Tanner and the Butchers' Dogge.—A country tanner that was running hastily through Eastcheape and having a long Pike-Staffe on his shoulder, one of the butcher's dogs caught him by the breech. The fellow got loose, and ranne his pike into the Dog, and killed him. The Butcher seeing that his dog was kill'd tooke hold of the Tanner, and carried him before the Deputy, who asked him, What reason had he to kill the dogge ?

For my own defence, Sir. London fashions are not like the Countries, for here the stones are fast in the streets, and the Dogs are loose, but in the Country, the dogs are fast tied, and the stones are loose to throw at them ; and what should a man do in this extremity, but use his staffe for his own defence ?

Deputy : Marry, if a man will needs use his staffe, he might use his blunt end, and not the sharp pike.

Tanner : True, but you must consider, Sir, if the Dog had used his blunt end, and runne his taile at me then had there good reason for me to do the like ; but I vow, Master Deputy, the Dogge came sharpe at me, and fastened his teeth in my breech, and I again ranne sharp at him, and thrust my pike into his belly.

Deputy : By my faith a crafty knave, if you will both stand to my verdict, send for a quart of wine, be friends, and so you are both discharged. —" 17th Century Story."

Wouldn't part.—The keepers were no match for Dan, and the squire at last hit upon an idea. He would buy Dan's dog.

"That's a sharp-looking dog you have, Dan. I've taken a fancy to him. I suppose a fiver would buy him?"

"No, sir," said Dan respectfully.

"Ten pounds, then?"

"No, sir."

"Good gracious, man; you, on the verge of starvation, and yet refuse ten pounds for a lurcher! You can't afford to keep a dog!"

"True, sir."

"Then, why do you?"

"I don't, sir! 'E keeps me!"

Not that sort of dog. — Stranger: "I want to buy a good watch-dog."

Dog Fancier: "Here's the one you want, sir. Trained by an expert. He can tell a insurance agent or a tax collector a mile off."

"And what will he do then?"

"Do? He'll chew 'em into soup bones."

"Well, he won't suit me."

"Why? Most people want a dog like that."

"Yes, I know; but I'm a tax collector, you see."

The lawyer's bill.—Mr. X, a lawyer, received at his office one morning a pork butcher, who said: "I want to know if I can get damages from the owner of a dog who has been helping himself to my meat."

Lawyer: "Certainly."

Butcher: "In that case kindly pay me 6s., for it is your dog that has eaten my sausages."

Mr. X. paid him.

A few hours later the lawyer's clerk presented himself at the butcher's with a bill for 6s. 8d. on account of the consultation had with the lawyer in the morning; and the crest-fallen tradesman had to pay.

Moral: To get the best of a lawyer you have to be 'cuter than a pork butcher!

Down on the Farm.—"You don't seem to be of as much use as I am," said the collie, boastfully.

"No?" replied the bulldog, quietly.

"No. You should see me go for the sheep when they start to run away."

"H'm! Wait till a couple of tramps come along, and watch me go for the calves when they start to run away."

Misunderstood.—Lady buying pup, bred from prize parents.

Dog Fancier: "The parents of this dog were never beaten, ma'am."

Lady: "Dear me! What well-behaved dogs they must have been."

With a joyful bark.—The

French papers have been breaking out into dog stories. This is from the "Matin":—

"Mme. Josephine Bousseron, residing in the Rue des Couronnes, went to the Boulevard de Belleville to do her marketing.

"On seeking for her purse to pay for a fish, she found to her despair that the purse was missing—stolen, doubtless. The poor woman almost wept over the loss, and was about to turn her weary steps to the police-station, to record the theft, when a poodle ran up, dropped her purse on the ground at her feet, and with a joyful bark made off."

Him alleddy dead.—An English resident at Shanghai, having made a good dinner from a tasty dish he did not know, called his cook, Wun Hoo, and congratulated him.

"I hope you did not kill one of those street dogs to provide the soup?" said his daughter.

Wun Hoo: "No killee dawg, missee," he exclaimed. "Him alleddy dead when I pickee up!"

Really worth it.—Mrs. Newrich: "But, Henry, how could you have given £5 for this dog? Is he really worth it?"

Mr. Newrich (with deep feeling): "Worth it? Ah, Emily, if you or I had the pedigree that dog has!"

Too much to expect.—Host: "Why did you strike my dog? He only sniffed at you."

Visitor: "Well, you didn't expect me to wait till he had tasted me, did you?"

No 'buts' about it.—The charge was one of keeping a dog without a license.

Clerk of the Court: "Do you wish the Court to understand that you refuse to renew your dog license?"

"Yes; but——"

"We want no 'buts.' You must renew the license, or you will be fined. You know it expired on January 1st.'"

"Yes; but so did the dog!"

A dog story.—A gentleman had a collie that tried the confidence trick. He came to the butcher one morning with a slip of paper in his mouth and dropped it on the floor at his feet. It was a signed order from his master for a piece of sausage. "I gave the dog the sausage," says the butcher. "He ate it and went home. Time after time the collie came with these orders to me, and finally I stopped reading them. The dog got as many as 20lb. of sausages from me in two months. But the master objected to pay. He said he had given the dog only a dozen orders, whereas I had honoured nearly a hundred. We watched the dog, and found that whenever a sausage hunger seized him he would hunt until he found a piece of white paper —any piece he could find—and bring it to me. Through my carelessness the collie had fooled me for two months."

Since deceased.—A dog who has eaten up a farm and a set of buildings has been found. This dog killed a neighbour's sheep. The neighbour offered to call it square if the dog was killed. The dog's master refused to agree to this, and a lawsuit came next. To pay the costs and damages assessed by the Court the owner of the dog had to mortgage his farm for £50. The mortgage had a bigger appetite than the dog, and soon his farm was gone, and the owner had to move away. The dog is now dead.

An old fable retold.—A dog was pursuing a rabbit, and had almost caught him, when a much larger rabbit came past. "Oho," said the dog to himself, "this little fellow is not worth while; I will catch the big one." So he followed it, but as the dog was already tired, and the rabbit quite fresh it was soon lost to his view. In the meantime, the little rabbit had also disappeared, and the dog had to go back home without having caught either one. He who is not content with little often gets nothing.

Mongols and Mongrels—Sir Henry Howarth, who wrote "A History of the Mongols," met at a reception a young woman who launched into a discourse on dogs, telling him she had three, all of good pedigree, adding, "Some of yours, no doubt, are clever."

"But I have no dogs."

"Oh, well, I mean those you have written about."

"But I have not written anything about dogs," said Sir Henry.

"You haven't! Why, I am sure somebody told me you had written a book on mongrels."

How did he know.—A retired colonel had for a neighbour a farmer, and a dog of the colonel's used to annoy the farmer's stock.

At last the farmer went to his neighbour and requested that the annoyance should be stopped, only to receive the reply:—

"How do you know it is my dog?"

"How do I know? Why, haven't I seen him?"

"You must bring me better proof," said the colonel.

Farmer: "All right, sir, the next time that dog bothers my cows, I'll bring you the proof in a wheelbarrow."

The dog never troubled the animals afterwards.

A kind o' gr'y'ound.—The cockney pedlar approached the dealer in dogs, and thus described what he wanted:—

"Hi, wants a kind of dog about so 'igh, an' so long. Hit's a kind of gr'y'ound, an' yet hit ain't a gr'y'ound, because 'is tyle is shorter nor any o' these 'ere gr'y'ounds, an' 'is nose is shorter, an' he is slim round the body. But still 'e's a kind o' gr'y'ound. Do you keep such dogs?"

"No," replied the dog man, "We drowns 'em."

A dog story.—A man who was looking after a large dog for a friend who had gone abroad was annoyed by the animal always sitting in his best arm-chair.

One day an idea struck him. He came into the room and found the dog in his usual seat, so he walked up to the window and called—

"Cats! Cats!"

Up jumped the dog and rushed to the window, while the man went and sat in the chair.

A few days later the dog entered the room while his master was sitting in his arm-chair. Going to the window he barked loudly.

The man got up to see what was the matter, and the dog secured the chair.

Retrieved his own tail.—A gentleman once possessed a valuable sporting dog, which was extremely clever in the retrieving of dead and wounded game. It had, in fact, never been known to lose a bird when brought down by the gun. The owner, however, was a remarkably bad shot, and one day, on firing both barrels hastily at a rabbit which ran unexpectedly across his path, he heard a mournful howl. The next moment his dog appeared carrying a black object in his mouth, and laid it carefully at his master's feet. The animal had retrieved his own tail.

In dogs and men.—A small but fighting dog was left in charge of a buggy while his master was in a shop. A large brindled cur came by, and seeing nothing about the buggy to guard it except the small dog, concluded to help himself to some provisions he saw in the trap, supposing that his size would cow the guard. The small dog made a running jump, climbed all over the brindled cur, and bit him in four different places within three seconds. It was a great surprise to the brindled cur, and, filling the atmosphere with howls he fled down the street. As the small dog quietly lay down again under the buggy he remarked softly to himself: "I have noticed in both dogs and men that nerve and activity count for a blamed sight more than size and hair."

Where is the dog.—A New South Wales farmer went out the other day and he tied his small dog to a fence. On his return he found a large carpet snake attached to the end of the leash, and no signs of the dog.

Rival dog fanciers.—The local dog show was over, and two of the village dog fanciers appeared before the bench, charges and cross-charges of assault flying about.

"Ah was ill, yer worship, an' 'e coom to me, an' 'e says, 'Why, Jim!' 'e says, 'doan't 'e worry thy 'ead about t' show. I'll take thy dog fer thee, an' see as it all reet, niver thee fear!' An' so, bein' as 'ow I was in the 'ouse wi' roomaticks, your worship, I let's 'im take the dog, an' a dirty trick 'e did me. Till 'e comes back I didn't know as 'ow 'e'd a dog entered; but 'e 'ad, an' 'e comes back an' 'e says, Jim,' 'e says, 'my owd dog got what they calls H.C.—'ighly commended.'

"'As it?' I says; 'an' what did mine get?'

"'Oh!' 'e says, wi' a spiteful sort o' smile, 'your dog got out of 'is pen, an' went a roamin' about before I could catch 'im, gettin' in the wrong pens, an' 'e got 'ighly delighted!'"

In China. — Hang-Chow's master, an Englishman in Hong-Kong, received a visit from his maiden aunt, who brought some domestic pets. These were handed over to Hang-Chow with orders to be careful with them, and at the same time to hurry up a dinner and show his skill as a cook. The aunt was so pleased with the flavour of the dishes that she wished to thank the cook in person, and his master brought in Hang-Chow, all smiles and bows. After receiving praises he spoke:

"Um! bow-wow, him makee velly good soup. an' talkee talkee bird (the parrot) makee one chop joss-cake!"

The rabbit began it.—This saying owes its origin to a German tale by Lamy: A dog following his master through the market snapped up a live rabbit in a poulterer's shop. The owner of the dog offered several times the value of the rabbit to appease the angry shopwoman, but she would have the offender go before the magistrates. A boy who had been looking on called the gentleman aside and offered (if paid for it) to state that the rabbit began it first.

A dog story.—"Yes, dogs are undoubtedly sagacious animals," he said to his friends; "but none of your dog stories will beat this. My friend Johnson had a most intelligent retriever. One night Johnson's house caught fire. All was instant confusion. Old Johnson and his wife flew for the children, and bundled out with them pretty sharp. Alas! one of the children had been left behind, but up jumped the dog, rushed into the house, and soon reappeared with the missing child, which he deposited on the lawn. Everyone was saved, but Rover dashed through the flames again. What did the dog want? No one knew. Presently the noble animal reappeared, scorched and burnt, with what do you think?"

"Give it up," chorussed the eager listeners.

"With the fire policy, wrapped in a damp towel, gentlemen!"

Very reasonable.—Purchaser: "Does any pedigree go with this dog?"

Itinerant Dog Vendor: "No, sir; I'm all out of pedigrease. But I don't mind chuckin' in a chain and a collar."

Oft tried fidelity.—Purchaser: "I would agree to your price if I were only sure that the little dog would be faithful."

Dealer: "Faithful? Well, I should say so. I have sold him half a dozen times already, and he has come back every time."

A good watch dog.—Gentleman: "But, I am afraid he wouldn't make a good watch dog."

Man (with bull terrier): "Not a good watch-dog! Why, lor' bless your 'art, it was only last week that this wery animal held a burglar down by the throat and beat his brains out with his tail."

No harm.—A tall official-looking man with a pocket-book in his hand called upon a farmer recently and observed: "I beg your pardon, Mr. Jones, but I believe you possess a—ah—yes, a black retriever dog." Visions of unpaid dog taxes burst upon Jones, and with great energy he replied: "Oh, no. Oh, dear, no. Nothing of the kind. He is a poor stray brute who followed me home, but he does not belong to me. Indeed, I've been going to take him to the police station half a dozen times." "Oh, indeed," said the stranger, "that is all right then. Only my client accidently shot the dog this morning, and I came round to compromise the matter by offering you five pounds, but, of course, if he is not your dog—why, good morning."

Good for rats.—"You said the darn dog was good for rats!" yelled the indignant customer, but the dealer only smiled.

"Well?" he grunted, deliberately.

"Well! He won't look at a a bloomin' rat!" and the irate person choked.

"Seems to me to be good for the rat, then. Wot more 'ave you to complain of?"

To kill a dog.—"Farmer Tompkins has got more nerve than any man I ever met."

"What now?"

"He came up to my place yesterday to borrow my gun, saying that he wanted to kill a dog that kept him awake at night."

"Well, what of it?"

"It was my dog he killed!"

A brute.—Collector: "It'll cost you 7s. 6d. for a licence for that dog, mum."

Mrs. Moggs: "Seven-and-sixpence, indeed! Why, that's all my old man had to pay for the licence to marry me!"

Mr. Moggs (from within): "Yes, but that animal's worth 'aving."

Too short.—A few weeks ago a dog show was held at a town not far from B——. One of the competitors was a man who was trying his luck for the first time. When the judges came round they eyed this man's dog and said it had some good points, but its legs were too short. "Wot do you know about dogs?" said the man, disgusted at such a decision. "Legs too short! Why, they are touching the ground, are they not?"

How can they?—"Good morning, parson!"

"Good morning, deacon! As I was coming along just now I saw a fight between a brindle bulldog and a mastiff. And, upon my word, deacon, more than fifty men were standing round. How can people take an interest in such things?"

"I dunno, parson. Which dawg won?"

Affectionate. — City man: "That's a fine bulldog. Does he ever become attached to strangers?"

Farmer Brown: "Occasionally he becomes attached to tramps, but we break the attachment with a chisel and a monkey-wrench."

CHAPTER VIII.

POULTRY, BIRDS, ETC.

Verra gratefu'.—Collector to farmer who has given a subscription to brass band funds: "I'm glad, Mr. Selkirk, ye appreciate the music sae muckle."

Farmer: "Hoots, man, I dinna care for your music, ava, but, ye see, yer band aye chases awa' the craws frae ma fields, an' I'm verra gratefu'."

The sin of the father.—"Hi! you young rascal, leave that bird alone, will you? Has he ever done you any harm?" said a traveller in a Somerset district to a sturdy urchin who was whacking into a gander with a big stick. "Noa, he ain't" responded the youngster; "but 'is feether bit I in the leg."

Thought he was a bird.—A parrot escaped from its cage and settled on the roof of the cottage of a labourer, who had never seen such a thing before, and who fetched a ladder and climbed up to it with a view of securing the handsome prize. When his head reached the roof the parrot said:

"What d'ye want?"

Very much taken aback, the labourer touched his cap and replied:

"I beg your pardon, sir, I thought you were a bird!"

Do poultry pay.—Father: "Now, see here; if you marry that young pauper, how on earth are you going to live?"

Daughter: "Oh! we have figured all that out. You remember that old hen aunt gave me?"

"Yes."

"Well, I have been reading a poultry paper, and I find that a good hen will rear twenty chickens in a season. Well, the next season that will be twenty-one hens, and as each will raise twenty more chicks, that will be 420. The next year the number will be 8,400, the following year 168,000, and the next 3,360,000. Just think! At only 2s. a piece we shall have £336,999, and then, you dear old dad, we'll lend you some money to pay off your mortgage."

Perhaps he kept chickens.—The following story is told in the "Life of Dean Stanley." A Sunday School teacher asked her pupils why Dives did not give the crumbs that fell from his table to Lazarus. The question was passed down the class, till one little girl said:

"Please, teacher, I think I know; perhaps he kept chickens!"

The Plymouth Rocks.—An Irish lady one morning took her servant girl to task for having boiled the breakfast eggs too long. "Why, Biddy," she said, "they are as hard as stones."—"Sure, ma'am," replied Biddy, "it's not the boilin' that made them hard; it's the fault of them new hens—the Plymouth Rocks."

Neighbour: "What beautiful hens you have, Mrs. Stuckup."

Mrs. Stuckup: "Yes; they are all imported fowls."

Neighbour: "You don't tell me so! I suppose they lay eggs every day?"

Mrs. Stuckup: "They could do so if we thought proper, but our circumstances are such that my hens are not required to overlay themselves."

Quite a prejudice.—Guest (at country inn): "It does seem rather strange, landlord, but it really appears to me that the eggs were fresher in London."

Landlord: "But that is only a prejudice, sir. It is from London we get them."

No explaining it.—"There's no use o' trying to explain it," said Farmer Corntossel.

"Tryin' to explain what?" inquired his wife.

"The way boys'll spend the whole day climbin' trees to rob birds' nests an' go to sleep before happast 10 in the mornin' 'ef you send 'em out to collect a few hens' eggs."

Self-supporting. — Milton: "Gibson doesn't seem to be

getting rich at poultry raising."

Bilton: "No; but he says his hens have taken to eating their own eggs, and he hopes that they'll at least become self-supporting."

Poultry Worries.—"Does it bother you much," inquired a farmer's wife of her neighbour, "Mrs. Pilkington, to keep the chickens out of the garden?"

"Yes," returned that good lady, "but what bothers me more is to keep the garden out of the chickens."

Betrayed himself.—In a certain Barkston Ash village there lives a character who was recently employed by a farmer to do odd jobs on the farm. A duck was missed, and the farmer suspected Bob to be the guilty party. Calling Bob to him he remarked: "Bob, what did you do with the duck you took last night?"

"Me!" said Bob; "I took no duck."

"Oh, but you did," said the farmer, playing the game of bluff, "for I heard it quacking beneath your jacket."

Bob fell into the trap. "You couldn't do that," he said, "for I twisted its neck."

Origin of species.—"Which did the Lord make first, Brudder Jefferson, de hen or de egg?"

"De hen, of kose—de egg comes from de hen."

"Yais; but de hen comes from de egg too."

"Now, see yair, Brudder Jefferson—if de Lord had made de egg fust, He'd had to make an incubator to hatch it."

Old heads are wiser.—"The farmer," said the young turkey, "seems to be very fond of me. He throws the choicest morsel of grain to me, and in many ways shows his admiration for me."

"Well," advised the old turkey, "I wouldn't let it go on if I were you. You are apt to lose your head over it."

Not a "breakfast" egg.—He was a waif from the slums having his first experience of the real country. They gave him a new-laid egg at breakfast as a great treat, but, after one spoonful he put it quietly aside, and devoted himself to the bread and butter. "Why, Pete," exclaimed the matron in charge, "don't you like your egg?"

"No, ma'am," he replied, deprecatingly; "it don't seem to have no smell nor taste."

She's a rooster.—Little Tommy had a number of pet chickens, but found it very difficult to tell which were hens and which roosters. There was one " frizzy " that specially puzzled him. One day, however, it gave utterance to an unmistakable " crow." Tommy rushed into the parlour, where his mother was entertaining visitors, and, almost breathless with excitement exclaimed: " Mamma, you know that little frizzly hen ? Well, she's a rooster."

Use for a naval base.—Two old Fifeshire farmers were having a crack one day about the new naval base, when one said :—

" Do you think there's ony use for it, Davie ? "

" Weel," replied Davie, " I dinna ken, but when they fire their big guns they'll frichten the craws awa' frae my tatties."

The cat's had chickens.—The old housekeeper met the master at the door on his arrival home. " If you please sir," said she, " the cat has had chickens."

" Nonsense, Mary," laughed he ; " you mean kittens. Cats don't have chickens."

" Was them chickens or kittens as you brought home last night ? " asked the old woman.

" Why, they were chickens, of course."

" Just so, sir," replied Mary, with a twinkle. " Well, the cat's had 'em ! "

She talked to him.—Once upon a time a youth who had commenced to navigate the sea of matrimony went to his father, and said :—

" Father, who should be boss—I or my wife ? "

Then the old man smiled, and said :—

" Here are a hundred chickens and a team of horses. Hitch up the horses, load the chickens into waggons, and wherever you can find a man and his wife dwelling, stop and make inquiry as to who is the boss. Wherever you find a woman running things leave a chicken. If you come to a place where the man is in control, give him one of the horses."

After seventy-nine chickens had been disposed of he came to a house and made the usual inquiry.

" I'm the boss o' this ranch," said the man.

" Got to show me."

So the wife was called, and she affirmed her husband's assertion.

" Take whichever horse you want," was the youth's reply.

So the husband said :—

" I'll take the bay." But the wife didn't like the bay

horse, and she called her husband aside and talked to him. He returned, and said: "I believe I'll take the grey horse."

"Not much," said the youth. "You'll take a chicken.

A sure sign.—Two boys in a rural district were one day discussing what it signified when the cuckoo is heard for the first time in the year. One said it was a sign of getting married, while the other said it was a sign that you were going to be rich.

A farmer overhearing them, said: "That cannot be true, because I have heard it many times, and I am not married yet, and I am certainly not rich."

Just then a local worthy, known as "Daft Jamie," was passing by, and the farmer said: "Jamie, can you tell us what sign it is when you hear the cuckoo for the first time?"

"Yes," said Jamie, as he took his pipe from his mouth. "It's a sign you're not deaf."

No questions asked.—The first slice of goose had been cut, and the minister of the Zion Church in the South looked at it with as keen anticipation as was displayed in the faces around him.

"Dat's as fine a goose as I ever saw, Brudder Williams," he said to his host. "Where did you get such a fine one?"

"Well, Mr. Rawley, when you preach a special good sermon I never axes you where you got it. Seems to me dat's a trivial matter, anyway."

Knowing hens.—Lady (to Mike, in charge of poultry yard): "How is it, Mike, you have 50 laying hens, and yet you only bring two eggs a day into the house?"

Mike: "Shure, mum, ain't they the cliver hens to know that there's only two of yez in it!"

Time no object.—An enterprising salesman from one of the large firms tried to sell an incubator to a farmer. His arguments did not make any impression, and as a clincher he said:—

"Look at the time it will save!"

Farmer: "Oh! what's the time to a settin' hen?"

Not disturbed.—Parke: "Do your neighbour's hens disturb you?"

Tame: "Not a bit. I have an excellent digestion."

The spoilt egg.—"Father," said an inquiring youth, when a hen sits on an egg for three weeks and it don't hatch, is the egg spoilt ? "

" As an article of diet, my son, it is henceforth a failure, but for political purposes it has its uses."

Enquire within. — Master Bobby's papa is the happy owner of an incubator. The other day, as the former was watching a chick breaking its way through its shell, he inquired :—

" I see how he gets out, but however did he go to work to get in ? "

Economic biology. — An American was giving a newcomer some points on poultry-farming. He said : " I make a considerable amount out of my chickens ; but then I work with care, and don't believe in wasting money. When I started I fed first of all on meal, then I mixed a little sawdust with it, and gradually increased until the chickens fed entirely on sawdust."

" But," said the young hand, " did they thrive on it ? "

" Thrive on it ! you bet they did."

" Did they lay ? "

" Never knew hens lay better."

" Well, anyhow, I don't suppose the eggs were fertile ? "

" See here my friend ; I set thirteen eggs under one hen and every one hatched out. Twelve of them had timber toes, and the thirteenth was a wood-pecker ! "

Cook's compliments.—Customer : " I thought I told you to get me a wing—and on no account a leg ? "

Waiter : " Yessir, I gave your message to the cook, an' 'e sez, ' My compliments to the gen'leman, an' tell 'im as ow the fowls in this 'ere hestablishment 'as ter walk as well as fly.' "

The wrong egg.—When General Lord Wellesley, afterwards Duke of Wellington, was in Calcutta, he one morning received a bad egg for breakfast, and sniffing it, he called to his valet :—

" Lamelle, a bad egg ! What an atrocious thing to have given me ! "

The valet hurried up with a serious face, and examined the egg closely, then exclaimed :—

" I entreat forgiveness, my lord ! The stupid servant has given your lordship in mistake an aide-de-camp's egg ! "

Starting in business.—Customer : " Are these the largest china eggs you have ? "

Storekeeper: "Yes, sir, they are."

Customer: "You see, I am starting in the poultry business, and I want to put these in the nests to give the hens an idea of how large to lay their eggs."

The sad faced man.—A good story-teller was making all around him laugh, except one sad-faced man. To him the speaker said: "You don't seem amused by my stories. Tell us one of your own."

"No, but I will ask you a conundrum. How do I differ from a stuffed turkey?"

The story-teller gave it up.

"Well, the turkey is stuffed with new chestnuts, and I am stuffed with old ones."

That's why.—"Maudie," said a father to his little daughter, "your school report is not nearly so good this term as it was last."

"Well, dad, last term you sent Mrs. Fizzleton a couple of ducks, and this term you didn't."

Shakespearean.—Which members of a poultry yard resemble two of Shakespeare's characters, "Macbeth" and "Macduff."

The cock, because he "murders sleep," and the hen, because she "lays on."

The price had gone up.—"Waiter! What's this? Half a fowl—five shillings?"

"Yessir. Most likely we shan't be able to get rid of the other half, sir."

At a neighbouring table a clever son of Israel, sniffiing a bargain, overhears the dialogue, and asks for the remains of the poultry. His turn comes to pay, and he finds he is charged seven shillings. When he starts raving he is told:—

"It was the best bit of chicken we had left, and everybody wanted it!"

Predestined. — A popular minister in Fifeshire, in the good old times, used at Christmas to be inundated with hampers.

One enormous turkey was sent to him by the thoughtful kindness of a member of his congregation, a neighbouring farmer; but, as the minister's family had already provided for the Christmas dinner, the bird was sent to the market and sold. A passer-by, seeing this fine specimen of poultry, said:—

"What a splendid turkey! Just the thing for the minister's Christmas dinner!"

To the minster it was again sent. The provident wife sent it off again to the market. Another friend, similarly struck with the splendid proportions of the turkey, purchased it and sent it to the minister. The good woman, not wishing to fly in the face of Providence, said at last:—

"It is clear that this turkey was meant for us," and so it formed part of the Christmas dinner.

A "revival" story.—Mr. Alexander, the evangelist, tells the following story: "There were two darkies over in my country named Moses and Ephraim, who went out one night to rob a hen-roost. Moses planted the ladder, climbed up the tree where the chickens were roosting, grabbed them round the neck one by one, and handed them down to Ephraim, who put them in a bag. About a dozen had been bagged when Moses suddenly stopped the proceedings.

"'What's the matter, Brother Mose?' asked Ephraim.

"'I'se jes' been thinkin' whether, now you and me's members ob de church, it's right for us to take all dis yer man's chickens.'

"'Brudder Mose,' said Ephraim, 'dat's a great moral question which you an' I an't got time to wrastle wid. Pass down anudder yaller-leg!'"

Not too old to learn.—Mrs. Younglove: "Our cook says those eggs you sent yesterday were old.'

Grocer: "Very sorry, ma'am. They were the best we could get. You see, all the young chickens were killed off for the holiday trade, so the old hens were the only ones left to do the layin'."

Mrs. Younglove: "Oh! to be sure. I hadn't thought of that."

Tiresome critics might well be met with a remark made once by Daniel Webster. When he was Secretary of State, he was one day reading at a cabinet meeting a draft of a message he had written for the President to transmit to Congress. As he went on, he was constantly interrupted by one of the members with suggestions, until, losing patience, he turned to him and said: "Sir, you might as well expect seven hens to lay one egg as seven men to construct one message."

Put himself right.—A negro, accompanied by his solicitor, was brought up before an American magistrate charged with stealing fowls.

The Judge sauntered into the court-room, and, after calling for order, looked round at the little company assembled. Pointing to the negro, he asked: "Are you the defendant in this case?"

"No, sah; no, sah; I ain't de 'fen'ant; dar's de 'fen ant ovah dar," pointing to his lawyer.

There was a general laugh in the court at this, in which even the Judge, after a brief struggle for composure, had to join.

The negro, seeing he had made a mistake, hastened to put it right.

"Yes," he said, "he's the 'fen'ant. I's de gentleman wot stole the chickens."

About Eggs.—Paddy Doolan went into a shop one day to buy eggs.

"What are eggs to-day?"

"Eggs are eggs to-day, Paddy,' replied the shopman, looking quite triumphantly at two or three young lady customers who happened to be in the shop.

"Faith, I'm glad to hear you say so," replied Paddy, "for the last ones I got here were chickens."

To contributors.—A lady called upon a rural editor and asked: "Could you use a contribution in your 'Household Department' this week?"

"Well," was the reply, "we could do with a couple of dozen fresh eggs and a nice ham, and a tender young turkey."

A modern parable.—Now it came to pass in the year set down in the almanac as 1905 that a certain man in a certain place bethought him to rise up and kneel down and dig unto himself one of those things called, in vulgar tones, a garden. And, lo! the name of this man was Legion, and he was seen of many in divers and sundry backyards, digging mightily for many evenings.

And it came to pass that when he had made an end of digging and had done poking seeds into the mud, that he sat him down in the kitchen and applied oil to exceeding many and great blisters on his paws. And as he did so he looked out on the rumpled mud and saw his neighbour's hens carefully picking up the seeds and stowing them away for reference for time to come.

Then he rose in great wrath and went out and said great, big, wicked words.

And his neighbour laughed like unto the merry hyena of the wide, rolling plains from whence cometh the blizzard.

Now this did not delight the soul of the certain man, and he paid $5 unto a man of the law to find out that it would cost at least $50 to make his neighbour keep his blamed hens at home. Whereat the certain man repented him of ever planting a garden, and went and did likewise no more. — DETROIT NEWS.

Wonderful! — A young married lady, who moved into the country from London, considered the keeping of hens a pleasant and profitable undertaking. As she grew more absorbed in the pursuit her enthusiasm increased, and when one day a friend inquired if they were good layers, she replied :—

"Wonderful! Truly wonderful! They haven't laid a single bad egg yet!"

Sign of the Times.—Dealer: "Why are the eggs dear? Scarcity, mum."

"But why are they scarce?"

"I don't know for sure, mum; but they do say that hens nowadays is actin' very queer—struttin' around, an' growing big combs, and spurs, an' tryin' to learn to crow, mum."

The Editor's compliments.—A friend of mine, a London editor, controls two daily papers and a farm in Warwickshire. There is a legend that the members of his staff who seek his special graces buy the editor's eggs.

"Do you know," one of them greatly daring, is reported to have said to him, "two of your eggs I had yesterday were not what you might call truly rural?"

"Indeed!" said the editor grimly. "And that article of yours in yesterday's issue didn't seem to me quite new-laid."

Oi'll mention it.—Mistress: "If you want eggs to keep you must lay them in a cool place."

Bridget: "Oi'll mintion it to the hens at wanst, mum."

Well it might be.—"I 'ope the duck was quite to your likin', sir?" said the waiter.

"Quite good, quite good. Indeed, I remarked how particularly tender——" "Aye, and well it might be tender, sir, for it was o'ny last evenin' as the pore bird was a crossin' the road, that it was run over by a heighty horse power motor car what was a——"

In the know.—Teacher: "What kind of a bird did Noah send out of the ark?"

Small boy: "A dove."

Teacher: "I'm surprised to find that the smallest boy in the class is the only one to know."

Big Boy: "Please, teacher, his father keeps a bird shop."

Birds can't read.—Mrs. Simple (to husband, pointing to notice of "Bird's nesting Prohibited"): "But Charles, dear, what's the use of putting that up, for the birds can't read."

His hottest corner.—Two troopers were recently relating to each other their roughest experience in South Africa.

No 1 said: "My hottest corner was in that terrible battle of Spion Kop."

"Oh, that's nothing," said No. 2, "my hottest corner was when two Boer women got at me while I was carrying off one of their ducks."

Still cackling.—Customer: "Really, now, are these eggs fresh?"

Grocer: "Madam, if you will kindly step to the telephone and call up our farm you can hear the hens that laid those eggs still cackling.

At a north country police court recently a miner was charged with stealing a hen, the property of a neighbour.

Prisoner: "The door o' my back yard wor open an' t'owd hen just walked in an' got shut up in t' coal-house somehow."

"But you kept the hen a week, and you knew the owner all the time?"

"I wor going to return it, yer worship, as soon as she'd done laying!"

Took orders.—In an Ohio town a Methodist church of that district held a conference, and for a week the place was filled with clergymen.

A few days after the conference was over, one of the leading ladies of the town drove out to a suburb to buy chickens of an old negress who had supplied the family for years.

Aunt Hanna: "I'm sorry, Miss Alice, I ain't got a chicken left. Dey all enter de ministry."

Why?—A boy of six came to his father the other day with the question—

"Why do chickens not have the same kind of mothers as other animals?"

His father replied that they did not need them, and then tried to explain to his young son Darwin's theory of the selection of species—that all animals had what they needed, nothing more, nothing less.

A moment's pause, and then, as if to give his father a chance to prove the theory, he asked—

"Then why weren't horses born with iron shoes on their feet?"

A cautious witness.—Not long ago a man was charged at a provincial court with trespassing, and also with shooting a number of pigeons the property of a farmer.

In giving his evidence the farmer was exceedingly careful, even nervous, and the solicitor for the defence endeavoured to frighten him.

"Now," he remarked sternly, "remember you're on oath! are you prepared to swear that this man shot your pigeons?"

"I didn't say he did shoot 'em," was the reply. "I said I suspected him o' doing it."

"Ah, now we're coming to it. What made you suspect that man?"

"Weel, firstly, I caught him on my land wi' a gun. Secondly I heerd a gun go off an' had seen some pigeons fall. Thirdly, I found four o' my pigeons in his pocket—an' I didn't think them birds flew into his pocket an' committed suicide."

An eating match.—A short time ago there was a famous eating match at a village in Yorkshire, between two men named Gubbins and Muggins, which caused a great deal of interest in the neighbourhood: a countryman, leaving the place a little before the match was decided, was stopped by almost every one on the road, with "Who beats? How does the match get on?" etc., to which he answered, "Why, I doan't exactly knaw — they say Gubbins'll get it; but I think Muggins'll beat un yet, for when I left he was only two geese and a turkey behind him."

Bed-time.—Mother: "Bed-time, Willie; little chickens always go to roost at sunset."

Willie: "Yes, ma, but hen goes with the chickens."

As the crow flies.—Sullen dissatisfaction hung like a thundercloud over the old farmer's weather-beaten face.

"Ye boast that there's fair play for everybody in this cattle show," he grumbled to a committee-man; but are ye acting up to your motto when ye calmly give a prize to a farmer as lives 14 miles away, when the rules distinctly state that every exhibitor must reside within a radius of 12 miles?"

"But you are calculating the distance by road, but we don't reckon it in that way," patiently explained the committee-man. "We reckon it as the crow flies."

"Well, it's your own show, and ye can please yourselves how you run it," rejoined the farmer, not yet resigned to his defeat; "but if that crow of yours wants to make out that

C—— is less than 14 miles away from here, it's high time ye wrung it's bloomin' neck and put a bit more trust in the map."

At an Hotel.—Guest: "Here, waiter, get me something else. I don't like chicken legs."

Waiter: "Not like chicken legs, sir! Why, here the ladies always has breasts and the gents legs."

Then you'll remember me.—Mrs. O'Rourke (to charitable old gentleman who is giving away poultry to the needy): "Long life to yer honour; sure, I'll niver see a goose agin but I'll think of yez."

Return the goose.—In one of his elections the late Mr. Shirley, M.P. for Doncaster, alluded to the iniquity of the absorption of common lands, and quoted these lines:—

Why prosecute the man or woman
Who steals the goose from off the common,
And leave the bigger scoundrel loose,
Who steals the common from the goose?

To his dismay an opponent answered in this wise:—

Our Shirley says, "Come, no excuse,
"Return the common to the goose;"
But this is how I read the summons,
"Return the goose unto the Commons."

Foul there.—During a slow game of football, when the spectators were getting rather impatient, a chicken, which had doubtless escaped from some adjacent farmhouse, ran on to the field of play.

Suddenly one of the men exclaimed "Fowl there!" The referee, who had evidently not been attending sufficiently to the game, immediately blew his whistle! Both players and spectators roared with laughter.

Stranger.—"How far is it to Bacon Ridge?"

Farmer: "Ten miles as the crow flies. Anything more I can do for you?"

Stranger: "Yes; you might lend me a pair of crow's wings."

Reason for all things.—Little Son: "Father, is there reason for all things?"

Father: "Yes, I suppose so."

Little Son: "Well, then, father, why do hens lays egg."

Father: "Because they can't stand them up on end."

About Chickens.—In a Berwickshire school the teacher was giving an object lesson on the chicken. "Now, tell me something strange about chickens," said she. "How they get out of the shells," exclaimed one boy. "Well," said the teacher, "that is wonderful, but I mean something more wonderful still." No one spoke for a little, and then one little boy held up his hand. "Well, Johnny?" said the teacher.

"How they ever got into them, ma'am!"

Appearances Deceptive.—First crow: "Come on! That's only a scarecrow."

Second crow (a little older): "What makes you think so?"

First Crow: "I've been watching it closely for 20 minutes and it hasn't moved a muscle."

Second Crow: "Huh! It's quite evident you've never had any experience of these labourers."

Adding insult to injury.—At a farmstead between Croxeth and Knowsley geese are "put up" to fatten for Christmas. One morning the bailiff on entering the feeding-house, found half a dozen missing and noticed a handkerchief tied round the neck of the gander, which was found to contain a note and sixpence and read as follows:—

Oh Mr. Wright we've come to-night
A long way we've had to wander;
We've taken six geese at a penny apiece,
And left the money wi' t' gander.

One better.—Two children at school were given to brag. One said, "I have a hen at home that lays an egg every day, and sometimes more."

"That's nothing," said the other; "my father laid a foundation-stone the other day."

Didn't want a lawyer.—Magistrate: "Your are charged with stealing chickens. Do you want a lawyer?"

Snowball: "No, yer honah."

"Why not?"

"If it please de Co't, I'd like ter keep dem chickens myself after habbin' all de trubble er gittin' 'em."

Suburban Chickens. — Customer: "But don't you think six shillings a terrible price for a chicken?"

Dealer: "Not suburban chickens, sir. Why, everyone of these fowls was raised on seed that cost two shillings per packet."

Discouraged 'em.—Stranger:

" Why don't you clear the rats out of your chicken-house ? "

Farmer Easie : " They don't do no harm."

" Don't they eat eggs ? "

" They used to, but not now. I think these new-fashioned china nest eggs has sort o' discouraged 'em."

The incubator. — Mabel's mother was showing her a brood of chickens hatched in an incubator. " They are poor little orphans," said the mother.

" An' is that the orphan asylum ? " asked Mabel.

They blushed.—Mrs. Newliwed (outside poulterer's) : " John dear, do you think turkeys are so good when they look so red about the head ? "

Mr. Newliwed : " No ; they're probably blushing to think what a price is asked for them. We'd better try a piece of beef this Christmas."

Out of Court.—Oldheimer (standing in his garden showing a friend the neighbour's new fence) : " You see, doctor, at last my neighbour has put up a new fence instead of the old hedge through which his chickens came and scratched up my garden."

Doctor : " How did you manage ? " Go to court about it ? "

Oldheimer : " Court nothing. Every few days I sent him a couple of dozen eggs and told him his hens had laid them in my garden. In less than a week I saw that fence go up."

A Mistake Somewhere.—At a public entertainment recently a conjurer had an experience which was comical, though disastrous from a professional point of view.

Having produced an egg from a previously empty bag, he announced that he would follow up this trick by bringing from the bag the hen that laid the egg. This little arrangement he had left to his confederate to carry out. He proceeded to draw the bird from the bag ; but what was his surprise on finding that the alleged hen was an old rooster, which strutted about the stage with ruffled feathers and offended dignity, and set up a vigorous crowing as if it had just awakened from its nocturnal slumbers. The whole audience shrieked with laughter, and the unfortunate conjurer made a bolt for the dressing-room.

One at a time.—A Ticket-Clerk in a theatre owned a parrot, and took him to the country for his summer holiday ; but one day the bird got out of the cage and disappeared. His owner found him towards evening, despoiled of half his feathers, sitting on the limb of a tree, while a dozen crows were pecking at him, and all the time the poor parrot, with his back humped up, was edging away from the crows and exclaiming, in imitation of his master:

"One at a time, gentlemen, one at a time."

A bit tough.—A gentleman in Lincolnshire sent a dead swan to the Athenæum Club, addressed to the secretary. A special dinner was to occur that week, and the committee without question turned the bird over to the cook.

At the dinner the swan, resting on a great silver dish, was a delight to the eye; but when it came to serving and eating the bird, no knife seemed sharp enough to cut it, and of course eating it was out of the question.

A few days later the donor met the secretary and said:—

"I hope you got my swan all right."

"Yes! That was a nice joke you played on us."

"Joke! What do you mean?"

"Why, we had the thing boiled for 13 hours, and even then we might as well have tried to cut through a rock."

"Why, I sent it to be stuffed as a curiosity in the club. That swan has been in my family for 280 years. It was one of the identical birds fed by the children of Charles I. My ancestor held the post of 'master of the swans and keeper of the King s cygnets. Well, I have no doubt it was a bit tough.

To correspondents. — The country editor is a cyclopædia. A subscriber sent him this query recently: "What ails my hens?' Every morning I find one or more of them laid over, to rise no more."

Answer: "The fowls are dead. It is an old complaint, and nothing can be done except to bury them."

By geese.—A gentleman asked a shepherd, whether that River was to be crossed over or not: Yes, says he, but going to try, flounc'd over head and ears. Why thou rogue, says he, did you not tell me it might be passed over? Truly, Sir, says he, I thought so, for my geese go over and back again every day.—OXFORD JESTS, 1684.

The Summer Boarder.—Farmer: "I'm goin' to kill a couple uv good fat hens for tewmorrer's dinner."

The Summer Boarder: "For Heaven's sake, kill the cocks.

The hens don't do any crowing."

Perverse.

The hen's a creature most perverse,
Displaying malice deep;
She stops when eggs are needed,
And lays when they are cheap.

The Incubator.—An old lady visiting an exhibition went to see some incubators which were on show, and, complaining of the expense of keeping fowls, said that, if they were cheaper, she would buy an egg-hatching machine. After she had asked various questions, the gentleman in attendance proceeded to show her the drawers in which were deposited the eggs in different stages.

"What," she said; "do you use eggs?"

"Certainly."

"Well, I consider it a perfect swindle—to pick the pockets of hard-working folks by selling them those frauds! Why, anybody can hatch chickens with eggs! I can do it myself!"

It wouldn't work.— Lowell once met an acquaintance (of dubious standing), whose cheerful, happy demeanour led him to ask the cause.

"Why, I've found a way to fortune. We know that the cause of the fine flavour of the canvas-backed duck is the wild celery on which it feeds. Now I propose to feed it to the barnyard duck, and supply the market."

Some weeks later, on meeting him, Lowell found him depressed. "Why, I thought the last time I saw you you were were going to make your fortune with ducks. Wouldn't it work?

"No, the d—n things won't eat it."

Wouldn't wash.—A poultry fancier, who also did a bit of local preaching, recently exhibited a Minorca cock. The judge, being suspicious of the colour of the comb, rubbed it with his handkerchief, when the colour came off, the bird being disqualified.

The following Sunday the owner, when holding his usual meeting, was addressing his flock upon the subject of brotherly love and exhorting them to lead honest lives, when a voice was heard to remark: "What 'ee paint yer comb for?"

About Rooks.—Not long ago a pair of rooks built their nest in one of a cluster of trees in a gentleman's grounds. The owner was delighted at the prospect of having a rookery practically at his back door, but the farmer who owned the surrounding land didn't look at the matter in the same light.

The farmer was no great lover of rooks, and he gave his sons orders to "pot 'em" at the first opportunity. One morning the farmer received this note from his neighbour :—

"Sir,—I wish your boys would let my rooks alone. I'm trying to make a rookery."

The farmer altered three words and returned the note.

"Sir,—I wish your rooks would let my crops alone. I'm trying to make a living."

Thought they sucked. — A simple-minded man, in a big manufacturing town, decided to keep fowls, so he bought a hen and ten chickens. He wrote to his brother to come and see them.

In a week's time the brother came, and saw the hen with two sickly-looking little chickens behind her. The brother, on seeing these, said :—

"I thowt tha towd me tha had ten chickens ?"

"So I had," replied the simple one, "but the others are dead."

"What's tha bin feedin' 'em on ?" said the brother.

"Nowt," replied the simple one, looking surprised. "I thowt they sucked."

"I've dropped an egg."— Mr. Choate's quickness at repartee is well illustrated by the following story : During a "week-end" at an English country-house his neighbour at breakfast one morning chanced to be a pretty American, who had come to misfortune in trying to manipulate her egg in the English fashion. With face full of dismay, she turned to him.

"Oh ! Mr. Choate, what shall I do ? I've dropped an egg !"

"Cackle, madam, cackle !"

Beats de debil.—During a visit to the south with an eclipse expedition, some years ago, an American professor met an old negro servant, whose duty it was to look after the chickens. The day before the eclipse took place the professor, in an idle moment, said : "Sam, if to-morrow morning at 11 o'clock you watch all your chickens you will find they will all go to roost."

When at the appointed time next day the sun in the heavens was darkened, and the chickens retired to roost, the negro's astonishment was great.

"Massa," he asked, "how long ago did you know dat dem chickens would go to roost ?"

"Oh, for a long time," said the professor, airily.

"Did you know a year ago, massa?"

"Yes."

"Then dat beats de debil! Dem chickens weren't hatched a year ago!"

Exasperating.—Small Boy: "What is a roost, papa?"

Parent: "A roost, my son, is the pole on which chickens roost at night."

Small Boy: "And what is a perch, papa?"

Parent: "A perch is what chickens perch on at night."

Small Boy: "Well, papa, could a chicken roost on a perch?"

Parent: "Why, of course?'

Small Boy: "And could they perch on a roost?"

Parent: "Certainly; of course!"

Small Boy: "But if the chickens perched on a roost, that would make the roost a perch, wouldn't it?"

Parent: "Oh, heavens, yes! I suppose so."

Small Boy: "But if just after some chickens had perched on a roost and made it a perch some chickens came along and roosted on the perch, and made it a roost; then the roost would be a perch and the perch would be a roost, and some of the chickens would be perchers and the others would be roosters, and——"

Parent: "Susan, Susan, take this child to bed before he drives me mad."

The incubator.—Mrs. Ruralles: "Your place is so large I wonder you don't keep fowls. It is so nice to have fresh eggs every day."

Mrs. Clyde: "But fowls are such a bother. Why couldn't we keep an incubator instead?"

How can it tell.—"Did you say a chicken chews its food with its gizzard?" asked the little boy with the high forehead.

"Yes, that is the process."

"If that is the case, how can a chicken tell whether it has the toothache or the stomach-ache?"

In Committee.—Egg Producer: "Do you want any fresh eggs to-day?"

Manager of Stores: "Yes, but the committee met this week and decided to get them at fourteen a shilling, instead of twelve."

Egg Producer (next morning): "Our hens had a committee meeting last night, and decided that they weren't going to lay their eggs at that price."

Blizzard or gizzard.—In an examination paper on the subject of inclement weather, Smith

Minor was asked to define a blizzard. He wrote: "Blizzard—a blizzard is the interior of a fowl."

The incubator.—Willie is a little boy, and a few days ago he wandered into his father's study, clasping in his hands a forlorn-looking little chicken, which had strayed from a neighbouring incubator.

"Willie," said his father sternly, "take that chicken back to its mother!"

"Ain't dot any mudder," answered Willie.

"Well, then, take it back to its father," said his father, determined to maintain parental authority.

"Ain't dot any fader," said the child. "Ain't dot any-thin' but an old lamp!"

Crows in the Cornfield.—The following clever way of keeping crows away from a cornfield is used by the Dutch farmer, and is practised to a certain extent in the eastern districts of this country. He makes some small caps of stout paper, and smears round the inner side of the mouth of each some bird-lime or other sticky stuff. In these he puts some grains of corn, and stands them about his fields by pressing their points into soft earth. When the crow finds one of these paper caps he thinks himself very fortunate until he attempts to peck at the tempting grain, when, to his astonishment, he finds the cap attached to his head—a regular fool's cap—which will not even allow him to see what course to take if he flies up. However, he succeeds in reaching some coarse grass or bushes, and after much bewildered scrambling and flopping about gets his head out of his undesirable cap, but ever afterwards avoids the field where there are more of them.

He meant well.—Young Jack came down from London t'other day. He kep' me and the missus up till arter 'leven o'clock a-tellin' tales about London and things. "Come, come," I say, "we'd best get to bed, else we shan't be up a-time t'get your breakfast ready, Jack." "P'raps O'll get it ready myself," says Master Jack. Well, O'm blowed, if that there Jack didn't slide down afore we was awake, an' when th' missus an' me got down there was th' tea an' boiled eggs all ready, and Master Jack a-laughing at us. The missus was a-talkin' when she cracked her egg. She stopped all of a sudden like; I cuts the top off a-mine.

"Jack," I say, "where did you find these 'ere eggs?" I say. "In the tin cupboard out at the back there," says Jack, airy like. "There was a dozen on 'em." "Jack," I say, "you meant well, mate; but that there tin cupboard, as you call it, happens t'be a inkybater, an' these 'ere what you bin a cookin' would a-bin black Minorca chicks by Friday."

The incubator.—Piker: "I understand that you filled your incubator full of cold-storage eggs. Hatch anything?"

Peaker: "I should say so! All the chickens came out with fur instead of feathers, and wore ear muffs."

The first steam whistle.—In 1833 one of George Stephenson's engines smashed a farmer's waggon and 960 eggs. "Dear me!" said the director, "this won't do. Can't you make your steam make a noise!" So Stephenson rigged up the first steam whistle.

Stuck up.—"Didn't you send any of your chickens to the poultry show?"

"No; 'I've noticed that when a hen requires a taste for society, she gets too stuck-up to lay eggs."

Cooked it.—Jones (who has a fancy for prize fowls): "Did a man bring a game bird here for me to-day, Bridgett?" Cook: "There was a cock left here, but I thought he was for dinner, so I cut off his head and trussed him." Jones: "Great Scott, woman! That was my splendid black-red gamecock that cost me five guineas."

Antediluvian Fowls.—A lady who kept poultry had, among others, some Andalusian fowls. One day she had one killed for dinner, which proved to be very tough.

"Rachel," she said to her servant, an elderly woman who had been with her some time, "what fowl is this? It seems to me a very old one."

"Well, mum," replied she, "it's one of them there Antediluvians."

A Bishop once asked a class of boys some questions in mental arithmetic, and received a let down. Said he:—

"Now, my little man, you there. If I were to shoot at a tree with five birds in it, and kill three, how many would be left?"

"Three, sir."

"No, no, my boy, there would only be two left."

"Please, sir, you said you shot three; only they would be left, t'other two would be flied away."

"Yes," replied the bishop; "you are quite right; you may sit down."

And he passed on to another class-room.

A Maltese Parrot.—Here is a tale of the maltese parrot. A very limited number of dogs are allowed on board a troopship, but there is no special limit as to birds. Tommy, embarking at Malta, had in his hands a long-haired white dog in a wicker cage with some feathers tied round its neck, and successfully brought it on board by affirming it to be a Maltese parrot.

The old lady entered the taxidermist's shop in a blaze of wrath, carrying a defunct cockatoo in a glass case.

"You can see for yourself, sir. You only stuffed my poor parrot in the summer, and here's his feathers tumbling out before your eyes."

"Lor' bless ye'm, that's the triumph of the art! We stuff 'em that natural that they moults in their proper season."

The Head Master: "Jenkins, what part in grammar is the word egg?"

Jenkins (sharp): "Noun, sir."

Master: "What is its gender?"

Jenkins (looking confused): "I don't know, sir."

Master (getting excited): "Is it masculine, feminine, or neuter, dunderhead?"

"Jenkins (brightening): "I can't say, sir, till it's hatched, sir!"

How to cook eggs.—Some time ago Bishop Paret, of Baltimore, was the guest of a family in West Virginia. Learning from the Bishop that he liked hard-boiled eggs for breakfast, the hostess went to the kitchen to boil them herself. While so engaged, she began to sing the first stanza of a well-known hymn. Then she sang the second stanza, the Bishop, who was in the dining-room, joined in. When it was finished there was silence, and the Bishop remarked, "Why not sing the third verse?" "The third verse?" replied the lady, as she came into the dining-room, carrying the steaming eggs. "Oh, that is not necessary!" "I don't understand," replied Bishop Paret. "Oh, you see," the hostess answered, "when I am cooking eggs I always sing one verse for soft boiled and two for hard-boiled!"

In the Spring of this year a farmer sent a young lad, who had just entered his service, down to a wheat field to see if there were any rooks among his wheat. The lad had only just come from a large industrial school in Yorkshire, and was not very familiar with the ways of rooks. When he returned from the field, the farmer asked him if there were any rooks there. The boy said he counted twenty-two there. "Did you send them away," asked his master. "No," said the lad; I thought they were yours!"

At a great sacrifice.—A creditor called upon a debtor whom he found at dinner, busy carving a turkey.

"Now, sir," said the visitor, "are you going to pay me soon?

"I should only be too glad, my dear sir; but it is impossible; I am cleared out, ruined; I haven't a stiver."

"Why, sir, when a man cannot pay his debts, he has no business to be eating a turkey like that."

"Alas! my dear sir," said the debtor, lifting the serviette to his eyes, "I couldn't afford to keep it!"

Old hen to chickens: "Sakes alive, children! what are you fighting about?"

"He has been snubbing me because I'm an incubator chicken!"

The Pope lost his dinner.—An Italian peasant arrived at the Vatican the other day, on his first visit to Rome, and, managing to pass the Swiss guard at the bronze doors, lost himself in a maze of rooms and passages apparently unguarded. At last he met a gendarme, who looked at him suspiciously and asked him what he wanted.

"The Holy Father."

"But that is impossible."

"But I have brought him to-morrow's dinner," and with that he hauled a good fat chicken out of his pocket, which immediately gave voice. Needless to say, both chicken and peasant soon landed in the piazza of St. Peter, and the Pope lost his dinner.

The real question.—"Which is correct," asked the visitor from the town, "to speak of a sitting hen or a setting hen?"

"I really don't know," replied the farmer's wife, "and what's more I don't care; but there is one thing I would like to know. When a hen cackles has she been laying or is she lying?"

Dooks and Geese.—At a recent big show in the north of Scotland opened by the Duke of —— two workmen were discussing the show and its exhibits, when the following conversation took place :—

First Workman : "An' fat think ye of the show ?"

Second do. : "Oh, it's rale guid."

First do. : "But hae ye seen the great Duke (meaning the Duke of ——).

First do. : "Na, na ; I hinna been doon amang the geese."

The feminine view.—"I say little woman, this out-of-the-way country place is a dull, dead-alive hole. I vote we chuck it and finish our holiday at Southend."

"You've no right to feel bored in a village where I can get a fowl for eighteenpence and cider at twopence a quart !"

Famous Eggs.—Breakfasting with some friends at Taunton, an eminent artist was strongly recommended to try a boiled egg.

"We are very proud of our eggs," remarked the hostess ; "they are really quite famous !'

Pleasant expectations thus aroused, the artist attacked the egg before him. It was unmistakably bad. After many apologies the hostess despatched the maid to the fowlhouse for another egg, but when this was brought it also proved unfit to eat. The mortified hostess told the girl to see if there were any more eggs obtainable, but the servant, newly engaged, hesitated.

"Well, Eliza,' said her mistress, "are there no more ?"

"Yes, ma'am," was the embarrassed reply ; "but that there black 'en do make such a fluster every time she 'as to get up !'

The ignorant girl had been unscrupulously despoiling a sitting hen.

Do poultry pay—Mr. Vernon like many other surburban residents, amuses himself by keeping fowls. It was his intention, when he first began it, to make it a self-supporting source of entertainment, and he cherished hopes of saving a little money in the supply of poultry and eggs for his own table. But "poultry food" costs money, and all the coops and others appliances which Mr. Vernon thought necessary cost much more than he had expected, so that it was only by the exercise of very great industry that he kept from losing instead of making money in his keeping of chickens. One day he found that his account for the week did not balance. He was behind. He sat and pondered over his column of figures for a little while, then put on his hat and went down to the poultry run.

Presently his little daughter, Eva, saw him coing back to the house, bringing a big fowl, headless. She ran out to meet him.

" Why, papa,' she exclaimed, " what did you kill him for ? "

" For dinner, my dear," answered her father. " He's worth five shillings, and I am that amount behind in my chicken account this week."

He took the fowl into the kitchen, and then went on into the library and took up his account book, credited himself with the price of the bird, and announced with pride at the the dinner-table that he had succeeded in balancing his account in a satisfactory manner.

" For your poor.''—Mother wit and a warm heart are possessed by Madame Yvette Guilbert. After one of the many charitable performances which she has given, the priest of the country village where it had been held entertained all the company at lunch. Madame Yvette found an egg on her plate, broke it, and ten gold pieces fell out. " You don't know my tastes quite well yet, Monsieur le Cure," she said. " I adore boiled eggs, but I eat only the white. I never touch the yolk, and I must leave it to you for your poor people."

Between bites.—" They say a carrier pigeon will go further than any other bird," said the boarder, between bites.

" Well, I'll have to try one," one," said the landlady; " I notice a fowl doesn't go far."

From Rhodesia. — A Rhodesian correspondent of the English " Field," writes: " On March 28th I sat a hen on twelve eggs. All went well until April 9th, when a large snake made its way into the sitting-house, and, after driving the hen off her nest, swallowed the whole of the sitting. I shot the reptile and on opening it up discovered that nine of the eggs were unbroken, so I rinsed them in warm water and placed them back in the nest. The hen took to them again quite calmly. This morning I found that the whole of the nine had proved their fertility, and the chickens appear quite healthy."

Who does the crowing.—Mrs. Crimsonbeak (during a quarrel): " Why, even in the poultry world the female chicken does all the work."

Mr. Crimsonbeak: " Nonsense ! "

" Doesn't the female chicken lay all the eggs ? "

" Yes, she does ; but that's not all the work."

" Well, it's the most important."

" Don't be silly. Who is it that does all the crowing."

Except crows.—A boy who was preparing for an examination in natural history at his school asked his father to give him some questions on the subject as a test of his proficiency. So the father said:

" Now, take the barn-door hen, for example, what does she produce ?

" Eggs."

" Quite right. And what do eggs produce ? "

" Fowls."

" Right again ; but what do we mean by fowls ? "

" Cocks and hens, of course."

" That brings us back again to the hens," said the father, " from which you have already said eggs are produced ; but can you mention anything which we get from the cocks ? "

" I have never learnt of anything coming from cocks except crows ! "

Eggs that exploded.—At a meeting of the Clogheen guardians the medical officer reported that the eggs supplied to the infirmary exploded like bombs immediately they were placed in hot water, and the patients were loud in their complaints. " Cannot a contractor who supplies infernal machines as human food be made amenable to the law ? " he asked.

Accommodating.—Customer : " You say these shilling a-dozen eggs are fresh ? "

Shopkeeper : " Yes, sir ; but if you have any doubts about it, perhaps I had better charge you eighteenpence."

The incubator. — Wilfred : " Mamma, we were up in Farmer Crosby's yard watching the eggs in his incubator."

His mother : " Did anything come out ? "

Wilfred : " Yes ; Farmer Crosby—and he chased us ? "

About Lord Eldon.—At the time Lord Eldon was plain Jack Scott, he received two days before Christmas a present of a fine turkey from an unknown friend, and a deliberation took place betwixt his wife and himself as to the best mode of cooking the bird. After some consultation the celebrated lawyer declared that it was better to divide the fowl and make two separate boilings of it. The lady assented. Half the fowl was already immersed in the boiling fluid when the announcement of a visitor threw the frugal pair into perturbation. The guest is introduced and recognised as an old friend, as he exclaims upon entering the room:—"My dear fellow, I sent you a turkey on the 23rd, and am now come to partake of it." The most intricate law suit never discomfited Lord Eldon half so much as this simple explanation. A new preparation was the consequence. The parboiled half of the turkey was taken from the fire, the two moieties carefully stitched together by the future Lady Eldon who was as good a seamstress as her husband was a lawyer and the fowl was served up to table, the seam being carefully covered over with celery sauce.

Quite funny.—Sir John Bell, Lord Mayor of London, lately said that some of the letters he received were quite funny. One from Vienna read: "I was delighted to hear that you had been made Lord Mayor, more especially as I understand that you are a farmer. May God give you health, strength, and a grateful heart to stand it. As you are especially interested in poultry farming, and it has been for years my earnest wish to get a good breed into my yard, could you kindly give me one cock and two hens in exchange for three birds of my breed here?" By the same post came a letter from a gentleman in Massachusetts asking for help in finding his long-lost brother.

CHAPTER IX.

SHOOTING.

A whole skin.—"Where," said the host to the old family servant after a day's shoot, "is Micky?"

"Sorrah wan o' me knows, Master Johnny."

"Why the divvle don't ye know? Is he in his skin, anyway?"

"In troth, Master Johnny, I think he's in most of it."

Impartial.—"Mr. Scatterton prides himself on being strictly impartial." "Yes," answered the unamiable man, "I once went shooting with him. He didn't seem to care whether he hit the rabbit, the dog, or one of his friends."

Hadn't reached it.—Lord Dudley was out shooting one day over a hilly and marshy bit of ground near Llandrillo, accompanied by a local inn-keeper, named Robert, whom he sometimes took with him as a guide. Coming to a suspicious-looking bit of turf, he said to his retainer, "Robert, has this bog any bottom to it?"

"Oh, yes, your lordship, it has."

Whereupon the Earl jumped on it, and was at once up to his waist and still sinking. "You rascal," he cried, "didn't you say this bog had a bottom?"

"And so it has, my lord; but you haven't reached it yet!"

The hare.—The Duke: "You would hardly believe, Lady Diana, what a shocking coward the hare is."

Her Ladyship: "Oh! I don't know. If the hare had your gun and you had his legs do you think you'd be any braver?"

Where the danger is.—"I should think you'd be afraid that some of these shooters would mistake you for the bear."

"Oh! that ain't where the danger is," said the guide, "So long as they take me for the bear, I'm safe. It's when they're shootin' at the bear that I have to look out."

The other Barrel.—Lord B—— was out shooting the other day, when one of the party, a novice at sport, unfortunately shot him in the legs. He fell and lay flat, and the keeper ran up exclaiming, "I hope you are not much hurt, my lord?"

"Oh, no," said his lordship, coolly.

"But can't you get up?"

"To be sure I could; but you see, if I got up he might let me have the other barrel."

"Confound your apologies! No, I'm not hurt much, thanks to my thick tweed coat; but what sort of a confounded sportsman must you be to take me for a partridge?"

Shooting amenities.—A gentleman out partridge shooting fired while one of his party was in the line of fire, fortunately without doing any harm.

"Excuse me," he said apologetically, "but I got quite muddled as to where you were."

Soon afterwards the careless one's hat was shot off, and the gentleman who had so nearly been his victim came up smilingly said:—

"I hope that's cleared your head."

About the rector.—Squire (interviewing keeper about his next shoot): "We must have another gun, Thomas. What about the rector? Is he all right?

Keeper: "Well, sir, 'e's a moderate fair shot at anything that's not movin'."

Why he ran.—Two men were out shooting: one had a licence, the other hadn't. A policeman approached, and the one that had a licence ran away.

The policeman was a good runner, and an exciting chase ensued over a mile and a half of nice ploughed field. At last the policeman got up to the runaway.

"Now, sir, where's your licence?"

It was produced.

"Then why did you run away?"

"Oh! I'm fond of exercise," answered the man; "but don't you think you'd better ask my friend if he has one?"

The friend was by this time about two miles off.

Would rather not.—"Who is that on my left?" inquired one sportsman of a gamekeeper one day when the season was at its height.

"That must be Lord Jay," said the keeper.

"Go and tell him where I am," said the other.

"I'd rather not," said the keeper. "Lord Jay halways fires when 'e sees hanything move."

No use.—Consider well your actions,
What's done you can't recall;
No use to pull the trigger,
And then try to stop the ball.

The cockney sportsman.—Forty years ago there was a "Rifle Movement," as there is to-day, and some stories were then told. Among them is one relating to Lord Wemyss, an old crack deer-stalker, who found to his mortification that, strive as hard as he could, he could not get into the first class. Among his more successful competitors was a by-no-means-distinguished-looking Londoner who gradually outstripped all his fellow shooters, and ended by carrying off the first prize. Lord Wemyss, curious to learn how he had gained his skill, asked him how he had acquired it.

"Oh," was the unpretending reply, "on cats in my garden at Brompton."

Partridges or promotion.—A colonel and a captain were out shooting together. The colonel walked some distance in advance of the captain. Suddenly a flock of birds arose, and the captain letting drive, spattered shot all about his superior officer. The captain hastened forward shouting his apologies. The colonel picked a shot out of his arm and said :—

" Look here, what are you out after to-day ? Partridges or promotion ?

Got safe home.—A party of amateurs some time ago arranged for a " shoot,' and ordered 30 pigeons from a dealer in a neighbouring town.

The shooting was of a really wonderful character, but the actual doings at the match need not be described in detail. The net results will readily be gathered from the following note, which was subsequently received from the dealer. It ran:

" Gentlemen,—I beg sincerely to thank you for your patronage, and to intimate that I shall be only too happy to supply you with any number of birds on future occasions of the sort. The whole of the 30, for which you paid me at the rate of 8d. per head, returned home in safety, and moreover brought with them a stray pigeon.

Consolation.—An Australian squatter had the misfortune to accidentally shoot one of the natives. He was entirely exonerated from blame, but, being a humane and sensitive man, the affair somewhat worried him, and he grew silent and gloomy.

At last his head shepherd, who was much attached to him —for they went out together from Scotland—received information which he thought would set his master's mind at rest, and hastened to impart it.

" Ye needna fret ony mair about the creature you shot, sir," said he, " for I have this vera morning been credibly informed by trustworthy eyewitnesses that there's hyndreds mair of them in the interior o' the country."

Discreet.—Landowner (to sportsman): " Do you know you are trespassing, sir ? "

Sportsman : " Well er—I'm sorry, er—but I didn't know, sir."

Landowner : " Can't you read ' private ' up here, sir ? "

Sportsman : " Excuse me, sir ; but I never read anything that is private."

No enemy left to love.—A missionary was spending some time in Texas, where he met with a fierce-looking man of the cowboy type, and begged him instead of fighting, that he should love his enemies.

" Anything but that, passon ; it's impossible."

"Impossible? How?"

"I an't got a enemy to love. I shot the last of 'em!"

Improving.—Not long ago a tradesman paid a vist to some friends in the country, and one morning he took out the gun, with him being—as on former visits—an old farm hand, whom we will call Jock. The visitor was a very bad shot, but a generous giver—facts well known to Jock.

A rabbit jumped up about 10 yards away. Bang went both barrels, but the rabbit escaped.

"Did I hit him, Jock?" asked Mr. M——, in an excited whisper.

"Weel, I couldna say ex-'zactly as you 'it 'im, but I must say as I never seed a rabbit wuss scared! Ye're improved vastly sin' last year, Mr. M——, an' if ye keeps on improvin' an comes agin next year why"—with a shake of the head—"summut'll happen to that rabbit!"

A certain sporting barber goes to great country houses in the shooting season, shaves the company in the morning, and acts as loader during the day. He was as near as possible shot by one of the sportsmen during the past season, the shot whizzing past his ear.

"A closer shave than you gave me this morning," was all the apology.

Generous.—"Smith sent his yesterday's bag to the hospital."

"How generous! What did it consist of?"

"One of the keepers."

A cockney, being out one day amusing himself with shooting, happened to fire through a hedge, on the other side of which was a man standing. The shot passed through the man's hat, but missed the bird.

"Did you fire at me, sir?" he hastily asked.

"Oh! no sir, I never hit what I fire at."

More in his line.—Fitz-noodle: "Weally, Giles, I've got a vewy poor bag."

Keeper: "You have, sir. If I might say so, sir, I think elephant shooting would be more in your line."

Cause for rejoicing.—Mrs. Rabbitt: "Oh! I'm so glad you're home again. I've missed you dreadfully."

Mr. Rabbit: "Thank you, my dear. I'm happy to say that the London Sportsman I met missed me too."

A Derbyshire squire recently invited some London friends down for a little shooting. One of the sportsmen, after shooting for three hours without success, was considerably annoyed by the keeper in attendance on him repeating after every miss —"I can't be mistaken surely." "For goodness sake be quiet," he at last shouted. "What do you mean with your everlasting 'I can't be mistaken'?" "Well, sir," was the reply, "if you 'adn't put a few shots through my 'at, peppered both my legs for me, and popped a full charge into my right foot, I'm blowed if I shouldn't think as 'ow you was a-firin' with blank cartridges."

Mark Woodcock.—A certain sportsman once displayed such a remarkable propensity for bagging the first woodcock and thus winning the half-soveriegn sweep, that his friends began to suspect something; in fact, they almost believed that he brought the bird with him. So the butler was told to examine his overcoat while the sportsmen were at breakfast. When the shoot began the customary thing happened. Mark! mark! I've got him," the sportsman cried, and everyone rushed to see the bird. "Here it is," he cried, and produced from his pocket a woodcock, plucked, trussed, and ready for the pot!

First rate shooting.—"Any good shooting on your farm?" asked a hunter, of a farmer. "Splendid," replied the agriculturist; "there's a canvasser man down in the clover-meadow, a peddler at the house, a county council candidate out in the barn, and two tramps down in the stock-yard. Climb right up over the fence, young man, load both barrels, and sail in."

Enigmatical.—The following was posted up in the county of Kent in the year 1821:—

"Notice is hereby given that the Marquis of Camden (on account of the backwardness of the harvest) will not shoot himself or any of his tenants till the 14th of September."

Both beauties.—A Darlington man went up into the hills for a day's rabbit-shooting, but failed to score a single hit.

He had to dine with several friends that evening, and as they knew he had been out shooting, he sent a boy into the village with instructions to get the two finest rabbits procurable, and to bring them to him while at dinner. The meal was not far advanced before he had told his friends of his day's adventures. Sport had not been very good, he said, but he had managed to bag two rabbits, anyway, and both beauties. Just then the boy entered the room, carrying a parcel which might have been mistaken for anything but rabbits. "These were all I could get, sir," said the lad, tearing away the paper from a couple of tins labelled "Best Australian Rabbit."

Lots of cover, little game.—Lord Henry Bentinck once happened to attend a church in the north of England, on a week-day festival, when the interior was decorated with flowers and evergreens, while very few worshippers were present. After the service the parson said to Lord Henry: "May I ask what you thought of the service?"

"As you have asked me, plenty of cover, but very little game!"

Or I shall die.—One morning Bismarck went out shooting with a friend, who slipped and fell in a bog hole, in which the more he moved about the more he sank. "Help me, Count, help me, or I shall die," he cried; and, in fact, he had sunk almost up to his neck.

"My good friend, it is impossible; I should die also, but this would be of no advantage to you. Rather than see you thus suffer, it would be better if I shot you through the head." So saying, he took aim with his gun, and said, "Keep still, for the love of God, or I may miss you!" The poor man, terrified made such an effort to keep out of the line of fire that he got out of the bog.

The Meenister's Goat.—One of Millais's favourite anecdotes related to an incident that occurred when he was shooting in Scotland with Mr. Reginald Cholmondeley and Sir William Harcourt. "One evening during a casual stroll, the sportsman"—the biographer does not say which—"spied a magnificent 'horned beast' grazing peacefully on their little hill. In the gloaming it loomed up as a stag of fine proportions, and, without pausing to examine it through a glass, he rushed into the house, and, seizing a rifle, advanced upon his quarry with all the stealth and cunning of an accomplished stalker. The crucial moment came at last. His finger was on the trigger, and the death of the animal was an absolute certainty, when a raucous Highland voice bellowed into his ear, 'Ye're no gaen to shute the meenister's goat, are ye?'"

A Zoological Conundrum.—Intending Tenant (to Lord Battusnatch's head keeper): "And how about the birds? Are they plentiful, Gaskins?"

Gaskins: "Well, sir, if the foxes of our two neighbours were able to lay pheasant's eggs, I should say there'd be no better shooting south o' the Trent."

The Duke of Devonshire was strolling, gun in hand, through one of his own fields near Baslow, when he shot a hare. Then a small boy jumped out from behind a hedge. "Here" Mester," cried he, peremptorily, "yo mustna touch that." "Why not?" asked the Duke.

"Why, its th' Duke's," answered the boy, "an' he'll have you locked up if he knows." "Oh," said the Duke, "then will you take charge of it?" "Ay, that I will," answered the boy, promptly; "my fayther's a keeper." Half-an-hour afterwards the boy and the hare arrived in the kitchen at Chatsworth. The Duke had taken a short cut home, and had the boy brought to him. The little chap was in distress when he saw the mistake he had made; but the Duke gave him a five-shilling piece, called him "a good lad," and sent him away rejoicing.

Lively shooting.—"The rummiest marster I ever 'ad," said an old gamekeeper in a northern county, "wur t'ould Parson Sharp.' He wur as blind as a bat, he wur." "And did he go shooting?" asked one of the interested audience.

"Shootin'? Yes—he shot reg'lar. But he couldn't see, he couldn't. When anythin' rose I used to cry 'Birds, sir!' and then I'd run behind parson, and the dogs 'ud run behind me, and we'd all go dancin' round behind t'ould gentleman, while he blazed away with both bar'ls."

The Gamekeeper's compliments.—A gamekeeper on a large estate in the North had a habit of expressing himself very neatly on all occasions. A noble lord one day said to him, "I suppose you've seldom met with a worse shot than me?" 'I've met with many a worse—for you misses 'em so cleanly!"

On another occasion he was shooting with a gentleman who missed everything he fired at. At last a pheasant flew up, the sportsman shot, some feathers flew.

Shooter: "I hit that time, Cox, and no mistake.

Cox: "Yes, sir, they will fly into it sometimes."

Except I'm druv.—"Seems to me you go shootin' a good many days when you ought to be 'tending to your farm."

"Well, I'm like that old nag

of yours—I don't work except I'm druv to it, an' then I don't do no more'n I can help!"

Legal Sportsmen.—The celebrated Lord Westbury was shooting in his coverts in company with Alexander Cockburn, then Attorney-General. Cockburn came to the end of a covert only to find Lord Westbury in process of a heated argument with his son as to which of them had shot the keeper. He turned to the keeper himself to inquire which it was, whereupon the man answered: "Both of them—confound it!" Subsequently, when Cockburn was arguing a case before Lord Westbury, and was at a loss for a certain date, his lordship observed, "Do you remember, Mr. Cockburn, it was such-and-such a day—the day, in fact, on which you shot my keeper."

He remembered.—The topic was shooting, and the time was after dinner, when more stories are told than at any other period of the day. Even the host's butler was on the alert, for he had helped his lord and master out of many an after-dinner difficulty.

"Ah," began the host, "how well I remember when I shot the right ear and the hoof of a deer with the same shot."

"Impossible!" exclaimed a languid youth who himself had made some mistakes with his gun. "However did you do it?"

The host, as was his custom in cases of emergency, turned to his butler. "James," he said, "how did I do that? Can you recollect?"

"Oh! yes, sir. Don't you remember, sir, the deer was scratching its ear with its hind leg just at the moment you fired."

"Ah! yes, yes, of course," said the host.

Not the word this time.—Senator Spooner, of Wisconsin is a successful hunter of big game. On one of his trips he had for his guide Bill Murray. They were out looking for bear or deer one day when Murray suddenly drew up his rifle and fired. The senator saw an animal fall heavily, and called: "We've got him this time, Bill." "I killed him plain enough," said the guide. Quickly making their way to where their quarry lay, they found a fine specimen of a Jersey calf. "We've killed somebody's calf!" yelled the guide. Senator Spooner gave him a withering look and said:

"William, you should be more particular in your choice of pronouns. 'We' isn't adapted to this particular instance."

The other barrel.—Guest (who has just given host a pellet in the leg): "Good heavens! What do you think I should do?"

Fellow-Guest: Do? Why, give him another barrel. Can't you see he's a 'runner?'"

The late Lord Cardigan always shot annually at the same place in Northamptonshire. The woods were difficult ones to beat well, being rambling and hollow, necessitating the use of a large number of "stops." These "stops" were generally small boys. But one year Lord Cardigan noticed that, instead of small boys the "stops" were grown-up men. He asked the keeper the reason, saying that it must come very expensive. "Well, you see, my lord," the keeper replied, "your lordship shot the boys down rather close last year."

The Professor.—Keeper: "I had a queer adventure this season with a gentleman whom I took for a university professor. We went out in one of your coverts, sir, together, but got separated before the professor bagged anything. I didn't miss him long before I was disturbed by the report of a gun, and instantly I felt the grass move about my feet. Then I saw the professor about seventy yards off, and he couldn't see me. I shouted just as he was about to fire again, and rushed towards him. 'Idiot,' he shouted, 'you have scared a beautiful pair of rabbits!' You see, sir, the learned old gentleman had been taking my leather gaiters for a pair o' rabbits."

Canna shoot baith.—"I fear, Duncan, that friend of mine does not seem over safe with his gun."

"No, sir, but I'm thinkin' it'll be all right if you wass to go wan side o' him and Mr. John the ither. He canna shoot baith o' ye!"

A sure shot.—Keeper on moor rented by the latest South African millionaire, to guest): "Never mind the birds, sir. For onny sake, lie down! The maister's gawn tae shoot!"—PUNCH.

The keeper's story.—A certain country squire, learning that his new gamekeeper had had a scrimmage with poachers, went down to the cottage to see him. The gamekeeper, who was young and enthusiastic, was a good deal knocked about, as was also a villager who had taken part in the battle; both were bathing their wounds. This was the story told to the squire: "I was walking round Hanger Copse, sir, Mike Farley here with me, when we came upon two rough customers in the lane carrying a basket," said the gamekeeper. "'What have you got in that basket?' says I. 'Nothing,' says the big 'un. 'I'm not so sure,' says I. 'Open it and let me see.' He looked ugly at that, sir, and got in front of the basket, and wouldn't let me come nigh it. So we went for 'em. I tackled the big 'un, and the little 'un went for Mike. We fought for more than twenty minutes, but we laid them out in the end, though we took plenty ourselves, too."

"And what was in the basket?" inquired the squire.

"Oh, there was nothing in the basket, sir."

Did not know.—The game warden of Colorado was walking out in the mountains the other day when he met a man with a gun, who said:—

"I killed one of the finest bucks yesterday I ever saw, and he weighed over two hundred." It was the season when deer may not be shot without subjecting the hunter to a heavy fine.

"Well, that is a fine one," said the warden. "And do you know who you are talking to? I am the chief game warden of Colorado."

The sportsman was only taken aback for a moment, when he said: "And do you know who you are talking to?"

The warden did not know.

"Well, sir, you are talking to the biggest liar in the whole State of Colorado!"

The Cockney Sportsman: "I suppose you find it difficult to keep up the supply of birds every year?"

Keeper: "'Twere at one time, sir; but since measter have let th' shootin' to th' Lunnon gents we allus 'as plenty."

A sure shot.—Early in September, while a shooting party were out for a day's sport, a raw young sportsman was observed by a keeper to be taking aim at a pheasant running along the ground.

Keeper: "Hi, you there, never shoot a running bird!"

Young Shooter: "What do you take me for, you idiot? Can't you see I'm waiting till it stops?"

So full of lead.—"Lend you my dawg to go out shooting with!" exclaimed Giles.

"With your permission, sir, no. Last dawg ever I lent to a party from London who wanted a bit of sport was so full of lead when he came back that the vicar took and mended the church window with it."

For safety.—A city gentleman was recently invited down to the country for "a day with the birds." Whatever his powers in finance, his shooting was not remarkable for its accuracy, to the great disgust of the man in attendance whose tip was generally regulated by the size of the bag.

"Dear me!" at last exclaimed the sportsman, "but the birds seem exceptionally strong on the wing this year."

"Not all of 'em, sir. You've shot at the same bird about a dozen times. E's a-follerin' you about, sir."

"Following me about? Nonsense! Why should a bird do that?"

"Well, sir, I dunno, I'm sure, unless 'e's 'angin' round for safety."

Snappit up.—Laird (to the gamekeeper): What terrible weather we have had this summer, Donald!

Gamekeeper: Aye, you're right, laird. Only three fine days in all the summer, an' twa o' them snappit up by Sundays.

CHAPTER X.

HUNTING.

Lunatics at Large.—An excellent example of the humours of sporting was recently afforded by a hare which led the followers of the Gravesend pack of beagles into the grounds of the Metropolitan Lunatic Asylum. A merry hunt was interrupted by an official, who called upon the party to quit the enclosure—a matter which proved not so easy of accomplishment. At the main gate the sportsmen were confronted by a porter, who refused point-blank to allow any of them to leave the confines of the asylum without an assurance from the superintendent that they were sane and not a posse of escaped lunatics.

A sly fox.—Some few years ago, when the late Tom Firr hunted the Quorn hounds, the following incident occurred: On three occasions a fox was found in Quorn Wood, and after running him to a spot six miles distant, the hounds were at fault, and could not run him another yard. On the fourth occasion, Tom Firr sent the first whip on in advance to the spot to see what occurred. There was a bed of wild mint there, and the fox, after rolling over and over in it, proceeded on his way. The mint destroyed the scent, and so baffled the hounds.

Had seen a fox.—Nimrod: "Hi, my man, have you seen a fox?"

Hedger: "Ay, that I have, surely."

Nimrod: "Where?"

Hedger: "Stoofed in glass case oop at the bar of the Jolly Varmers."

For a holiday.—Some time ago, when the members of a certain hunt turned up at the appointed place, they found a large and very mixed company awaiting them. One of the most striking figures at the meet was Mr. J.——, the local coal merchant, who had borrowed his mount for the occasion from the shafts of one of his coal-carts that same morning.

"That horse looks as if he wanted to lie down and sleep, J——," observed a friend to the coal merchant.

"Oh, he'll soon wakken up when he gits into the country," said J——, who weighs at least fifteen stone. "E's been varry hard worked lately—been doing 'is ten hours a day, in fact. 'E's been out wi' three loads this morning, and as 'e looked a bit fagged, I thowt as 'ow I'd better give 'im a bit of a change, so I browt 'im efther t'hoonds for a 'olliday like!"

A slight misunderstanding.—Owing to the large number of puppies this season, the East Kent Hunt have advertised for "foster-mothers." Among the replies received by the secretary was the following:—

"Dear Sir,—In reply to yours I beg to offer my services. I am thirty-five years old, strong, and very fond of children."

A question of "hands."—Sportsman (who has just come off over the tail): "You silly ass, you needn't laugh. Can't you understand the reins were so slippery I couldn't get any hold!"

Earned his preferment.—Once when a Duke of Grafton was thrown into a ditch, a young curate, who had been closely competing with him for pride of place, shouted, "Lie still, your grace," and cleared him and his hunter and the fence at a bound. So pleased was the duke with the performance that he declared he would give the young divine his first vacant living, and not long afterwards carried out the promise, vowing that if the curate had stopped to pull him out of the dyke he would never have patronised him.

A suggestion.—A summons has been served on a well-known M.F.H. in Leicestershire for not having collars on his pack of hounds, with owner's name and address engraved thereon. We venture to make a further suggestion. All hounds must be muzzled and led on a chain while hunting.—PUNCH.

The unlucky dreamer.—A tale is told of an enthusiastic fox-hunter who ruefully inspected his idle stud one morning when the country was frost-bound. To him came his stud-groom in a great state of importance and excitement. "Sir," he exclaimed, "I knew this was coming; it's a fact—I dreamt of it, and," he concluded impressively, "it's coming harder, sir, for I dreamt it lasted six weeks!" His master stared at him aghast, then remarked, "Well, if you don't dream a thaw before Saturday night, I'll sack you.'

How long ago.—Breathless Hunter: "I say, boy, did you see a hare run by here?"

Boy: "Yes, sir."

Hunter: "How long ago?"

Boy: "I think it'll be three years next Christmas.

Not 'arf! "Here, you boy, open that gate again. Why did you shut it after letting that man through?"

"That gentleman gave me sixpence to open the gate. You don't think I was going to keep it open and let all the hunt through for sixpence, do yer?"

Feeling for the break.—Smith was a great cyclist, but had very rarely been on a horse. One day, when staying with a sporting uncle, he thought he would like to follow the hounds, which were to meet near by; so he borrowed a young horse from his relative which was not much accustomed to the hunting field.

At first he went steadily, until the horse, being startled by a rabbit darting from a clump of grass, broke into a mad gallop. The rider was flung forward on to the horse's neck.

"What are you doing, my lad, with your arms there?" jokingly called out his uncle.

"I'm feeling for the brake," was the muffled reply, "but I can't find it!"

Pungent.—A friend of the late Lord Norbury, a Colonel Pepper, having just purchased a horse, took him out for a day with the Queen's County Hounds, and during the run the horse gave him a tremendous fall.

At dinner that evening the colonel was telling his lordship of his purchase and of the heavy fall he had had. "But I have not given him a name yet," said Colonel Pepper; "will you suggest a suitable one, my lord lord?"

"Oh," said Lord Norbury at once, "call him Pepper caster."

Ladies first; Grooms second.—A sporting farmer, who in the hunting field had waited patiently for seven ladies to go through a gap in a fence, was suddenly charged by a pushing groom.

To him he spoke: "Please remember when riding over tenant farmer's land that it is ladies first, gentlemen second, farmers third, and grooms last."

Hints to Beginners.—A warning to those who hunt from town.—Cabby (gazing after sportsman in pink): "Ain't 'e a toff? Got 'isself up like a bloomin' oleograph, 'e 'as."

Sport in the home.—"We had been running for 25 minutes," he explained, "and hounds going fairly straight, must have covered close on five miles, when down I came a most awful purler!"

"How?"

"Why, the fact is, my leathern steed shied at the commode and chucked me slap into the middle of the washstand!"

Altogether.—Returning from hunting one day, George III. entered affably into conversation with his wine merchant, Mr. Carbonel, and rode with him side by side a considerable way. Lord Walsingham was in attendance; and, watching an opportunity, took Mr. Carbonel aside, and whispered something to him. "What's that? What's that Walsingham has been saying to you?" inquired the good-humoured monarch. 'I find, sir, I have been unintentionally guilty of disrespect. My lord informed me that I ought to have taken off my hat whenever I addressed your Majesty; but your Majesty will please to observe that, whenever I hunt, my hat is fastened to my wig, and my wig is fastened to my head, and I am on the back of a very high spirited horse, so that if anything goes off we must all go off together ! ''

Fox the Quaker.—A Quaker said a few words to a certain country parson, better known for his fox-hunting than for his parish duties.

'' Friend, thou'rt clever at fox-catching, I believe ? Nevertheless, if I were a fox I would hide where thou wouldst never find me.''

'' Pray, where would you hide, sir ? ''

'' I would hide in thy study, friend.''

Making progress.—She (to riding-master) : '' Well, sir, do you think I make any progress ?''

Riding-Master : '' Certainly ; you fall better than you used to do when you first began.''

Alone he did it.—Annie Seed : '' Oh, Mr. Tallyheau, you should have seen Mr. Seldham-Hunt take that high hedge ! ''

Mr. Tallyheau : '' The idea ! I didn't think the horse he rode was much of a jumper.''

Annie Seed : '' Oh, the horse didn't take the hedge ! Mr. Seldham-Hunt did it alone.''

The bag fox.—Railway porter (who has been helping lady to mount) : '' I hope you'll 'ave a good day, ma'am.''

Lady Diana : '' I just hope we'll find a fox.''

Porter (innocently) : '' Oh, that's all right, ma'am. The fox came down by the last train ! ''

Foxhunter logic.—'' I dislike everything belonging to hunting,'' said a lady to an old fox-hunter ; '' it is so cruel.''

'' Cruel ! '' said the old man, with apparent astonishment ; '' why, madam, it can't possibly be cruel, for '' (logically holding up three fingers in succession, '' we all knows that the gentlemen like it, and we all knows that the hosses like it, and we all knows that the hounds like it ; and,'' after a long pause, '' none of us can know for certain that the foxes don't like it.''

Bagged the dog.—A farmer who resides near Thirsk tells of an experience he met with some years ago. Going one morning to open the sliding door of his poultry shed, he found that the place had been raided by a fox, which was still inside. Reynard appeared to have worked up the slide little by little until he effected an entrance, when it dropped and left him a prisoner. The farmer informed a representative of the hunt, and the two decided to turn a dog in and then hold a bag over the hole. There was a swift rush into it, and the mouth was at once shut and held tightly. But, alas ! they had bagged the dog, and the sly fox, bolting out immediately after, was quickly out of sight.

What about Samson.—A street preacher who had been haranguing an audience in Hawick Market Place, at the close of his address invited all anxious inquirers to state their difficulties, and he would have great pleasure in answering them.

A person with sporting proclivities wished the preacher to explain " by what means Samson caught the three hundred foxes he set adrift among the Philistines' corn, when it took the Duke of Buccleuch's hounds a whole day to catch one."

The Fox as game preserver.—The animals on which the fox usually preys are often left untouched round his own home ; and it is even asserted that nothing is killed on the side of the hill in which that home is made. Some curious instances with regard to his habits in these respects are given in " Nature Notes." In a small patch of nettles within a few feet of the mouth of the foxes' earth a partridge placed her nest, and brought off her brood. Round this nettle-bed the cubs were constantly to be seen, and in it they played hide-and-seek. In another case the entrance to an earth was surrounded by five or six rabbit-holes, the tenants of which were unmolested by their next door neighbours. In a third a litter of cubs was placed in a large pit surrounded by fencing, and in which there were a number of rabbits. None of these were attacked by the cubs, though they would seize a dead rabbit in full sight of the person who had shot and thrown it to them.

In Kilkenny.—An M. F. H. received the following letter from a lady whose holding is within the radius of his hunt :—

" Honoured Sorr,—Out of the kindness of your heart and the largeness of your purse would you be good and send a poor woman ten shillings ? The fox is after stealing my best gander.—Bridget O'Hara."

Not to-day.—Member of Hunt (to farmer) : " I wouldn't ride over those seeds if I were you. They belong to a disagreeable sort of fellow, who might make a fuss about it."

Farmer : " Well, sir, as him's me, he won't say nothing about it to-day."

CHAPTER XI.

RACING.

Cleaned out.—A rider in a point to point steeplechase in Kent recently had a bad experience. He was welshed of a fiver, he for half an hour was lying under another man's horse, a thief went to the tent and stole his bag containing his clothes and gold watch and chain, and finally he had to go home wrapped in a blanket.

Pleasures of hope.—"I hope," said the serious friend, "that you haven't been betting on the races?" "I hope so, too," said the young man with the red necktie and the restless eye. "I hope I shall wake up to-morrow and find out that the whole thing was a wild dream."

An assumption.—A story is told of a former Archbishop of York. He was driving on the box seat into Doncaster during race week, and thinking about anything rather than horseflesh, when the driver pulled out his watch with the remark:

"We'll be in time after all, I think."

"In time for what?"

"Why, the St. Leger of course."

"The St. Leger? Oh, yes, to be sure! But I never go to race meetings."

Driver: "Ah, well, you're like me, I suppose. I always did like a real good cock fight a sight better."

Shoot 'em!—The late Earl of Glasgow was one of the most unlucky of racehorse owners.

"I tell you what it is, my lord," said the trainer, "if I owned such a lot of brutes, I would shoot 'em."

"Shoot 'em!" repeated the Earl, in wild amazement. "Shoot all my horses?"

"Yes, I would shoot 'em!"

"Then shoot 'em!" And in spite of all entreaties to the contrary, the Earl insisted upon the order being executed.

An overdose.—Scene—West End Club. Time—9 p.m., 1st June, 1904.

Enter member, looking miserable.

A Friend: "Well, Jimmy, how goes it? What price the Derby?"

Jimmy: "Simply damnable! I'm absolutely cleared out."

Friend: "Thought so! Overdose of Epsom."

Knowing. — "Does your

husband take as much interest in horse-racing as he used to ?"

"Yes, Charlie can always tell the day before a race which horse is going to win and the day after why he didn't."

Better luck.—"What luck did you have at the races ?"

"Better than last year."

"You didn't give your money to the bookmakers, then ?"

"Yes, I did. But last year I had my pockets picked before I got to the course."

A railway deal.—"Did you say Farmer Hiram lost that fifty pounds of his in a railway deal ?"

"Yes."

"I didn't think he was a financier."

"He ain't. This deal was in a smokin' car, going to the races. He met the three-card-trick man."

The knowing ones.—Wife: "Charley, dear, don't you think it would be better for you to let me pick out the horses you bet on ?"

"You don't know anything about horses."

"I don't. But I've noticed that the people who know all about them are the ones who lose their money."

Bury ten! A backer who frequently had to ask for "time," and eventually died owing a large sum to the Ring, by whom he had been well treated, was dining at a well-known betting club. A bookmaker had not long before died "broke" and a subscription of £1 each was got up to bury him. The backer, on being told what was the business, pulled out £10, and said, "A pound each to help to bury a bookmaker! Here, take this 'tenner,' and bury ten."

Cleared out.—Fair Sportswoman: "How much have you cleared on the day's races, captain ?"

The Captain: "My pockets."

The wife of a sporting gentleman has written to the Society for the Prevention of Cruelty to Animals to know if something can be done to prevent horses being "scratched." She is sure it must be very painful, because her husband is sometimes quite upset, and she heard him groan in his sleep about horses being "scratched."

A Persian Derby.—"One horse will arrive before another, I know; but which it is I do not care," is a remark attributed to the Shah of Persia, and it expresses the views he once held on horse-racing. Later on he found out that there was money in the sport. He started a

Persian Derby, and himself entered twenty-seven horses amongst the three hundred that ran. For every horse a considerable stake had to be deposited. Those horses that did not win, of course, did not deceive anything, but those that did win did not get anything either, because they had been so insolent as to beat the Shah's horses; and to punish the owners for their crime, the victorious racers were confiscated for the benefit of the imperial stables.

Room for another.—" Look here, sir," cried an indignant reader of the daily sporting paper, bursting into the editor's sanctum flourishing a recent copy of the paper. " You've got nine prophets on your paper, and every one of them gave a different horse as the certain winner of the great Massingham Handicap yesterday; there were ten runners—and damme, sir! the tenth horse won!"

" Is that correct, sir?"

" Yes; look at it yourself."

" Then all I can say is that we've got room on the paper for another blooming prophet!"—Sporting Times.

Much safer.—" Women always look for a chance to spend money," he observed. " When ever they open a newspaper they begin to study the advertisements."

" Well, Charley, dear, that is much safer than studying the racing entries."

Going to the horses.—" A lot of people are going to the dogs," said a misanthrope. " Not to the dogs," answered a man who disapproved of the institution known as the turf—" to the horses!"

Some good out of evil.—Jacob: " How did you make your money?"

Isaac: " Racing."

Jacob: " I never knew you betted."

Isaac: " I didn't. I started a pawnshop just outside the course for them as wanted a ticket home after ' backing the winner!' "

Honestly run.—" Did you ever see a horse race that you could say was absolutely honestly run?"

" I think I did, wunst," said Bill. " The feller that won it had stolen the hoss, and he kept ahead of us."

A safe thing.— A relative travelling with George Fordham, the famous jockey, asked him for a " safe thing " for a five-pound note. Fordham's reply, as coming from a jockey, is worth noting:—

"Put it in your trousers pocket," he said, "and get your wife to sew the top up. That is the 'safest thing' for a fiver at Newmarket that I know of."

Hunt Steeplechase Season in the North.—Candid Friend (to aged competitor in the Farmers' Race, who has been jumped off): "Man, Sandy, ye should ha' rosined yer breeks. If it didna help ye tae ride, it might mak' ye stick tae the kirk on the Sawbath.—PUNCH.

"Certainties." — A tipster advertised that for a certain consideration he would wire back a number of absolute certainties. A fool sent him ten pounds. All the "certainties" lost, and now the man wants his money back. Did he ever try to get butter out of a dog's throat? We are almost tired of denouncing the advertising tipster who sends "certainties" as a delusion, a snare, and a fraud. The only certainty about the matter is that the tipster will get the money and keep it, and his client will part with his money and see none of it back.—SPORTING TIMES.

An Innocent Abroad.—A story is told in connection with last Ascot race-meeting. An American who was used to going into racing-booths in his own country, ordering luncheon and paying a dollar, found himself hungry at the Royal meeting, so he walked into the first tent handy and told the attendant to give him something to eat. The man put a sumptuous luncheon before him, to which, as well as to the champagne, the visitor did ample justice. He then handed the attendant five shillings, received his thanks, and was bowed out of the tent, inwardly congratulating himself on the moderateness of the charge. An English friend whom he met outside said, "I did not know you knew Lord H.?"

"Neither do I."

"Oh, I beg your pardon, I thought you did, as you came out of his tent!"

Backed the right horse.—"Did you ever make any money backin' horses, Milligan?"

"I made forty quid wance."

"How did you do ut?"

"I backed him down a pub. cellar, an' sued the publican for leaving the flap open."

A clever tipster.—On one occasion the sporting man was away, and Blanchard was asked to do the tips for a big race on the following day. He knew nothing whatever of racing, so he put the names of the horses engaged into a hat, and he " went " in big type for the two he drew out. They finished first and second. His reputation as a sporting prophet was made, and he would never run the risk of spoiling his record, for he absolutely refused ever to give a tip again.—SPORTING TIMES.

A Tod Sloan story.

It must have been a proud moment—not to say a scoop—for a well-known horse-journalist on the other side when, only recently, he bought the wine and got the great little Tod Sloan to relate the story of his most masterly piece of horsemanship—winning a forlorn hope on a horse called Joe Miller; one that could go, but was the biggest loafer that ever wore a saddle.

" However did you manage it ? " he queried.

" By touching his pride," answered his Todlets. " Soon as the flag fell an' we were off I just whispered in his ear, ' Joe, you're running against a lot of crabs—a good horse like you ! Now, just for the sake of old times, show your heels to these crawfish, will you ? '—an' by gee, sir, Joe did ! "

CHAPTER XII

POLITICS.

" Herr Gobden."—

The German traders lifted
Their foaming goblets high,
And drank to Richard Cobden,
Whose name shall never die.
They roared aloud his praises,
And gave him three times three
For where without " Herr Gobden "
Would German business be ?
" By Cobden," England answered,
" For us Free Trade was won,
And most of it at present,
By Germany is done."

The income-tax. — Farmer Jones : " What's your opinion about the income-tax ? "

Farmer Giles : " Well, I've been reading a lot lately about farmers and income-tax, but seems to me with this free trade I see more of the tax and less of the income ! "

So reasonable.—John Bull: "Here's a nice thing! I used to manufacture these goods myself a little while ago."

Mr. Asquith: "Come, now, John, don't be unreasonable. He gives you the job of carrying them—until he's able to do it himself!"

All grass.—Tariff Reformer: "Can't you see that a tax on imported corn would improve the price you receive for your crops?"

Farmer: "Noa, that I can't!"

Tariff Reformer: "Nonsense, man! Let me explain."

Farmer: "Don't 'ee trouble, mister; my varm be all grass!"

Cheaper to import.—It is not at all unlikely that a cry for Protection may be raised by the Irish Home Rulers, for the small farmers of the Distressed Isle are beginning to feel the pinch of foreign competition. The contractors who supply forage for the cavalry in Ireland find it cheaper to import their hay from abroad than to buy it from the Farmers.—SPORTING TIMES.

The Temptation.—

Beneath the tree old Satan stood,
Said, "Pluck the fruit; behold! it's good.
Be ruled by me, accept Free Food,
And ban Protection."

Deceived by that alluring cheat,
Our parents plucked it and did eat,
Its aftertaste they found unsweet—
They'd lost Protection.

The only remedy.—Farmer Coates: "Protection is the only remedy for agricultural depression and other free trade ills."

Farmer Dods: "Yes, I've found that out a long while, since my trade got so 'free' that I had none left at the finish, and had to seek 'protection' in the Bankruptcy Court."

Election Amenities.—During the election contest in Hastings a donkey was seen perambulating the parade bearing the inscription on boards 'Brothers and sisters vote for Free Trade."

A backslider.—At a Radical meeting in the Weald of Kent a farmer said amidst loud cheering:

"My father was a Free Trader, I have always been a Free Trader, and I always mean to be a Free Trader, but I think it would be a good thing if the Government would put a forty shilling import duty on hops."

On this the Radical candidate groaned, and the Nonconformist minister turned up the whites of his eyes.

"He dunno where he are," shouted a voice from the back of the hall.

Happy England.—
The kitchen cupboard's empty
the rent is overdue,
The missus feels it badly,
the kids is cryin', too,
I'm gettin' sick an' weary of
trampin' round the town
For the off-chance of workin' ten
hours for 'arf a crown;
But this is still my comfort—the
tariff bogey's laid,
An' livin's cheap in England
because we have Free Trade.
My Sunday togs are 'anging in
uncle's shop this day,
The kids is all in tatters, my
clo'es are all decay.
Yet moochin' slow an' 'ungry
along the streets I go,
An' ain't I proud an' 'appy to
see the drapers show!
Lord, but they're cheap, them
garments, an' mostly foreign
made,
"Thank God," says I, "in
England we 'aven't lost Free
Trade."
I'm sorry for them people in
lands beyond the sea
Wot 'aven't got enlightened the
same as you an' me.
They're workin', yus, they're
workin', an' earnin' money too,
But, Lord, the price of livin'! It
knocks me 'ow they do.
Their hours is pretty easy, but,
blow me, when they're paid,
Look wot it costs to keep them in
lands without Free Trade.
The mills is lyin' idle, the farm's
is runnin' out.
An' no mistake there's 'unger
an' idle men about,
But don't be mean an' narrer,
look fairly round the case,
Ain't we got cheaper livin' than
any other place?
I am a bloke as always will call
a spade a spade,
An' this is 'appy England
because we 'ave Free Trade.
—Sydney Bulletin.

Not sure about it.—The Earl of Dalkeith was once canvassing the county of Midlothian. Among the voters was a tough old fellow to whom a captain accompanying the candidate said: "This is Lord Dalkeith. Of course you know him?"

"Na, na, I dinna ken him," was the answer.

"At all events," continued the captain, "you know his father, the duke?"

"Oh! aye, I ken the duke! He's a gran' man, the duke!"

"Then you'll surely vote for his son?"

"I'm no so sure about that, captain. It's no every coo has a calf like herself!"

The good time coming.—

Speaking of famous "solutions" of the Irish question, Lord Morris said he had been listening "to talk about the prosperity of Ireland" as long as he could remember—above sixty years—and during all that time it had always been just "going to come." It reminded him of the vet.'s bill on which was the item, "to curing your honour's horse till it died."

Do as I do.—Hodge: I be never quite certain what they do mean at the meeting, you know, squire.

Squire: Well, you do exactly as I do and you'll be all right.

From a rural voter to his M.P.—You're a fraud, and you know it. I don't care a rap for the billet or the money either, but you could hev got it for me if you wasn't so mean. Two pound a week ain't any moar to me than 40 shillin's is to you, but I objekt to bein' maid a fool of. Soon after you was elected by my hard workin', a feller here wanted to bet me that You wouldn't be in the House more than a week before you made an ass of yourself. I bet him a Cow on that as i thort you was worth it then. After i got your Note saYin' you deklined to ackt in the matter, i driv the Cow over to the Feller's place an' tole him he had won her. That's orl I got by howlin' meself Hoarse for you on pole day, an' months befoar.

Rotten.—There is a historic incident of a young Tory heir to a peerage being pelted with rotten eggs while making a political speech.

"Ah," he remarked, wiping the mess from his face, "I have always said that the arguments of my opponents were unsound."

With the brains.—A Newton Abbot butcher tells this story: "A little girl came to my shop yesterday afternoon and asked for a sheep's head. 'Do you want a Tory or a Radical sheep's head?' I asked. 'Please, sir, she replied, 'I want a Radical sheep's head because father is a Radical.' So I just scooped the brains out and gave her the empty head. In a few minutes she returned. 'Please,' she said 'mother is willing to give twopence more if you will let her have a Tory sheep's head with the brains in it.'"

Didn't want to boast.—"Are you a British subject?" asked the official on the steamboat stage at Calais of the passenger who was about to put his foot on the gangway to go on board. "Yes," he replied in a whisper, "but I don't want to boast about it while this Government is in power—don't tell anybody?"

An M.P.'s post bag.—Members of the House often have a warm time with their rural constituents. One of the New South Wales members has received this letter from his district: "Dear Mister,—Sumtime ago I writ you, asking if there were anything the government cud do to make a nagging wife behave herself. I an't herd from yu, and things is no better. Will you please let me me no if yu kin git me one of them poison snakes from Afrika at the Agricultural Department. I have allers voted for yu, and this is mitey little to ask."

And at home it is the same.

"Dear Sir,—My dear wife died on Friday last. Got her safely in the ground on the Tuesday after, but am £3 2s. out of pocket by the transaction. I am hard up, and can barely afford this sort of thing. I know I shall not appeal in vain to your assistance."

Another:—

"Dear Sir,—I voted for you at your last election, and have lost heavily by it. A pal of mine said he had got a dead cop for the Liverpool Cup. Said he would not give me the tip unless I promised to vote against you, as he said he had his shirt on the other chap. I said I would vote for you in any case, and I did, but my pal's tip was the winner, and, therefore, I have missed a big chance. Should you feel inclined to assist me I should be more willing to vote for you next time."

What will he do next.—Sir Wilfrid Lawson, in his best days in the House, was always saying good things. Mr. Chamberlain often came in for notice. Here is one of his observations concerning the right hon. gentleman: "Certainly he (Mr. Chamberlain) has taken to very extraordinary courses lately. One hardly knows where to find him. He is like a farm servant I heard of the other day, who did very extraordinary things. One day the farmer in whose service he was went into a barn and found that the man had hanged himself. Looking at him with astonishment, he said, 'I wonder what the man will do next?'"

Order! Order!—Mr. Johnson, whom Indiana sends to Congress, is famed for his cleverness in debate. Recently he called an Illinois Congressman an ass. This was unparliamentary, and had to be withdrawn.

Mr. Johnson said: "I withdraw the language, Mr. Speaker, but I insist that the gentleman from Illinois is out of order."

"How am I out of order?" yelled the man from Illinois.

"Probably the veterinary surgeon could tell you," replied Mr. Johnson.

This was admissable on the records.

"The onluckiest thing."—Old Farmer Peapod always believed that Parliament could do anything and everything.

So, on his last visit to market, a few of his friends were discussing the latest news when he came on the scene.

"Weel," he said, "an' what's Parliament doin' now, Bill."

"A bad thing for us, Dan," he replied. "They've just passed a bill adding two months on to the winter."

"Well, I never," he said; "if that beant the onluckiest thing that ever 'appened. An' 'ere am I right out o' fodder."

The popular candidate.—"Why didn't you vote for my friend?" asked the politician. "He's the most popular man in the State."

"That's the reason," answered Farmer Corntossel. "I never yet see a man that made a business of bein' popular who had much liking for hard work."

"Upon my head."—One of the most amusing things said by Lord Beaconsfield was at the moment of his entry into public life at High Wycombe. As the two candidates stood side by side addressing the people, Mr. Disraeli's opponent, a county man of influence, said that he was "standing for the seat upon the constitution of the county, upon the broad acres of his fathers, upon law, property, and order.

"And what does Mr. Disraeli stand upon?" cried a farmer in the crowd.

"I stand," said the future leader of his party, rising without a moment's hesitation, "upon my head." It was thought, by Mr. Disraeli, the smartest thing he ever said.

Too near home.—An old Rhode Island farmer, having lost all his money, turned socialist, and set out to convert a neighbour of his.

"Now, Ezra," said the neighbour, "let me understand ye. Do you mean everything should be shared?"

"That there's precisely what I mean."

" Well, if ye had two heifers, would ye give me one ? "

" I would."

" If ye had two horses, would ye give me one ? "

" Certainly, sir, certainly."

" If ye had two pigs, would ye give me one ? "

" Ah, there ye're getting too near home. Ye know I've got two pigs."

Stop your braying.—At a recent political meeting at which Mr. Chamberlain was speaking a man in the room kept on asking, " Are you going to tax my food ? " and repeated the question. At last one of the audience shouted out, " Stop your braying ; he ain't a-going to tax thistles ! "

Cackler, M.P.—" Do you know," asked a farmer of a politician, " the difference between yourself and my old speckled hen ? " The politician gave it up.

" Well, the difference is this : she never cackles till she's laid her egg, and you are cackling all the time without ever laying any eggs at all."

Mighty mixed.—" Things is gettin' mixed, Sophy," said Farmer Hodge, mighty mixed."

" What's the matter ? "

" The politicians are all tryin' to tell the farmers about farmin', an' the farmers are trying' to tell the politicians about politics."

Spoke from his hat.—A short time ago a young candidate for Parliament was addressing an open-air meeting near Ipswich. He held his hat in his left hand, put his written speech in the bottom, and began to read it.

Presently the speaker was interrupted by an old farmer with " More in thee 'at than in thee 'ead, lad ! "

A politician.—A farmer in America had a son, and did not know what business to start him in. So he put him up in a room in which there was nothing but a Bible, an apple, and a dollar. He decided that if after a short time he found the boy eating the apple he would make him a farmer ; If reading the Bible, he would train him for the Church ; and if he had pocketed the money he would make him a stockbroker. Entering, he found the boy sitting on the Bible and eating the apple, with the dollar in his pocket. He became a " politician."

The man for him.—Sir Henry Smith was canvassing in presence of numerous friends, and on asking a farmer for his vote, the man replied, "I'd vote for ye, Sir Henry, as usual, only you're such a fool."

"Fool, am I?" retorted Sir Henry, "then I'm the very man to represent you." This diamond shaft went to the farmer's heart, and he promised his vote.

Politics and Pigs.—The late Rev. J. C. Egerton, M.A., held that promises which had been leisurely "draaed through" the brains of his humble parishoners often yielded conclusions quite as reasonable as those reached by more professed thinkers, and conclusions at times far more originally expressed. He says: "Many years ago I heard from a parishoner an opinion of politics, which I felt to be no mere second-hand cynicism, but the genuine belief, however much mistaken, of a dweller in the country, who, thinking for himself, had come to doubt the existence of political honesty. 'Well,' he said, 'in my opinion, politics are about like this: I've got a sow in my yard with twelve little 'uns, and they little 'uns can't all feed at once because there isn't room enough, so I shut six on 'em out of the yard while t'other six be feeding, and the six as be shut out they just do make a hem of a noise till they be let in, and then they be just as quiet as the rest.'"

The Political Farmer.—The political farmer (despondently): "Somehow I don't seem to make farming pay."

"Maybe you haven't tried the right way."

"Yes, I've done everything. I've tended meetin's, and jined clubs, and voted for every candidate that said he knowed the way to help us along. But it don't seem to do no good, and I must say I'm gettin' clean discouraged."

Same as yours.—One of the wisest speeches ever made by a country chap was that of a man who, during one of the Belfast riots, was asked by a mob what his opinions were.

He glanced at their weapons, their bludgeons, and their blunderbusses.

"Gentlemen, I am of the same opinion as that gentleman there with the big stick."

Took him down.—"I stand," said a Western stump orator, "on the broad platform of the principles of '98, and palsied be mine arm if I forsake 'em."

"You stand on nothing of the kind," said a little shoemaker in the crowd; "you stand in my boots that you never paid me for, and I want the money."

The law of heredity.—A popular priest was speaking at a Kerry meeting in support of a young landlord for a rural district council:—

"He is a landlord, I admit," said his reverence, "but had he been able to choose his position before he was born, he might have selected another station in life. He can't help being what he is, because he inherited the name. Can any one here deny that he is a good landlord?"

A Voice: "Ah, yer riverence, that may be thrue, but then we had to shoot his father!"

At an agricultural meeting.—People have an idea that agricultural labourers are stupid. There never was a greater misconception. If I had a weak case to present I would inconceivably rather submit it to a town audience than to an agricultural one. Indeed, the only time I was let very much down was at an agricultural meeting in the village of Braunton, near Barnstaple. In the middle of my speech a man got up and said: "I should like to ask 'ee a question about that."

I said: "Perhaps you had better wait until the close of my speech, and I'll do my best to answer you."

He persisted, however, which brought another man to his feet, shouting: "Sit down, you ass!"

An altercation of a wholly personal and uncomplimentary character followed between the two disputants, when a third man got up and said: "Sit down, both of 'ee; you'm both asses!"

In a moment of extreme unwisdom I turned on the three of them, and said: "there seems to be an unusual number of asses here to-night, but, for heaven's sake, let's hear one at a time."

Whereat the first gentleman, pointing a long finger at myself, returned: "Well, you go on, then."—Dr. T. J. Macnamara.

CHAPTER XIII.

GARDEN.

The cockney garden.—While stationed at Newcastle, in Natal, one company was ordered on detachment to a small town called Utrecht. As they were going to stay there for a long time it was proposed by the officer in charge to have a garden and grow their own vegetables. A full private, a cockney, was selected for the gardening. He planted the seed in a heap, and they came up in great bunches. The officer, on a tour of inspection, asked what they were.

"They are radishes, sir."

"I didn't know they grew in bunches like that."

"Well, that's how we sell 'em in London."

A riddle.—Why is a Welsh garden like a weather-beaten old ship?—Because it is pretty sure to have several leeks in it.

Hoaxed.—A very lazy man was once asked by his wife to dig up potatoes in the garden. After digging for a few minutes he went into his house and said he had found a coin. He washed it, and it proved to be a five-shilling piece.

Presently he returned to the house again, and said he had found another coin; he washed the dirt off it, and this time it was half-a-crown.

"I have worked pretty hard," said he to his wife; "I think I'll take a short nap." When he awoke he found that his wife had dug up the rest of the potatoes, but she found no coins. It then dawned upon her that she had been hoaxed.

Makes no difference.—Seedsman: "What kind of seeds would you like?"

Suburbs: "Any kind, so long as they're cheap. You see, it makes no difference to me, as the chickens always scratch them up before they get time to sprout."

Among the cabbages.—A man in Somerset had a fine bed of cabbages, to which some of his neighbours helped themselves, so he thought he would try and catch the thieves, and one night he lay in the garden with his head about even with the cabbages. He had not been there long before he heard some one walking towards him. It was a woman, who began to feel the cabbages until she came to the owner's bald head, and was about to use her knife, when the man shouted out: " 'Old 'ard, missus, that's my 'ead!"

An argument.—A worthy Yorkshire canon, who had been displeased by his gardener, sought an interview with the offender in order to reprimand him. Knowing that if he was able to avoid the interview until his master's wrath had abated, he would come off more easily the man kept out of his way. A few days afterwards, however, when the storm was quite over, master and man came face to face in one of the hothouses, and the canon asked: "Why have you avoided me in so pointed a manner of late, Johnson?" To which the gardener replied: "Now I'll put it to you as a man, sir: Would you, if you could help it, stand in front of a canon to be blown up?"

Soldiers' Gardens.—General Lord Mark Kerr, when commanding the Poona division, vigorously encouraged soldiers' gardens. One day, taking an early stroll in mufti, he saw some privates at work. Much pleased he remarked:

"Well, my men, nice thing gardening is, isn't it? I see you take an interest in it?"

"Do I?" rejoined Tommy. "That's all you know! We have got an old general here who's mad on it, and we are here on fatigue duty to-day."

Active growth.—"My turnips," said Will Loyre, "be so large that they're a shovin one another out of the ground."

"Same thing as my 'tater patch," said his companion. "I see the ground one morning a'eavin', and, thinking it were a mole, I says to my dog, 'Jack, go for him, but I'm danged if that what was a-movin' wasn't one of my bloomin' Magnum Bonums a-growin'!"

Champion potato.—The average Irish farmer still clings to the Champion potato, in spite of constant and wide-spread failure, and as a correspondent says, "he will doubtless continue to grow it long after it has caused his death from starvation."

All expectation.—"The saddest thing in old age," Jefferson, the actor, said, "is the absence of expectation. You no longer look forward to things. Now a garden is all expectation, and in that you often get a lot you don't expect. Therefore, I have become a gardener. My boy, when you are past seventy, don't forget to cultivate a garden. It is all expectation."

More practical.—"My dear boy," said a kind-hearted schoolmistress to an unusually promising scholar whose quarter was about up—"My dear boy, does your mother design that you should tread the straight and thorny path of the professions, the intricate and narrow way of the ministry, or dwell amid the flowery fields of literature?"

"No, marm," replied the juvenile prodigy; "dad says he is going to set me at work in the tater patch."

Wasteful.—Countryman, after quietly gazing at a suburban garden, which among other "ornaments," boasts several marble statues: "Jest see what a waste! There's no less than six scarecrows in that little ten-foot garden patch, and any one of 'em alone would keep off all the crows from a five-acre lot!"

A vocal cow.—This advertisement comes from Cambridge: "Wanted, a steady, respectable young man to look after a garden and milk a cow who has a good voice and is accustomed to sing in the choir."

The indiarubber plant.—"Did you break that india-rubber plant?"

"That ain't no india-rubber plant. I pulled at it until all the leaves came off, and it didn't stretch a bit."

From a gardening contemporary.—Everything in this department was in excellent condition. The vines, peaches, and pigs were in splendid bearing form.

Very likely.—"What are you doin' you young rascal?" said a farmer to a small boy under a tree in his orchard, with an apple in his hand.

"Please, sir, I was goin' to put this 'ere apple back on the tree, sir!"

Humulus.—A Kentish farmer who has a beautiful house is very partial to climbers, and the following advertisement he could not resist: "Humulus, 6d.; grand climber; grows 14 feet; throws out a bold flower and good leaves." He sent his money, and was dangerous to approach the following day. The climber was simply a hop plant, of which he had ten acres in front of his house. It was the "Humulus" that trapped him.

The farmer's boy.—Visitor: "Digging potatoes, eh?"

Farmer's Boy: "Yes."

Visitor: "What do you get for digging potatoes?"

Boy: "Nawthin', but I get somethin' fer not diggin' 'em."

Visitor: "Indeed? What would you get for not digging them?"

Boy: "Licked."

A terrible warning.—A farmer who was much troubled by trespassers during the nutting season consulted with a botanical friend, who told him the technical name of the hazel. Eventually the farmer placed the following notice at conspicuous points about his premises:—

"Trespassers take warning! All persons entering this wood do so at their own risk, for although common snakes are not often found, the Corylus Avellan abounds everywhere about here, and never gives warning of its presence."

The crop was unmolested that year.

Split pea-seed.—An order has lately come to a London seed-house for some split-pea seeds from a parson—doubtless not of the old sort. It is, perhaps, a result of the University extension movement into what are called the great towns.

How his garden grew.—The lord of Acacia Villa was more than angry. For the fourth time this spring the seeds which he had sown in the largest bed of his small garden had been scraped up. He therefore despatched his servant to The Lilacs to inform the lady thereof that her cat should be shot.

"It's not my cat," said the lady of The Lilacs. "It's the dog from The Willows that scratches up your seeds."

It might be so, for perhaps the dog was an educated one, and could climb garden walls. So the owner of the flower-bed waited for further evidence.

In time he got it, and once more his retainer called upon the lady of The Lilacs.

"Please, ma'am," said the girl, "master thought you'd like to know that the dog from The Willows has taken the liberty of having kittens in our bicycle shed, and he's given your cat the job of nursing them!"

CHAPTER XIV.

HOUSEHOLD AND HOME.

Prepared.—The vicar of a little parish in Devonshire always felt it to be his duty to give each couple a little serious advice before he performed the marriage ceremony, and for this purpose he usually took them aside one at a time, and talked very soberly to each of them regarding the great importance of the step they were about to take, and the new responsibilities they were to assume.

One day he talked in his most earnest manner for several minutes to a young woman who had come to be married.

"And now," he said, in closing, "I hope you fully realise the extreme importance of the step you are taking, and that you are prepared for it."

"Prepared!" she said, innocently. "Well, if I ain't prepared, I don't know who is. I've got four common quilts, and two nice ones, and four brand-new feather beds, ten sheets, and twelve pairs of pillow-slips, four linen tablecloths, a dozen spoons, and a new six-quart kettle, and lots of other things."

A true ghost story.—Two young ladies on a visit to a house which possessed a haunted room begged their hostess to let them sleep in it for a night, and, their wish being readily granted, the young ladies went to bed and soon fell fast asleep. About midnight the door opened, a tall figure stalked into the room, and, seizing the bedclothes at the foot of the bed took them off and disappeared, leaving the girls too terrified to stir hand or foot until daylight, and very cold. They dressed early and sat on their bed until it was time to go down to breakfast, discussing with each other their awful experience, but it seemed too preposterous. The solution of the mystery was revealed to them at breakfast. Then an old Indian officer remarked, "I couldn't sleep for the cold, so I took the liberty of going to the spare room and taking the clothes off the bed, and even then I wasn't warm."

Served him right.—The noise made by the burglar in the Fergusson pantry, slight as it was, disturbed the light sleeper in the bedroom above, and the burglar was surprised a moment later to find himself covered with a revolver in the hands of a determined looking man in a night shirt.

Burglar: "I hain't done nothin' but eat a few cold victuals, mister."

Fergusson: "I see, you have been eating the remains of a strawberry shortcake my wife made for dinner last night. Do you know what I'm going to do with you?"

"Turn me over to the police, I s'pose," gasped the helpless thief.

"Worse than that," said Fergusson, "I'm going to make you eat a quart of patent health food. It's pretty dry eating, but you'll eat every particle of it or I'll bore six holes through you. There it is, in that big bowl. Turn yourself loose on it!"

With grim determination, Fergusson stood over him till it was finished, after which he picked up the luckless scoundrel, who had fallen exhausted to the floor, and threw him out of the open pantry window.

Travelling in Ireland.—There is a good opening for anyone who wishes to start an hotel in the picturesque parts of Ireland. A traveller lately staying at an inn there was called rather earlier than he wanted to be, and he asked to be let alone. Half an hour later the landlady came to his door and said, "Surr, will you please get up?"

"What's the matter now?"

"Oh, surr, it's two men want their breakfast at 8 o'clock, and I can't lay the table till I have got off your top sheet!"

He'd like to know.—A farmer's boy in Barren County, Kentucky, advertised for a wife. He says:—

"He wants to know if she can milk,
And make his bread and butter;
And go to meeting without silk,
To make a 'show and flutter.'"
"He'd like to know if it would hurt
Her hands to take up stitches;
Or sew the buttons on his shirt,
Or make a pair of ———."

The tramp's advice.—Housekeeper: "You promised that if I'd give you a good meal and a suit of old clothes you'd tell me how to keep the premises from tramps."

Tramp: "Yes, mum, an' I'm a man o' me word, mum."

"Well, what am I to do?"

"Never give 'em anything, mum. Good morning, mum."

A Laundry in the Philippines.—A sojourner in the Philippines says in a letter to friends at home: "I want to go home. I want some washing done. I send you under separate cover a handkerchief and collar just back from the laundry here. Take the handkerchief out and bury it, and save the collar as a souvenir. They take the clothes down to the river, hard water and partly salt, souse them in, take them out, lay them on boards, and beat them with stones until full of holes, and pound the buttons off. Then they smooth them out with a plank."

To stay his appetite.—Housekeeper: "Now, you clear out right off, or I'll call the man."

Tramp: "Please, mum, I only wanted to borry a Bible, if you have one to spare."

"Bibles? I've got about fifteen."

"Well, mum, will ye please lend me one a few minutes? I want to read about Belshazzar's feast. Mebby it will stay my appetite till I get to some house where people has fewer Bibles an' more pies."

A steady job.—Woman (to tramp): "Can't you get any work?"

Tramp: "Yes, ma'am; I was offered a steady job by the old man who lives just down the road."

"What did he want you to do?"

"Ma'am he wanted me to get up at four in the morning, and milk 17 cows, feed, water, and rub down four horses, clean the stables, and then chop wood until it was time to begin the day's field work."

The book canvasser.—The woman had her arms in the wash-tub, and was scrubbing one garment after another. A book canvasser knocked at the front door until he was tired, and then went around to the back, where the woman was bobbing up and down over the work.

Canvasser: "Good morning, madam."

Woman: "Good mornin'."

"Pleasant day," observed the book agent, sparring for an opening.

"Good enough."

"Excuse me, madam, but I have here a work that I would like to show you."

"Have you, really?" answered the woman. "Well, I've got a lot of work that I'd like to show you." She took one soapy hand out of the tub and waved it at him.

And the book agent, finding

his " work " covered with soap-suds, also thought it best to quit.

As his mother used to do.—

He criticised her puddings, and
he didn't like her cake;
He wished she'd make the biscuit
that his mother used to make;
She didn't wash the dishes, and
she didn't make a stew,
And she didn't mend his stock-
ings—as his mother used to do.
Ah, well, she wasn't perfect,
though she tried to do her best,
Until at length she thought her
time had come to have a rest;
So, when one day he went the
same old rigmarole all through
She turned and boxed his ears,
just as his mother used to do.

That jug.—Mrs. Chatterton: " Bridget, that jug you broke this morning belonged to my great-grandmother."

Bridget: " Well, Oi'm glad ov that! Sure, Oi was afraid it was something yez had just bought lately."

All the harder.—Bridget: " Oi can't stay, ma'am, onless ye give me more wages."

Mrs. Hiram Offen: " What! Why, you don't know how to cook or do housework at all."

Bridget: " That's jist it, ma'am, an' not knowin' how, sure, the wurk is all the harder for me, ma'am."

Prosaic.—" I shall never permit myself to become a household drudge," said the newly-married woman; " I shall try to improve my mind." " That is a good idea, my dear, but don't let your literary pursuits eat up all your talents. There are times when currant jelly appeals to a man even more than current fiction."

Where Woman's time goes.—" Please state to the Court exactly what you did between eight and nine o'clock on Wednesday morning," said a juvenile counsel to a delicate-looking woman in the witness-box.

" Well," she said, " I washed the three children and got them ready for school, and sewed a button on Johnny's coat, and mended a rip in Nellie's dress. Then I made the beds, watered my plants, dusted the parlour, and set things to rights, cleaned the lamps, combed baby's hair, sewed a button on one of her shoes, swept out the hall passage, and brushed and put away the children's Sunday clothes, cut and brought the vegetables from the garden, wrote a note to Johnny's Sunday-school teacher asking her to excuse him for not being at school on Sunday, and sat down and rested for a few minutes before the clock struck nine. That's all.

Domestic science.—Daughter: "Yes, I've passed the Oxford and Cambridge exam.; but now I must inform myself in psychology, philology, bibli——"

Practical Mother: "Stop right where you are. I have arranged for you a thorough course in roastology, boilology, stitchology, darnology, patchology, and general domestic hustleology."

The editor's needs.—From a Dakota agricultural paper: It is reported that one of our neighbouring fastidious newly-married ladies kneads bread with gloves on. The incident may be somewhat peculiar, but there are others. The editor of this paper needs bread with his shoes on, he needs bread with his shirt on, he needs bread with his pants on, and unless some of the delinquent subscribers of this old "Farmers Friend" pay up before long he will need bread without a d——d thing on, and North Dakota is no Garden of Eden in the winter time.

Modesty rewarded.—Du Guesclin, the greatest soldier of his time, in peace went about simply dressed and without escort. One day he was going to dine with a friend, and in the simplest apparel. The lady of the house stopped him, and, taking him for some menial, asked him to help her in the kitchen, as her husband was out, and she might be late. Du Guesclin took off his coat and started splitting wood. When the master of the house came in, he said:—

"What means it, my lord, that you are here working?"

"I am merely reaping the reward of my modest looks," replied the marshal.

A vegetarian.—Dressmaker: "And would you have leg of mutton sleeves, madam?"

Customer: "Most certainly not. I am a vegetarian!"

To make sure.—Old Lady (to London cabby): "Now I want to go to my dressmaker. I've lost the address, but it's a small house beyond Oxford Street, down a street on the right, and the number's over the door."

Cabby: "Well, mum, won't you please come up and drive yerself, so we might be sure of not making any mistakes."

Had a relapse.—Butcher: "I tell you, ma'am, that bacon's as right as you are."

Customer: "I tell you it's bad."

Butcher: "How can that be? Why it was only cured last week."

Customer: "Then it must have had a relapse, that's all."

In butcher's shop.—Boy: "My mother sent me back to let you see what a big bone there was in the pound of beef she bought last night, and she wants another pound without bones."

Butcher: "Tell your mother the next time I kill a cow without bones I'll send her a leg for nothing."

Explanation wanted.—We read in an Irish paper that a police magistrate complained in a case in which the prisoner was charged with selling putrid beef, "that no explanation was given to him of the beast having died before it was killed."

Goat flesh for mutton.—A favourite device in certain stations abroad was to palm off goat-flesh for mutton. A zealous quartermaster in the Ionian Islands, suspecting this practice on a certain occasion, thought he would assuredly defeat it by ordering that all the legs of mutton sent in by the butchers should have the tails attached. The Greek contractor smiled knowingly, but promised compliance, and for the next few days every joint was delivered in the manner required. The quality of the meat, however, did not improve; on the contrary, it had a more "goaty" flavour than ever, and loud were the complaints of the soldiers. At last the mystery was solved, as one day the inspecting officer picked up a leg of mutton to weigh it, and the joint fell to the ground, leaving the tail in his hand. It had merely been sewn on.

A phenomenon.—A phenomenon is reported from Christchurch, New Zealand. The local mutton, for some unknown reason, has been giving forth a phosphorescent glow, and according to one account it is no uncommon sight to see economical householders reading by the light of their meat. It is no doubt on the way to our markets.

Canned "beef."—One of the latest of the embalmed beef stories comes from Rockbury, Virginia, where, in a can of preserved beef shipped from Chicago there was found a metal dog license tag, No. 13,506. No other trace of the dog was found in that tin.

The prize sheep.—A butcher bought a prize sheep at the Cattle Show, and hung it out at his shop. A day of two afterwards the following dialogue took place:

Butcher's Man: "Mrs. Jarvey wants a leg off the big sheep."

Butcher: "Very well, tell her she can have it, but don't take any more orders for legs. I've sold over a dozen to come off that animal already."

For a black eye.—An Aston lady, with a worried look on her face and a "football" edition of the evening paper in her hand, recently walked up to a meat stall and began turning over the stray pieces labelled "All choice!"

"Wot d'yer want now, missus?" inquired the proprietor.

The lady said she wanted a piece of beef.

"When you was 'agglin' for the mutton you bought 'arf an 'our ago you told me as 'ow you couldn't eat beef," said the butcher.

"No more I carn't," answered the lady, "but I reckon I shall want a bit o' beef to put on a black eye afore the morning. My 'usbin's bin to a football match an' is team's lorst!"

Tinned beef.—"I want some don't - know - what - you - may - call - it," said the facetious man in the grocer's shop.

"Here you are, sir," replied the grocer, handing him a sample of American tinned beef.

The Christmas-box. — Mr. Labouchere tells a story touching the new Secret Commission Act:—A friend of mine, who is of a waggish turn, received a visit from his butcher just before Christmas. The butcher asked if there was any objection to the cook receiving her usual Christmas - box. "What is the usual Christmas-box?" asked my friend. The butcher evaded an answer, but on pressure thought it would not be more than half-a-sovereign. "Well, look here," said my friend, "if it is worth your while to pay my cook half-a-sovereign for the chance of keeping my custom, it must be well worth your while to pay me a sovereign for the certainty of it. So you send me up thirty shillings, and I will give the cook ten."

He has not yet received a remittance.

A vocation.—Village Doctor: "And what do you intend to make of this little man, Mrs. Brisket?"

Proud Mother: "Butcher, sir. 'E's bound to be a butcher. Why, 'e's that fond o' animals, we can hardly keep 'im out o' the slaughter-'ouse!"—PUNCH.

The art of cookery.—Mr. Bowler: " I should like to know what good all these cooking-school lessons are doing our daughter."

Mrs. B.: " Everything she cooks she brings home."

" Yes, and none of the family will touch 'em, and the things are just thrown away."

" No, they are not. She gives them to beggars."

" Huh! What good does that do?"

" We are getting rid of the beggars."

The Calf's Head.—The wife of a farm hand bought a calf's head and put it on to boil, leaving her little boy to mind it while she went to church close by. The clergyman had reached his " fifthly, my brethren," when a small boy poked his head into the door and whispered " Mother—mother, you needn't wink and blink at me, but you'd better come home quick, for the calf's head is buttin' all the dumplings out of the saucepan."

Jump-short pie.—A clergyman in Norfolk entered a parishoner's cottage the other " noon time," and was invited to partake of some " jump-short " pie, on which the family were about to dine.

" It's very nice—tastes like lamb. Why do you give it such an odd name?"

" Well, sir," said the host, " it is lamb. You see sir, the young lambs in the marshes try to jump over the dykes, and some of 'em jump short, tumble in, and get drowned. Then we fish 'em out, and my old woman puts 'em into a pie. Have another helping, sir?"

The rubber cow.—" Well," remarked a gentleman, as he courageously attacked a particularly tough steak served up to him at a restaurant. " I have heard of the iron horse and the golden calf, and now I seem to have encounttered the india-rubber cow!"

Baked chicken is off.—" The Bill of fare for Sunday dinner will be shredded chicken instead of baked chicken," announced the old Yankee farmer to the group of city boarders. " H'm!" grunted one pessimist, " what caused the change?" " What caused the change? Why, by heck, one of them thar racing automobiles just ran through my whole flock of poultry."

The sarcastic guardian.—Fish and potato pie not being relished by some of the inmates of the Truro Workhouse, it has been determined that experimentally the Friday's dinner for the next six weeks shall consist of rabbits.

"As an alternative diet," suggested a sarcastic guardian, "try pheasants!"

Got mixed.—Beef was very scarce in Ladysmith during the siege, but General Sir Ian Hamilton, then a colonel, insisted that "horse is not half bad when properly cooked, and when one is used to it. In fact," he said, concluding a discussion, "I have a joint cooked to-night, which I hope you will all sample. Of course, there's beef, too—to-night."

Every one at the table preferred the beef, with the exception of Colonels Ward and Ian Hamilton, who ostentatiously carved generous slices from the "horse-flesh."

The dinner was nearly over, when one of the servants whispered a communication to Ward. Up he sprang. "I'm distressed, gentlemen," he announced to the startled company "a silly mistake has been made, The joints were mixed up somehow, and you have been eating the horse! I'm really annoyed. But I hope you'll be convinced now that the meat is splendid eating. I'm sure you all seemed to enjoy it!" Glances were exchanged, moustaches were twilled. Nobody seemed ready with a response. Then a voice from the bottom of the table piped up: "Oh! don't distress yourself, Ward. I thought some mistake had been made, so I just changed those dishes as they stood on the sideboard. It was you and Hamilton had the horseflesh all right."

Not that kind of egg.—He was a vegetarian, his family were out of town, and he went to a restaurant for breakfast, seating himself next to a stranger. The vegetarian took occasion to advertise his creed by telling the stranger that all meat was injurious, and that the human diet should be strictly vegetarian.

"Well," said the stranger, "I seldom eat meat,"

"But," argued the vegetarian "you have just ordered eggs, and eggs are practically meat, because they eventually become birds."

"The kind of eggs I eat never become birds," replied the stranger quietly.

"Good heavens, man," cried the vegetarian, "what kind of eggs do you eat?"

"Principally boiled eggs," said the stranger.

Pneumatic bread.—"I wanted ter ax yer," said the new coloured servant, with much embarrassment, "ef yoh would hab any objections to my bakin' some home made bread?"

Wife: "But the baker's bread is quite satisfactory."

Servant: "I didn't speck ter make it foh you all. I was axin' yer as a pus'nal favoh. I hasn' got myse'f usenter to dis here baker's bread. When'I bites inter a piece an' doesn' fin' nuffin but a hole I feels dis-app'inted. I knows I's way behin' de times. Dey kin put wind in baloons an' bicycle tires, an' I ain't got nuffin to say. But when it comes to pneumatic bread, I gibs up."

Disillusioned.—Spouter: "On the surface things are often right, but it is when we explore the depths of things that we see the deceptions of our fellow-creatures."

One of the Crowd: "Say, guv'nor, you've just been buy'in a barrel of apples, ain't yer?"

The conjuror and the Orange.—Robert Houdin, the most famous sleight-of-hand Frenchman, was accosted on the Boulevard by a retailer of oranges.

"Well, my lad," said Houdin "how do you sell them?"

"Two sous a piece, monsieur," said the boy.

"That is a high price indeed," replied the artist; "however, I will try them." Cutting an orange into four pieces, he produced a twenty-franc gold piece from the inside. "Behold!" said he, "how your fruit repays me for your extortion. Come, I can afford to buy one more." And he repeated the same experiment as before. Houdin now offered to come to terms for the whole basket, but the astonished lad ran off with joyous alacrity, and, reaching home, began to quarter the contents of the whole basket, but found none that contained golden seeds.

The wrong basket.—Customer (to dealer): "Say, there must have been some mistake about those apples you sold me yesterday."

Dealer: "What was the matter with them?"

"Nothing. That's just it. There were no bad ones at the bottom of the basket."

"So you got 'em, did you? I picked them out for myself."

A miser.—A Tipperary boy said of a well-to-do but miserly farmer: "He is worth two thousand pounds to my knowledge; but I would not nail up a fruit tree with his clothes."

Tomatoes is a hextra.—Smith: "Look here, Brown, we'll soon decide the matter; let's ask the waiter. Waiter, are tomatoes a fruit or a vegetable?"

Waiter: "Neither, sir. Tomatoes is a hextra."

The proof of the pudding.—"What do you think of the pudding, dear?" said the young wife. "I made it out of Mr. Shouter's cookery book.

"Oh, that accounts for it. I suppose it's the leather binding that makes it so bad." replied the brute.

The conscience clause.—A school teacher put the following problem in arithmetic to his class:

"If one horse can run a mile in one minute fifty-five seconds and another a mile in two minutes, how far would the first horse be ahead at the end of a race of two miles?" A scholar returned the question with the following note attached:

"Please, sir, mother says I must never have anything to do with horseracing."

To sweeten.—Among the cookery recipes in a popular journal is the following:—

Steamed Cherry Pudding.—Cut an ounce and a half of dried cherries in small pieces. Put two ounces of breadcrumbs, half a pint of milk and ONE OUNCE OF CASTER OIL into a saucepan, and let it simmer for five minutes. When cool, stir in two beaten eggs, and the cherries, etc., etc.

Come to terms.—A dispute having long subsisted in a gentleman's family between the maid and the coachman, about fetching the cream for breakfast, the master one morning called them both before him, that he might hear what they had to say. The maid pleaded that the coachman was lounging about the kitchen the greater part of the morning and yet would not fetch the cream for her. He saw she had not a moment to spare. The coachman said it was not his business.

"Very well," said the master, "but pray what do you call your business?"

"To take care of the horses and clean and drive the coach," replied he.

"You say right," answered the master, "and I do not expect you to do more than I hired you for; but this I insist on, that every morning, before breakfast, you get the coach ready, and drive the maid to the farmer's for milk; and I hope you will allow that to be part of your business."

The coachman and the maiden soon after came to terms.

The Duke's arms.—Among the stories that amused Queen Victoria was that told by the late Duchess of Athole of a comical advertisment regarding the Dunkeld and Blairgowrie coach, which was posted in the village of Dunkeld, in Perthshire.

The coach was named "The Duchess of Athole," and the inn from which it ran was "The Duke's Arms."

The notice ran as follows:—

"The Duchess of Athole leaves the Duke's Arms every lawful morning at six o'clock."

A recommendation.—"What sort of a man is your coachman?" was asked recently.

"He drives with great difficulty and drinks with great ease."

A ready retort.—A Scottish nurse was out in her master's garden with a baby, and the gardener inquired:—

"Is't a laddie or a lassie?"

"A laddie," said the nurse.

"Weel," says he, "I'm glad a' that, for ther's ower mony women in the world."

"Hech, mon!" says the nurse, "did ye ken ther's aye maist sawn o' the best crop?"

Can be seen.—The scarcity of servant girls led Mrs. Vaughan to engage a farmer's daughter from a wild district of Ireland, and her want of town ways has led to scenes.

One afternoon a lady called at the Vaughan's, and Kathleen answered the call.

"Can Mrs. Vaughan be seen?"

"Shure, an' Oi think she can; she's six feet hoigh, and four feet woide! Sorrah a bit of anything ilse can ye see whin she's about."

Useful indoor and out.—"Can any lady or gentleman recommend a man and wife (Church of England), man useful indoor and out. Principal duties, large flower garden, small conservatory, draw Bath chair, wait at table, keep lamps, and wear dress suit except in garden. Clothes and beer not found. Family, lady and child, lady help, house, and parlour maid kept. Must not object to small bedroom. Wife, plain cook (good), to undertake kitchen offices, dining room, and hall (wash clothes). Wages for the two, £50; all found."

CHAPTER XV.

HEALTH.

'Ceptin for that.—"Have you taken anything for your cold ?" asked a doctor of a hungry-looking man, who came to him complaining of being "all run down." "Well, I ain't bin takin' much o' anythin', doctor, that is, nothin' to speak of. I tuk a couple o' bottles o' Binkham's bitters a while back, an' a bottle o' Quackem's invigorator, with a couple o' boxes o' Curem's pills, and a lot o' root bitters, an' quinine my old woman made up. I've got a porous plaster on my back, an' a liver pad on, an' I'm wearin' a' lectric belt an' takin' quinine and iron four times a day, with a dose or two o' salts every other day. 'Ceptin' for that, I ain't takin' nothin !"

The restaurant rabbit.—A gentleman relating the incidents of his travels while in Paris, says :

I entered a restaurant and ordered a rabbit. I was green—verdant as the first cucumber—or I should not have done this. The rabbit came, and I offered a share to an old Frenchman opposite, whose eyes were fixed upon my plate ; but he bowed a negative.

"Monsieur has not been long in Paris ?" he said.

"No. I have just arrived," I answered.

"Monsieur is going to eat that ?"

"Yes. May I offer you a slice ?"

"Monsieur will allow me to make a small observation ?" inquired the Frenchman, with a grimace.

"Certainly," I replied, becoming alarmed.

"Monsieur, that rabbit once 'mewed' he replied.

A veteran.—During the late autumn manœuvres an officer making his inspection after mess, addressed a corporal with :

"Rations all right ?"

"Yes, sir."

"Any complaints ?"

"No, sir ; but the men think if the cow they had for dinner had lived a bit longer it might have been recommended for the long-service medal !"

Her grandmother as well.—The late Rev. Peter Mackenzie, the celebrated Wesleyan minister, on account of his great geniality was often consulted by poor people about all kinds of things. One evening a servant girl, who was living some distance from her home, came to see him in great trouble because she had seen her mother in a dream, and she was afraid it boded ill.

"What did you have for your supper?"

"Half a pork pie."

"Well, if you had eaten the other half you would have seen your grandmother as well."

Whose baby.—Cheeky boy (to his schoolmaster): "Did you hear, sir, about that baby that was fed on elephant's milk, and gained 7 lb. a day?"

Schoolmaster: "No, I didn't Whose baby was it?"

Boy: "The elephant's baby, sir."

The patent food.—Lady: "Is this a patent food?"

Grocer: "Yes, ma'am. It's very dear. It looks like dog biscuit and tastes like nothing, but boiled with plenty of good milk they say its nourishing."

Even more marvellous.—She (glancing over an illustrated paper): "Don't you think those horseless carriages are very wonderful, Harry?"

He: "Yes, but I know of something that would be even more marvellous."

She (much interested): "Oh, what?"

He: "Horseless Sausages."

Not quite the same.—Mr. Stoutun (at a fashionable watering place): "You recommend spare diets, long walks, and plenty of exercise. Why, I could do all that at home, and save the enormous expense of this place."

Doctor: "Yes, my dear sir, I know. But a patient so stout as you needs plenty of worry. The high prices here will go a long way to reducing your weight."

Looked bad.—"I am glad to see you on your feet again, Mr. Burrows," said Miss Parshaw graciously. "You looked very bad the last time I saw you."

"You must be mistaken, Miss Parshaw," said Burrows. "I have never been ill. Where did you see me last?"

"You were in the park on horseback."

Sidney Smith's Pleasantry.—When the physician, Sir Henry Holland, told Sidney Smith that he had failed to kill either one of a brace of pheasants that had risen within easy range near the latter's home, the divine asked, "Why did you not prescribe for them?"

On'y savinty-foive. — While passing through a village a tourist saw an old man seated at a cottage door devouring huge hunks of bread and bacon in a ravenous manner. He remarked :—

"Look here, my good man, you shouldn't eat so rapidly at your time of life! Think of your digestion!"

"My di-gestion be orlright, and Oi beant old. Oi be on'y savinty-foive."

"Then you don't consider that old?" the tourist asked. "What age was your father when he died?"

"Feyther? Feyther beant dede; he be oopstairs putten gran'feyther to bed!"

Vigorous at 82.—Mr. H. G. Davis, the man who at 82 was vigorous enough to be Democratic candidate for the vice-Presidency of the United States the other day, says his rules of good living and long life are as follows :—

"I sleep eight hours every night.

"I eat three square meals in 24 hours.

"I drink a little wine at times, but that is all.

"I do not use tobacco in any form.

"I take a good long walk every day."

A stranger asked one of his neighbours if he did not think Mr. Davis was getting too old to do business.

"Think so? I guess you haven't swapped horses with him lately, have you?"

Sheep's heads for ever.—Douglas Jerrold was once invited to a sheep's head supper. One gentleman present was particularly enthusiastic on the excellence of the dish, and throwing down his knife and fork, exclaimed : "Well, sheeps' heads for ever!"

Jerrold : "There's egotism."

What is in us.—A western school teacher said : "Do not attempt any flights of fancy; be yourselves and write what is in you." The following day a pupil handed in—

"We should rite what is in us. In me there is my stomach, lungs, heart, liver, two apples, one piece of mince pie, three sticks of candy, a hull lot of peanuts and my dinner."

Too much of a good thing.—There are many good things of which even the very poor may get more than is sufficient. A tired and hungry man fell from utter faintness by the roadside. A crowd had gathered, when an onlooker hurried himself forward shouting :

"Stand back! Give him air!"

The fainting man rallied and sat up.

"Air!" he gasped. "Give me air! Why, gentleman, I have had nothing but air for the last fortnight."

That grew underground.—During the Christmas holidays a party was held at a friend's, when one of the company, a young lady, was relating that the doctor had forbidden her to eat anything that grew underground. Potatoes and various other vegetables were enumerated, when an old man exclaimed—"Nor wild rabbits!"

Hard times.—City Doctor (to hard-pressed farmer): "Your daughter wants tone. Send her to the seaside, and give her salt water baths."

"'Deed, doctor, in these hard times, wad a guid stiff pickle at hame no dae?"

A prescription.—Lady (at a fashionable garden party, trying to get a prescription on the cheap): "But tell me, doctor, dear, how am I to lose in weight?"

Doctor: "Try my butcher, my dear madam; you will find you will soon lose in weight there."

Only fair.—"These shoes, doctor," said the cobbler after a brief examination, "ain't worth mending."

"Then, of course, I don't want anything done to them."

"But I must charge you two bob, just the same."

"What for?"

"Well, sir, you charged me a pound the other day for telling me there wasn't anything the matter with me."

Before the doctor comes.—Doctor: "Mrs. Brown has sent for me to see her boy, and I must go at once."

Wife: "What is the matter with the boy?"

Doctor: "I don't know; but Mrs. Brown has a book on 'What to do before the doctor comes,' and I must hurry up before she does it or the boy will be dead."

And still alive.—There is a story of a woman who pleaded inability to pay rates on account of long sickness, and the fact that she had been attended by no less than four doctors. "What," said the judge, "four doctors, and you are still alive! That will do, my good woman. You can go."

The charm that failed.—"Have you tried anything for your rheumatism?" asked the doctor of the farm labourer who had consulted him. "Iss, sure, surr. I did been to an ould gipsy 'ooman, an' she did tould me to carry a 'tater in my pocket,'' replied the patient, producing a dried-up tuber from his inside breast pocket. '' I 'ave carry it for three months, but it done me no good.''

Inside information.—A story is told by an American Congressman of a small boy, green apples, and Christian Science.

'' I found one of my constituents,'' said he, '' trying to give some medicine to a young son who had eaten too many green apples, while a Christian Science neighbour was assuring the boy that there was nothing at all the matter with him.

'' 'I think I ought to know, groaned the boy; 'guess I've got inside information' ''

Mostly fools.—A celebrated quack was once visited by an old acquaintance from the country, who addressed him as '' Zam.''

'' I'm glad to see thee'st got on so vinely, Zam,'' said the rustic. '' But how is't, man? Thee know'st thee never had no more brains nor a pumpkin.''

Taking him to a window, the quack bade him count the passers-by.

'' How many have passed ? ''asked the quack after a few minutes.

'' Nointy or a hundred.''

'' And how many wise men do you suppose were among this hundred ? ''

'' Mayhap one.''

'' Well, all the rest are mine.''

His auld sel' noo.—'' Hoo's the auld laird the day ? '' asked a Highlander of a friend who was a servant at the '' big house.'' '' Gettin' better, thank guidness ! '' was the reply. '' He's beginnin' tae throw the medicine battles to the doctor, an' tae sweer at the meenister. Ay, the laird's gettin' his auld sel' noo ! ''

No cure for indigestion.—

He ate pork chops and sausages,
And pies and fried potatoes,
His soups were full of onions and
Of garlic and tomatoes.
He ate salt mackerel and cheese,
And pastries and bananas,
And after having finished these,
He smoked a few Havanas.
And yet he oft, in mournful tones
Was heard to ask this question
''Why is it that I cannot find
A cure for indigestion ? ''

Laughter is beneficial.—Man is the only animal that laughs, and as laughter is beneficial it is a sin for us to substitute drug-taking for laughter, said the Rev. Frank Crane in his address to the National Druggist's Association, Chicago. '' Laughter increases the blood-circulation. It enlarges the heart. It expands the lungs. It 'jiggers' the diaphragm. It promotes the circulation of the spleen. Beware of theologians who have no sense of mirth; they are not altogether human. Keep your chin up. Don't take your troubles to bed with you; hang them on the chair with your trousers or drop them into a glass of water with your teeth."

The Chinese physician.—Sir G. Staunton related a curious anecdote of old Kien Long, Emperor of China. He was inquiring of Sir George the manner in which physicians were paid in England. When, after some difficulty, his Majesty was made to comprehend the system, he exclaimed:

"Is any man well in England that cannot afford to be ill? I have four men to whom the care of my health is committed; a certain weekly salary is allowed them, but the moment I am ill the salary stops till I am well again. I need not tell you my illnesses are usually short."

Foot and mouth.—An old gentleman while suffering from gout used to make use of most violent language. His son on one occasion in writing to a friend remarked, "You will be sorry to hear that the governor is down with the foot and-mouth disease again!"

A powerful drug.—"The principal ingredient in all these advertised patent medicines is the same."

"It must be a powerful drug. What is it?"

"Printer's ink."

How do you feel.—Dr. Bird was once the guest of Captain Burton, the explorer, and one night, when Burton had been telling of an Arab attack which ended fatally for his assailant, the doctor provoked from him one of the most cruel retorts ever made at a doctor's expense.

"How do you feel, captain, when you kill a man?" said he.

Burton paused a moment, and then replied, slowly: —

"I don't know, doctor. How do you?"

Since you left.—A parish doctor, having obtained a better practice elsewhere, engaged the sexton to remove his furniture.

Afterwards the doctor sent an account for medical attendance, and the sexton sent his bill for the removal.

This the doctor said was a gross overcharge, and that if the sexton could get work removing furniture at the same rate, he might give up grave-digging.

The sexton replied :

" Dear sir,—I would be very glad to get steady work at anything, as there has been almost nothing to do in the churchyard since you left."

No reason to complain.—Gentleman, to gravedigger hard at his work : " Well, John, how's the world using you ? "

" Oh ! pretty weel, sir ; 'deed, I've nae reason to complain, for I've plenty of work to dae. Ye see, we've gotten two doctors here noo."

Misunderstood.—An old negro in Carrollton was ill and called in a doctor. He did not get any better, and another doctor was sent for. He felt the pulse a moment, and then looked at the tongue. " Did the other doctor take your temperature ? " he asked.

" I don't know, sah. I hain't missed anything but my watch as yit, boss."

Lost weight.—Doctor : " If you do as I tell you, you will soon feel lighter and better."

Patient : " Thank you, doctor. How much do I owe you ?"

Doctor : " Two guineas, please."

Patient (handing them over) : " You are quite right ; I feel much lighter already ! "

Prison dietary.—A prisoner, an Irishman, asked one day to see the prison doctor. Asked what his trouble was, he replied :—

" Docthor, I've come to ask you to ordher me something more to ate. Whin i come in here I could hardly see my toes, and now I could blow me nose wid the skin of me belly."

Drink your ale.—A farmer went to Abernethy complaining of discomfort in the head—weight and pain. The doctor said : " What quantity of ale do you take ? "

" Oh ! I taaks my yale pretty well."

Abernethy (with great patience and gentleness) : " Now, then, to begin the day, breakfast, what time ? "

" Oh ! haafe past seven."

" Ale then—how much ? "

" I taaks my quart."

" Luncheon ? "

" At eleven o'clock I gets another snack."

" Ale then ? "

" Oh ! yes ; my pint and a haafe."

" Dinner ? "

" Haafe past one."

" Any ale then ? "

" Yees, yees ; another quart then."

"Tea?"

"My tea is at haafe past five."

"Ale then?"

"Noa, noa."

"Supper?"

"Noine o'clock."

"Ale then?"

"Yees, yees; I taakes my fill then, I goes to sleep afterwards."

Like a lion aroused, Abernethy was up, opened his street door in Bedford Row, shoved the farmer out, and shouted after him: "Go home, sir, and let me never see your face again. Go home, drink your ale and be damned."

That stopped it.—A doctor in Ireland, having quarrelled with the priest, found soon after that he was being called out at night for trivial cases. One winter's night he was sent for to a place several long miles away. He went, and found an old woman with a slight touch of bronchitis. So, after reflection he said: "My poor, good woman, you've only a few hours to live, and must send for Father O'Leary at once." They ran for the priest, but after his reverence's visit the doctor got no more bogus night calls.

Not a bird doctor.—Ethel Reddy: "Mamma, won't you please ask Dr. Doce to look at my little sick ducklings?"

Mrs. Reddy: "No, no; run away! Dr. Doce isn't a bird doctor."

Ethel Reddy: "Well, papa said last night he was a quack doctor."

One good turn.—An old sexton was lettering a tombstone in a graveyard in Yorkshire when he was stopped by the doctor.

"Why, John, you have spelt that wrong."

"Have I, doctor? Well, well, pass it over doctor. I have covered many a mistake of yours and said nothing."

For heaven's sake.—Joseph Jefferson, the actor, was taken ill while visiting at the home of a friend, and the wife of his host became alarmed over his condition, and, being of a religious turn, wished to instil in the mind of the actor her belief in the necessity for spiritual help. A call to his room with a poultice gave her an opportunity.

"Mr. Jefferson," she said, shifting the poultice from one hand to the other," for the sake of your soul I—I would like to pray for you."

"Thank you, dear madam," he said; "you may—for my

sake, but for heaven's sake put on the poultice."

His choice of weapons.—A story is told of two of the most noted of Germans. Virchow had severely criticised Bismarck in his capacity as Chancellor, and was challenged to fight a duel. The man of science was found by Bismarck's seconds in his laboratory, hard at work on the discovery of a means of destroying trichinæ, then making great ravages in Germany. "Ah: " said the doctor, " I have the choice of weapons. Here they are! " He held up two large sausages, exactly alike in form. " One of these sausages is filled with trichinæ; it is deadly. The other is perfectly wholesome. Externally they can't be told apart. Let his excellency do me the honour to choose whichever of these he wishes and eat it, and I will eat the other! "

She was satisfied.—The poor lady was suffering from hallucinations, believing that she had some live animal inside her. The doctor, with the husband's full approval, put her under chloroform, and when she awoke showed her a dead lizard, telling her that she had been operated on, and that this creature had been extracted.

All went well for a fortnight, when the lady complained once more of strange sensations, and said that the lizard had left seven young ones behind it.

" Impossible, dear lady," said the doctor; " the lizard was a male." She was satisfied, and the pain vanished.

A drastic cure.—A gentleman who had for years been abusing the pleasures of the table, at last found his health in such a state that he went to consult a celebrated physician, Dr. Spring, of Watertown. The doctor quickly perceived the nature of his disease. " I can cure you, sir, said he, " if you will follow my advice."

The patient promised to do so.

" You must steal a horse."

" What! steal a horse? "

" Yes, you must steal a horse. You will then be arrested, convicted and placed in a situation where your diet and regimen will be such that in a short time your health will be perfectly restored."

The dyspeptic Emperor.—Addison tells in the SPECTATOR an old story of an emperor who had dyspepsia, and whose doctor ordered a hole to be bored in an axe-handle, and some medicine poured into it instead of into his mouth. Then the emperor was ordered to use an axe in chopping till his hands became moist with sweat. This, it was said, would cause them to absorb the drug, and produce a cure. The story goes that the prescription succeeded, and that his majesty became sound and well once more in his digestive organs.

One in ten.—A quack doctor was asked by a physician how it was that he contrived to live in style while he (the physician) could hardly live.

"See, how many people pass us lately; and how many of them do you think have common sense?"

"Possibly one in ten."

"Why, then, the one goes to you and I get the others."

The Stomach-ache.—Queen Alexandra, when Princess of Wales, came one day upon a little boy who was crying. He was in charge of a comfortable old lady, who seemed quite unmoved by his grief.

"What is the matter?" inquired the Princess. "Is he ill?"

"Well, ma'am, he isn't hexactly ill, but no stomach carn't stand nine buns—and shop 'uns too!"

Consolatory.—A little child ate everything she fancied, until she became ill of indigestion and died.

"What a comfort," exclaimed the bereaved parents, "now that she is gone, to recall that we never denied her anything!"

The grass cure.—The simple pastoral habit of eating grass is, they say, a sovereign cure for dyspepsia and other ills which afflict us. The originator of the new cult is a Spaniard, who experimented with a grass diet. Dry bread and grass are the odd combination which form the daily meals of the sufferer from gastritis. He does not, however, swallow the grass, but merely chews it, and absorbs the juices. The grass eaters are hardly likely to have an extensive following, although the habits of dogs and cats, who devour grass as medicine, is certainly a fact in support of the new idea.

Irish humour.—In spite of the hardships of the poor harvesters from Ireland their humour never leaves them.

"You've a cowld, Mrs. Leary," said one of them to her crony sone day.

"Indeed, and that's very true, Mrs. Mahoney."

"And where did you get that, honey?"

"Sure, and I slept last night in a field, and forgot to shut the gate."

Faith in drugs.—This was the subject under discussion when an elderly physician who had spoken against the practice of "dosing" by laymen, told this story:—"I had a patient once who complained of pains in her right arm. She was otherwise well and strong, and looked upon the little ache as nothing serious. Weeks after she had been to see me she met me and said that she used the liniment I gave her on her bad arm every single night, and that when she did not use it she could not sleep. One night she retired before making the application, but reached from her bed to the table, got her liniment bottle, gave her arm a good rubbing and felt better for it, and went to sleep. When she awoke the next morning she found that she had taken the wrong bottle, and had applied copious doses of black ink. It did her as much good as my liniment.

Not yet decided.—Reporter: "To what do you attribute your great age?"

Oldest inhabitant: "I bain't sure yet, sir. There be several o' them patent medicine companies as is bargainin' with me."

Subcutaneous. — A labourer had got hurt—not much more than a scratch, it is true, but his employer had visions of being compelled to keep him for life, and had adopted the wise course of sending him at once to the hospital. After the house surgeon had examined him carefully he said to the nurse:

"As subcutaneous abrasion is not observable I do not think there is any reason to apprehend tegmental cicatrization of the wound."

"Well, you're a wonderful thought-reader, doctor. You took the very words out of my mouth. That's just what I was going to say."

The quick change.—"Is this the office of Quigley's Quick Cure?"

"Yes."

"Gimme six bottles for my wife."

"Tried all other remedies without success—eh?"

"No, she ain't ill at all; but I saw in your advertisement where a woman wrote, after taking six bottles, 'I am a different woman,' and I have hopes mine may prove so too."

That pork!—Doctor: "I must know what you have eaten

to-day, in order to understand your stomachic disorder."

Patient: "Oh, doctor, only a little pork. It was left over from last week, and was perhaps not quite fresh."

Doctor: "Would it not have been more sensible to let the pork spoil entirely, rather than to upset your stomach?"

Patient: "But doctor, you can cure a diseased stomach, but what can you do with spoiled pork?"

Part of the treatment.—Patient (to pretty nurse): "Will you be my wife when I recover?"

Pretty Nurse: "Certainly."

Patient: "Then you love me?"

"Oh no; that's merely part of the treatment. I must keep my patients cheerful; I promised this morning to run away with a married man who had lost both of his legs."

Schweinfurth and Bismarck.—The circumstances of Dr. Schweinfurth's first diagnosis of the ex-Chancellor of Germany's case brought out the characteristics of the two men. When the physician entered Prince Bismarck's study the latter was absorbed in a mass of State papers. Dr. Schweinfurth at once began questioning him about his symptoms.

Prince Bismarck: "I am very busy. I didn't send for you to ask me questions, but to tell me what's the matter with me."

Doctor: "I see you've sent for the wrong man! What you want is a vet."

Bismarck: "How so?"

Dr. Schweinfurth: "A veterinary surgeon is the only one who prescribes for his patients without asking them a question."

All he had.—"I'm a confirmed dyspeptic; that's the reason I look so bad," said Mr. Collander, gazing almost enviously at the red-bronze face of his former schoolfellow, who had dropped down from the country into Mr. Collander's city office.

"What you need is simple country food, man," said his old friend, clapping him heartily on the shoulder. "Come and visit my wife and me on the farm for a while, and we'll set you up. It's rich city living that's too much for you. Now take breakfast for instance. All I have is two good cups of coffee, a couple of fresh dough-nuts, a bit of steak with a baked potato, some muffins, and either griddle-cakes or a piece of pie to top off with. What do you have?"

"A cup of hot water and two slices of dry toast. But if you think a simple diet like yours would help me I will make one more attempt at it."

The green apple.—"No, sir," said the doctor, "I wouldn't have that apple tree cut down for money. It's as good as green crabs for the stomach-ache"

"But you never get any fruit from it," argued Brown; "the boys steal all the apples before they are half ripe."

"That's just it," replied the doctor, with a quiet smile. "That tree stands me in a good £50 a year."

Her symptoms.—Farmer (to medical man): "If you get out my way, sir, at any time, I wish you'd stay and see the missus. She says she ain't feeling well."

Physician: "What are her symptoms?"

Farmer: "I don't know. this morning, after she had milked the cows and fed the pigs, and got breakfast for the men, and washed the dishes, and built a fire under the copper in the washhouse, and done a few odd jobs about the house, she complained of feeling tired-like. I can't think what can be the matter with her."

Chiefly rheumatics.—The simple old Sussex countryman enjoys talking to the swells from town, and adding to their stores of information. It is not fair, however, to the countryman to use such big words. Recently a visitor to an East Sussex village, in conversation with an old inhabitant, said: "I suppose you have suffered a good deal from the rural exodus about these parts?"

"No, sir," said the old villager, "it be chiefly rheumatics, but this influenzie do upset some of the folks, surelye."

The "peck of dirt."—"Everybody, you know, eats his peck of dirt before he dies," was the old estimate. "You're a hundred years behind the times In these days of sausage factories pie manufactories, refreshment rooms, glue jellies, canned rabbits, and game and fowls kept like mummies in cold stores, man eats his peck of dirt once a month."

A terrible curse.—Preaching to his flock on drink, an Irish priest, in the course of his sermon, said: "Whisky, my brethren, is a curse, a terrible curse; it makes you bate your wives, starve your children, shoot at your landlords; and, worse than all, when you've had too much of the cursed stuff, it makes you miss them too!"

CHAPTER XVI.

DRINK.

Epistaxis.—On the way to the police station the prisoner received an injury to his head and had to be attended by a doctor, who gave the following certificate: "Drunkenness, contused wounds on head and epistaxis."

Mr. Plowden: "I wish you would tell the doctor who attends to these cases at the station to try to describe what he has to say in English. He tells me that the prisoner is suffering from epistaxis. I do not know the least in the world what that is; therefore I am none the wiser for the certificate.

The clerk then handed his worship a dictionary.

Turning to the word Mr. Plowden said: "I see it means bleeding from the nose. Now why couldn't the doctor say that instead of saying he was suffering from epistaxis? However, I am glad it is nothing worse, for really I thought it was something so serious as to cause me to stay my hand before passing sentence. I should not like to punish a man suffering from epistaxis."

Kivered too much.—Former Congressman Tucker, of Virginia, tells a story of a Virginian who had been indulging too freely in the bowl. Looking round at his companions, the Virginian boasted, "Gentlemen, I can lick any man in Richmond." Nobody took up the challenge, and the Virginian returned to the charge. "Gentlemen" he said, "I can lick any man in the whole State of Virginia." The words were hardly uttered before a tall, lean, sinewy man from the western part of the State gave the boaster a thrust that sent him sprawling on the floor. The Virginian had a sense of humour and as he picked himself up he turned to the group and drawled, "Gentleman, I'm ready to acknowledge that I kivered too much territory."

Ready for him.—In certain public-houses cheese and biscuits are provided for customers during the opening hour.

A man went into one and called for a drink. When the barman brought the drink in he also brought a fresh supply of cheese and biscuits, and placed them within reach of his customer, who ate the lot to one glass of beer. The barman on seeing this said:—

" Ye must hev been hungry, mate. When are ye coming back ? "

" Wey, aa'll be back next Sunday."

" Aa'll reet. Aa'll hev a truss of hay reddy for ye."

For his oilcake sake.—A foxy sort of person is the rural J.P., who also is the only corn and cake merchant in the district; yet the rural " drunk " is sometimes foxier.

" Very sorry, yer washup," pleaded the latter from the dock, " but I came sixteen mile inter town yesterday to buy a ton o' oilcake. Meetin' a ole friend or two, an' not bein' used to strong ale, two or three cans knocked me over, an' I was run in afore I'd had time to git the oilcake."

" Discharged," said the bench promptly. " Go and buy your oilcake and get back home." All the rest of that day the J.P. waited vainly for his oilcake order.

That's why.—" Why haven't I a hundred-acre farm as well as that man riding by in his carriage ? " yelled a red-nosed anarchist as he glanced at the crowd.

" Because he saved his money and bought his farm, and you poured your money down your throat," responded a man on the back seat; and the orator asked no more conundrums.

Convinced.—A temperance lecturer, who wished to prove to his audience the deadly power of whisky, caused a drop of water to be magnified and thrown upon a magic-lantern screen.

The picture was a terrible one. Worms bigger than pythons, crabs bigger than elephants, spiders the size of a ship, fought together in the drop of water like fiends in the infernal regions.

The lecturer now caused a drop of whisky to be added to the water.

The effect was marvellous. The liquor killed all those ferocious horrors instantly. Their vast claws and tentacles and feelers stiffened. All became peaceful and still.

An old lady in the front row whispered hoarsely in her husband's ear :—

" Well, Jabez, that settles me. I'll never drink water again 'thout puttin' some whisky in it."

To a Gouty friend.—Dear drinker of all sorts and kinds of brews,
Smoker of weeds innumerable and good;

Inhaling cigarettes as hourly food
That e'en thy lungs may have perpetual booze;
Seeker afar, all gouty things to choose,
All potables with rheumatiz imbued,
All edibles that most should be eschewed—
To visit thee, how could King Gout refuse!

"The horse did no harm," said a man charged with being drunk at the North London Police Court while in charge of a horse and cart.

"The horse had much more sense than you," said Mr. Fordham. "Sober horse, man drunk. The man made a fool of himself, horse was quite harmless. Fined 10s. or seven days."

The consumer gets.—From one bushel of barley a distiller gets four gallons of whisky. Of this the retailer gets 50 per cent. of the selling price, the distiller 25 per cent., the Government 10 per cent., the Farmer 10 per cent. — and the consumer gets 10 days or forty shillings.

The greasy pole.—It was election day in a little Dorset village, and all the natives had a holiday, and were enjoying themselves at booths and merry-go-rounds in the public park.

Jack Saunders, the farmer's handy man, had made unsuccessful attempts to climb the greasy pole and annex the leg of mutton which hung thereon.

At length, his patience exhausted and his money all spent, he wended his way homewards in a somewhat muddled condition. He chanced on the road to meet his employer, who, anxious as to the election, inquired:

"What is the state of the poll, John?"

"Gad, zir, I 'oóden 'vise 'ee to try it, vur never zeed 'un greasier in all my life."

Father Doolan to Irish turf-carter, half tipsy at mid-day: "Pat, Pat, this will never do! You must really go and take the pledge at once."

Pat: "Thin, bedad, yir riverince, I will require to part wid mi ould pony, for not a fut will he stir past a public-house until I go in."

Whisky.—Wigg: "There is one class of men that whisky has never been known to injure."

Wagg: "And that is?"

Wigg: "The men who leave it alone."

Josh Billings on Whisky.—The potato has eyes, but, like the Sadducees of old, they see not.

Potatoes dwell in the ground, and are az prolifick as a hen's nest.

They are planted in hills, one potato in a hill, and they giv yu back twenty for one. This is generous.

The only mean thing that a potato kan be made to do iz to turn itself into whisky.

Whisky kan be made out of potatoes, and there ain't no liquid, nor no solid, known to man, that is haff so mean and low-lived as potato whisky.

When a man gits so lo down that he iz willing to drink potato whisky for the sake of gitting drunk, hiz boddy—and I have a good mind to say his soul—isn't worth saving.

If thare is deviltry ov enny kind that kan be got out ov man, whisky is sure to develop it.

All along o' they cards.—A country minister who invited his flock once a year to supper in the schoolroom, intrusted his "handy man" with the delivery of the invitation cards. A day or two before the function his reverence found his man sitting by the roadside in an advanced state of hilarity, and oblivious to all earthly conditions.

"Good gracious, Jenkins! what does this mean? How did you get into this shocking state?"

"It's all along o' they cards, sir. I takes 'em round, and this 'un asks me to take a nip, and that 'un asks me to take a nip, and so I gets like this."

"Why, this is terrible! Are there no temperance people in the parish?"

"Lor, yes, sir, lots of 'em, but I sends their cards by post."

Not to swallow them.—An Irish priest had laboured hard with one of his flock to induce him to give up whisky. "I tell you, Michael," said the priest, "whisky is your worst enemy, and you should keep it as far from you as you can."

"Me enemy, is it, father?" responded Michael. "And it was your riverence's self that was tellin' us in the pulpit only last Sunday to love our enemies."

"So I was, Michael," rejoined the priest, "but I didn't tell you to swallow them!"

Why he didn't.—Two gentlemen shooting in Scotland sat down to lunch. On taking a bottle of whisky out one of them noticed that the cork had been tampered with, and, knowing the character of their gillie, at once accused him of having been at the lunch-basket.

"I fear that you have been drinking the whisky, Sandy."

"Na, na, sir, I hae not, fur the cork would na come oot!"

One from China.—A man, who had got very drunk, set off to cross a mountain by night. Overcome with the drink, he sank down on the edge of a precipice, and was soon fast asleep. Just then along came a tiger; and creeping up to the sleeping man, the animal began to sniff at his face, puzzled perhaps by the smell of the drink. One of the tiger's whiskers ran into the man's nose, and tickled him so much that he gave a loud sneeze, at which the terrified tiger started so violently that it fell over the precipice and was killed.

Told by Dean Hole.—One day, at Caunton Church, during morning prayer, a member of the congregation was distinctly tipsy; this man had been at a wedding the day before and had not slept off his drink. After a while Dean Hole stopped reading for a few moments, and said sternly:—

"Are you fit to remain in God's house?"

The man got up as well as he could, and, with the help of James Blackney, left the church. After service Hole said:—

"James, what did you do with him?"

The reply was: "I put him on a tombstone, sir."

Hole: "Couldn't you put him under it?"

CHAPTER XVII.

TRAMPS, BEGGARS, TRESPASSERS AND POACHING.

In defence of tramps.—"You condemn us tramps, but there's one thing ma'am, to give the devil his due, you will admit in our favour, ma'am; you don't hear of us indulgin' in labour disputes, and we do not worry people about an eight hours' day!"

The stress of competition.—Mrs. Goode: "You are the sixth man who has asked me for something to eat to-day."

The Tramp: "I s'pose so.

If de competition in dis life gits any wus, some of us'll have to go to work."

The new woman.—A tramp rang the bell of Dr. Mary Morrison's house the other day, and when a pleasant woman came to the door he asked her if she would be so kind as to ask the doctor if he had an old pair of breeches to give a poor man.

"I'm the doctor," said the smiling woman.

He fled.

Fate is agin me.—Lady: "Ain't you ashamed to be begging on the streets?"

Beggar: "Well, yes. I'd sooner do it in de pulpit or at a church bazaar, but fate is agin me."

A stopper.—Visitor: "Are you bothered much by beggars and tramps?"

Farmer: "Not now, but I used to be a good deal."

"How did you stop it?"

"I tacked up a notice beside the kitchen door, and the tramps back away out as soon as they catch sight of it."

"I suppose it's 'Beware of the dog!'"

"Oh no, It's just 'Good workmen wanted.'"

Getting used to it.—Farmer (to tramp): "You said you were going to lead a more industrious life, and here you are lazily watching them ploughing but doing nothing yourself."

Tramp: "Well, governor, you know these sudden changes are dangerous. I'm first trying to get myself used to the sight of work."

Under the greenwood tree.—Tramp: "Why don't yer come in the shade, Bill? You be puspiring like an ordinary common workman out there."

Go to the ant.—The tramp approached the proud citizen, and asked for alms.

"'Go to the ant, thou sluggard.'"

"'Taint no use, mister. Me aunt's jist as tight-fisted as me uncle an' all de rest uv me relashuns. I fear I'll have to go to work at last."

A privileged profession.—Lady: "Why is a strong man like yourself found begging?"

Tramp: "Ah, madam, it is the only profession in which a gentleman can address a beautiful lady without the formality of an introduction."

Well frequented.—A stranger, passing along a road in Scotland, was surprised at the solitude in which he found himself, having met no one upon the road so far as he had gone.

Coming up to a poor man who was breaking stones by the wayside, he asked him, by way of drawing on conversation, if this road was well frequented.

"Ou ay," said the man, "it's na sa ill; a beggar gaed by yesterday, and there's yoursel' the day."

Congratulations. — Tramp: "Beg pardon, sir, but I haven't had anything to eat for a week."

Philanthropist: "Let me congratulate you. It must be a great saving to you, and you're looking so well—you don't look bilious, or in any way out of condition!"

The rolling stone.—Jack London, the novelist, was praising the tramp.

"Many a tramp," he said, "is more intelligent and honourable, and has a happier life, than the average rich man. Some tramps are renowned, too, for their honour.

"I once knew a tramp named Boston Jack. It is said that Boston Jack knocked on the back door of a farmhouse one July afternoon and asked for assistance.

"The farmer's wife said: 'Why don't you go to work? Don't you know that a rolling stone gathers no moss?

"'Madam, without evading your question, may I ask of what practical use moss would be to a man in my condition?"

In an old waistcoat.—A rough looking individual came to the lone farm where little Willie lives and grasped him by the collar. "If you don't tell me where your father keeps his money, I'll knock yer 'ead orf yer shoulders an' arfter that I'll eat yer."

"Oh, please don't do that, sir. You'll find all the money we've got in an old waistcoat in the kitchen."

Two minutes later a bruised and battered wreck was shot through the door, and sat for a while on the ground. "That kid's too smart—never said a word about the ole man inside that weskit."

For a shilling.—A Scottish farmer, returning from market, had his trap held up by a couple of footpads. But they did not know him. He declined to give up his cash bags, and followed up his refusal by such vigorous resist ance that before long he both the footpads securely had bound and lying in the bottom of the trap. He hailed them off to the police, and they were duly brought before the magistrates.

"It wis gey plucky o' ye tae handle the prisoners in yon fashion," said the baillie.

"Aye, bit I wisna gaun tae lose ma money," said the farmer.

"Whit money had ye?"

"Oh, ah'd thruppunce ha'penny."

"Poors above!" burst out one of the prisoners, "it's a guid job he hadna' a shillin'. He'd 'a' killed the pair o' us."

He didn't complain.—As I was going through the fields to my work one morning at six o'clock I met an old man who had been sleeping on some hay. I was going on taking little notice, when the man stopped me and asked for a match. I gave him a few, then he said: "It's early to go to work." "Yes," I said, "but don't you get tired doin' nothin'?"

"Terrible, but I never complain. Everybody has their troubles."

Must be somewhere.—The squire of a certain parish going the round of his domain, met with a poor navvy trespassing. 'What are you doing here, sir?" said the squire; "don't you know that no one is allowed to trespass here?"

"Wey, sor, aw didn't knaw who's grund it is; but aw've n'yyen o' my awn, an' aw mu' be on somebody else's. Aw cawnt walk under the grund."

First-rate Scarecrows.—Overheard some time ago. Tourist: "Do those scarecrows save your crops?"

Farmer: "They work first-rate. You see, every tramp that comes along crosses the fields to see if the clothes are worth stealing, which they ain't, and that scares the crows away. Good idea, ain't it?"

On the mend.—Beside a straw stack sat a tramp—a jolly tramp and a wise—who, while he patched his tattered coat, did thus soliloquise:—"It seems to me that my lone life doth ever downward tend, and drags me into wretchedness, but still I'm on the mend. And when I need a little cash I make no loud laments, but by a straw stack sit me down and gather in my rents."

Ruined by motors.—"Well, my man, and what are you begging for?"

"I 'ates to arsk yer for charity, sir, but I'm one of them unfortunit persons wot 'as bin ruined by motorin'."

Old Gentleman (who hates

motors): "Oh, indeed; poor fellow! Were you run over?"

"No, sir; but, yer see, before motors became popular I used to 'old 'osses' 'eads outside the 'otels."

Too slim for him.—A Norfolk squire was lamenting the increase of poaching to his keeper, who told him that a man named Richards was the most notorious poacher in the neighbourhood.

Soon after the squire happened to meet Richards, who asserted that he could get game whenever he wanted it, keepers or no keepers.

Squire: "Well, if you bring me a hare to-morrow from my own estate, I'll give you a guinea for it."

"What! and you a J.P.?"

"Oh, that'll be all right."

"Well, then, done, sir."

Next day the poacher arrived and was shown into the study.

"Well, have you got him?"

Richards opened the sack, out of which jumped a fine hare, which rushed round the room seeking to escape.

"Why haven't you killed it?"

"Because, sir," said the poacher, with a grin, "I haven't a licence!"

That a' depends.—A well-known poacher, who lived upon the Border, was brought before the magistrates on a charge of illegal fishing, and, having been found guilty, was fined thirty shillings or 10 days' imprisonment. On his pleading poverty the Court asked him how long he would require to make it up. "Weel, yer honours," he replied, scratching his head, "that a' depends on hoo the fish come up the watter."

Walter Scott when practising at his profession had the happiness of restoring to society a rascal in the shape of a poacher, whose acquittal he obtained. When the verdict was given the lawyer whispered to his client: "You are a lucky beggar!"

Prisoner: "I quite agree with you, sir, and I will send you a hare to-morrow."

Poacher or keeper.—A peasant girl went two or three times to a rectory with a hare and other game for sale. The rector, wishing to ascertain how she came by them, asked her where she got them.

"Sure, your reverence," said she, "my father is poacher to Lord Clare."

Found in a man trap.—A Scottish laird plagued by poachers procured a cork leg dressed in a stocking and shoe, and sent it through the neighbouring villages by the town crier, who proclaimed that it had been found in a man-trap on the previous night in the grounds of the laird, who desired to return it to its owner. There was no more poaching after that.

A work of necessity.—The Rev. P., of the Magdalen Islands, Canada, was on his way to a lonely part of his parish one Sunday morning. Nearing the church, he was horrified to see the son of the family with whom he expected to dine stalking rabbits with a gun.

"My boy," he said, "do you know it is Sunday?"

"Yes," said James, not recognising him; "but this is a work of necessity."

"And how is that?"

"'Cause the parson's comin' to dinner, and we've got nothing to give him."

In a friendly way.—When charged with trespassing in search of game, a notorious poacher declared that he had only been hunting for primroses.

"Primroses!" said the prosecuting lawyer. "Was your dog looking for primroses when the gamekeeper caught him with a live rabbit in his mouth?"

"No, he worn't. That poor rabbit was lame, and t' dorg had just nipped it up in a friendly way to carry it back to its warren, when along came t' gamekeeper. It's a pity if one animal can't do another a good turn wi'out somebody makin' a crime of it!"

Didn't use no tackle.—Some years ago, before a severe winter, a man was hauled before a Bench of West Riding Justices for being found on game preserved land. On being searched, several dead rabbits were found on him, and a small piece of freshly cut turnip, but no nets or gear of any kind.

"How is it," asked the magistrate, "that you are found in possession of these rabbits? Where is the tackle you caught them with?"

"Didn't use no tackle."

"Well, how did you catch them then? Confess, and I'll deal lightly with you."

"Well, your worship, it was this way. You see, sir, that snow being on the ground, food is hard to get for rabbits and such like, so I take a piece of fresh turnip, rubs my head with it, and goes and lies down near a rabbit hole, and out they come and sniffs at it, then nibbles, and I grab 'em, breaks their necks, when up comes this 'ere keeper 'and swears I'm poaching."

Hard times.—A Scotch poacher, given the option of paying a fine or going to prison, asked for time to pay. "What do you want time for?" asked the sheriff.

"Weel, ma lord, it tak's some time to mak' up a big fine nooadays, when fowks grudge half a croon for a hare!"

The wily preacher.—The other day, in a country town, situated in a fine sporting district, a police officer came face to face with a well-known poacher, who was carrying a splendid hare.

"Caught again, Bill," exclaimed the officer. "So you've gone back once more to your old games?"

"Not me. What do you take me for?" replied Bill. "Why, I've bought this thing at the game and poulty dealer's."

"A good yarn that," laughed the other. "Just fancy you buying a hare!"

"Then all I can say is you must come and ask him," said Bill.

"Of course I must," responded the officer, and they started for the dealer's.

"Oh, yes," said the shopman. "I sold him that hare, and he gave me four shillings for it, and I know it's the one, because he asked me to mark it, as the police would be sure to catch him with it, and want to run him in, so I nipped a bit off the right ear."

The police officer was thunderstruck, but Bill, was of course, allowed to go. The officer was sure that somehow he was sold, and one day, he found out how he had been cheated. On that morning Bill had snared no fewer than six hares; and after getting the dealer to mark a hare which he purchased, he went and marked the poached ones exactly like it, and was thus enabled to dispose of them without detection.

Hard lines.—"Dis tramp's life is tough, Bill. I ast fur bread and would have got a stone only de leddy couldn't trow straight."

CHAPTER XVIII.

MILITARY.

Plain Speaking.—It is told of the late Sir William Olpherts that one day an officer came to him with a pitiful tale of his men's discontent with their vegetable rations; they were an Irish regiment, and they wanted potatoes. But in those early Anglo-Indian days potatoes were not always available in remote districts. Mutiny was feared. "Hell-fire Jack," in command of the district, promised to put an end to the trouble. He ordered a full-dress parade of the potato-loving soldiers at noon, and rode up in the sweltering heat to inspect the ranks himself.

"Now, my men," he shouted, "I want you to speak out plainly. I hear you want potatoes—do you?"

"We do, sir!" came from their parching throats.

"Then you won't get 'em!" replied Sir John. "You're good soldiers, I admit, but if you expect God Almighty to grow potatoes on the dry plains of India specially to please you, you're damneder fools than I take you for. Dismiss!"

He meant "taters."—Scene: Soldiers' barrack-room at Dinner time. Orderly Officer (inspecting men's dinner) asks:—

"Any complaints, men?"

Voice from the end of the table: "Yes, sir."

Officer: "Well, what is it?"

Voice: "Spuds is bad, sir."

Officer: "Spuds is bad? Haw-er" (turning to sergeant), "Spuds is bad. Haw! What does he mean by spuds, Sergeant Murphy?"

Sergeant (glaring at culprit): "The man is higgerunt, sir. He means taters."

Pink combinations.—A Jew who had been supplying the troops in South Africa was found to be double-dealing with the enemy and was banished, and his goods thrown about the veldt. A number of Kaffirs working in the horse hospital near found among them some pink combinations, and soon arrayed themselves in these. When the vet. came to inspect his invalids he saw them being groomed by Kaffirs in this extraordinary rig, and nearly expired with laughter.

A rale friendly feeling.—An

Irish landlord embarking for England in command of an Irish militia regiment was accosted by one of his tenants on the quay. "For God's sake your honour, don't go and be massacred by them Boers." The colonel hastened to explain that he was only going to England, not to South Africa, adding: "Besides, if I were going out to be shot, I'd give the preference to one of my own tenants." "Sure, and that shows a rale friendly feeling between us," said the delighted tenant, gripping him warmly by the hand.

All bone.—Orderly officer to men at dinner: "Any complaints?"

Irish private: "Yis, sor. The mate's all bone, sor!"

The animal's fault.—"What are you doing there, Mike?" You are wanted as an ornament for one of His Majesty's horse, and not to be sweeping the ground like a broom!"

Mike: "Oi know that, sorr; but it was the animal's fault intirely."

In a balloon.—Two army doctors, while ballooning, lost trace of their whereabouts, and, seeing a rustic in the fields, gradually descended, and when nearly overhead one of them called out:

"Hi, there, Johnny, where are we?"

Boy: "Why, ye be in a balloon, beant ye?"

"Tell it to the marines."—This phrase as an expression of incredulity is traced to Pepys, the author of the DIARY, and it is said by him to have originated with Charles II. The story goes "that his light-hearted Majesty was strolling in the shade with Pepys, Secretary to the Admiralty. 'I had speech yestere'en at Deptford,' said Mr. Pepys, 'with the captain of the Defiance who hath but lately returned from the Indies, and who told me the two most wonderful things that ever I think I did hear in my life.' Among the stories told were of fish flying in the air. 'Fish flying in the air!' exclaimed his Majesty. 'Ha, ha, a quaint conceit, which 'twere too good to spoil wi' keeping! What ho! sir'—he turned and beckoned the colonel, Sir William Killigrew, of the newly raised maritime regiment of foot, who was following with the Duke of York. "We would discourse with you on a matter touching your element. What say you, colonel to a man who swears he hath seen fishes in the air?"

"'I should say, sire,' returned the sea soldier simply, "that the man hath sailed in southern seas. For when your Majesty's business carried me thither of late I did frequently observe more flying fish in one hour than the hairs of my head in number.'

"'Mr. Pepys,' said the King, 'from the nature of their calling no class of our subjects can have so wide a knowledge of seas and land as the officers and men of our loyal maritime regiment. Henceforth, ere ever we cast doubts upon a tale that lacketh likelihood, we will first tell it to the marines.'"

Disarmament and a parable.—The SPECTATOR discusses the question of disarmament, and concludes with Æsop's fable of the cock and the fox, which, it thinks, fits the situation:—

"A cock sat on a tree-top. 'Come down,' said the fox from below, 'I have great news for you!'

"'What news?' asked the cock.

"'All the birds and the beasts have sworn peace. There will be no more war, but we shall all live like brothers now. Come down then, that I may congratulate you!'

"The cock did not answer, but strained his neck as if looking at something in the distance.

"'What do you see?' said the fox.

"'A pack of hounds.' Upon this the fox started up to go.

"'Surely there is no need to hurry,' said the cock, 'now that all are at peace!'

"'No—no!' said the fox, making off, 'but they have not heard the news.'"

He came to life.—Two of the Dorset Imperial Yeomanry captured a mounted infantryman on Salisbury Plain during manœuvres. They explained to him that by all rules of the game he must be a dead man, and asked for his ammunition. This he gave up. Next they asked him for his bread and cheese and whatever his flask contained. The corpse put spurs to his horse. "Dead or not, you'll have a rough time before you get my vittals," he shouted, as he went off at racing pace.

A vocation.—Farmer Jason: "So you want a job, eh? What can yer do?"

Frisbie: "Nothin'."

Farmer Jason: "Well, I can't give you a job of that kind but it seems to me yer might get a place somewhere as a war correspondent with the Japanese."

Maybe.—An officer of a regiment was inspecting his company when he came to an Irishman who had evidently not shaved for some days.

"Doyle, how is it you have not shaved this morning?"

"Oi have, sorr."

"How dare you tell me that," said the officer, "with a beard on you like that?"

"Well, sorr, it's loike this. There's one looking-glass in our room and there was nine of us all shaving at the same time, and maybe oi shaved some other chap's face."

A Tiger story.—An officer of the Bengal Lancers who was seized by a tigress owed his escape to a curious accident. The tigress seized him by the breast of his coat and shook him until he became unconscious. On recovering, he heard a strange noise at a little distance as if some one was sneezing violently. It was the tigress herself. He slowly turned round and gave a furtive glance in that direction. He could hardly believe his eyes. There was the tigress slinking off with her tail very much between her legs, and sneezing violently and making the most piteous grimaces. The truth dawned upon him like a flash of lightning—in the operation of shaking his snuff box had flown open from his waistcoat pocket, and the tigress had received the contents in her face.

The safest place.—General Lee used to tell a tale of an old negro who fought through the war. The General asked him where he had seen the best time during the whole of his campaign.

"At Chickamauga: because I found the safest place on the field as soon as the firing began."

"How did you manage that?"

"I knowed I'd be safe, 'cause I shipped for the place whar de ginirils was."

A slate wanting.—A well-known eccentric Perthshire colonel, when walking, came upon an old man busy at work thatching a wayside cottage.

Said the Colonel: "Man, ye're makin' a grand job o' that."

Thatcher: "Ay, no' sae bad."

Colonel: "Do you think you could do anything to this?" showing his bald pate.

Thatcher: "I'm afraid not sir. That's raythe oot o' my line. I'm thinkin' it's a slate it wants."

Rough and ready.—General Grant used to tell a story of an old carpenter who had served under Jackson. Stonewall had come to a stream, the bridge over which was burned. The engineers and the draughtsmen were summoned, received their orders, and retired to prepare their plans. Two hours later the carpenter waited on Jackson, and said: "General, that bridge is finished, but them air pictures ain't come yet."

The orderly room.—Present: The commanding officer, adjutant, sergeant-major etc., and a recruit brought up for attestation.

The Commanding Officer: "What religion do you belong to, my man?"

The Recruit (recollecting himself): "Christian, sir, please."

Commanding Officer: "Oh, of course; but what denomination?"

The Sergeant-Major (coming to the rescue): "Tell the commanding officer where you go to on Sundays?"

The Commanding Officer: "Yes, where do you go on Sundays, my man?"

The Recruit: "Rattin' mostly, sir."

"Never a waur rider."—A young officer, riding through a Scotch village one day in full uniform, and mounted on a splendid horse, was much annoyed by a lad following him along the street. At last he said to the boy:

"Did you ever see a war-horse, before, my lad?"

"Yes," said the boy, "I have seen a waur (worse) horse many a time, but never a waur rider."

But the horses.—Field-Marshal Lord Ligonier was the first Commander-in-Chief at the Horse Guards, and was buried at Westminster Abbey. Soldiering agreed with him, for he was 92 when he died, although he had taken part in the Duke of Marlborough's campaigns and many others. Once, before his regiment, the 4th Horse, was sent on foreign service, it was reviewed by George II.

"Colonel" (as he then was), said the King, "your men have the look of soldiers, but their horses seem poor. How is that?"

"Sir," answered Ligonier, "the men are Irish, and gentlemen, too; but the horses are English."

And still two miles. — A regiment of regulars was making a protracted, weary march along a heavy country road, and the men, eager for food and rest, were impatient to reach habitation.

A man on horseback rode past.

"Say, friend," called out one of the regulars, "how far is it to the next town?"

"Matter of two miles or so. I should think," came the answer. And the rider vanished.

Another long hour dragged by, and then the soldiers came upon a labourer.

"How far is the next town?" they asked, eagerly.

"Good two miles!" said the labourer, and proceeded on his way.

Half an hour's further marching brought them to a third wayfarer.

"How far to the next town?" they once more asked.

"Not far," came the encouraging answer. "Only two miles!"

Through the general atmosphere of depression rang the voice of an optimistic sergeant:

"March, boys—march for your lives!" it cried. "We're holding our own, anyway!"

The wondrous thing.—Many stories used to be told in the Middle Temple of the late Mr. Baker Greene.

For years he was surgeon in a cavalry regiment, and on his departure for India was continuously dunned by his long-suffering tailor, who at last, in despair, begged his debtor to take care of his health.

This was the reply:—

"I have received the hypocritical letter hoping that I will take care of my health in order to live to pay your bill. These are your chances so far. I attend every cholera case in camp, and make a special study of small-pox. I swim every morning in a lake swarming with alligators. At the recent attack upon a hill fort I went with the forlorn hope, and was one of the three who returned unwounded. To-morrow evening, alone and on foot, I shall go into the jungle and wait for the man-eating tigress as she returns at dawn to her cave and her cubs. If it be she who falls I shall spend my leave in the fever-haunted jungles of the Terai, following up big game, and if I survive I shall cool myself by joining a party to ascend the peak of Dhawalagiri, whose snow slopes and glaciers are as steep as your prices."

And the wondrous thing is that the tailor was paid.—SPORTING TIMES.

CHAPTER XIX.

LAW.

The ass was missing.—An eminent judge used to say that in his opinion the best thing ever said by a witness to a counsel was the reply given to Missing, the barrister, at the time leader of his circuit. He was defending a prisoner charged with stealing a donkey. The prosecutor had left the animal tied up to a gate, and when he returned it was gone. Missing was very severe in his examination of the witness. "Do you mean to say the donkey was stolen from the gate?" "I mean to say, sir," giving the judge and jury a sly look, "that the ass was Missing."

Try something else.—Mr. Justice Lawrence recalls a colloquy between a prisoner on his trial for horse-stealing and himself.

Judge: "Why did you steal the horse?"

Prisoner: "To earn my livin'."

Judge: "Bad way of earning your living, isn't it?"

Prisoner: "Must do something."

Judge: "So you must. Try six months' hard labour."

Not so large.—The witness: A witness was being examined in a court of law the other day. The question was about the size of certain hoof-prints left by a horse.

Counsel: "How large were they? As large as my hand?"

Witness: "Oh, no; it was just an ordinary hoof!"

And everybody laughed.

A question of identity.—The lawyer does not always get the best of the cross-examination. Sir Frank Lockwood was once examining a farmer in a case which turned on the identity of certain cattle.

"Are you certain these were the prosecutor's beasts?" was the question.

"I am," said the farmer.

"But you were some distance away from them at the time. At what distance can you be certain it is a beast you are looking at?"

"Oh, about as far as you are from me."

More's the pity.—It once fell to Lord Morris's lot to hear, at Coleraine, a case in which damages were claimed from a veterinary surgeon for having poisoned a valuable horse. The issue depended upon whether a certain number of grains of a particular drug could be safely administered to the animal. The dispensary doctor proved that he had often given eight grains to a man, from which it was to be inferred that twelve for a horse was not excessive.

"Never mind yer eight grains, docther," said the judge. "We all know that some poisons are cumulative in effect, and ye may go to the edge of ruin with impunity. But tell me this, the twelve grains—wouldn't they kill the devil himself if he swallowed them?"

Doctor: "I don't know, my lord; I never had him for a patient."

Judge: "Ah, no, docther, ye nivver had, more's the pity. The old bhoy's still aloive."

Weight of evidence.—In an Irish police-court the magistrate was about to pronounce sentence on an Irishman for the theft of a goose.

"And it is on the oath of thim two witnesses that yer honour is going to condemn me?"

"Certainly," said the magistrate,

"Oh, murther! to condemn me on the oaths of two spalpeens who swear they saw me take the bhird, when I can bring a hundred who will swear they didn't see me do it!"

None of us.—Some time ago, in the court of a certain Scottish burgh, a man was charged with the theft of a pig. The worthy Bailie, in sentencing the prisoner, remarked that pig-stealing in the burgh had lately been too rife, and finished his peroration thus:—"And unless I make an example of you it's very certain none of us will be safe."

Precisely.—"Do you or do you not know the fence between the farm of Patrick Barney and Timothy Sullivan?" asked a judge of a witness.

"I do, yer honour."

"And have you at any time crawled under that fence?"

"Niver, yer honour."

"Perhaps you may be able to state positively whether you have or have not climbed over that fence?"

"I have, yer honour."

"Now, Mr. Witness, remembering that you are giving your testimony under oath, you will be so good as to state to the Court and jury precisely what part of that fence it was which you climbed over?"

"The top, sorr."

Could not lie.—Sheriff Rutherfurd, of Edinburgh, was rarely heard to perpetrate a professional jest, but when he did unbend the joke was a good one. On one occasion he had before him two horse dealers. There had been a good deal of hard swearing on each side, and it was averred by one of the dealers that the horse which he had bought could not lie down. Sheriff Rutherfurd heard all the evidence in the case, and then, looking over the bench down to the parties, he remarked that it seemed to him that the only one connected with this case that could not lie was the horse.

Hoist with his own petard.—A country magistrate, Mr. W., was once asked by a man to buy a pheasant.

"What is the price?" asked Mr. W.

"Three-and-six, sir," said the seller.

"I will buy it," said his honor.

After the sale Mr. W. asked the man to show his licence to sell game, telling him he was a magistrate, and should have him prosecuted if he hadn't one.

The licence was promptly shown.

"Very good," said Mr. W. "Now you can have the bird back for half-a-crown, as I only bought it to test you."

"Agreed!" said the man, and the bird was again transferred.

"Now show your licence to sell game," said the last buyer, "or I will inform the Excise."

Ultimately, Mr. W., seeing he was done, gave the man a sovereign to keep the matter quiet.

He could not swim.—Two men were sentenced by a self-appointed Court to be hanged for horse stealing. The place selected for the execution was the middle of a trestle-bridge spanning a river. The first noose was insecurely tied and the prisoner dropped into the river. He swam to shore and made good his escape. As they were adjusting the rope for the remaining prisoner, the latter drawled: "Say, pals, make sure of thet knot this time, will yer?" 'Cause I can't swim."

The best way for you.—Uncle Eph was before the Court on the same old charge. After the evidence, the judge, with a perplexed look, said: "But I cannot comprehend, Ephraim, how it was possible for you to steal those chickens when they were roosting right under the owner's window, and there were two vicious dogs in the yard."

"It wouldn't do you a bit of

good, jedge, for me to 'splain how I cotched 'em,'' said Eph. '' You couldn't do it if yer tried forty times, and yer might get a hide full of buckshot de berry fust time yer put yer leg over de fence. De bes' way for yer to do, jedge, is fer yer to buy yer chickens in de market.''

Why mercy should be shown.—'' You admit you stole the melons ? '' said the judge.

'' Oh, yes, suh—I stoled um ! ''

'' And yet you ask for mercy ? ''

'' Yes, suh—kase de white man kotched me fo' I had a chance ter eat um ! ''

In legal phraseology.—'' If I were to give you an orange,'' said Judge Foote, of Topeka, '' I would simply say : 'I give you the orange,' but should the transaction be entrusted to a lawyer to put in writing he would adopt this form : 'I hereby give, grant, and convey to you all my interest, right, title, and advantage of and in the said orange, together with its rind, skin, juice, pulp, and pips ; and all rights and advantages therein, with full power to bite.' ''

A case of "Jury's prudence." '' I remember,'' said the Irish Chief Justice Morris, '' when the jurors were taken in alphabetical order. Ten men of the name of Murphy were on the jury, all first cousins of a farmer named Murphy in the dock. The other two jurymen were Moriartys, but what chance had had they against ten Murphys and the Murphys were so busy talking to the Moriartys that nobody listened to me. Without leaving the box the jury acquitted the prisoner.''

'' What sort of law do you call that ? '' asked a Saxon standing by.

'' I should say it was a case of jury's prudence,'' said his lordship.

A farmer's dance in Kentucky.—Up in Clay County, once upon a time, a Christmas frolic ended in a tragedy. Old Mrs. Philpott was a witness.

'' Tell us about the fight,'' said the Judge.

'' I never seed no fight.''

'' Well, then, tell us what you did see.''

'' Cy Sewell he gives a Christmas dance, and me and a lot of others wuz thar. The boys and girls got to dancin', and as the boys went dancin' round and round they got to slappin' each other, an' finally one boy he slapped another boy harder than he 'lowed to an' knocked him down. An' the boy that got knocked down he jumped up an' jerked out a big knife and whacked the fellow that knocked him down right across the middle, from side to side. An' then the brother of the fellow what got cut he pulled a British bulldog an' he leg go six 44's right squar at the fellow that had the knife; an' just then Bill Smiley—Bill's a cousin of Jake Haynes what gat shot—come runnin' out'n old man Sewell's room with a double-barrel shotgun an' let off both barrels in the crowd, an' old Sewell he got excited an' jerked a Winchester rifle out'n from under the bed an' went to pumpin' lead into the gang; an' by that time the house was full o' smoke an' flashin' an' hollerin' an' I seed thar was goin' to be a fight, an' I left the house."

He will deserve it.—An old and well-to-do farmer, dictating his will to a lawyer said:—

"I give and bequeath to my wife the sum of £100 a year. Is that writ doon?"

"Yes," said the lawyer, "but she is not so old but she may marry again. Won't you make any charge in that case? Most people do."

"Ah, weel. write again, and say: 'If my wife marry again I give and bequeath to her the sum of £200 a year.' That'll dae, eh?"

"Why, that's just double the sum that she would have had if she had remained unmarried," said the lawyer. "It is generally the other way."

"Aye," said the farmer, "but him that taks her wull deserve the bit of money."

He could remember.—It was a right-of-way case, concerning an ancient footpath over the fields of an estate which had passed lately from an old family into the hands of a rich upstart. The dispute was carried to the law courts, and the lawyer appearing on behalf of the new land-owner cross-examined a venerable yokel who had testified that to his own personal knowledge there had been a right of way over the disputed land ever since he was a boy of five.

"And how old are you now? asked the lawyer.

"Eighty-five, sir."

"But surely you can't remember things which occurred when you were a boy of five, eighty years ago?" said the lawyer, in affected incredulity,

"'Deed an' I can, sir. I can mind a year afore that, when

your feyther, sir, 'owd Skinflint George' us called him—"

"That will do you may stand down," said the lawyer hastily, reddening furiously as a titter ran round the court.

——"got a walloping from Mother Buncombe——"

"Stand down, sir!"

—"for chatin' her two-year-owd lass ——"

"Do you hear? Stand down!"

—"a farden out o' the change ō' a thruppny-bit!" concluded the venerable witness, triumphantly, as he slowly left the box.

Had he known it.—A highwayman sentenced to be hanged in a country town, order was sent to the carpenter to make a gallows; which he neglecting to do, the execution was forced to be deferred, for which the judge was not a little angry, who sending for the carpenter, asked him why he had not done it? Why, sir, said he, I have done two already, but was never paid for them; but had I known it had been for your worship, I would have left all other business to have done it.

Writ serving in Galway.—The following quotation is from an affidavit made by a process-server who had met the fate of all bailiffs daring to invade the sacred precincts of a Galway gentleman's residence:—

"And this deponent further saith, that on arriving at the house of the said defendant, situate in the county of Galway aforesaid, for the purpose of personally serving him with the said writ, he, the said deponent, knocked three several times at the outer, commonly called the hall, door, but could not obtain admittance; wheron this deponent was proceeding to knock a fourth time, when a man, to this deponent unknown, holding in his hand a musket or blunderbuss, loaded with balls or slugs, as the deponent has since heard and verily believes, appeared at one of the upper windows of said house, and, presenting said musket at this deponent, threatened that if this deponent did not instantly retire, he would send his, this deponent's soul to hell; which this deponent verily believes he would have done, had not this deponent escaped. — SKETCHES OF THE IRISH BAR.

An old 'un.—A justice of peace overtaking a parson upon the road between London and Bow, told his companions that he would have a joke with him: and so, coming up to him, said, "Sir, you don't follow your

Master's rule, for he was content with an ass, but you ride a very fine horse."

Parson: "The reason is, because the King has made so many asses justices, that a clergyman cannot get one to ride on."

Not my way.—"I hope," said a client, who was a baker, to his lawyer, about to furnish a bill of costs, "that you will make it as light as possible."

"Ah," said the lawyer, "you might perhaps say that to the foreman of your bakery, but that is not the way I bake my bread!"

A spendthrift. — Judge: "You say that your parent is mentally incapable of taking care of his money, and you wish a guardian appointed? Well, what proof have you that he is a spendthrift?"

"Why, he has been known to attend every market within twenty miles of home for several years past."

"Petition granted," said the judge.

Left himself out.—A gentleman, who knew something of law, lived in an Irish village, and was in the habit of making the wills of his poorer neighbours. At an early hour one morning he was aroused by a loud knocking at his gate, and, putting his head out, asked who was there. "It's me, your honour, Paddy Flacherty. I could not get a wink of sleep, thinking of the will. I've not left myself a three-legged stool to sit down upon!"

Acquitted this time.—After hearing a claim for £4, the value of two lambs alleged to have been killed by a dog, Judge Scully at Hastings County Court gave judgment for the defendant.

There was a prima facie case, said his Honour, but not sufficient evidence to show that the dog had done the damage.

The defendant asked what the judgment meant.

Judge Scully: "It means that the dog is acquitted this time, and that he had better not do it again."

A sad use for a K.C.—Mr. Marshall Hall, K.C., tells the following story of a County Court action in which he took part: "I remember, many years ago, being taken down to a County Court. I looked at the brief, and found that the whole amount to be sued for was £6, while my own fee was more than five times that sum, and I could not make the matter out. It was an action for trespass—seizing a horse in execution; and the sort of horse it was can be imagined, and in the end I won. The case took the whole day. Then when it was all over, I heard that there was a bet of £500 depending on the result of the case. The parties were all horsey people, and they knew they would get a fair run for their money, and they used me for the purpose of a gamble."

There you have me.—Judge (to farmer who defended his own case with some temper): "What do you suppose I am on the Bench for?"

"Ah! There, my lord, you have me!"

Turned up smiling.—Sir William Wightman held office in the old Court of King's Bench far beyond the prescribed time, and at last he took a sort of farewell of his brother judges. However, he turned up smiling again at Westminster Hall.

"Why, Brother Wightman," said Sir Alexander Cockburn, "you told us that you intended to send in your resignation."

"So I did," said Sir William; "but when I went home and told my wife she said, 'Why, William, what on earth do you think that we can do with you messing about the house all day?' So you see I was obliged to come down to Court again."

Not before witnesses.—His Honour: "You are charged with stealing chickens. Have you any witnesses?"

Prisoner: "I have not. I don't steal chickens before witnesses."

A "question of taste."—A Welsh County Court Judge recently had before him a case in which a printer sued a pork butcher for the value of a large parcel of paper bags with the latter's advertisement printed thereon.

The printer having no suitable illustration to embellish the work, thought he improved the occasion by putting an elaborate Royal Arms above the man's name and address, but ultimately the latter refused to pay.

The Judge, looking over a specimen, observed that, for his part, he thought the lion and unicorn were much nicer than an old fat pig.

"Oh, well," answered the butcher, "perhaps your Honour likes to eat animals like that, but my customers don't. I don't kill lions and unicorns. I only kill fat pigs!"

Verdict for defendant.

One for him.—Defendant's

Counsel : "How do you know they are your ducks ?"

Farmer: "Oh, I should know them anywhere." (Describes their peculiarities.)

Counsel: "Why, those ducks can't be such a rare breed; I have some very like them in my own yard."

Farmer: "Very likely, sir. They're not the only ducks I've had stolen lately."

Two blacks never make a white.—It is related of Lord Brampton when he was plain Mr. Hawkins, and yet a barrister, that he was one day arguing a case before a magistrate, who snappishly told him that two blacks did not make a white.

"They may sometimes," replied Hawkins, promptly,

"Indeed, how so?" asked the magistrate.

"A pair of black Spanish fowls may be the parents of a white egg," was the answer, which sent the court into convulsions.

Fair and frail.—At a fair in Ireland the day finished with a fight with shillelahs for the settlement of old feuds. One man was killed in the melee, and his assailant was brought up for manslaughter. A doctor testified that the victims' skull was very thin. The man was found guilty, and before sentence was passed the judge asked him whether he had anything to say.

"No, yer honour, only might I ask 'Was that a skull for a man to go to a fair wid?'"

A good man.—Judge: "Do you know this man?" Witness: "Oi do that yer 'anner." Judge: "Is he a man of high moral character standing well in the community?" Witness: "By me sowl Oi don't know yer maning." Judge (irritably): "I mean, sir, is he a good man?" Witness: "Och, by the saints and that he is. He defayted the best man in his district, in a fair stand-up fight."

On the evidence.— Justice Lawson summed up in the case of a man who was charged with stealing a pig. The evidence of the theft was quite conclusive, and, in fact, was not combated; but the prisoner called the priests and neighbours to attest to his good character. "Gentlemen of the jury," said the judge, "I think the only conclusion you can arrive at is, that the pig was stolen by the prisoner, and that he is one of the nicest men in the country."

The benefit of the doubt.—A gamekeeper pounced upon a

poacher in the act, with ferret, rabbit, and net. The man's defence was that he knew nothing about the matter except that he heard a noise and got over the hedge to see what it was when the keeper seized him. The Bench gave him the benefit of the doubt. "Can I be tried agen for this?" said the man.

"No," was the reply.

"Not niver no more?" he repeated, and received the same answer.

"Then will you be good enough to tell 'em to hand me over ma ferret and ma net."

Didn't want to hear more.—It was an action for damages against the owner of a dog which had worried some sheep and counsel for defendant took the line that it was plaintiff's own dog which was the culprit. The cross - examination proceeded thus:—

Counsel: "You admit the defendant's dog and yours were alike?"

Plaintiff: "They are as much alike as two peas."

Counsel: "When you saw the dog worrying your sheep, how far were you away?"

Plaintiff: "About a hundred yards."

Counsel: "And yet you are able to swear that it was the defendant's dog and not yours? Pray, how do you manage to be so positive?"

Plaintiff: "Well, you see, first of all, my dog had been dead two days——" But counsel did not seem to want to hear any more.

Magnanimity. — Captain "Josey" Little, the famous gentleman rider of a past age, like most other gentleman riders, was in a chronic state of impecuniosity. At length it became necessary to deal with his debts, and he invited his creditors to meet him at the office of his solicitor. A pile of bills and acceptances stood on the table, with which Captain Little with impulsive honesty proceeded to deal.

"These must be paid," he said, "if it takes my last shilling to do it. Pay 'em 6d. in the pound!"

"Captain," said his lawyer, enthusiastically and with much earnestness, "you're heart's too big for your breast; your banking account won't stand it."

His first offence.—"Do you know of any mitigating circumstances in your case?" said a Texas justice to Sam Johnsing, accused of stealing.

"Lemme off dis time."

"Is it your first offence?"

"Fust offence, sah."

"How did you manage to get the chicken so cleverly, without disturbing the dog in the yard?"

"Dat comes from practice, your worship," said Sam, who felt flattered by the remarks of the court.

All the difference.—A case was being tried recently respecting the soundness of a horse, in which a clergyman, not educated in the school of Tattersall, appeared as chief witness.

He was a bit confused in giving his evidence, and a blustering barrister, who examined him, exclaimed:

"Pray, sir, do you know the difference between a horse and a cow?"

"I acknowledge my ignorance," replied the clergyman; "I hardly know the difference between a horse and a cow, or a bull and a bully; only that a bull, I am told, has horns, and a bully"—bowing to the counsellor—"has none."

What they said.—Baron Dowse once had a case in which the accused man understood only Irish. An interpreter was accordingly sworn. The prisoner said something to the interpreter.

"What does he say?" demmanded his lordship.

"Nothing, my lord," was the reply.

"How dare you say that when we all heard him? Come sir, what was it?"

"My lord," said the interpreter, beginning to tremble, "it had nothing to do with the case."

"If you don't answer, I'll commit, you, sir!" roared the baron. "Now, what did he say?"

"Well, my lord, you'll excuse me, but he said: 'Who's that old woman with the red bed-curtain round her sitting up there?'"

At which the Court roared.

"And what did you say?" asked the baron, looking a little uncomfortable.

"I said: 'Whist, ye spalpeen! That's the ould boy that's goin' to hang yez!"

The "gentleman rabbit."—At Bow Street Police-office a respectably-dressed woman applied to Mr. Marsham for advice. "I have got a gentleman rabbit, and my young man lodger has got a lady rabbit."

Mr. Marsham: "Well, what of that?"

"Well, unknown to me, my lodger took my gentleman rabbit to see his lady rabbit."

Mr. Marsham: "What was the result?"

"Nine little rabbits, your Worship." (Loud laughter.)

Mr. Marsham: "That is very satisfactory."

Applicant (indignantly): "Not at all. Why, he only wants to give me one rabbit as my share of the litter."

Mr. Marsham: "That is not a bad share. I suppose your rabbit suffered no harm."

"Didn't he, though? Why the other one tore all the hair off the poor dear's back." (Laughter.)

Police-sergeant Ford, warrant officer, was directed to suggest to the lodger that he should give his landlady at least two rabbits.

To suit their convenience.—Charles James Fox and his secretary, Mr. Hare, who lived with him, were both noted for their impecuniosity, and their creditors spent much time in dunning them. One morning before daylight there was a violent ringing at their door, and Mr. Fox, going to the window, saw a group of creditors below.

"Are you fox hunting or hare hunting this morning, gentlemen?"

"Come, now, Mr. Fox," one of them called up, "tell us when you are going to pay that bill. Just set a date, and we will leave you in peace."

"All right," was the reply. "How will the Day of Judgment suit you?"

"Not at all. We'll all be too busy on that day."

"Well, rather than put you to any inconvenience, we'll make it the day after."

It wouldn't do.—A young constable had the week previously hauled up before the Bench an offender charged with snaring a rabbit on a preserved estate. As the remanded case came on for a second hearing, the supposed defunct animal, which seemingly appeared as fresh as ever, was duly again in evidence, and the delinquent in the dock exchanged a meaning and significant glance.

"And so my client is charged on remand with stealing or ensnaring a rabbit," at once began the wary lawyer, calmly—"the one produced, eh?"

"Well—er—no, not the one produced," stammered the disconcerted Robert, "but one exactly like it. You see," he went on, "when the case were put off last week, I ses to myself as that there rabbit won't keep till next Bench day that's certain, so I'll have a pie made of it and get a fresh one from the keeper a day or two before the time in place of it. It'll be as broad as 'tis long!"

But it wasn't, for after the roar of laughter which greeted this explanatory statement had subsided the magistrate announced that "the prisoner was discharged."

The choice of ——.—Here is a story of a white man in America who was arrainged before a coloured Justice of Peace for killing a man and stealing his mule. The comparative enormity of such crimes varied with the soil upon which they were committed. In this case the deed was done in Arkansas, near the Texas border.

There was some rivalry between the States, but the coloured Justice tried to preserve an impartial frame of mind.

"We's got two kinds ob law in dis yere Cawt," he said. "Texas law an' Arkansas law. Which will you hab?"

The prisoner thought a minute, and then said he would take Arkansas law.

"Den I discharge you fo' stealin' de mule, an' hang you fo' killin' de man."

"Hold on a minute, Judge," called the prisoner. "I would rather have the Texas law."

"All right. Under de law ob Texas I fine you fo' killin' de man, an' hang you fo' stealin' de mule!"

They tried again.—At the trial of a Mexican cowboy on a charge of horse-stealing, a jury had been gathered, put into a room, and some time later a dozen men burst in, demanding the verdict.

"Not guilty," answered the foreman.

Laying hands on pistols, the intruders slammed the doors with: "You'll have to do better than that. Try again."

In half an hour one of the men opened the door once more. "Your opinion, gentlemen?"

"Guilty."

"Correct! You can come out. We hanged him an hour ago."

Did it strike them.—Mark Twain had finished his speech at a recent dinner party, and, on his seating himself, a lawyer rose, shoved his hands deep into his trouser pockets, as was his habit, and laughingly inquired of those present at the society dinner: "Doesn't it strike this company as a little unusual that a professional humorist should be funny?" When the laughter that greeted this sally had subsided, Mark Twain drawled out:

" Doesn't it strike this company as a little unusual that a lawyer should have his hands in his own pockets ? "

Out West.—In a rural Justice Court out West the defendant in a case was sentenced to serve thirty days in gaol. He had known the Judge from boyhood, and addressed him as follows :—

" Bill, old boy, you're not a-gwine to send me ter jail, air you ? "

" That's what," replied the Judge. " Have you got anything to say agin it ? "

" Only this here, Bill ; God help you when I git out ! "

What need more to ask.—Counsel : " Do you understand the nature of an oath ? "

Witness : " Sir ? "

Counsel : " Do you understand the nature of an oath, I say ? "

Witness (impressively) : " Sir, I have driven a keb in this city for nigh on forty year."

Law and Custom.—One of the American Ambassador's legal stories told at a gathering of lawyers related to a Texas Judge before whom a prisoner was brought, charged with horse-stealing. The Judge promptly sentenced the prisoner to be hanged, but his lawyer interrupted.

" You can't hang this prisoner according to law, your honour," he said.

" Guess, you're right," said the Judge. " Well, I'll discharge him ; and I guess it's up to the boys to hang him according to the regular custom."

He gruppit me.—A Dumfriesshire gentleman caught a boy in his garden stealing apples, and handed him over to the police. He was brought up before a Baillie the next morning, As it was his first offence the Baillie let him off, but told him never to yield to such a temptation again, adding : " Ye should have flown from the Evil One." The boy, thinking he referred to the gentleman, said : " So I did, sir, but he gruppit me afore I got ower the fence ! "

The desired effect.—An action was being tried before Lord Coleridge for damages for the death of a sheep dog, a winner of many prizes at bench shows, and counsel for the defence was endeavouring to show that the dog had "had his day," and that damages should be nominal. Lord Coleridge, however, was sweetly slumbering, and counsel felt the necessity for rousing him, if possible. So, gradually raising his voice, he asked one of the plaintiff's witnesses :

"Is it not your experience as an exhibitor that when an old dog has taken his place regularly on the bench for many years he gets sleepy and past his work?" The laughter that followed had the desired effect.

The seriousness of it.—Two neighbours had a long litigation about a small spring, which they both claimed. The Judge, wearied out with the case, at last said: "What is the use of making so much fuss about a little water?"

"Your honour will see the serious nature of the case," replied one of the lawyers, "when I inform you that the parties are both milkmen."

Circumstantial evidence. — During an adjournment of the Molineaux trial in New York, District-Attorney Osborne discussed one afternoon the value of circumstantial evidence with a group of reporters.

"Suppose," he said, "that I am talking to a milkman. This milkman claims there is no water in his can of milk. He tells me that he milked the cow himself; that he washed out the can; that he strained the milk—and, then, while he is speaking, out leaps a frog from the can. That frog's evidence is circumstantial, but, nevertheless, it is much stronger than the man's, which is direct."

He felt it.—"What is this man charged with?" asked the police justice.

"Stealing a dog, your honour.

"Well, sir, what have you got to say for yourself?"

"Your honour, if you'll make it embezzlement I'll plead guilty. I may be a thief, but I've got feelin's, and it looks so small to steal a dog."

Legal advice.—"It's this way," explained the client. "The fence runs between Brown's place and mine. He claims that I encroach on his land, and I insist that he is trespassing on mine. Now, what would you do if you were in my place?"

Lawyer: "If I were in your place, I'd go over and give Brown a cigar, have a drink with him, and settle the controversy in ten minutes. But as things stand I advise you to sue him by all means. Let no arrogant, domineering, insolent pirate like Brown trample on your sacred rights! Assert your manhood and courage. I need the money!"

Weight of testimony.—Solicitor (to Irish client who has been arrested for horse-stealing):

"Now tell the truth; it's no use concealing it if I am to do any good for you. Did any one see you steal the horse?"

Murphy: "Yiss, sorr. There was wan man seen me steal the horse an' he's goin' to come into coort and swear to it, the low, contimptible blackguard."

Solicitor: "In that case I'm very much afraid it'll go hard against you. You can't escape with evidence like that."

Murphy: "But, sorr, look ye here. Oi can bring twinty men an' more that'll swear they didn't see me steal the horse."

A good record.—In a rural justice court in Georgia recently an old negro, whose testimony had been questioned, said in his own defence:—

"Jedge, I'm a good man. I been a-livin' roun' heah ten years. I an't never been lynched; en de only horse I ever stoled throwed me en broke my two legs!"

For disgracing the profession.—Sergeant Davy, a distinguished English lawyer at the time of Lord Mansfield, being once called to account by his brethren on the Western Circuit for disgracing the profession by accepting silver of a client, he replied: "I took silver because I could not get gold; but I took every sixpence the fellow had in the world, and I hope you don't call that disgracing the profession."

Bacon's Abridgement.—When Andrew Jackson, the seventh President of the United States, was a young man he practised at the bar. It was his habit to carry in his saddle bags when he attended Court a copy of Bacon's Abridgement, and to make frequent appeals to it in his cases. This precious book was always done up in coarse brown paper, and the unwrapping of the volume was a very solemn function as performed by Jackson.

During a certain trial on one occasion, however, a fellow-lawyer procured a piece of bacon the size of his book, and while Jackson was addressing the Court, he slipped out the bacon from its wrapping and substituted it for the legal manual.

At length Jackson had occasion to appeal to Lord Bacon. While still talking he raised the bearskin flap of his saddle-bags, drew out the brown paper package, carefully untied the string, unfolded the paper with decorous gravity, and then, without looking at what he held in his hand, exclaimed triumphantly:—

"We will now see what Bacon says!"

What wonder that the Court-room rang with laughter at his expense.

A good reason.—In the bankruptcy Court a young gentleman who went the pace was asked by the judge if he could give any reason for the failure of a man with his ample means and good education.

"Oh, yes, easily—fast women and slow horses!"

"I'll give you the cow."—"I had a case," said a lawyer, "in which a man was arrested for stealing a cow. He was held over for the grand jury on preliminary hearing, and he sent for me. His letter ran something like this: 'Dere Sir,—I am in Jale, and the man sayes I am likely to goe to the pen. I did not steel the cowe and I am purfuctly innercent. Please gete me out, if it are the last act of yure life. This is not a nice place. Pleese do get me out. I think I can pay you sum day. I did not steel thes cowe. Tell the Judge that. And if You can get me off free I am willing to do all I can for you. If you do I will give you the cowe.—Yours truly, Bill Smith.'"

The hanging Judge.—Lord Norbury was commonly known as "the hanging judge." "Ah! my lord, give me a long day!" implored a prisoner on a certain 20th of June.

"Your wish is granted!" said Norbury, with a leer. "I will give you until to-morrow, the longest day in the year!"

Counsellor O'Grady tells us that the only occasion on which Lord Norbury was known to weep was at a performance of "The Beggar's Opera," when a reprieve arrives for Captain Macheath. Curran had a sly hit at this side of the judge's character one day at dinner, when the former was carving a joint of roast beef. "Is that beef hung, Mr. Curran?" queried the Chief Justice. "Not yet, my lord!" was the reply. "You have not tried it!"

"Duke's and fules."—A Scotchman, giving evidence at the bar of the House of Lords, in the affair of Captain Porteous, and telling of the variety of shot which was fired upon that unhappy occasion, was asked by the Duke of Newcastle what kind of shot it was? "Why," said the man, in his broad dialect, "sic as they shoot fules (fowls) wi', an' the like."

"What kind of fools?" asked the Duke, smiling at the word.

"Why, my lord, dukes (ducks) and sic kin' o' fules."

Seeing and Knowing.—An eminent judge, who was trying a right-of-way case, had before him a witness who was telling the jury that he had "knowed the path for 60 yeer, and my feyther tould I as he heered my grandfeyther say—"

"Stop!" said the judge; "we can't have any hearsay evidence here."

"Not," exclaimed Farmer Giles. "Then how dost knaw who thy feyther was 'cept by hearsay."

Judge: "In courts of law we can only be guided with what you have seen with your own eyes, and nothing more or less."

"Oh, that be blowed for a tale," replied the farmer. "I ha' a bile on the back of my neck, and I never seed un, but I be prepared to swear that he's there, I do!"

This second triumph on the part of the witness let in a torrent of hearsay evidence about the footpath which obtained weight with the jury, albeit the judge told them it was not testimony of any value, and the farmer's party won.

Succinct.—She was sworn, and counsel asked her if she had seen the cow straying on the line.

"Yes, I seed it."

"Did you see the engine strike the beast?"

"Yes, I seed it."

"Then tell the Court in your own words, as shortly as possible, exactly what happened."

"There ain't nothin' to tell," said the old lady. "It just tooted an' tuck 'er."

It was out in Kansas, a man brought an action to recover some land that had been outrageously filched from him. His case was a good one, but the other side had doctored its witnesses—had even doctored the plaintiff's witnesses, too—and up to that time, when he stood in court, not a jot or tittle of testimony in the plaintiff's favour had been recorded.

He, as soon as he was sworn turned to the judge and said:—

"Sir, I brought this suit, and yet the evidence, excepting my own, is all against me. Now I don't accuse anyone of lying, but these witnesses are the most mistaken lot of fellows I ever saw. You know me. Two years ago you sold me a hoss for sound that was as blind as a bat. I made the deal and stuck to it, and this is the first time I have mentioned it. When you used to buy my grain, judge, you stood on the scales when the empty wagon was weighed, but I never said a word. Now, do you think I am the kind of man to kick up a rumpus and sue a fellow unless he has done me a real wrong? Why, judge, if you'll recall that sheep speculation you and me ——"

But at this point the judge, very red in the face, hastily decided the case in the plaintiff's favour.

Providential.—"Old man had his left leg cut off by a railroad."

"You don't say!"

"It's a fact; an' he made enough out o' it to paint the house, take the mortgage off the mule, an' buy Sue a pianner."

"My! but ain't Providence on the side o' some folks?"

How he shot the dog.—A negro was brought up on a charge of shooting a dog, and the following dialogue took place:—

Magistrate: "Did you shoot that dog with malice aforethought?"

Nigger: "No, sah! Didn't have no mallets. Shot him with a gun."

Magistrate: "You do not understand. I will put it in another way. Did you shoot him in self-defence?"

Nigger: "No, sah. I shot him in de tail when he jumped de fence."

Got mixed up.—Judge B—— was noted for the way he got mixed in his charges to the jury. On one occasion a case was tried before him, the facts of which stood thus. Smith brought a suit against Jones upon a promissory note given for a horse.

Jones's defence was that at the time of purchase the horse had the glanders (of which it died), and that Smith knew it.

Smith replied that the horse did not have the glanders, but the distemper, and that Jones knew that when he bought it.

The judge charged the jury "Gentlemen of the jury, pay attention to the charge of the Court. You have already made one mis-trial of this case, because you did not pay attention to the Court, therefore I intend to make it so clear this time that you cannot possibly make a mistake. This suit is upon a note given for a promissory horse. I hope you understand that. Now, if you find that at the time of the sale Smith had the glanders, and Jones knew it, Jones cannot recover, That is quite clear, gentlemen, I will state it to you again. If you find that at the time of the sale Jones had the distemper, and Smith knew it, then Smith cannot possibly recover. But, gentlemen, I will state it a third time, so that you cannot possibly make a mistake. Now, if, at the time of sale, Smith had the glanders, and Jones had the distemper, and the horse knew it, then neither Smith, Jones, nor the horse can recover. Let the record be handed to the jury.''

Out West.—Will your honour please charge the jury ? '' asked an Arkansas lawyer at the conclusion of a horse-thief trial.

'' I will,'' replied his Honour. '' The court charges each juryman one dollar for drinks and six dollars extra for the one who used the Court's hat as a spitoon during the first day of the sessions.''

" Deduction is the thing,'' declared the law student. '' For instance, yonder is a pile of ashes in our yard. That is evidence that we have had fires this winter.''

'' And, by the way, John,'' broke in his father, '' you might go out and sift that evidence; it would do a lot of good on the lawn 1 ''

Chapter XX.

EDUCATION.

Education sometimes a drawback.—'' Edication,'' said Farmer Jones, '' is a mighty good thing, but sometimes it may do harm. I oncet knowed of a case where edication came purty nigh droundin' a pretty young lady.''

'' How was that ? ''

'' Well, she fell into the pond, an' instead of hollering out, politely remarked, ' I am within measurable distance of extinction.' ''

'' An' the fool of a farm hand that heard her lost five minutes makin' up 'is mind whether to pull her out or go home fur a dictionary.''

Education and starvation.—District Visitor : '' John Pickakse, I hear you keep your son away from school. Don't you think you are very foolish to injure his prospects ? ''

Flourishing Labourer :—'' Whoy, marm, that 'ere's jest wy I am a-tryin' to perwent them a-gittin' 'im and educatin' of him, They might make a pore starvin' clerk of him, and I wants him to earn a good livin', like 'is father.''

The Encyclopædia.—" We-ell, some ways I'd like to an' some ways I wouldn't," said honest Farmer Bentover, when the suave seller of big books had paused in his siren song. " Ye see, if I was to sign for that 'ere cyclopedee in 47 parts, including the index an' appendicitis, I'm sorter afraid I'd hev to work so hard to pay for it that I'd be too tired to enjoy readin' it ; while if I read it at my leisure, as I'd 'ort to, in order to git the good of it, I wouldn' hev time to earn the price."

The odd shillings.—Professor Lushington, the scholarly Professor of Greek, Glasgow, was a retiring man, who mingled little with the outside world. A farmer, accompanied by his son, waited upon him to enter the lad in the Greek Class. After having received all the necessary information, the farmer said, " What's your charge for the class, sir ? "

The Professor : " The class fee is three guineas."

Farmer : " Ah ! sir, ye maun drap the odd shillings ! "

Too old for that.—One of the students in an American university, wishing to do something during his vacation, introduced a new encyclodædia into the country districts, and at one place he found an old farmer working in the fields.

" I'd like to sell you a new encyclopædia."

" Well, young fellow, I'd like to have one, but I'm afraid I'm too old to ride the thing."

His eddication.—Uncle Reuben : " Farmer Wheatley's boy is home from College. He told me his eddication is finished."

Uncle Hiram : " His eddication can't amount to much."

" Why not ? '

" If it did he wouldn't think it was finished."

Not an undertaker.—I don't see any use in my son Benjamin studyin' Latin, pessimistically said a certain honest but somewhat moss-grown farmer, addressing the principal of the village academy. " I want him to get the kind of education that will be of value to him in after life, and not a lot of things that isn't no good to nobody. I hope I make myself clear."

" But, my dear sir," expostulated the educator, "Latin is one of the foremost essentials of a liberal education. It broadens the mind, strengthens the intellect, and——"

" Tut, tut ! What I want him to learn is somethin' that will strengthen his financial grasp, so to speak. Latin is one of the dead languages, isn't it?"

"Yes; but——"

"Very well, then; it won't be of no manner of use to Benjamin. He's going to be a farmer, ye see, not an undertaker."

Physiology.—A country school teacher in New Jersey recently introduced the study of physiology. A few days later she received the following note: "Dear Miss A,—Please don't learn my Mary Ann any more about her insides. It ain't nice, and besides, it makes her think her vittels disagree with her."

On breadmaking.—A schoolmaster writes:—"I am at the head of a town school, and a short time back gave breadmaking to a class of boys as the subject for an essay. One of the essays began in schoolboy English—'The first thing in breadmaking is to boil the potatoes, and then you must peel them and mash them carefully. Then you must mix them with a little water, and set them in a warm place till they begin to ferment,' &c. Flour was not mentioned in the course of the essay. The boy's father is a baker!"

A good excuse.—A Board school teacher says that one of his pupils recently came to school bringing the following letter of excuse from his mother: "Dear Sir,—Please excuse my boy a-scratching hisself. He's got a new flannel shirt on."

The season for apples.—The teacher was telling about the different seasons. He asked: "Now, one of you boys, tell me which is the proper season to gather apples?"

Johnnie: "When the dog's chained."

How could she.—At a school in the country the sentence, "Mary milks the cow," was given out to be parsed. The last word was disposed of as follows:

"Cow is a noun, feminine gender, singular number, third person, and stands for Mary."

"Stands for Mary!" said the excited pedagogue; "how do you make that out?"

"Because," answered the intelligent pupil, "if the cow didn't stand for Mary, how could Mary milk her?"

They shook hands on it.—Farmer (at country school): "Be you the teacher?"

"Yes, sir."

"So it was you who thumped my boy Tom yesterday?"

"I did punish an unruly scholar."

"Punish! Well I should say so. You stamped on him, an'

slugged him, an ended by kickin' him clear across the playground. Is that correct ?"

"Pretty near."

"Let me shake hands with you. I have to admire a man who can knock out my son Tom, for I'll be hanged if I can do it."

Schoolboy "howlers."—The historical and other "facts" given here are taken from schoolboys' examination papers (says the "University Correspondent"):—

Doomsday Book.—A book signifying that each man should have seven feet of land for a grave.

What is a watershed. ?—A shed for keeping water in.

A watershed is a house between two rivers so that a drop of water falling on one side of the roof runs into one river, and a drop on the other side goes into the other river.

Scutage was a way the Anglo-Saxons had of ploughing the ground.

The Feudal System lies between the Humber and the Thames.

The principal products of Kent are Archbishops at Canterbury.

The chief clause in Magna Charta was that no free man should be put to death or imprisoned without his own consent.

A ruminating animal.—A Board school teacher recently explained to his pupils that "a cow is a ruminating animal, because it chews the cud."

The following day, in order to test the memory of his scholars he asked:

"What is a ruminating animal ?"

A chubby little arm went up at the foot of the class, and a squeaking voice piped out:

"Please teacher, a roomating animal is a animal wot chews her cubs. We had a white mouse wot ate five of them."

At a fancy dress ball for children, a policeman stationed at the door was instructed by the committee not to admit any adults. Shortly after the beginning of the ball an excited woman came running up to the door and demanded admission. "I'm sorry, mum," replied the policeman, "but I can't let anyone in but children." "But my child is dressed as a butterfly," exclaimed the woman, "and has forgotten her wings." "Can't help it," replied the policeman, "orders is orders, so you'll have to let her go as a caterpillar."

Precautionary.—The school

authority of a certain village took it into their heads lately that they would have the children's eyesight examined by an oculist. This was done, and the parents of those children whose eyes were found to be in any way affected were communicated with.

Accordingly, the head-master wrote to the father of Willie Thompson :—" Dear sir,—I beg to inform you that your son William shows signs of astigmation, which ought to be attended to at once.—Yours faithfully."

Willie's father replied :—

" Dear sir,—I don't quite understand what it is Willie has been up to now, but I have walloped him to-night ; you can do it again to-morrow morning.—Yours faithfully."

What's the harum.—Two Irish farmers who had not seen each other for a long time met at a fair. They had a lot of things to tell each other.

" Shure, it's married I am," said Murphy.

" You don't tell me so ! " said Moran.

" Faix, yes," said Murphy, " an' I've got a fine healthy bhoy which the neighbours say is the very picture of me."

Moran looked for a moment at Murphy, who was not remarkable for his good looks, and then said :—

" Och, well, what's the harum so long as the child's healthy ? "

A born financier.

Willie had a savings bank :
'Twas made of painted tin.
He passed it round among the boys
Who put their pennies in.
Then Willie wrecked that bank and bought
Sweetmeats and chewing gum,
And to the other envious lads
He never offered some.
" What shall we do ? " his mother said ;
" It is a sad mischance ! "
His father said : We'll cultivate
His gift for high finance."

SPORTING TIMES.

The prodigal's return.—At a certain small farm there was a happy fireside gathering, for the youngest son, the scapegrace of the family, had returned from his wanderings ; penniless, it is true, but the uncrowned hero of a hundred fights.

As he told of daring encounters with wild beasts in distant lands, the father's heart glowed with pride, and, turning to his eldest son, a plodding, thrifty fellow, whose timidity with respect to animals was unconquerable, he jokingly exclaimed :—

"Well, I wonder what animal you could keep at bay?"

"I? I keep the wolf from the door."

His good points.—They were discussing the vagaries of a prodigal son, who had returned after a more than usually wild outbreak.

"You must, at any rate, admit he has good points," urged the loving mother, as usual.

"So has a porcupine," said the parent.

Didn't hear it.—Farmer Jones: "That there notice zez 'Shut the gate!'"

Tommy Brown: "Please, sir, I didn't hear it!"

His autograph.—A boy was recently presented with a jack-knife, with which, boy-like, he cut and marked everything that came in his way, from the dining-room table to the trees in the orchard. A few days after he had become the happy possessor of the knife the father was startled by seeing two men bringing home the boy in a sad state, his face cut and covered with blood.

"Nobody didn't hit me," he said to his father between his sobs; "it was only a mule kicked me in the eye!"

"A mule kicked you in the eye, eh? Haven't I told you a thousand times that mules were not fit things for boys to fool with?"

"I wasn't fooling with him at all," said the boy. "I was only trying to cut my name on his back!"

Not a small bull.—Tommy (to father): "Is a streamlet a small stream?"

Father: "Yes, my son."

"Is an owlet a small owl?"

"Yes, Tommy."

"Is an egglet a small egg?"

"Well, yes, you might call it that."

"Then what is a bullet? 'Tisn't a small bull, is it?"

Willie's Wisdom.—Willie had been naughty, and his father was going to whip him.

"My son, do you know why I am going to whip you?"

"Yes, dad," replied the little fellow, "it's because you're bigger'n I am."

He knew better.—A London Sunday school was having its annual holiday. Bread and butter was handed round, followed by slices spread with marmalade. One of the female teachers noticed one of her favourites would not touch the marmalade, and asked him why. "Because, mum," said he, "I works where they makes it!"

The colour line.—"That youngest boy of yours does not seem to be a credit to you," said the white man to the darkie Uncle Mose.

"No, sah. He is de wustest chile I has. He is mighty bad. He's de white sheep of de fam'ly, sah."

Not olive branches.—"John, what are the chief branches of education in your school?"

"Willow branches, sir; master's used up nearly a whole tree."

A bad example.—Despite the notice against smoking, a friend tells me that a boy entered the monkey's house at the Zoo recently puffing at his cigarette as large as life and twice as natural. The keeper eyed him for awhile in silence. Then he tapped him on the shoulder. "Put it out, dear child," he said. "You'll teach the other young monkeys bad habits."

Whatsoever a man soweth.—The Sunday-school superintendent was illustrating the text, "Whatsoever a man soweth, that shall he also reap." "If," he said, "I want to raise a crop of turnips," what sort of seed must I sow?" "Turnip seed," said the class. "And if I want to raise a crop of tomatoes what seed must I sow?" "Tomato seed," said the class. "Very good. Now, if I want to raise a crop of good manhood, of noble strength, of rigid well-doing, what kind of seed must I sow then?" A visitor, who kept count, reports that half the school said "Turnip seed," while the other half went solid for "Tomato seed."

CHAPTER XXI.

RELIGION.

The Sexton and the goat.—Several ladies were engaged in decorating the church in a southern village when news was brought them that a goat was making a meal of a "Peace on earth, goodwill toward men" design in yew leaves.

The sexton rushed to the rescue, but the goat repelled his attack.

"Make haste, Johnson, and get up," said the vicar's wife from a place of safety; "it's starting to eat again."

"Let him eat again, ma'am,"

gasped the sexton. "I'm a-goin' to wait till he's got some goodwill to man inside 'im."

Jacob's ladder.—Dr. Wilberforce, when Bishop of Oxford, was at a Sunday-school where the verses descriptive of Jacob's ladder were read. "Is there any little boy or girl," said the Bishop, "who wishes to ask any question as to the passage which has just been read?" After a short pause a small boy said: "Please, sir, the angels had wings, and why did they require a ladder?" "A most natural question," said the Bishop. "Is there any other little boy or girl who can give an answer?" On which a little girl said, "Perhaps, sir, they was moulting!"

High or low.—Some years ago a clergyman went to an hotel to order a dinner for a number of clerical friends.

"May I ask, sir," said the waiter, "whether the party is High Church or Low Church?"

"Now what on earth do my friends' opinions matter to you?"

"A great deal, sir. If High Church, I must provide more wine; if Low Church, more wittles."

The blade of grass.—A certain minister, during his discourse one sabbath morning, said: "In each blade of grass there is a sermon."

The following day one of his flock discovered the good man pushing a lawn mower about his yard, and paused to say: "Well, parson, I'm glad to see you engaged in cutting your sermons short."

Boiled the prayer book.—Some years ago a thrifty old cottager, named Bethia Rummy, attended service every Sunday morning at the little Church of St. Elzevir, distant some two miles from her cottage, on a hillside in Derbyshire.

As regular in her provision for temporal wants as she was in attendance to spiritual necessities, her custom was to place a piece of bacon in a pot near the fire to be ready cooked against her return. Then with her big prayer-book wrapped in a snowy handkerchief, Bethia trudged off to St. Elzevir's.

One Sunday, however, she came late and flustered to her usual place, just in front of the reading-desk, and, to her vicar's astonishment, remarked, as she unfolded the snowy handkerchief:

"Lawk a daisy me! if I haven't biled the Prayer-book and brought the bacon to church!"

The Church Bazaar.—Mr. Surplice: "Oh, Mrs. Dash, the church bazaar is not so bad; it brings the church people together."

Mrs. Dash: "Mr. Surplice, after you have been in this parish a while longer, you will understand that for true peace and amity our church people need to be kept apart."

Their manners and morals—A parson in Leicestershire appears to have a poor opinion of some of his flock, as told in HORSE AND HOUND:—

When commenting upon hunting men and women, he remarked: "It is terrible how they have deteriorated; most of those who come here now have the manners of the stable-yard and morals of the poultry-yard."

Both doing well.—A well-known New England farmer of the old type has two grown-up sons. According to the BOSTON JOURNAL, one is an excellent preacher of the Gospel, while the other is a liquor dealer.

The old man was asked what his sons did for a living.

His answer was characteristic and concise: "One is serving the Lord, the other the devil, and both are doing well."

The look of a thing.—A young minister was settled in a country district, where his house was a long way from the church. He was fond of horses, and not only drove about the district tandem fashion during the week, but shocked some of his congregation by driving tandem to and from church on Sunday.

One of his elders went into the vestry at the close of a Sunday service, to remonstrate with him.

"Why?" said the minister, "what is there wrong driving them tandem more than abreast?"

"It disna' look weel on the Sabbath," replied the elder.

"Look!—what about the look? It's a mere matter of taste."

"But," persisted the elder, "there's something even in the look of a thing. Now, when ye're gie'en the Benediction, ye haud up your hands so"—and the other imitated the minister's gesture with outspread and uplifted hands. "But suppose ye put your thoomb to your nose, and spread out your hands tandem fashion in front this way—wad there be no a guid deal in the look o' that?"

Don't come here to gossip.—One of the fiercest agitations which ever swept over Ireland was that in the early Thirties for the abolition of the tithes paid to the clergy of the Established Church. The tithe-proctors—the men who collected the impost, or, in default of payment, seized the stock of the Catholic peasants—were objects of intense popular hatred. As an old, simple priest sat in the confessional of a country chapel, awaiting penitents, a rough youth entered to confess his sins. What he had to relate to the priest was very sanguinary indeed. "Four murthers!" exclaimed the good father, in horror. "Now will ye have me believe ye've been killin' all yer family?" "No, yer riverence, they wasn't me own flesh and blood at all," said the penitent. "And who wor they, thin?" inquired the confessor. "Well, Father, they wor tithe-proctors.' "Tithe-proctors is it ye say?" exclaimed the priest. "Now, why didn't ye tell me that at first, and not be takin' up me time that way? Get out of here! Ye don't come here to gossip, but to confess yer sins."

By their fruits.—A country minister in America took leave of his congregation in the following way:—

"Brothers and sisters, I come to say good-bye. I don't think you love me, because you have not paid my salary. Your donations are mouldy fruit and wormy applès; and the Scripture saith, 'by their fruits ye shall know them;' Brothers I am going away to a better place to be chaplain of a penitentiary. I go to prepare a place for you, and may the Lord have mercy on your souls! Good-bye."

Parson and Bishop. — A stranger travelling in Norfolk asked a countryman the way to a particular place, and was told to go along a road until he came to a "parson," and then turn to the right, going on till he reached a "bishop," when he would be all right.

"But I may walk a long way without meeting either a parson or a bishop."

Native: "I see you don't belong to these parts. Here we call a sign-post a 'parson," because he points the way others should go, but does not go himself; and a broken-down post a 'bishop,' because he neither points the way nor goes himself.

The "Squishop."—In many parts of Sussex the incumbents of the districts, especially in the south, hold land, and occupy a position midway between squire and parson, and it became the fashion among the more homely folk to call them "squarsons." One morning the late Bishop Wilberforce, who possessed the most extraordinary talent for throwing himself into all sorts of different occupations and mastering their technic almost by intuition, was taking an early constitutional and lighted on a rustic hoeing turnips in a fashion to cause himself the greatest fatigue with the minimum of result. The Bishop took the hoe, and in a short time showed him a more workmanlike mode of using it. In astonishment the man said:

"Who may ye be, a squarson?" "No, my man," said his lordship, "I'm a squishop."

Thae drucken societies.—John Brown, a farmer in a northern parish, was waited upon by a deputation from the church of which he was a member with a proposal that he should become an elder. "Weel," replied John, "I ha'e nae objections mysel', but you had better speak to the wife aboot it."

Accordingly they proceeded to explain to Mrs. Brown the object of their visit, when she with a record of some of her husband's former exploits, horrified them by exclaiming: "'Deed, no, he'll dae naething o' the sort. He's into far ower many o' thae drucken societies already."

Solomon and the sower.—One boisterously windy day a clergyman despatched a message to his servant to sow a portion of a field known to them both as the "bank." In no very amiable mood, the man made his way to the study.

"Dae ye want me to sow the bank?" he inquired, somewhat sternly.

"Yes, John, I do," replied his reverence.

"Ye canna sow in sich a day o' wind," explained John.

"Well," replied the minister, "you know Solomon says: 'He that considereth the wind will not sow.'"

"I dinna care a button what Solomon says. I fancy he kens as little about farmers' work as you dae, or he wadna hae said ony such thing. Naebody but daft folk wad think o' sawin' in such a wind. Solomon may say what he likes, but him and you both wadna mak' a guid ploughman between you."

On a rail.—"What's become o' Parson Jenks, who came out here to preach?" asked a friend of a Dakota man.

"Well, you see, he made a

sort of a bad break, and we just firmly passed him along to some other community. We didn't like his style somehow. We found it necessary to help him out of the neighbourhood on a rail."

"I am astonished! You did a great injustice to a worthy man I am certain. What were the charges against him?"

"Why, in his sermon one Sunday he got goin' on about the Holy Land, and said they could rise bigger wheat over there than we could in Dakota, and then went on to quote something that I don't believe was ever in the Bible about the seed falling in some particular kind of sile and increasing a hundredfold. Just as soon as he said that I and Deacon Penny rose right up to and went out and got a rail, and Deacon Jones and the members of the choir brought the reverend gentleman out and set him on. I tell you no man can preach to us who goes on reflecting on Dakota's wheat-raising."

The quick and the dead.—The following notice was lately fixed upon the church door at a village in Hertfordshire and read in the church: "This is to give notice that no person is to be buried in this churchyard but those living in the parish, and those who wish to be buried are desired to apply to me. E. G., parish clerk."

Comparisons are——.—Parson (who has just arrived for the first time at his new country living): "I say, porter, my arrival seems to have caused a great deal of excitement in the village."

Porter: "Yes, sir; but it's now't to when the dancing bear was here yesterday."

Better late than ——.—When the Rev. Dr. —— obtained the honorary degree of Doctor of Divinity, a farmer in the parish took an early opportunity of stating the news to his shepherd, with whom the minister was a particular favourite. "You'll be glad tae hear, John, that the University has conferred on oor minister a doctor's degree." "Weel," said the shepherd, "I'm no the least surprised at that, for mair than twenty years since he cured a dog o' mine o' a colic."

Considerate.—Curate: "And how did you like my harvest sermon, Mr. Wurzel?"

Mr. W.: "Not bad, sir! not bad at all, considerin' yer total hignorance of the subject."

Degrees of affinity.—A new curate at a village in Dorset met a farmer's boy while going his rounds, and in the course of conversation the boy said his parents had an aunt living with them.

The parson, not understanding the boy clearly, asked :

" Then do I understand that your aunt is on your father's side or on your mother's ? "

" Well, zumtimes one and zumtimes t'other, 'cepting when feyther whacks 'em both."

The gamekeeper and the parson.—Rector (on his way to church, meeting a gamekeeper) : " Come, my good fellow, how is it I never see you at church ? "

Keeper : " Well, sir, I don't wish to make your congregation smaller."

Rector : " I don't see how you could."

Keeper : " Well, sir ; you see if I came to church, some of the others would go poaching."

A sporting offer.—There has just died in Sydney the widow of Canon Smith, who, while incumbent of St. Barnabas', solicited Sir Hercules Robinson for a contribution to the rebuilding fund, then lagging dolefully.

" Look here," replied Sir Hercules, " I've backed the double event at Randwick to win me a pretty big stake ; if it comes off I'll give you five per cent. of the pot for your church, and God bless you ! "

" Amen ! " cried the Canon devoutly, and—sure enough, up they rolled !

In a country church.—The vicar of a country church who had for some time been much troubled by members of the congregation coming into church very late—indeed, only just in time to hear the sermon—was determined to put a stop to the practice.

One Sunday morning, when giving out the text of his sermon, he noticed a farm labourer entering the church. Pausing after giving out his text, and hoping to shame the late-comer, he called out from the pulpit :—

" Mr. Churchwarden, will you please find the gentleman who has just come in a comfortable seat ? "

Farm Labourer : " Thank yer kindly, parson, and would yer kindly gi' us the text again ? I didna quite catch it."

His last end.—" ' And his last end is worse than his first,' " quoted the Sunday-school teacher. " What does this refer to, children ? "

" A hornet," said the freckled boy, who had just joined the class.

They went fishing.—Bishop

Beckwith, of Georgia, was fond of sport, and one day was out with a dog and gun and met a member of his parish, whom he reproved for inattention to his religious duties.

"You should attend church and read your Bible."

"I do read my Bible, bishop, and I don't find any mention of the apostles going a-shooting."

"No, the shooting was very bad in Palestine, so they went fishing!"

Wants stopping up.—The congregation had suffered much discomfort from a draught in church. The matter came up for discussion at the vestry meeting, when various remedies were suggested. After much talking the vicar spoke to an elderly parishioner, who had hitherto been silent, and he replied:—

"Well, sir, bein' as you've appealed to me, I can only say that agen you're 'alf-way thro' t' sermon we begins to feel like as tho' theer's a deal o' waste wind about."

"Possibly our friend finds my discourses to be of a breezy character."

"Dear, dear, no, sir! My meanin's this. When we've bin perched i' one spot for well-nigh fifty minit a-list'nin' to yer, we're more'n ever persuaded theer's a 'ole someweer wants stopping up!"

The bishop's choice.—The late Bishop of London was once ordered by his physician to spend the winter in Algiers. The bishop said it was impossible; he had so many engagements. "Well, my lord bishop," said the specialist, "it means either Algiers or heaven."

"Oh, in that case," said the bishop, "I'll go—to Algiers."

It's the ither.—An old Scottish farmer who had led an intemperate life lay on his deathbed. The parish minister was called in. "I am very pleased to observe that you are afraid to meet your Maker," said the clergyman as he noticed the anxious look on the face of the dying sinner.

"Na, na," said the old man, "it's no Him I'm feered for, it's the ither birkie."

The gadarene swine.—A story is told of Dean Burgon, when Vicar of St. Mary's, Oxford. He was preaching one Sunday evening on the swine possessed with the devils, and had been rather long in his discourse, so, after saying, "They all ran violently down a steep place into the sea," he glanced at his watch and added, hastily, "And there we must leave them until next Sunday evening!"

A change o' pasture.—A minister met a Scotch farmer from a neighbouring parish, and mentioned that he was to preach in his parish church next Sunday, as he had arranged an exchange with his minister. "A'm glad o' that," said the farmer. "Sheep aye like a change o' pasture, whether it's tae better or tae waur. Oor grass is gae bare enoo, and it's seldom gude at ony time."

At the wrang end.—John Clark, farmer, of Hightown, was an attender at the kirk, though he had a poor opinion of the minister's preaching. Ere long he met him at a party, and the farmer made up his mind that though a poor preacher, he was a very good dancer. A friend meeting the farmer at a fair said to him, "Hightown, how is the new minister getting on? What kind of a man is he?"

"Ah weel, he's a rael nice, free man, but tae tell ye the truth, a' think he's clever at the wrang end."

His conscience betrayed him.—In the life of R. S. Hawker, the famous vicar of Morenstow, Mr. Byles relates the following: One day a labourer at Tamerton came to Hawker in trouble, saying that a sack of potatoes had been stolen from his garden and would his reverence kindly help him to discover the thief. "Well, well," said Hawker. "we will see about it after church." He was taking the sermon that day, and he preached on the eighth Commandment. "And now," he said, "I have a sad tale to tell. One of our neighbours has missed a sack of potatoes from his garden, and the thief is even now sitting among you. He has a feather on his head!"

A man in the congregation was observed to put his hand to his head, and so the guilt was brought home.

Not such a fool.—A late bishop, during his annual confirmation visit to a country church, was surprised and annoyed to find one-half of the churchyard under a seemingly flourishing crop of potatoes. Upon coming out of the church after the confirmation ceremony was over, he turned to the clergyman and said: "Mr. Vicar, I see that you have potatoes planted in God's acre." "Yes, my lord," replied the vicar, "and an excellent crop I expect, too." "Well, sir," rejoined the bishop, "I trust that when I come here next year I shall not find a crop of potatoes in the churchyard, sir." "Oh, no, my lord, I hope I am not such a fool as that. I propose to rotate the crops—cabbages next year, my lord.'"

A Bishop on strong language. — A colonial visitor once called upon the late Archbishop Magee and used very strong language in the course of conversation about some theological questions. The Bishop remonstrated.

"Well, my lord," said the visitor, "you must excuse me; I am a plain man, and call a spade a spade."

"Oh," said the Bishop, "I'm surprised and pleased to hear that. I should have thought from what I have heard you say that you would call it a blooming shovel."

The minister's horse.—Many stories are told of the wit of Dr. Mason, once pastor of the Scotch Presbyterian Church in New York. He was a great preacher, but many of his most telling lessons were given in private rather than in the pulpit. He had a great fondness for horses, of whose good points he was said to be a judge. On one occasion a brother minister met Mason and stopped to ask his opinion of the animal which he was then driving. Dr. Mason surveyed the horse carefully, and finally pointing to the animal's knees, which were bent, said, "That is a good sign for a minister, but it is a very bad sign for a minister's horse."

Lay membership.—The Americans are an inventive people. Mr. Herman, a layman, has organised the chickens in the neighbourhood of a Wesleyan Methodist Church into a missionary society to raise funds to aid the church. Each hen is a lay member, so to speak. The farmers of the neighbourhood have agreed to give to the church the eggs that their hens lay on Sunday. Mr. Herman will stamp each egg with the date on which it was laid. He has agreed to realise one penny on each egg, no matter what may be the market price.

Commontaters. — A country clergyman one day received a visit from one of his parishoners, who had a large sack on his back. "Good morning, Giles," said the Vicar. "What can I do for you?" "Plaze, zur," said Giles, "in your sarmon last Zunday you said the commontaters didn't agree with you, an' zooa I brought 'ee zum o' my very best kidneys!"

"Give him a pony."—A popular sportsman in Nottinghamshire lay ill recently. While he was so confined the curate of the parish called upon the wife, and said, "I have come to ask if Mr. N. will give us a contribution to our fund for the deserving poor?" Mrs. N. proceeded upstairs to her invalid husband—a most kindly-hearted man—and informed him of the curate's mission. "Oh, give him a pony," said the weary sufferer. Downstairs goes Mrs. N., and reported the answer. "But, my dear madam," said the curate, "we have no use for a pony; it would only be an incubus!" Upstairs again went the good lady, and repeated the remarks of the curate. The sufferer raised his head. "What! Is he as green as that? Then give him only a fiver!"

That is the system.—There was a good deal of the Sir George Boyle Roche about Major O'Gorman. It was always doubtful whether his "bulls" were not deliberate, and whether he was not laughing in his sleeve at the House of Commons which thought itself laughing at him. One night in the course of a speech he referred to the old tithe system in Ireland, by which one-tenth of the produce of the holding of the Catholic peasant went to support the Established Church. "The poor man," said the Major, "was robbed by that accursed tithe system of fully one-tenth of his hard earnings—nay, he was sometimes deprived of as much as one-twentieth."

The pulpit was occupied.—A curate went to preach in a very quiet Warwickshire village, where a strange parson was unusual. He was met by the verger, who anxiously asked him if he would preach from the chancel.

Curate: "Why, my good man?"

Verger: "Well, yer reverence, it's like this. I 'ave a duck in the pulpit sitting on fourteen eggs."

The miraculous.—A story is told of the well-known Irish priest, Father Tom Maguire. A farmer, it seems, once asked his Reverence what a miracle was. "Well," replied Father Maguire, "walk on before me and I'll see what I can do for you." The farmer complied, and as he did so the priest gave him a well-aimed kick that made him howl with pain. "Did you feel that?" inquired his Reverence. "Begorrah, I felt it sure enough." "Well," Father

Maguire replied, "it would be a miracle if you didn't,"

The smoked hams of Bayonne are the most delicious in France. The bishop of that city being on a visit to Paris, called on the great wit of the time, Piron. The wag with his habitual gaiety, said to the prelate in greeting him :—

"My lord, I have a great veneration for the hams of your diocese."

A pessimist.—The incumbent of a country vicarage had long a thorn in his side in the shape of a crusty old farmer, who delighted in opposing the vicar in every way. The parson, having been offered another living, accepted it, and, taking leave of the parish he called upon the farmer, when he was touched by the man's evident regret. "Why, I thought you would be glad to get rid of me!" exclaimed the vicar. The farmer shook his head solemnly. "Well," he said, "you see, sir, I've lived here for nigh on forty years, and my experience of our parsons is that there's never a bad 'un goes but a wuss 'un comes."

Worse than all.—"What keeps our friend Farmer Brown from Church?" said a clergyman. "I hope it is not agnosticism."

"No," said the sexton; "it's worse than that."

"Worse than agnosticism? Is it deism?"

"Worse than that, your honour."

"Worse than deism? I trust it is not atheism?"

"It is worse than that, sir; it is rheumatism."

A whale's different.—A coloured preacher took some candidates for immersion down to a river in Louisiana. Seeing alligators in the stream, one of them objected.

"Why, brother," said the pastor, "can't you trust the Lord? He took care of Jonah, didn't he?"

"Y-a-a-s, but a whale's diff'rent. A whale's got a memory, but ef one o' dem 'gators wus ter swaller dis nigger, he'd jes' go ter sleep dar in de sun an'fergit all 'bout me."

His choice.—The celebrated Archbishop Whately, keen wit as he was, once met his match in an Irish jarvey. As they were driving along the Archbishop asked him :—

"Paddy, if the devil had his choice between you and me at the present moment, which of us do you think he would take?"

"Me, to be sure, my lord."

"Why so?"

"Because it would be his only chance with me; as for your grace, he's sure of getting you any time."

His belief.—An Englishman touring in Ireland wished to discover the religion of his Irish guide, and inquired: "Paddy, what's your belief?"

"Wisha, then, your honour," Paddy replied. "I'm of my landlady's belief."

"What's that, Paddy?"

"Sure, and I'll tell you. I owe her five half-years' rent. She believes that I'll never pay her, and that's my belief, too."

That he would.—A tract distributor, the other day, in a new settlement out west, popped his head into an Irishman's cabin and asked him "if he would accept a tract on the Holy Land?"

"Yes, bejabers, I'll take a houl section, if ye'll pay my passage."

His pickings. — Captain Spencer, senior prison missioner of the Church Army, tells a story of a certain convict's philosophic view of his existence. "Well, my man," asked Captain Spencer, "what do you do when you are out of prison?"

"Well," said the convict, "in spring I does a bit of pea-picking, and in the summer time I does a bit of fruit-picking, and in the autumn I does a bit of hop-picking."

"Oh!" said the captain; what happens after that?"

"Well, now, mister," replied the convict, "I may as well be honest, and tell you that in the winter time I does a bit of pocket-picking."

The missioner, in amazement, asked finally, "And what happens then?"

The convict answered laconically: "Why, here I am doing a bit of oakum-picking."

About his soul.—One day, in a western town of the United States, a farmer of the neighbourhood called on the parson, and was told by his daughter, ten years old, "Papa, I am sorry, is not at home; but if it's about your soul you have come, come into the study and I'll talk to you."

Lay members.—"I know what the preacher meant when he spoke of the lay members this morning," remarked little Fred on his way home from Church.

"What did he mean, dear?" said his mother.

"He meant chickens," answered Fred. "I heard him tell papa the other day that there was a lot of gossiping old hens in his congregation."

The jumble sale.—The other day a certain East-End clergyman, carrying his overcoat, met one of his parishioners. The day was pretty warm.

"You hardly want your overcoat to-day, sir," said the parishoner.

"I know," was the vicar's reply; but my wife is interested in a jumble sale, and when I carry my clothes about with me I know where they are."

A good shepherd.—Not very long ago the Bishop of Truro, accompanied by his wife, was strolling along one of the country lanes in his diocese.

Suddenly there appeared a drove of runaway bullocks, followed by a gesticulating countryman.

When the latter saw the bishop, he shouted to him to head off the fugitives. Always good-natured, his lordship did not hesitate for a moment, but waved his hat, and succeeded in turning the cattle.

When he came up to the farmer, the latter was much embarrassed at discovering the bishop's identity.

"I'm very sorry——" he began.

"Well," said the bishop, "I'm supposed to be a shepherd of sheep, you know, not of bullocks."

"Then," replied the farmer, "I'm happy to be one of the sheep."

Painfully frank.—In preaching funeral sermons, clergymen often have a hard course to steer, but here is an instance where it was all plain sailing. A minister, who flourished in a rural district in the West of England a good many years ago, was strictly honest, but a painfully frank old man. One day he was approached by one of his flock, a man of doubtful reputation, who said:

"Look'ee here, pazzon! I want to make a request of 'ee, an' 'tis this: I want 'ee to promise you'll preach my funeral sermon, if so be you outlive me."

"Why, certainly, Bill— certainly."

"An' I want 'ee to preach it from the words, 'An honest man is the noblest work of God.'"

"I'll do it, Bill—I'll do it for you with pleasure," replied the parson. "And I'll add that I'm sorry there's such a very poor specimen in the coffin."

CHAPTER XXII.

LOVE AND MATRIMONY.

In the North country.—" I hear, John, that you are lately married," said a north-country young lady to a farmer. " Who is your wife ? "

" Well, miss, I don't quite know."

" How so ? Where did you meet her ? "

" Aweel, ye see, miss, I went to the market, and as I was going I seed a canny lass walking along the road, and I says, ' Will you come into my cart, and I'll take you home ? ' ' Ay,' she says, and up she came. ' Are you going to the market ? ' ' Ay,' says she. ' What for ? ' says I. ' To get a place,' says she. So I set her down in the market and left her ; and as I came back in the evening the lass was again walking up the hill. Again I spoke to her, and asked her, 'Have you gotten your place ? ' ' Nay,' she says, ' I haven't.' ' Will you come into my cart ? ' ' Ay,' says she. So she got up again, and I asked her, ' D'ye think my place would suit you ? ' ' What place is that ? ' said she. ' Why, to be my wife,' says I. ' I don't mind,' says she. So we got wed, and she's a rare good wife.

Fortune out of weeds.—Mabel : " There's Mr. Stubbs. He's the only farmer on record who has made his money out of weeds."

George : " He surely didn't do that ? "

Mabel : " Yes, he did."

George : " How, pray ? "

Mabel : " Married a widow."

In 1915.—If slang continues in its career the following dialogue will be a fair sample of love-making about the year 1915 :—

He : " Say, you're a peach ; you're the whole orchard, and there's not a caterpillar on you."

She : " There's one not far away from me, though ! "

He : " Oh, I'm not in my serious clothes. Say, I've a hunch that I could make you as happy as a rat in a cheese. Are you on ? "

She : " I'm on the fence."

He : " Well, that's better than not being within a mile of the game. Can you see me at all ? "

She : " Can't help it. You're plainer than a blood-and-thunder advertising poster."

He : " Let's quit sparring for wind. Let's clinch. Why can't we go as a team ? "

She: "Nit! We don't match."

You mustn't.—She lived in the country, and he from the town for the summer fell in love with her. But her heart was in the keeping of a neighbouring farmer's son, and she could not return his affection. She told him so that night on her father's porch, where the honeysuckles hung low in the moonlight.

"If you do not marry me," he whispered, "I'll drown myself."

"Oh, don't," she said, for her heart was tender, though another's. "You mustn't," laying her soft, white hand on his arm; "There's no place wet enough except our well, and, oh! what shall we do for our tea water if you jump in there? I was never struck with your appearance, and how much worse you would look coming out of the well!"

Nothin' easier in life.—A small farmer went into a bank in Limerick, when the following conversation took place between him and the manager:

"Good mornin' yer honner: I called about a little business, and though there's other banks in the town I thought I'd give yer honner the compliment."

"Well, Tom, I'm glad to see you; and what's the business?"

"I hear the interest in Widow Brady's farm is to be sould soon, yer honner; and I want to 'rise' five hundhred poun' to buy it."

"Nonsense, Tom, how could you ever pay the money back, if I lent it to you?"

"Oh, there's nothin' asier in life. Shure me young Jim 'ud get it in a fortin when he marries."

"And may I ask, Tom, what age is the young fellow?"

"He's just three year ould, yer honner!"

A grass widow.—Two children were playing on the side-walk, and a lady passed them. "She's a grass widow," remarked one.

"What's a grass widow?" asked the other.

"Gracious! Don't you know that?" the first replied scornfully. "Why, her husband died of hay fever."

Scarce complimentary.—One day, a few years ago, Mr. O'Brien, a land agent in the West of Ireland, met a countryman, and, having heard of his marriage, saluted him with, "Well, Pat, so you have taken to yourself a wife?"

"Yis, yer honour, I have."

"Well, here am I, and I can get no one to take me, and I feel lonely sometimes."

"I think I can put yer honour in the way."

"How, Pat?"

"Do as I did; go where you are not known."

The argument. — An Irish workman had leave to attend a wedding. He turned up the next day with his arm in a sling and a black eye.

Master: "Hallo! what is the matter?"

Man: "Well, sir, I saw a fellow swaggering about with a swallow-tailed coat and a white waistcoat. 'And who might you be?' sez I. 'I'm the best man,' sez he; so one word led to another, and we tried to settle the argument. He was not a bad man aither—he left his mark on me!"

Sowed in haste.—Visitor (to Irish farmer going to races): "Ever thought of marrying?"

"No; I married first. Sowed my crops too early."

The new woman.—"What does this here 'New Woman' talk mean, John?"

"It means, Maria," replied the old farmer, "that women be a-takin' men's places. You'll find the plough where I left it; an' when you sharpen the axe you can go on cutting up that cord wood in the yard, and I'll have supper ready when you get home."

They wilt.—"Which weeds are the easiest to kill?" asked young Flickers of Farmer Sassfras, as he watched that good man at his work. "Widows' weeds," replied the farmer. "You have only to say 'Wilt thou,' and they wilt."

They reconsidered the matter.—Sometimes the Irish co-operative banks have odd applications for loans. It is understood, of course, that loans are only given for a good use, such as for buying a pig, or seeds or manure or farm implements. One evening a young man came before the committee of a bank in the county Mayo, and asked for a loan of £2. He was asked why he required it, and said that it was to buy a suit of clothes. The committee demurred at first that they had no money to lend for this purpose. "Well, the case is this. I'm fond of Nora Carty, and she has a noice little farm as well. Now, I'd have twice as good a chance with her if I had a decent suit of clothes to my back instead of these rags."

The committee reconsidered the matter, advanced the money, and the boy won Nora Carty and her farm.

Girls in Papua, or New Guinea, have poor chance to elope. Their dads force them to sleep in a little fibre-built house on the topmost branches of a tall tree; then the ladder is taken away, and the old man and woman can take it easy.

Never idle.—"Did you marry an industrious, hard-working man?" said her old friend.

"Yes, indeed," said the girl with the picture hat; "Harold is never idle. He plays golf all summer and cards all winter."

The very ground.—She: "He declares he loves the very ground I tread on."

He: "Ah! I thought he had his eyes on the estate."

Matrimony and purgatory.—An Irish priest while catechising a class of girls, with a view to confirmation, asked, "What is matrimony?" on which one of the girls, mixing it up with another thing, replied "A state of punishment in which men are placed for a time to fit them for a better life." His curate said, "Put her down to the bottom of the class"; but the priest with a twinkle in his eye, said:

"Lave her where she is; for aught you or I know she may be right afther all."

Attractivity.—Professor Smith was once lecturing on natural philosophy, and in the course of his experiments he introduced a good powerful magnet, with which he attracted a block of iron from a distance of 2 ft.

"Can any of you conceive a greater attractive power?" asked the lecturer.

"I can," answered a voice from the audience.

"Not a natural object?"

"Yes, indeed. When I was a young man there was a little piece of natural magnet done up in a neat cotton dress as was called Betsy Maria. She could draw me 10 miles on Sunday over ploughed land and pasture in any weather. That magnet o' yourn is pretty good, but it won't draw so far as Betsy Maria!"

Not so much profit.—The Laird: "You are a lucky man, Andrew. I hear you are going to be married again."

Andrew: "Aye, I'm thinkin' aboot it."

The Laird: "And the lady has a bit of money, hasn't she?"

Andrew: "Aye, she has a pickle."

The Laird: "And so had your first and second. You've been fortunate, eh?"

Andrew: "Weel, a wee bit, but no' that much. Ye see,

what wi' the expense o' gettin' them into the hoose, an' the expense o' gettin' them out o' the hoose, there's no' much profit left in it."

Roses all the way.—In his parish magazine a vicar of a well-known church in the south of England says: "Perhaps some of you noticed the singularity in the last banns of marriage published in our church namely, between Charles Rose and Rose Charles, the bride lost her surname Charles, but married a Charles Rose, and so became not only Rose Rose, but also Mrs. Charles Rose, instead of Miss Rose Charles.

Working for nothing.—Mrs. Mann (meeting former servant): "Ah, Mary, I suppose you are getting better wages at your new place?"

Mary: "No, ma'am, I'm working for nothing now—I'm married."

The unvarnished truth.—A Kansas editor tried the experiment of telling the rural unvarnished truth in his journal for one week. He didn't get beyond the first day. This item appeared on Monday: "Married—Miss Sylvia Rhode to James Carnahan, last Sunday evening at the Baptist Church. The bride was a very ordinary girl, who doesn't know any more than a rabbit about cooking and never helped her mother three days in her life. She is not a beauty by any means, and has a gait like a fat duck. The bridegroom is an up-to-date loafer, has been living off the old folks all his life, and don't amount to shucks, nohow. They will have a hard life while they live together." The editor is still in the hospital.

A queer fee.—A Southern State minister tells this:—"One of the queerest fees I ever received was from a young negro for whom I performed the wedding ceremony at my own home. At its close, and just as the party of five or six were leaving, the bridegroom said:—

"'Yo' will find de fee for yo' kindness out in a co'nah ob de porch, sah.' I followed the party out to the porch, and when they had gone I looked in a corner, where I found a pair of fine fowls tied together by the legs. They set up a lusty squawk as I picked them up. The bridegroom had said, as he went down the steps, that they were ob his own raisin',' but I never felt quite sure of that."

The last message.—Two men were crossing a field in which a bull was grazing. As they advanced, the bull drew himself together and came to them. One man made for the nearest fence. The other saw no way of escape, as the brute came for him pell-mell. Twice round that field they went like mad. The third time round he shouted to his mate: "Give my best love to Bridget. This is the last time round!"

Jilted.—Harry: "She has jilted me, and I know I shall die. The disappointment will kill me!"

Aunt Hannah: "I know how disappointments affect one, Harry. But you will get over it. I felt just as you do now when I set that yeller hen on 13 eggs and only just got one poor chick out of the lot."

In a Yorkshire County Court, recently, a buxom farm lass was called as a witness in a case where there was a dispute as to the ownership of a cow. The girl happened to mention that her sweetheart knew something about the matter. "Oh," said the County Court judge, "then we had better call him into Court." The girl blushed furiously. "It wean't be any good, sir." she protested. "Ah'm fair put to it to get him to coort when we're alone, an' A'hm sure he won't do it before all you gentlemen."

What God has Joined.—Dr. Carmichael, the new Bishop of Montreal, an Irishman, tells a story about a clergyman who was examining a Sunday-school class, and who chanced to ask one of his small pupils why it was cruel to cut off dogs' tails. One child replied that it was cruel because of the text in the Bible. "What text, my dear?" asked the puzzled clergyman. The child replied: "What God has joined together let no man put asunder."

Ill-cooked joints. — Sydney Smith once wrote that "frequently it is that those persons whom God hath joined together in matrimony, ill-cooked joints and badly-boiled potatoes have put asunder."

The cold shoulder.—There is a maiden named Dorothy, whose father came to her one evening and said:—

"Look here, Dorothy, I don't like young Barnes coming here so much. Next time he comes just give him the cold shoulder."

"But, papa, he is a vegetarian."

Love Lane.—A short time ago a young couple on holiday in a Welsh town walked out towards the country. Eager for information as to their whereabouts, the lady accosted a farm labourer.

"What road is this ?"

"It is not a road. It is Love Lane."

"Where does it lead to ?" she asked.

To her utter confusion and that of her companion, he answered seriously—"To the asylum."

Maiden Simplicity. — Young William Evergreen and Maria Knewsome were walking along a lonely country road near Kildare one fine evening. William was carrying a large tub on his head and a live pig in a sack on his back, when suddenly Maria exclaimed :—

"Oi be afear'd Bill ! Oi be fear'd !"

"What be'st fear'd on, great stoopud, w'en Oi be 'long wid 'ee," was Bill's reassuring response.

"Oi be fear'd you'll get a-kissin' an' a-coortin' o' me, Oi be !" replied the tremulous maiden.

"'Ow can Oi git a-kissin' an' a-coortin' o' ye w'en Oi 'a got this great tub on me 'ead an' a pig on me back ?" reasoned William.

With true maiden simplicity Maria replied : "C'u—c'u'dn't you put that pig on the groun an' turn that tub atop on 'im, and set down on't, an' pull me 'side of ye, if ye was amind to 't, eh ?"

The leg up.—Arry and Araminta strolled lovingly adown the green and perfumed meadow, prating playfully of love.

In the course of their perambulations they chanced upon a bull — a skittish bull ; for his head lowered coquettishly, charmingly he pawed the ground, and then —

"Oh !" cried Araminta to her valiant swain, "he's making straight towards us ! What shall we do ?"

"Here," roared the resourceful gentleman, "don't stand there doing nothing ! Come and help me climb this tree !"

CHAPTER XXIII.

MOTORING AND CYCLING.

Cyclists will oblige.—At the bottom of a steep and dangerous hill is a small cottage garden, cut off from the road by a ditch and a low stone wall.

On many occasions the owner of the garden has been heard to complain of the conduct of "them there cycling fellows, a-coming tearing doon the hill an' a-knockin' ma wall aboot!"

Of late he has found one or two injured wheelmen in the garden itself, despite the notice on the board to the effect that trespassers would be prosecuted.

Quite recently he took this board down and replaced it with the following—which can easily be read from the road:—

"Notice! This plot is for cabbiges. Cyclists will oblige by stopping in the ditch!"

He wondered.—A somewhat hasty and generous motorist, driving at rather more than regulation speed in a West Derby lane, overtook a man and a dog. The man jumped to one side; the dog was killed. Instantly the motorist stopped, leapt from his car, pressed three sovereigns into the man's hand, and fled. The man gazed at him, and then at the money.

"He is very kind," he said softly to himself; "but I wonder who owned the dog?"

At a meeting of the Westbury District Council, the chairman made the important statement that "Dust raised by motor-cars killed the flies on the turnips." Perhaps this will encourage the motorists to persevere.

He was lying on a bit of grass at the cross-roads. A motorist stopped and asked the way. The man jerked the toe of a boot in the proper direction.

"If you can do a lazier thing than that, I'll give you a shilling."

The man inclined his head towards his left-hand trouser pocket. "Put it there," he murmured.

Bicycle or cow.—Even the latest inventions cannot do away with all time-honoured methods. A farmer of the old school made this very plain the other day. His wife wanted some tacks, and he went into the village ironmonger's to buy a package. The shopkeeper thought he saw an opportunity. "I'll tell you what you want," said he. "You want a bicycle to ride round your farm on. It'll save you time and money. They're cheap now, dirt cheap at £10." The farmer scratched his chin. "I'd rather put the money into a cow," he said "But think," replied the shopkeeper jocosely; "think how foolish you'd look riding round town on a cow." "Well," said the farmer, "I don't know. Perhaps I shouldn't look so much more foolish than I should milkin' a bicycle!"

Bysickles repared.—Under the spreading chestnut tree, the village smithy stands; but there the smith no longer wields the sledge with sinewy hands. The olden sign of "Blacksmith's Shop" there greets the eye no more; but "Bysickles repaired" is seen above the smoky door.

Right for the Zoo.—Dressed in the latest motor-cycling costume with goggles all complete, the motor cyclist gaily toot-tooted his way by Regent's Park towards the Zoo.

Suddenly he dismounted, and said to an urchin: "I say, my boy, am I right for the Zoo?"

"You may be all right if they have a spare cage, but you'd ha' stood a far better chance if you'd 'ad a tail!"

Troubles enough. — "Why don't you get an automobile?"

"My dear sir, I don't need it. I have three life insurance policies and several boils on my neck, my wife's a nag, my barley crop has failed—so I have troubles enough already."

Mr. Dooley on Automobiles.—"Mr. Dooley," in his "Dissertations," has a few words on automobiles: "Do I think th' autymobill has come to stay? Sure I'll niver tell ye. I've seen all th' wurrld but me on roller skates. I've seen ivrybody ridin' a bicycle but me. Tin years ago, whin ye'er son was holdin' on to ye'er ar-rms as ye reeled up th' sthreet on a wheel, sayin' ye're prayers wan minyit an' th' revarse another, ye tol me that th' bicycle had come to stay because it was nicissry to get round quick. To-day ye blush as I mention it. Th' autymobill will stay till it gets cheap enough fr ivrybody to have wan. Whin th' little, eager messenger-boys is dashin' up th' sthreet in a eighty-horse power Demon Terror th' rich will be flyin' kites or runnin' baloons, an' ther'll be a parachute foorce iv polismen chase thim acrost th' skies."

Might have been worse.—A London music-hall manager was doing a spin on his bicycle, and on his way to Twickenham he ran into a man who was carrying a sack of potatoes. The man went one way, the tubers another, but both were unhurt. The manager congratulated him on his escape, and gave him half-a-crown as a solatium. "It might have been wus," said the man, picking up the contents of the bag, "if they had been heggs; but, thank the Lord, taters don't burst."

Wont carry cider.—Farmer: "Well, George, I haven't seen you on that there bicycle as you bought lately."

George: "No, farmer. He bean't no good to I. He can't find his way home, an' he won't carry cider!"

Outclassed.—Two skunks were sitting in a fence corner discussing the subject of smell when a gasoline automobile went by One looked at the other and said "O! Moses! what's the use of all our efforts?"

Thinks ye're another ass.—Coster (to motorist, who is sounding an alarm): "If yer stop tootin' that bloomin' 'orn I'll get 'im to go on directly; but while ye're makin' that noise, 'e thinks ye're another ass, and 'e'll see you blowed before 'e'll be dickertated to by you!"

The quick and the dead.—"Now, Johnnie," said the Sunday-school teacher, "can you tell me the difference between the quick and the dead?"

"Yes, miss," said the young hopeful, "the quick is them as gets out of the way of motor-cars, and the dead is them as doesn't."

A motor won't do.—"There's nothing a motor won't do," said the pushing agent.

"I know there is," said the farmer. "When I come home from market on Fridays I can drop the reins on the old mare's neck and she'll take me home safely. Now a motor——"

The agent left.

Won't jump.—Rustic (to motorist who has charged the hedge): "It's no good sir. They things won't jump!"

A garage.—Casey: "Phwat's a garage?"

Reilly: "Sure, it's wan o' thim horseless livery stables."

The regulation speed.—As a ploughman was about to cycle through a certain village another man on a motor bicycle drew up. "What's the meanin' o' a' they notices stuck ootside the toons noo?" queried the ploughman. "That," replied the motorist, "means you've got to pass through the village at ten miles per hour."

"Ten miles i' the hour!" ejaculated the ploughman. "Its easy enough for you motor chaps to do that, but hoo the dickens do they think I can keep it up on this auld bone-shaker o' mine?"

Other times, other ways.—Old coachman (exercising superseded carriage horses): "Well, all I can say is, when the ladies went out with me, they used to take a pride in makin' themselves look nice; but when they goes out in that bloomin' thing, they looks like patients out of one of them eye and ear hospitals!"

The speed limit.—Irate motorist (finding himself obstructed in a narrow country lane): "Now, then, Turniptops, wake up! I don't want to be stuck here all day!"

Countryman: "Aw doan't see what tha' 'es to grummle abaht. Awm goin' as fast as thee!"

In doubt.—Cy.: "I say, neighbour, does your horse git skeeren at these here automobeels?"

Neighbour: "Weel, he do git mighty narvous when them things come along; but one p'int I an't sartin on—whether it's the machine thet skeers him, or them fellers with goggles on what's in it."

Equal to the emergency.—Old Colonel MacWhizzeeo's friends, when they see his crimson visage flashing past in a cloud of dust and a motor-car, wonder why he is never fined for driving at an excessive speed. "Presence of mind, my boy," the Colonel will say, with a wink, "Be equal to any emergency, and, like me, you'll never be summoned, let alone be fined."

One of the Colonel's friends was fortunate enough one day to be with him in the car and witness his presence of mind and capability of coping with an emergency.

The Colonel ran over a farmer's dog and killed it. Before the farmer could roar "Stop!" the Colonel had pulled up his car and had seized the farmer by the collar, thundering, "Your name and address, scoundrel!"

"My name and address!" gasped the indignant farmer. "What for?"

"For aiding and abetting your dog in an attempt to wreck my car by creeping under the wheels!" roared the colonel.

And jotting down a few

meaningless hieroglyphics, he resumed his reckless journey.

How they settle it.—" One summer morning," said a motorist who was recounting some of his adventures, " the approach of a great flock of sheep obliged me to pull off the narrow country road. I halted my car, and watched with interest the passage of the sheep, the intelligent dogs, and the shepherd. I had a short talk with the shepherd about his odd and difficult trade.

" ' Look here," I said, ' what do you do, driving sheep like this on a narrow road, when you meet another flock coming the opposite direction ? ' "

" ' Well,' said the shepherd, ' ye just drive straight on, both of ye, and the one that has the best dogs gets the most sheep.' "

Sensitive.—A Dublin jarvey, who had just affixed his horse's nosebag, turned to the driver of a broken-down motor 'bus close by and shouted out: " Now, then, be aff wid yer ould oilbox, sure the shmell of it spoils my 'orse's dinner."

We are often asked whether poultry-farming can be made to pay, and a correspondent now tells us that since he has trained his chickens to run into the roadway at the sound of a motor-horn, he has managed to get such good compensation prices from motorists that he has been able to buy a pianola on the instalment plan.

An unfortunate.—Well, my man, and what are you begging for ? "

" I 'ates to arsk yer for charity, sir, but I'm one of them unfortunit persons wot 'as bin ruined by motorin'."

But he knew.—The guide was showing the visitors round the slaughter-houses.

" Now," said the guide, " of course you don't know anything about cutting up pigs."

" Don't I ? " chuckled the chauffeur. " Maybe you never saw me going down a rural road at fifty miles an hour."

When is a pig.—Passer-by: " Is that your pork down there on the road, guv'nor ? "

Farmer: " Pork ! What dy'e mean ? There's a pig o' mine out there."

Passer-by: " Ah, but there's a motor-car just been by.'"

CHAPTER XXIV.

GOLFING.

The dog was mad.—"I say," drawled an individual who was showily dressed in golf costume, and whose legs appeared to be such as could hardly be expected to support an average barndoor fowl, "your dog has bitten me; is he all right?"

"What do you mean by 'all right?'" inquired the person addressed, behind whom an artful-looking terrier had taken refuge.

"I mean, is he—er—mad?"

"Well, I'm a bit unsartin about 'im now. Did you say 'e bit you?"

"Yes; in the calf of my leg."

"Then he's mad, you may depend upon it; for dogs that are sane don't go round bitin' broom-handles and golf-sticks, and sech like!"

Improvement. — Cyclist: "Hallo, Bertie! Whatever are you doing in this out-of-the-world place? Aw—you seem busy."

Bertie: "Oh, didn't you hear that my pater apprenticed me to farming? I am very busy. You see, this piece of moorland up here was no good before I came, but with a lot of work, I've turned it now into very good golf links."

An enthusiast.—As an illustration of the enthusiasm with which golf is pursued the follow ing anecdote is told of a well-known Scotch author and a young friend of his. The two had spent the whole day on the links, and had had some close and exciting matches. As they left for home the elder man remarked —

"Do you think ye could play to-morrow, laddie?"

"Well," answered the youth. "I was to be married to-morrow; but I can put it off!"

CHAPTER XXV.

FISHING.

No liar.—Simpson (to fishmonger): "Just throw me half a dozen of those trout."

Fishmonger: "Throw them?"

Simpson: "Yes, then I can go home and tell my wife I caught 'em. I may be a poor fisherman, but I'm no liar."

Out of harm's way.—"Father," said Farmer Jones' boy, insinuatingly, as he leaned on his hoe, "Tommy Perkins says the fish are bitin' very freely up the brook to-day."

"Well, you tell him if he'll come over here an' help you with yer hoein'——"

"Yes?"

"They won't git a chance to bite him."

Cruel sport.—Benevolent Old Gentleman: "Don't you think fishing a cruel sport?"

Fisherman: "I should just think it was. I've been sitting here five hours and never had a single bite, and I've got three wasp stings, and been eaten up with flies, and the sun's taken all the skin off the back of my neck!"

A day's fishing.—They had been out fishing all day, and when they had left their boat and had gone up to the hotel a curious looker-on saw the old boatman counting some things that lay in the boat.

"Many fish?"

"No. Many empty bottles!"

Not in his line.—Vicar: "Well, gentlemen, what can I do for you?"

Spokesman: "Please, sir, we be a deputation from farmers down Froglands Parish, to ask you to pray for fine weather for t' harvest."

Vicar: "Why don't you ask your own vicar?"

Spokesman: "Well, sir, we reckon 'e be'unt much good for this 'ere. 'E do be that fond of fishin'."

The patient angler. — "A friend of mine," says ex-President Cleveland, "was once travelling on foot through a section of West Virginia, well known for its excellent fishing-grounds, when he chanced upon an old angler of the old school—a venerable old countryman who, as he sat on the bank, looked as if time and the world might pass away without disturbing his content. 'Have you fished long in this stream?' asked my friend.

"'Twenty-three years.'

"'Get many bites?'

"'Two years ago, in this very spot, I had a fine bite.'"

He didn't know.—A well-known actor not long back spent his holidays in a certain district in Berkshire. Being fond of fishing he decided to have a day's angling in the river Kennet. He had only just commenced operations when he was accosted by a keeper, who asked him "by what right he dared to fish in that place."

The former, assuming a most tragic attitude, and with a tone full of dignity, replied —

" By what right, do you say ?—

" By that great right the vast and towering mind
Has o'er the instinct of the vulgar kind."

The keeper, quite astonished by the imposing tone of his reply, withdrew, saying:

" Beg your pardon, sir; I didn't know that."

His object.—A visitor in a small village, watching an old rustic fishing in a shallow stream, noticed that for half an hour the hook was never drawn from the water.

" Are there any fish in that stream ? " asked the visitor at last.

" No, sir, I don't think so," replied the old man.

" But you seem to be fishing."

" Yes, sir."

" Then, what is your object?" was the next question.

" My object, sir, is to show the wife that I've no time to peel the potatoes."

Concerning eels.—In a Belgian paper a story is told by M. Fiston of certain observations which he had made upon the habits of eels. He had planted at a distance of about one hundred and fifty yards from the bank of a river where eels were plentiful, several lines of peas. As the peas reached maturity he noticed that some of the pods were gnawed through with an even clean cut, and he at once attributed the damage to field mice. But his gardener one day informed him that he had visited the ground very early in the morning and saw several " serpents " come from among the peas at his approach and go to the river. The next morning M. Fiston himself went to the field, and threw a stone into the middle of the peas, when at once out came a dozen eels, which fled towards the stream.

He didn't care for salmon.—In some parts of the Canadian back country the recurrence of boiled salmon, broiled salmon, salmon cutlets, and salmon steak at every meal becomes, after a few weeks, monotonous. To the native palate, brought up on it, this constant reappearance of the self-same dish is a matter of course; but to the newly arrived tourist it grows at last into a sad object.

" Is there nothing else for breakfast ? " said one such victim of colonial hospitality, as a whole fish and a pot of mustard were laid before him on the table,

"Nothing else! Why, there's salmon enough for six, ain't there?"

"Yes, but I don't care for salmon."

"Well, then, fire into the mustard."

Quite another thing. — The Duke of —— was once a guest at a dinner when he was unexpectedly called upon to respond to a toast. Recovering somewhat from his surprise, his grace said that this situation reminded him of the case of a friend who got an involuntary bath while fishing at Hampton Court. With no little difficulty he was rescued, and after he had regained his breath and was in a fairly comfortable condition, his rescuer asked him how he came to fall into the water.

"I did not come to fall into the water," replied the unfortunate man; "I came to fish."

CHAPTER XXVI.

TRAVELLING.

A pious wish.—The tourist in Ireland left the train at every station, and went ahead to the luggage van to ask if his trunk was safe.

"Are you quite sure," he asked for the sixth time, "that my trunk is safe?"

"Begorra, I wish the Lord had made ye an elephant, instead of an ass," said the guard, "an' then you'd always have your trunk in front of you."

Railway life in Central Africa.—Douglas Freshfield's account in the ALPINE JOURNAL of his expedition in South Africa is interesting. The party saw no lions, but at a railway-station which they came across there was a story that a station-master had recently sent two telegrams; "Please send further police protection. Men very brave, but less so when lions begin roaring," and "Please let 10 a.m. run up the platform, disregarding signals. Signalman up post, lion at bottom."

Respectful advice.—Artemus Ward was travelling on a slow-going Southern road soon after the war. When the conductor was punching his ticket, Artemus remarked: "Does this railway company allow passengers to give it advice, if they do so in a respectful manner ?" The conductor replied, in gruff tones, that he guessed so. "Well," Artemus went on, "it occurred to me that it would be well to detach the cowcatcher from the front of the engine and hitch it to the rear of the train. For, you see, we go too slow to overtake a cow but what's to prevent a cow strolling into this car and horning a passenger ?"

Where ignorance is bliss.—A man who was travelling through Arkansas on horseback stopped before a mountain region farmhouse to inquire the way. "What's the news ?" asked the mountaineer as he leaned his lank frame against the fence.

On finding that what had become a part of history was news to him, the traveller asked why he did not take some periodical, that he might keep in touch with the world.

"Wal, when my pa died ten years ago, he left me a stack of newspapers three feet high, and I an't done readin' o' 'em yet."

It's an ill wind.—A gentleman who was on a walking tour, after travelling over many weary miles of rough country, arrived in an exhausted condition at a straggling village, only to find it quiet and deserted. All the shops were shut, and every house was locked. Finally he espied a surgery, and, thinking that the doctor would at least offer him a chair and some refreshments, he rang the bell. "The doctor's locked the 'ouse up and gone to the football match, sir," he was informed by the coachman, who slouched lazily up from the backyard.

"Oh! that's the attraction, is it ?" remarked the weary tourist. "I really thought it was a funeral."

"So it may be in the end, sir, for, if our lads lose, they've vowed to kill the other team, and if the other team lose they've vowed to kill the referee. So, whatever happens, master's sure of a bit of business!"

The pass was made out.—A railway employee applied to one of his directors for a "pass" to visit his family.

"You are in the service of the company ?" said the director.

"Yes."

"And you are paid regularly ?"

"Yes."

"Well, now, suppose you were working for a farmer instead of for a railway company, would you expect him to take out his horses every Saturday night and carry you home?"

"No," replied the railway man, "I shouldn't expect him to do that. But if he had horses out, and was going my way, I should call him a mean fellow if he didn't give me a lift."

The pass was made out.

According to Act of Parliament.—At a railway station in Kent, the door of the carriage was opened to admit a tall man with a slender girth, who tried to wedge himself in between two burly farmers; but, finding it hard, he said: "Excuse me, sir, you must sit up a bit. Each seat is made for five persons; and, according to Act of Parliament, you are only entitled to eighteen inches of room."

"My good sir," said the farmer, "although you have been fortunate enough to be constructed according to Act of Parliament, you can hardly blame me if I am not built that way."

Weeds in Louisiana. — A Louisiana railway driver was acquitted of neglect in running over a man, because "the weeds on the track grew so high as to obscure the person."

In Kentucky.—Shortly after a new administration took hold of a well-known southern railroad a great number of claims were preferred against the company on account of horses and cattle being killed along the line in Kentucky. To make matters worse, it appeared that every animal killed, however worthless it may have been before the accident, invariably figured in the claims subsequently presented as being of the best blood in Kentucky. One day, in conversation with one of the road's attorney's, the president became very much excited in referring to the situation. "Do you know," he exclaimed, bringing down his fist on the desk by way of emphasis, "I have reached the conclusion that nothing in Kentucky so improves live stock as crossing it with a locomotive."

The force of habit.—Railroad claim-agents have little faith in their fellow creatures. One said recently: "Every time I settle a claim with one of these hard-headed rural agents who wants the railroad to pay twice what he would charge the butcher if he gets a sheep killed, I think of this story, illustrative of the way some people want to hold the railroad responsible for every accident, of whatever kind, that happens. Two Irishmen were driving home from town one night when their buggy ran into a ditch, overturned, and they were both stunned. When a rescuer came along and revived them, one of them said: "Where's the train?" 'Why, there's no train around,' he was told. 'Then where's the railroad?' 'The nearest railroad is three miles away,' he learned. 'Well, well,' he commented. 'I knew it hit us pretty hard, but I didn't suppose it knocked us three miles from the track.'"

CHAPTER XXVII.

PUGILISM AND WRESTLING.

About Tom Cribb.—At one time Barnes, editor of the Times, when at Cambridge took some lessons in the "noble art," and much fancied his powers. One day, in the fields, he met a rough-looking fellow sitting on a stile, whose manner he did not like. Barnes told him he would have to thrash him if he did not behave himself. The man laughed. "Young man," he said, "I am Tom Cribb." This led to a cessation of hostilities and a pleasant dinner and other happy relations between the editor and the renowned champion of England.

Presidential athletes.—George Washington was a strong man, and a famous wrestler. He was never thrown, which meant much, for wrestling was a favourite amusement with Virginians. Lincoln, too, excelled in the same sport.

"It is a curious thing," Lincoln said, when Washington's prowess was mentioned to him, "but that is just precisely my record when I was a youth. I could outlift any man in Illinois, and I was never thrown. If George were round now I should be pleased to have a tussle with him, and I rather believe that one of the plain people of Illinois would be able to keep up his end against the old Virginian."

Threw him over.—A Scotch farmer famed for his strength, was often challenged by people from a distance who had heard of his reputation. One day there arrived from London Lord W., a well-known amateur pugilist.

He found the Scot working in a field.

"Friend," said his lordship, after first tying his horse to a tree, "I have come a long way to see which of us is the best wrestler."

Without saying a word, the farmer seized him round the middle, pitched him over the hedge, and resumed his work.

His lordship slowly gathered himself together, whereupon the farmer said :

"Well, have you anything more to say to me ?"

"No," replied Lord W., "but perhaps you'll be so good as to throw me over my horse."

It was a famous victory.—The foreign and dusky potentate had been brushing up his knowledge of English history.

One day his motor drew up close to the famous Marston Moor, and beckoning to a typical countryman who was resting on a gate near by, he said :

"My friend, is it not that it is that there was a great battle fought here ?"

"Well, yes," said Hodge, scratching his matted poll, "a did have a few rounds here wi' Jem Clodd, of the Manor Farm, but that was a year ago, and a never dreamed your honour would have heard about it !"

He couldn't hit Jess.—The North Atchison boys tell a story of Joe Henderson, the father of Jess, the athlete, who was thought to be the strongest man in town. When Jess was about fifteen years old, and after he had taken boxing lessons several months, his father attempted a little punishment. After trying his best he couldn't hit Jess, so he went into the house and said to his wife : "Mamma, what's the matter with our Jess ? He needs a licking, but I can't hit him."

Wrestling for rent. In some cantons of Switzerland public wrestling matches are held once a year, at which nearly every one is present. At Grenchen, recently, a property owner and his tenant wrestled for a year's rent as stakes. The tenant won.

CHAPTER XXVIII.

PASTIMES.

There or thereabouts.—Ambassador Choate tells a story of a Bishop of Rochester, who was so fond of cricket that he used to play with a local team, and one day when the bishop was batting the bowler pitched very wide.

"Please keep the ball in the parish!" said the bishop.

The next ball the bowler sent in caught the bishop full in the waistband, the bowler observing:

"I think that's somewhere about the diocese, my lord."

Time to interfere.—Mr. Justice Hawkins, when on circuit, finding a long summer evening drag on his hands, took a turn in the lanes, and, staying at a rural inn for a cup of tea, his ears caught the charmed sound of the falling ninepins. The company eyed the newcomer with greedy eyes, thinking they would lead him on to an advantageous game.

The learned judge played, and in a very short time relieved every gentleman in the place of his spare shillings.

Then the landlord thought it time to interfere, and, touching his lordship on the back, said: "Look here, my fine friend; we have had your sort here before, and if you don't want to shake hands with the police, you'd better get out of this!"

Not to undeceive.—"Does that young Featherhead play poker?" asked Jarvis of an acquaintance. "No," was the reply, "but he thinks that he does, and we are careful not to undeceive him."

How's that, umpire?—To entertain the tenantry at one of his country seats, a certain noble earl on Whit Monday got up a cricket match between local scratch teams, but at the last moment it was found they were an umpire short. The earl's valet took the post; and no sooner had his lordship come to bat than he was caught by the wicket-keeper during the first over. Being doubtful of having touched the ball, however, the peer turned to his servant with:—

"How's that, umpire?"

"Your lordship is not at home to-day—beg pardon, I mean your lordship is out!

And even the archbishop's butler smiled.

A professional point of view.—He was an old farmer, on a visit to town, and he saw two young fellows playing chess.

"Excuse me," he said, "but the object of both of you is to git them wooden objects from where they are to where they ain't?"

"Yes."

"And you have to be on the look-out for difficulties?"

"Constantly."

"And if you ain't mighty careful, you're going to lose some of 'em?"

"Yes."

"An' then there's that other game that I see some of you dress up for, and play with sticks an' a ball?"

"You mean golf?"

"Yes, is that game amusin'?"

"It is, and the exercise beneficial."

"Well, if you young gentlemen want to really enjoy yourselves and get beneficial exercise you come over to my farm an' get me to let you drive pigs. You'll git all the walkin' you want, an' the way you have to watch for surprises, an' slip about so as not to lose the pigs, will make you forget for a time your domestic cares."

CHAPTER XXIX.

MUSIC.

Tinned music. — A phonograph had been introduced into the village "public," and the landlord, after running off several records, asked one of his audience—a big agricultural labourer—what he thought of the invention.

"Wey," he replied, "Aa nivver could get on wi' tinned meat, and Aa'm hanged if I like tinned music!"

Voice culture. — Farmer Haynes: "What's that noise?"

Mrs. H.: "It's Jane cultivating her voice."

"Cultivating, eh? If I'm any judge, that's harrowing."

Thanks be.—Mrs. Casey: "Sure th' goat has ate all av Maggie's piano music!"

Mr. Casey: "Thanks be for that! Now, if he'd only ate th' peanny, Oi'd pension him fer loife!"

CHAPTER XXX.

THEATRE.

The evening's amusement.—A visitor to a country town asked the local policeman when the theatre opened.

" We have no theatre here."

" Well, the music-hall, then?"

" No, nothing of that kind here."

" Have you no evening amusement at all ? "

" Oh, yes," said the policeman. " If you will wait till nine o'clock you'll see them shunting the goods train ! "

Dissipation.—Farmer's Boy: " Father, can I go to the circus to-night with Hiram Homespun ? "

Father: " No. 'Taint more'n a month since yer went t' the top o' the hill to see the eclipse o' the moon. 'Pears to me, yew'er getting dissipated and kinder reckless."

An indignity.—The old type of travelling actor was moving his company on the cheap, and a kindly stationmaster had smuggled them into goods trucks and had sent them off at goods rates, The train stopped during the night at a wayside station, and the stationmaster looked out of the window and inquired of the guard as to what he had in the train.

" Oh ! manure and actors."

A head appeared from a cattle truck, exclaiming: " So help me bob, guard, you might have said ' actor-r-rs ' first."

In a loose box.—Mr. John Hare sent his coachman to a theatre to secure stalls. The man who knew more about the stables than theatres returned with an awkward message.

Mr. Hare: " Well, did you get the stalls ? "

Coachman: " No, sir, the stalls were all taken up; but they told me they would be pleased to—to "—he scratched his head, " to put you in a loose box, sir."

On tour.—" I'm afraid," said the actor when a cabbage came within an inch of his nose, " that somebody in the audience has lost his head."

Long steps.—A story is told of a talk between Mr. Sanger, of circus fame and a bore.

" What steps would you take, sir, in the event of that tiger getting out ? "

" Very big ones."

CHAPTER XXXI.

WEATHER.

The safest course.—"On the whole," said the aged weather prophet, "I have found that the safest course is to predict bad weather."

"Why?" asked the neophyte.

"Because people are much more ready to forgive you if the prediction does not come true."

The barometer. — Tourist: "Fine weather, Sandy. What's the day going to be."

Sandy: "Well, I'm thinking it'll may be rain."

Tourist: "But the barometer is rising, Sandy."

Sandy: "Ay, but it's verra little heed the weather hereabouts pays to the barometer."

That kind of rain.—A minister when praying for rain was anxious that there should be no mistake, and accordingly framed his petition after this fashion:—"Oh Lord, Thou knowest we do not want Thee to send us a rain which will pour down in fury and swell our streams, and carry away our ridges and haycocks and farms; but, Lord, we want it to come down drizzle-drozzle, drizzle-drozzle for about a week.—Amen."

Providential. — "How's times?" asked the tourist. "Pretty tolerable, stranger," responded the old man, who was sitting on a stump. "I had some trees to cut down, but the cyclone levelled them and saved me the trouble." "That was good." "Yes; and then the lightning set fire to the brush pile and saved me the trouble of burning it." "Remarkable! But what are you doing now?" "Waiting for an earthquake to come along and shake the potatoes out of the ground."—CHICAGO NEWS.

Not change. — Doctor: "What you need is a change of climate."

Patient: "Change of climate! Why, I have nothing else. If the climate would only keep the same a few days running I think it would be all right."

In a country paper describing the effects of a late thunderstorm, it was stated, "Several cattle were killed, but fortunately no lives were lost."

The bright side.—A farmer, driven to the roof of his flooded farm, was gazing over the rising waters. "Washed all your fowls away ? " asked a man in a boat below. " Yes, but the ducks swam."

" Tore up your orchard trees ? "

" Don't mind it much. The crop would have been a failure."

" But the water is right up at your windows, man ! "

" Well, them windows wanted washing."

The barometer. — A sheep farmer in the Cheviot hills had been told that it was useful to have a barometer in the house, for it would let him know when the weather would be good or bad. He was accordingly persuaded to procure an instrument which he hung up in his lobby, and saw every day without much edification. At last there came a spell of rainy weather, while the barometer marked " set fair." The rain continued to fall heavily, and still the hand on the dial made no sign of truth. At last he took the instrument from its nail, and marched with it to the bottom of the garden, where a burn was rushing along. He then thrust the glass into the water, exclaiming, " Will you believe your ain een noo, then ? "

The Glebe Farm.—When Wilberforce was rector of Brightstone, in the Isle of Wight, he was waited on by an old farmer, who much wished to rent the glebe land.

" Why," asked Wilberforce.

" Well," said the old man, " when t'other parson was here he used to farm it hisself, and there being little of it, he always got in his hay before anybody else. Then he clapped on the prayer for rain ! "

Domestic weather forecasts.—When you see a man going home at two o'clock in the morning, and his wife is waiting for him, it will probably turn out stormy.

When a man receives a bill for goods his wife has bought unknown to him, look out for thunder and lightning.

When a man goes home and finds no supper ready, the fire out, and his wife cabin-hunting, it is likely to be cloudy.

When a man promises to take his wife out to a party and changes his mind after she is dressed, we may expect a heavy shower.

Dinna forgit.—The spring had been a dry one, and the crops were somewhat backward, but at last a nice gentle rain was falling, which bid fair to mend matters considerably. Said Sandy M'Tavish to Alec M'Nab when they met outside the village inn, " Hech, mon, here's just what we're wantin' the noo. It's a magnificent rain bringin' things oot o' the groun." "Whist, mon, Sandy," said Alec with a shudder. "Dinna forgit that I've twa wives there."

The rainbow.—The solutions of problems in natural philosophy given by boy scholars are sometimes very amusing. A boy in a public school in Maine, being asked why the rainbow is circular in form, answered that "it was fixed so that teams might go under it."

Non-Intervention. — The deacon prayed fer rain six days an' nights on a stretch, an' when the rain come——"

"What then ?"

"Drowned two of his best cows, an' washed the foundations from under his house. An' now he says that hereafter he's a good mind to keep quiet an' jest let Providence run the weather to suit itself !"—ATLANTA CONSTITUTION.

A second flood.—Some time ago when Mr. Balfour was going through a village near his Scottish home at Whittingehame he was accosted by one of the old men of the place.

On being presented with a shilling, he whispered to Mr. Balfour: "Man, dae ye ken what I'm gaun to tell ye ?"

"No," said the Statesman.

"Weel," he said, "it's gaun to rain seventy-twa days."

Mr. Balfour, thinking to have some fun with him, replied: "That cannot be; for the world was entirely flooded in forty days."

"But," returned the old fellow, "the world wisna sae drained as it is noo."

Then Noah knew.—Some years ago a class of boys was under examination in Sussex. Among the questions was, "How did Noah know there would be a flood ?" "'Cause," shouted a confident urchin, "he looked at Moore's almanac.'

Cause and effect.—Sunday School Teacher: "Johnny, can you tell me what caused the Flood ?"

Johnny: "Yes, ma'am, rain."

For shelter.—Sandy Thompson had a wife whose tongue was quite equal to the task of "deaving the miller." One very wet, windy night as the minister was passing the farmer's house he was surprised to see Sandy standing in the midst of the rain. "Dear me," said the minister, "what are you doing outside on a night like this ?"

" Oh, I'm shelter'n frae the storm. Man, it's naething outside tae what's it's inside."

The black ram.—Sir Isaac Newton was once told by a shepherd boy that it was going to rain, though the sky was cloudless. As it proved true Sir Isaac told the boy he would give him a guinea if he would point out how he could foretell the weather so well.

The boy pocketed the gold, and said :

" Whenever you see that black ram turn it's tail towards the wind, sir, it's a sure sign of rain within the hour ! "

A judgment.—Parson (to farmer whose barley is sprouting) : " Miserable weather, Mr. Roots ! "

Farmer : " Aye, it be a sort of judgment on them folks as was so plaguey anxious to pray for rain last July." (Parson hurries on).

A sure sign.—Mr. Tyers, the proprietor of Vauxhall Gardens, was a worthy man, but indulged himself a little too much in querulous complaints when anything went amiss ; insomuch that, he said, if he had been brought up a hatter he believed people would have been without heads ! A farmer once gave him a humorous reproof. He stepped up to him very respectfully, and asked him when he meant to open his gardens. Mr. Tyers replied, the next Monday fortnight. The man thanked him, and was going away ; but Tyers asked him in return what made him so anxious to know.

" Why, sir," said the farmer, " I think of sowing my turnips on that day, for you know we shall be sure to have rain."

Rather dry.—" What did you think of my lecture ? " asked a speaker of an old farmer.

" It was right enough," said the farmer, moodily, " but a couple of hours' rain would have done it good ; it was rather dry."

Got twins.—The hot weather last year in America was the cause of an amusing incident at Bilville. A book agent travelling there was asked by a farmer to wind up the bucket from a well : " It seems to me," said the agent as he tugged at the windlass, " that your bucket's mighty heavy."

" Yes, it's got the twins in it."

" The twins ? "

" Yes ; lowered 'em down to cool off 'bout a half-hour ago. This hot weather mighty bad on babies."

A noisy sunset.—Hearing the report of the evening gun from

Edinburgh Castle, an old lady from the country inquired, as she walked down Princes Street with her son, what the sound was.

"Oh! I suppose it's just sunset," was the off-hand reply.

"Sunset!" exclaimed the old woman, with open-mouthed astonishment. "Mercy me! does the sun gae down here wi' a bang like that!"

Partridge's Almanac.—One of the most celebrated almanac makers of former days was one Partridge, and of him a rather good story used to be told.

He was travelling in the country, and stopped at an inn for dinner. He prepared to resume his journey, when the ostler advised him to stay where he was, as it would certainly rain.

"Nonsense!" said Partridge and proceeded on his way.

He had not gone far, however, when, sure enough, a heavy shower of rain fell. Struck by the man's prediction, he rode back, and offered the ostler half-a-crown if he would tell how he knew.

"Well," replied the man, with a grin, after getting the money, "the truth is we have an almanac of Partridge's here; and he is such a liar that, whenever he promises a fine day we always know it will be the opposite.

"Now to-day, your honour, is set down as a fine day in the almanac."

That's why.—"Why, Pat, there used to be two windmills there."

"Thrue for you, sir."

"Why is there but one now?"

"Bedad, they took one down to lave more wind for t'other."

CHAPTER XXXII.

INSECTS.

The moth it seems a careless thing;
It flutters by on gaudy wing;
And yet this treacherous beast, alack,
Will eat the clothes right off your back!

Hard times.—First horse-fly (humped up in the shade, watching the automobiles whizz by): "By my troth, Cecilia, but it's hard times we've been seeing since those things came."

Second horse-fly: "You may well say so, Horatio. Heaven knows it's a hard future for horseless flies!"

The last of the mosquitos.—"I guess you don't know what flies are in this country," observed the Yankee. "Way over in Ohio I missed a cow. I found her skeleton on the ground, and the last of the mosquitos a-sittin' on a fence pickin' his teeth with one of her ribs."

He found it.—City Visitor: "What makes little Tommy cry so, Mr. Leeks?"

Farmer Leeks: "Well, the fact is, he went out this morning to find a hornet's nest for his natural history collection, and ——"

City Visitor: "And the poor boy couldn't find one?"

Farmer Leeks: "No! the poor boy found one."

To cure fleas.—Customer: "Have you something that will cure fleas on a dog?"

Druggist: "I don't know. What is the matter with the fleas?"

So big.—"I haven't noticed any mosquito netting around here," remarked the visitor who was making his first trip to Swampville-on-the-Sound.

"No," answered a native, "they are so big we use mouse-traps."

Insects as food.—"Having personally eaten some hundreds of species of caterpillars," says M. Dagin, a French entomologist, "raw, broiled, boiled, fried, roasted and hashed, I find most of these pleasant to taste, light and digestible." But the despised cockroach of our kitchen is what M. Dagin waxes most enthusiastic over. "Pounded in a mortar, put through a sieve and poured into beef stock, these creatures make a soup preferable to bisque." Nevertheless, a Chinese proverb runs to the effect, "If your stomach is delicate, abstain from the cockroach!"

What d'ye lacke.—A country fellow walking London streets, and gazing up and down at every sight he saw, some mockt him, others pulled him by the Cloake, in so much he could not pass in quiet. He thought hee would requite them for their kinde salutations, with something to laugh at; and, comming to Paul's gate, where they sell pinnes and Needles, the boyes being very saucie, pulled him by the cloake, and one said, What lacke you friend ? another, What lacke you Countryman ?

I want a hood for a Humble Bee, and a payre of Spectacles for a blind Beare; which so amazed the boy, that he had nothing to reply, and the Countrey Man went laughing away. — "Pasquil's Jests" about 1650.

CHAPTER XXXIII.

RATS AND MICE.

A trial of rats.—Chassanee was one of the earliest famous French lawyers; he won his first laurels in a trial of rats in Autun (1445). In the Middle Ages wild and lower animals were tried like persons, and the most ridiculous performances took place. The inhabitants of a district being annoyed by rats, these were cited, and Chassanee had been selected as their counsel. The rats not appearing on the first summons, Chassanee secured an extension of time by arguing that all his clients being summoned, including young, old, sick, and healthy, great preparations were necessary. The rats still failing to appear, Chassanee denied the legality of the summons under certain circumstances. A summons from the court, he argued, implied full protection to the parties summoned, both on their way to it and on their return home; but his clients, the rats, though most anxious to obey the Court, did not dare stir out of their holes on account of the number of evil-disposed cats kept by the plaintiffs.

"Let the latter enter into bonds under heavy pecuniary penalties that their cats shall not molest my clients, and they will appear." The plaintiffs declining to be so bound, the case was dropped.

Looking for another.—There is a brave woman in Paris. She saw a mouse, and when the mouse ran she ran too—not in the opposite direction, but after it. The result was that she fell through a hole in the floor. Beneath the floor she discovered a brass box, and in the box gold coins to the value of £200. She is now looking for another mouse.

An official rat catcher.—Among recent announcements

is one that the County Council has appointed an official rat-catcher. The report of proceedings being brief, we are unable to say whether he is to be paid on the scale of wages laid down by the Amalgamated Society of Rat Catchers.

The Pied Piper.—"Dad," said Teddy, "it isn't true, is it?"

"What isn't true, my son?" asked his father.

"Why, this about the Pied Piper of Hamelin. Is it true that he could play on his pipes so fascinatingly that the rats would come out of their holes and drown themselves?"

"Well, I dunno," said Teddy's father. "It might be. Your Uncle Tom can play the cornet so that it will frighten a cow into the river, and make all the dogs in five miles growl. Yes, I daresay it's true."

Wanted rats.—The following announcement was given to the world in 1816:—"Wanted immediately to enable me to leave the house which I have for the last five years inhabited, in the same plight and condition in which I found it, 500 live rats, for which I will gladly pay the sum of £5 sterling, and as I cannot leave the farm attached thereto in the same order in which I got it, without at least five millions of dockens (weeds), I do hereby promise a further sum of £5 for the same number of dockens."

Rattin' wi' pigs.—A benevolent old gentleman, while rambling through a wood met a man who boasted that he owned the seven best rat-catchers in England. He had all the seven frisky dogs with him as usual.

"My good fellow," said the gentleman, "why do you waste your time bothering with these ridiculous dogs? Wouldn't there be far more profit in keeping the same number of pigs?"

The owner of the dogs looked pityingly at his questioner.

"What do you take me for? A fine fule I should look rattin' wi' pigs."

CHAPTER XXXIV.

FUNEREAL.

The corpse spake.—In old days it was rather a common custom among the poorer Irish when they were not able to afford a coffin for a relative to make the corpse beg for it, the body being placed on a bier on the footway outside the door on a Sunday, with a plate to receive the coppers of the people as they passed to Mass. But sometimes this practice led to imposture, and once the body of a man lay outside a cabin while the people placed their pennies or half-pennies on the plate. A poor woman came, and, putting down a sixpence began to gather pennies from the plate. "Arrah, ma'am," cried the corpse; "be ginerous wance in yer life, and lave the change."

Fond of society.—The wish to be buried with their own people is characteristic of the Irish. A new graveyard was opened near a village in County Limerick As an old woman lay dying, her grandchildren tried to persuade her to be buried in the new ground, instead of the old, overcrowded graveyard. "Indeed and I won't be buried there," cried she. "Is it in that could and lonesome place ye want to lay me? Shure I'd never be comfortable there wid not a bone of wan belongin' to me. No; take me to Kileely graveyard, which is full of dacent people."

Made a clean sweep.—Those who have had enough of the amateur noise-maker will read with sympathy this extract from the "Gold Coast Journal": "We report with deep regret the death of Madame Aframmah, of Low Town, which took place on the evening of the 12th inst. She was buried next day with the Amateur Brass Band."

Keep's a'!—The late Rev. Mr. Barty, of Ruthven, was a man of humour, and many stories are told of him. A vacancy having occurred in the office of gravedigger, one Peter Hardie, sought for it. The parish is small, consisting of five farms. The rate per head having been duly fixed, the minister and Peter were just about to close the bargain, when Peter said: "But am I to get steady wark?"

"Keep's a'! Peter," answered Mr. Barty, "wi' steady

wark ye'd bury a' the parish in a fortnicht ! ''

A delicate plant.—A farmer had died suddenly at the age of 60. He was very much respected and the funeral party were bewailing his lost and speaking of his good qualities. His father was still in the land of the living, hale and hearty, at the great age of fourscore years and ten. '' It's a sad loss,'' mourned he, '' I always told my wife that we should never be able to rear him.''

Ought to have tatered it.—A rural dean, some years ago, went to pay an official visit to one of his clergy, and in the churchyard he found a crop of barley !

'' I do not think this quite a proper thing to have in the churchyard.''

The old churchwarden, who was standing by, replied : '' That's just what I have been telling of him. He ought to ' tatered ' it fust.''

An epitaph.—

Poor Peter Staggs now rests beneath this rail,
Who loved his joke, his pipe, and mug of ale ;
For twenty years he did the duties well,
Of ostler, boots, and waiter at the Bell.
But death stepp'd in, and order'd Peter Staggs
To feed the worms, and leave the farmers' nags,
The church clock struck one—alas ! 'twas Peter's knell,
Who sigh'd, '' I'm coming—that's the ostler's bell ! ''

An Irish country wake.—'' So you were at poor Rafferty's wake. Was anybody sober ? ''

'' Nobody but Rafferty.''

Sport at a funeral.—Of Lord Spencer it is related that on one occasion when he was Lord-Lieutenant of Ireland he was out hunting, and came across a funeral procession. He drew on one side out of respect for the feelings of the mourners, when suddenly the hounds came by in full cry. The bearers dropped the coffin, and with the mourners ran for all they were worth after the hounds, and he was left with the corpse.

Not more than once.—The stranger strolled through the village streets until he arrived at the cemetery, says the old story. The gravedigger was hard at work excavating a grave.

'' Do people die often hereabouts ? '' asked the stranger.

'' None of 'em ever died more'n once since my time.''

Inappropriate to the occasion.—Three American commercial travellers met at a small country hotel. They were sitting on the porch, swapping yarns, when a farmer drove up.

"None of you fellers is a preacher, I suppose? You see, my hired man's dead. The reg'lar minister's out of town, an I don't want to put the poor feller away without no religious doins' of any kind, so I thought as how maybe one of you might help me out."

It was finally decided that the traveller for windmills should say something for the dead. The landlord took them out in his wagon that afternoon. Several farmers were around the coffin. The windmill man braced up.

"My friends, death is sad. But, sad as it is, it must come to all. Hardly was our friend here prepared for death when along it came—and—he took to his bed. He had been carrying water for the stock farm a long way off. The exertion pulled him down. Had this farm been supplied with one of our 'None-Can-Beat-It' windmills, capable of pumping 200 gallons a minute, this man's life would——"

"Hold up a bit," interrupted the farmer. "I've got that very kind of a windmill, an' if the pesky thing hadn't got out of order an' fell down on Jim he'd be here alive now. Proceed, brother, but like as not you'd better skip windmills."

Left.—In the country an old farmer died who was reputed to be rich. After his death, however, it was found that he died penniless. His will was very brief. It ran as follows:—

"There's only one thing I leave. I leave the earth. My relatives have always wanted that. They can have it."

A stayer.—In many Scottish families the old manservant is something of an institution. He enters the service of a family when a boy, adheres faithfully to his place for a long number of years, and only resigns when the infirmities of age are upon him. In time he becomes rather imperious, and claims as his right little things that were at first granted to him as favours.

A lady tells a story illustrative of this. Her coachman—who had been in the service of the family in her father's time—gave her great trouble, and she determined to see what effect dismissal would have upon him. Calling him into her presence, she said with as much asperity as she could command:

"John, you must look out for another situation. You will

leave my service at the end of the month.''

'' Na, na, my lady,'' he said. '' I drove you to the kirk to be baptised, I drove you to your marriage, and I'll stay to drive you to your funeral ! ''

CHAPTER XXXV.

MISCELLANEOUS.

Pleasures of town.—'' Have you many town advantages here ? '' asked the visitor of the native of the country town.

'' We've got a telephone line and electric lights, and overhead trolly trams, and they are always tearing up the streets.''

The wreckers.—Looking over the storm-swept Pentland Firth, with its dangerous rocks and fierce currents, a tourist remarked to the Orkney pilot : '' This must be a great place for wrecks.

'' Wracks, man,'' he shouted, '' there's mony a braw farm in Orkney got out of wracks, but the Breetesh Government has put a leethouse here, and yon,'' pointing to the double lighthouse on the Skirries, '' yon's twa—there is no chance of wracks for a puir fisher body noo ! ''

All face.—A recent Governor of Canada, well wrapped in furs and a heavy coat, was conferring with an Indian chief on the shores of one of the great lakes in the depth of winter. The latter, clothed in a single blanket was walking over the frozen ground in apparent comfort. On being asked how he could keep warm, he replied, '' You do not cover your face.''

'' No,'' said the Governor, '' but I am used to that.''

Indian : '' Good, me all face.''

Un Milord Anglais.— Lord Hertford rented a residence in the Rue Lafitte. One morning his servant awoke him and informed him that some people had come to look over the house.

'' The house,'' exclaimed his lordship. '' I have taken it myself ! ''

'' Yes, my lord, but the landlord wants to sell it, and some intending purchasers have come to inspect it.''

'' Tell the landlord I'll buy his house, and not to wake me again.''

O-blitherated. — In some country districts of Ireland it is not unusual to see the owners' names simply chalked on carts in order to comply with the regulations. This custom lends itself to mischief on the part of boys, who sometimes rub off the lettering and therefore get the owner into trouble with the police. A case of this kind having occurred, a constabulary sergeant spoke to a countryman whose name had been wiped out unknown to him.

"Is this cart yours, my good man?"

"Af coorse it is; do you see anything the matter wid it?"

"I observe that your name's o-blitherated."

"Then you're wrong; me name's O'Reilly, an' I don't care who knows it!"

On a ranch.—In his "Story of the Cowboy," Hough gives the following quarterly report of a foreman to an Eastern-American ranch owner:—'Deer Sur, we have brand 800 caves this roundup we have made sum hay potatoes is a fare crop. That Inglishman yu lef in charge at the other camp got too fresh an' we had to kill him. Nothing much has happened sence yu lef. Yurs truly,—JIM."

What he thought of it.—"What do I think o' London ask ye,?" said old John——, a Dundee worthy, on being asked his opinion of the great metropolis. 'What do I think o't? It's just a lump of guid ground spoilt with stane and lime."

Cryptogamic.—Willie: "It's always in damp places where mushrooms grow, isn't it papa?"

Papa: "Yes, my boy."

Willie: "Is that the reason they look like umbrellas, papa?"

His mail bag.—Postman: "Here's a letter for your folks."

Farmer: "Well, well! That's two letters we got this fall. People must think we don't do nothin' but write."

One good turn.—En Fiacres: "Dites donc, cocher, tachez de marcher un peu plus vite."

"Ah! j'veux pas surmener, Cocotte. Je suis membre de la Societe protectrice des animaux."

"Eh, bien! moi, je suis membre de la Societe de temperance; vous n'aurez pas de pourboire."

A politician.—Reunion electorale dans un pays vinicole.

"Je demande au candidat quelles mesures il prendra contre le phylloxera qui ravage nos vignes?"

"Citoyens, je viens de vous declarer deja que je suis pour le soufrage universel."

The straight tip.— First waiter: "Did that Arizona ranchman give you a tip?"

Second Waiter: "I should say he did. He told me if I didn't step lively he'd blow my whiskers off with his revolver."

No celery.—At an hotel one of the party asked, "Have you got any celery, waiter?"

"No, sir. I relies on my chances when gentleman like you come, sir!"

A practical Socialist.—"Father says," he remarked calmly, "as them 'ere mushrooms is as much our'n as your'n You din't sow 'em! They growed promisc'ous like."

"Oh, that's it, is it?" retorted the farmer. "Very weel, here's summat else in t' hedge as I didn't sow, and yo' can hev the benefit on't," with which he cut a serviceable switch from the hedge and gave a thrashing to the youngster.

"Noo then," he remarked, when he had finished, "just you trot off home and tell your father as Aw've a duck-pond on t' farm. Aw niver sowed that, nar dug it aythur, for that matter. It coom sorter promisc'ous like, and if 'e'll just stroll round Aw'll see as 'e gets his share o' that!"

The naturalist rebuked.—The reverend gentleman was a keen naturalist, and had a remarkable knowledge of fungi. One day, when calling upon old Miss Locke, he was embarrassed when she reminded him of the time that had elapsed since he last paid her a visit.

"If I were a toadstool," she said, "you'd have been to see me long ago!"

The flour of the family.—An ingenious observer has discovered that there is a remarkable resemblance between a baby and wheat, since it is first cradled, then "thrashed," and finally becomes the "flour" of the family.

Where the body was.—An Irishman took a contract to dig a public well. When he had dug about 25 ft, down he came one morning and found it caved in—filled in nearly to the top. He looked cautiously round and saw that no one was near; then took off his hat and coat and hung them on the windlass, crawled into some bushes, and waited events. In a short time the people discovered that the well had caved in, and seeing Pat's hat and coat on the windlass they supposed he was at the bottom of the excavation. Only a few hours of brisk digging cleared the loose earth from the well. Just as the eager citizens had reached the bottom, and were wondering where the body was, Pat came walking out of the bushes and thanked them for relieving him of a sorry job.

These women.—They were talking in the village pub. of triplets and the King's bounty. An old villager, who had been nodding over his ale, suddenly woke up.

"They be main wonderful, these women," he said. "Down at the Soak, when faather was a boy, he remembered one that had quadrupeds."

Much cry.—Among the minor farming industries of America is the raising of frogs for table. Jim Withee, the veteran tavern-keeper and horse-trader, tells a story of the Presidential campaign of 1900. An acquaintance remarked to Jim that Bryan would be elected; that all the people were talking that way.

"Bryan!" snorted Jim. "Bryan! Bryan reminds me of a young farmer who came to my hotel one day and asked if I did not want some frogs' legs. I told him I guessed not, but asked him how many he had. He said he had 'about a million,' whereupon I told him to bring in a few dozen and I would have them served, and, if the boarders liked them, I would buy more occasionally. He went away, and I did not see him for about two weeks, when he again appeared and wanted to sell some frogs' hind legs. I asked how many he had, and he replied, 'Six.' I said, 'Are you not the fellow who came in here before, and said you had a million?' 'Yes,' said he, 'I thought I had a million, but I was going by the noise they made.'"

Breakfast at five.—"I suppose you won't want to get up very early in the morning," said the eastern counties farmer as he lighted the guest from town to his room.

"No; I am rather a late sleeper."

"All right; then we won't have breakfast till five o'clock."

It was Christmas night, and Brown had a merry party. He said that all present should ask a conundrum or pay a forfeit.

Jones: "Why is this room like a nobleman's park?"

No one answered the question, so Jones gave a sly look at the ladies present, and replied: "Because there are so many 'dears' in it."

They're a' Dukes.—The late Duke of Buccleuch returned to Drumlanrig after a considerable absence. Shortly after his return he was sauntering along the banks of the Nith, when he met an elderly man who had long been employed on the estate. The Duke shook him cordially by the hand, and with characteristic kindness inquired after his health and welfare generally. "A'm very weel, thank your Grace for speirin'. A'm rael pleased tae see your Grace back again ; they're a' Dukes when you're awa' ! "

Financial.—Mr. J. H. Moore, the chief of the bureau of manufacturers of the Department of Commerce and Labour, is noted in Philadelphia for his perspicacity, and his advice upon financial matters is valued highly. A young woman the other day said to him :—

"I have inherited five thousand pounds, and hesitate whether to invest it in Government bonds, which pay only 3 per cent., or in Zaza Gold Mine stocks, which pay 15 per cent."

"If you want to dine well," he said, "choose the gold-mine investment. But take the other if you want to sleep well."

Who's your friend ?

That man's my friend who just
  steps in
To see me makes his errand
  spin
Then says : "I'm off—I must
  not stay—
I see this is your busy day."

Census taking.—The census-taker rapped at the door of the little farmhouse and opened his long book. A girl of about 17 came to the door.

"How many people live here ? " he began.

"Nobody lives here. We are only staying through the hop season."

"How many of you are here ? "

"I'm here, father's in the barn, and Bill is——"

"See here, my girl, I want to know how many inmates there are in this house. How many people slept here last night ? "

"Nobody slept here, sir. I had the toothache dreadful, and my little brother had the earache, and the new hand that's helping us got sunburnt so on his back that he has blisters the size of eggs ; and we all took on so that nobody slept a wink all night long."

Not so bad after all.—"What does 'P.G.' stand for ? " asked Mr. Justice A. T. Laurence, at the Anglesey Assizes, in referring to the village of Llanfair P.G., where an offence was alleged to have been committed.

"It is the shortened name of

a village.'' replied Mr. J. Bryn Roberts, M.P.

The village in question is Llanfairpwllgwyngyllgogerychwyrndrobwllandysiliogogogoch, a name which when pronounced without a stop is awe-inspiring. But Welsh names are "descriptive," and "St. Mary-Church-by-the-white-pool," etc., is not so bad to the native as it looks.

About President Roosevelt.—William T. Dantz, who was with President Roosevelt while he was a Western rancher, relates an incident illustrative of the President's temper—although, he says, it is the only time he ever knew it to get away from him. It was during the last round-up of cattle, and Roosevelt and Dantz were saddle-comrades and bedmates. It was a stormy night, and they went to bed—which consisted of tarpaulin-covered blankets on the wet ground—tired and hungry, the rain having drowned the cook's fire.

"Hardly had we turned in," says Mr. Dantz, "when a night-rider slashed a wet lariat across our bed, calling out. "All hands turn out; cattle breaking away." With a groan I slipped out sideways and groped in the darkness for my pony's picket line. Suddenly I heard a burst of picturesque language, the gist of which was a general malediction on the country, the man who made it, the men who lived in it, and the fool that would leave God's country for such a —— wilderness."

Potatoes and pedigree.—A fellow was one day boasting of his pedigree when a wag who was present remarked very sententiously:—"Ah! I have no doubt. That reminds me very much of a remark made by Lord Bacon—'They who derive their worth from their ancestors resemble potatoes, the most valuable parts of which are under ground.'"

The family tree.—"Young man," said the farmer, "I must say you've done a lot of talking about your family tree. Anybody would think you owned a timber-yard. Come out into the lane a minute."

The youth in golf clothes went with him.

Pausing by a birch tree, the farmer said, "I want you to take partic'lar notice of this."

"What for?"

"That's our family tree. That's what has heightened our ideals and stimmylated our energies. That has furnished switches for four or five generations of us."

The typewriter.—Old Farmer: "No, I don't want any more labour-saving machines. I've tried enough of 'em. There's a typewritin' machine my wife spent all her egg money to buy for me. Just look at the confounded swindle."

Friend: "What's the matter with it?"

Old Farmer: "Why, you can't even write your name with the thing unless you know how to play a church organ."

Want to know it.—Everyone has heard of the man who preferred tough beef-steak to tender because it went further. Similar to this spirit was the attitude of a prosperous farmer who went to a well-known coachbuilder to order a family carriage.

"Now I suppose you would not want rubber tyres?" said the builder.

"No, sir," replied the farmer warmly. "My folks ain't that kind. When we're riding we want to know it."

Bad to beat.—The father of James Hogg, the Ettrick Shepherd, was a proud sort of man, and never liked to admit that he was ever beaten. This led him into some queer excuses at times. He and his son went to the hills one winter morning to see whether the sheep were safe. The old man having gone too near the edge, where the descent was very steep, the snow gave way, and he fell to a considerable depth. Alarmed for his father's safety, Hogg looked over the cliff, and saw him standing seemingly unhurt. When his father found that he was being noticed, he shouted out: "Man, Jamie, you were aye fond o' a slide. Let me see you do that."

Just a few words.—"Have you anything to say before we eat you?" said the King of the Cannibal Isles to a missionary.

"I have. I want to talk to you a little on the great advantages of a fruit diet, for the growth of which your islands are so well suited."

An Edison joke.—Edison is a bit of a wag in his way, and he knows how to choke off too inquisitive visitors to his laboratory.

"What is that?" asked an interviewer, pointing to a queer-looking model.

"That," replied the inventor gravely, "is a motor to run by sound. You attach it to a cradle, and the louder the baby howls the faster the cradle rocks. I ought to make a fortune out of that; don't you think so?"

Law-abiding to suit.—"I was

driving through an Irish county with a dare-devil kind of Jehu," says a writer in a contemporary, "and I said to him: 'This is a grand country, and everything in it tending to prosperity! It's a pity you are not a more law-abiding people.' 'Law-abiding!' he cried, in a high key. 'Sure, we're the law-abidingest folks anywhere this blessed day, excep' when we gets a good chance! Now, we're comin' up to a turnpike here, just round the corner, and will yer honour pay, or shall I make a dash?'"

A new one on Washington.—"Come on, George," cried one of young Washington's playmates, "we're going in swimming."

"Can't very well do it, fellows," said the future father of his country. "I've got to stay here and chop some wood."

"Been kneeling over some more cherry trees?"

"Yes," answered George. "I cut down dad's favourite tree, and now he's making me cut it up."

"Oh! well," cried one of the boys as the crowd started down the road towards the swimming hole, "you always were a cut-up, anyway."

Take notice.—On the banks of a rivulet near Strabane there is said to be a stone bearing the following inscription that is intended to be of service to strangers: "Take notice, that when this stone is out of sight it is not safe to ford the river." A surveyor of the roads in Kent is said to have set up a finger-post bearing the statement: "This is the bridle-path to Faversham. If you can't read this you had better keep the main road."

Enclosing a Common.

A Lord, that purpos'd for his more availe.
To compass in a Common with a rayle,
Was reckoning with his friend about the cost,
And charge of every rayle, and every post:
But he (that wisht his greedy humour crost)
Said, Sir, provide you posts, and without fayling,
Your neighbours round about will find you rayling.

Cause for thanksgiving.—Farmer Snadbitter: "Hello, Josh! Ain't ye workin' to-day?"

Farmer Pildecker: "Naw. Thanksgivin'."

"Thanksgivin': Why! Thanksgivin' don't come for a month or two yit."

" I know ; but ye see I've married off four daughters, Bill's jined the standin' army, and a sewin' machine agent run off with the old woman ; so if I ain't got cause to knock off for a special Thanksgivin', then you'll have to p'int out the whyfore that's all ! "

Professor Townley was a book-worm, and a man of the city. The country had known him not till a friend persuaded him to rusticate for a short period.

One morning his host observed the professor intently watching something in the garden, so he went to see what it was.

" This is doing me a world of good ! " said the professor. " Just look how your cat is tearing that mouse to pieces."

" For my part," said his host, " I think it rather a revolting sight, and I'm surprised you should find amusement in it. You're a member of the Society for Prevention of Cruelty to Animals, are'nt you ? "

" I was," said the professor ; " but since I've been staying here I've been chased by a bull bitten in the leg by a dog, kicked over a fence by a horse, and butted through a thorn hedge by a ram."

One more for the dog.—Sahib (to Native Bill Collector) : " Well, what do you want ? "

N. B. C. : " Four rupees wheel-tax one dog-cart, Sahib ; two rupees tax each two ponies, and one rupee one bicycle. Total, nine rupees, Sahib."

Sahib : " How do you know what I've got ? You've been asking my servants. And the next time I catch you here I'll set my dog on to you. Do you understand that ? "

N. B. C. : " Yes, Sahib. One rupee more dog tax."

The laird's breeks.—The beautiful Duchess of Gordon was once scouring the country electioneering. She called at Craigmyle, and having heard that the laird was making bricks on the property for the purpose of building a new wall, she opened the subject of her errand with the tactful remark : " Well, laird, and how do your brick's come on ? " Good Craigmyle's thoughts were much occupied with a new part of his dress, which had lately been constructed, so, looking down on his nether garments, he said, in pure Aberdeen dialect : "Muckle obleeged to yer Grace, the breeks war sum ticht at first, but they are deeing weel eneuch noo."

Harsh.—Trespasser (who has fallen in pond) : " Help ! help ! I can't swim ! "

Irish Farmer: "Come out of thot, ye villain!"

Trespasser (chokingly): "Help me out—I'm d-drowning!"

Irish Farmer (not moving): "If ye dare to git dhrowned in my pond, ye dirthy spalpeen, Oi'll have ye locked up!"

Grown up. — "How's your son, Uncle Mose?"

"He's doing right well, sah. You'd be s'prised to see him, sah."

"I suppose he's got over all his childish tricks. Probably he'd consider robbing an orchard pretty small business now?"

"Yes, indeed, he would, sah He wouldn't rob anything smaller den a bank now, sah."

On an ocean liner.—Among the latest attractions of an ocean liner is a fish-pond from which passengers may choose which they like for breakfast or dinner. Kippered herrings, bloaters, and Finnan haddies will be seen swimming about waiting to be cooked. The next liner should have a kitchen garden, in which the people can watch their favourite vegetables growing, and a vineyard for the production of the wines.—Sporting Times.

Money in it.—"Do you know that there is money in Angora goats?"

"I know that there is in one. It ate a vest of mine, and there was a bank-note in one of the pockets."

Dreams go by contraries.—An old Irish gardener, meeting his master, after the prolonged absence from the estate, touched his finger to the tip of his cap and said:—

"Good morning, yer honour. Glad am I to see yez. Oi had a fine drame of ye last night."

"Indeed, Michael!" remarked the employer. "what was the dream?"

"Oi dramed that ye gave me a fine box o' tobaccy, an' that her ladyship, yer honoured wife, gave me humble Biddy a little caddy o' th' best tay."

"Ah, Michael, but you know dreams always go by contraries."

"Then," said Michael, "my-be ye'll be after giving me wife th' tobaccy, an' her ladyship'll give me th' tay."

A Christmas box?—"Why, I don't know, you, my friend."

"Then please ask your gardener. He lends me your wheelbarrow whenever I want it!"

T. Beaty Hart, Bridewell Printing Works, Mill Road, Kettering.